UNDER THE ROSE

KATHRYN NOLAN

That's What She Said Publishing, Inc.

Editing by Faith N. Erline
Cover by Kari March

ISBN: 978-1-945631-74-0 (ebook)
ISBN: 978-1-945631-59-7 (paperback)

082220

For my grandfather, who passed away two months before this book was released.

My grandfather lived all 89 years on this earth with an uncomplicated joy. His zest for life was contagious. He used to wear these yellow-tinted aviator sunglasses that—as he'd tell every friend and stranger alike—made each day seem filled with sunshine.

My grandfather believed that every stranger should become your friend. That a simple 'hello' on the street should turn into a conversation. He believed songs were to be whistled and music was for dancing; that crab cakes should only come from Maryland and cheesecake should be enjoyed plain (no cherry topping!). My grandfather believed all dogs should be adopted and loved (which is why he had so many of them). He was a Navy veteran who visited other vets in the hospital when they were alone. He was a husband who loved his wife for 66 years—having married her after a quick, six-week courtship. My grandfather could charm every person he met—and there wasn't a party he didn't like. In fact, my grandfather was the party.

When I was a little girl, my grandfather would sit and listen patiently until I finished my many long, rambling stories—even if he was late to work. Amidst his boundless energy, he still believed in giving you his undivided attention. And he would gladly make room in his heart for anyone that sought refuge there.

But most importantly, my grandfather believed his children and grandchildren should receive his truly unconditional love—a love filled with his uncomplicated joy. My grandfather loved all of us deeply until the last day of his life. And, of course, he was still making jokes.

1

SAM

I had been banished to the land of private detectives.

"My father and I appreciate your discretion," I said as smoothly as I could manage. "Especially during this difficult time."

Abe's usually impassive features softened. "Agents go through difficult situations all the time, Samuel. I told your father that you were welcome as our consultant for as long as it takes. It helps to stay busy."

I nodded. "Thank you, sir."

Although what helped even more was having a father who was acting Deputy Director of the FBI. "Consulting on cases with a firm of private detectives" was an interesting way to describe what this situation really was. I was hiding.

I was stranded at Codex until my father released me.

"I'd appreciate it if the details of my current situation were kept private from your team," I added.

Abe lifted a brow. "You're here to provide valuable insight and nothing else. Codex is lucky to work with an FBI agent of your caliber."

It was a tiny act of kindness. Yet my gratitude for my former instructor threatened to sweep me away. Abraham Royal was a stern-looking white man in his early forties, his dark hair graying at the temples. His expectations were ruthlessly high. But he had an unyielding loyalty to those he respected.

Banishment or not, it was comforting to be back under his careful supervision—and to know I still had his respect.

"Selfishly, I'll admit that I'm glad to introduce you to another side of criminal justice," he said. "The FBI isn't the only agency that can hunt down stolen books."

I allowed a slight smile. "I don't doubt it. But I'm a Bureau man, through and through."

He made a sound of disapproval as he leaned against his mahogany desk. "You always have been. I'll just have to be content with having the Deputy Director in my debt."

"His gratitude for this will certainly pay off for Codex," I said. "He pulls all the strings, as you know."

Abe's expression was cryptic. "That he does." His eyes flicked to the clock on the wall. "The rest of the team will arrive in a minute. I haven't made them aware that you're coming. The element of surprise is a crucial part of my leadership style."

"And teaching style."

"That is correct," he admitted. "I don't miss the Bureau worth a damn. But I miss teaching at Quantico. It's inspiring being in the room with those new recruits, all so eager for the future." He looked at me, as if waiting for my agreement.

Inspiring. It was a bizarre word coming from a man renowned for his seriousness. Had there been *eagerness* brimming over in those training rooms? Because I'd assumed every other future agent had felt as terrified and anxious as I had.

"Yes, sir," I finally said. "What's your team like here?"

"Perfect."

"That's high praise," I said.

"When you can handpick your team, it improves everyone's morale—and effectiveness—tenfold. These detectives are sharp, focused, hard-working." He tilted his head. "Funny."

Abe was not a man known for his humor. But there was a lightness to him I'd never seen when we'd worked together at the Bureau. It was telling that he'd left and founded his own private detective firm within that same year. My former instructor had been a model of virtue. He'd also been permanently furious and endlessly agitated, not one to sit still for long without a cause.

"Funny and hard-working," I said. "Sounds like a good fit for me for a few weeks."

"You look like you could use a laugh," he said. And this time, the compassion in his face was so obvious I had to look away. Voices echoed in the narrow stairwell behind us, then a door opened. Abe's body language grew even lighter, almost jaunty, as a tall Black man and a dark-haired white woman strode into the room.

Abe Royal was *happy*. Yet if you listened to my father—and I never had a choice not to—any person who abdicated their responsibility to the Bureau was bound for mediocrity.

"Henry, Delilah, good morning," Abe said. "I'd like to introduce you to our new consultant, Special Agent Samuel Byrne. We worked together during my last year in the Art Theft unit."

"And he was my most terrifying instructor at the FBI's training academy," I added.

Abe looked pleased at the description. "Thank you for that, Sam."

"New consultant?" the dark-haired woman asked.

Abe shrugged. "Surprise," he drawled.

The man stepped forward first. Like Abe, he wore an expensive suit. "I'm Dr. Henry Finch. In my former life, I was a rare book librarian working in Oxford at the McMaster's Library."

"Henry's boss was Bernard Allerton," Abe said. "They worked together for more than a decade. Henry was the one who confronted Bernard with the evidence that Interpol and the FBI are still working through."

Bernard Allerton was the most famous rare book librarian in the world—and for years, federal agents like Abe had suspected the man of orchestrating the theft of rare manuscripts and antiques on a grand scale. Six months ago, Bernard had fled Oxford and was still on the run.

"Bernard Allerton was your *boss*?" I asked.

Henry nodded gravely. "It took me a long time to believe he was a criminal," he said. "The man's an expert in manipulation."

"That's certainly what Abe and I believed back when we worked together," I said.

Maybe this banishment *would* be interesting.

"I can confirm your beliefs were accurate." Henry shook my hand firmly before sitting.

The dark-haired woman stepped close. She had pale skin and bright blue eyes. And an expression of absolute distrust on her face.

"Delilah Barrett," she said. "I'm a former police detective."

"Ah." I nodded. "Makes sense now."

"Delilah treats everyone like a potential suspect," Henry explained. She glanced over at him, and her entire body relaxed.

"Old habits, I'm afraid." She looked contrite.

"You don't have to apologize," I said. "I spend all my time with the Bureau. I treat everyone like a suspect too."

She sat in front of me. "I definitely remember those days."

"Sam is a talented agent," Abe said, "and he'll be an asset to us these next few weeks. His knowledge of rare book theft rivals our own. And with the festival this weekend and our other open cases, I thought an extra set of hands would be helpful."

She smiled broadly—Abe's trust in me was all the evidence that she needed to do the same, it seemed.

"You should know," he continued, "that Henry and Delilah are also engaged."

I watched the pair share a secret, romantic look while Abe bristled behind his desk.

"Abraham Royal has allowed two of his employees to be engaged?" I asked, stupefied.

"Yes, well, my only other option was losing them both. And that was never an option," he said.

"He's getting soft," I told Henry and Delilah.

"I wholeheartedly agree," she stage-whispered.

"*Soft* isn't in my vocabulary, trust me," Abe replied.

"Noted, sir," I said. But I shot a secret grin at the couple. Abe *was* happy here.

"What do you think of our operation?" Abe spread his palms out, indicating his cozy office. Codex was located on the second story of a used bookstore in Philadelphia's historic district. This floor had exposed brick walls, colonial-era fireplaces, and ceilings so low I kept hitting my head. A fitting location for a firm that specialized in retrieving stolen rare books.

"I'm looking forward to working with the team," I said,

surprised to find that it was the truth. "Why don't you get me up to date on any active cases or investigations?"

Henry leaned forward, adjusted his glasses. "At the end of February, Delilah and I went undercover as a married couple to garner the trust of Philadelphia's wealthiest heiress, Victoria Whitney. We believed she had stolen The Franklin Museum's copy of *On the Revolutions of Heavenly Spheres* by the astronomer Copernicus."

"Spoiler alert—she *had* stolen it." Delilah's sly look betrayed all I needed to know about how this duo had gone from fake-married to real-engaged. "We were recently alerted by Abe's contact at the FBI that Victoria was just released from her house arrest. And Alistair Chance, the partner she rolled on, is about to start a five-year federal prison sentence."

"Victoria and Bernard had a wild romance years ago, and she was still receiving stolen books as gifts—maybe from him—until the day he fled," Henry said. "Whether she still communicates with him, we can't confirm. The cases we've closed recently don't appear to be interconnected but seem opportunistic in nature. If Bernard is pulling the strings from Europe, we haven't seen it."

"Interpol agents have potentially spotted Bernard in London," I said.

"Unconfirmed?" Henry asked.

"Unfortunately," I said. "Photos are blurry, at best. Sources are nonexistent. No action on his credit cards, bank accounts, or his passport. The man has successfully disappeared. Interpol has managed to keep his name from the papers both here and abroad. The majority of the world is still under the impression that Bernard Allerton is just a librarian."

Henry glanced at Abe. "The day I met Abe, he told me a

man like Bernard would have been prepared to stay underground for a very, very long time."

"Abe is right," I said. "The Bureau is extremely frustrated with their search. They're worried he'll continue to elude them for years."

Abe tapped his pen on the desk. "Yes, well, we'll see about that."

"Is Codex searching for Bernard Allerton?" I asked.

"Let's just say Bernard wouldn't want to meet any of us in a dark alley," Delilah said.

I was enjoying this unexpected curiosity beckoning me like the crook of a finger. The two weeks since my incident had been unbearably lonely—and solidified my suspicion that I was truly a workaholic with no hobbies except going to the gym. The thrill of the hunt—the comfort of working with a real team—felt strange and new.

"Our biggest priority right now is the 60th Annual Antiquarian Book Festival," Abe said. "It's being hosted at The Grand Dame Hotel here in the city."

"We believe it's a hotbed of criminal activity," Henry said.

"Any time you have book buyers in a room with booksellers, someone's breaking the law," I agreed.

"Our thoughts exactly," Delilah said. "We have a few open cases from local clients with cold trails and no leads. Our plan is to hit the festival, working undercover as potential buyers, see if we can shake down a few sources."

"I'd like to see you in the field, Sam," Abe said. "Back in your Quantico days, I remember you as being the most talented undercover agent in your class."

"That's kind of you, sir," I said, swallowing the hard truth. I *was* talented—but the real undercover genius had been my irritating, frustrating, genius rival. The woman I'd been competing against—and arguing with—since I was eighteen goddamn years old.

But that woman didn't matter, no matter how persistently she appeared in my thoughts even seven years later. What *did* matter was Abe giving me the chance to prove myself, post-incident.

The office door flew open, and a hurricane of limbs and laughter crashed into the room.

"Sorry I'm late *again,* but Federal Donuts was a madhouse, and I pulled an all-nighter trying to crack a mystery I think you guys are going to *freak* about. Abe, don't look at me like I broke your ridiculous *code of conduct and honor* by being all of ten minutes late."

The blur of chatty limbs spun around as if sensing my presence. In her arms was a box of donuts. And stuck in her messy blonde bun was a trio of pens—that habit had annoyed me to no end back in our Quantico days.

The donuts hit the ground.

"*Byrne?*" Behind her big glasses, Freya's green eyes were wide with shock.

"Evandale," I said calmly.

Her cheeks flushed pink with anger. My fingers clenched the arm of my chair.

"Oh, and I forgot to mention," Abe said. "The third member of our Codex team, Freya Evandale. You two were in the same class at the training academy, remember?"

"Oh, we remember," Freya said, chin raised in our old ready-for-battle position.

I felt my nostrils flare, heart rate already hammering at her nearness. Apparently, the land of private detectives contained my irritating, frustrating, genius rival.

And she was even more beautiful now than the last time I'd seen her.

2

FREYA

Samuel Byrne was a mirage caused by sleep deprivation.

He had to be.

Because there was *no way* my archnemesis was in Abe's office. *At Codex.*

Sitting in *my favorite chair.*

We continued scowling at each other with a box of piping hot donuts between our feet.

My nemesis still had the audacity to look like Captain America—brave, broad-shouldered, handsome. Except I'd known this man for a long, long time. And beneath that superhero facade was a tightly-wound company man in serious need of a vacation.

"I was just telling the rest of the team about Sam's new position here at Codex," Abe said. "He'll be consulting on cases for a few weeks. In the field, when he can be."

A smirk tugged at the corners of Sam's mouth. My cheeks flushed hotter.

No. Not a mirage.

This was a fucking *nightmare.*

Henry picked up the box and flipped the top open, releasing the tantalizing scent of fresh-baked cinnamon and sugar. "You two went to school together?" he said, ignoring our attempts to murder each other with our eyes.

Delilah took hold of my wrist, tugging me next to her on the couch and placing a donut in my hand. My gaze was still leashed to Sam's—a nonverbal duel I was unwilling to lose.

"We, uh..." Sam started. "Freya and I went to Princeton together."

He broke our stare down first. *Point for Freya.*

"I didn't know that," Abe said, forehead pinched.

"Not that many people do," I said. "Sam and I had the misfortune of running our campus's Criminology Club together. When we weren't stuck in all of the same classes."

We'd competed against each other for club president so viciously our classmates assumed we shared political aspirations. We didn't. Our shared aspiration was *winning.*

"Our glorious leader *does* know that Sam and I spent four months together at Quantico before I dropped out." I leveled Abe with a searing glance. His hands went up in surrender—then paused to pick an imaginary speck of lint from his pristine suit. "Funny you forgot to mention to either of us we'd be working together."

"Didn't see the need," he said airily. "And besides, I would have hired Samuel whether you liked it or not."

"Well, it's certainly fine by me, sir," Sam said, jaw clamped tight.

"And me as well," I said swiftly. I avoided Delilah's bemused expression—worried I'd crack beneath the pressure of it. My best friend still carried the bloodhound instincts that had made her such a remarkable police detective. Later, she'd be grilling me like I was a hostile suspect.

"Moving on," Abe said, "there is one more piece to this

situation that I have kept from the three of you. I taught Sam at Quantico, along with Freya. We worked together in the Art Theft unit my last year with the Bureau before I left to found Codex. As I was leaving, Sam agreed to bend a few rules to keep me apprised of what was going on in the world of rare book theft." He nodded at Sam. "You technically all know Sam as my contact at the FBI."

My blood chilled. Abe's connection to the FBI was a legal gray area that Codex cheerfully operated in. There were certain things private detectives couldn't pursue; we were paid by clients to retrieve stolen goods, not to bring criminals to justice. But if we *stumbled into* anything illegal we made sure to document it for Abe's contact. It was a two-way relationship—sometimes when the FBI was stuck on a case, they shared details with us too.

Anything to get the damn book back, as Abe would say. And apparently that contact had always been Sam.

"Seems like we've been working together for a while now, Evandale," Sam said. His blue eyes were dark, confident.

"Seems like we have," I said, silently fuming.

"It makes Sam's role as consultant an even better fit, given he's been supplying vital information for some of our cases the past three years," Abe said.

I narrowed my gaze at my boss—and he replied by holding out a second donut on a plate. "I know you take bribes in the form of cinnamon and sugar."

I took the plate slowly, not sure if I was in the forgiving mood yet. My brain couldn't process this new, glaring reality—the man I used to compete with all through school and during my training was suddenly sitting in the Codex office like he'd always worked here.

I felt like a college freshman again, instantly trying to prove myself.

How was that *possible?*

And worse, in the seven years since I'd washed out of Quantico, I'd ceased being a rising star. I was sitting next to a badass police officer, a rare book librarian who spoke four languages, and a former FBI agent so supremely talented that his leaving to start a private firm sent shockwaves through the industry.

Oh, and Sam, a highly trained and decorated federal agent.

Me? I was a glorified computer nerd with a love for wizards and baked goods.

"So now that we're all on the same page," Abe continued, "let's get to work. I want our focus to be getting Sam up to speed on any open cases and figuring out how we're going to work the book festival opening tomorrow. I want strategies." He looked right at me. "And later, I want a summary from you of the new code words you mentioned."

Sam's stare slid my way, curious.

"And I want the two of you partnered on the next case we catch."

I shook off the fog of Byrne's irritating good looks. "What? Me and Delilah?"

"No. You and Sam."

"You're joking," I sputtered.

Abe flashed a rare grin. "Come now. Have you ever known me to tell a joke? The two of you were expert partners at the academy. There should be no problem here, correct?"

Sam cleared his throat. "Actually, sir, if I may—"

"We'll probably kill each—"

Abe held up a palm. "Scratch that. I wasn't actually

asking for anyone's opinions. The next case that walks through those doors will be handled by the two of you. Together."

The first day I met Sam, I was instantly wary of the arrogant jock who swore he knew *everything* there was to know about fighting crime. We were only eighteen, but he was already confident. Brash. Brilliant.

And fucking *hot*.

That first day we met, every brain cell had flashed the same word, over and over. Now, against my better judgment, I allowed my gaze to land back on Byrne's. And there went my brain cells, agitated with a threat I thought I'd *never* see again, declaring the presence of my sworn adversary and all that he represented.

Danger, danger, danger.

3

FREYA

My cursor hovered over a phrase that lacked gravitas but piqued my interest: *We're certainly looking forward to having an empty house this weekend.*

It was probably a banal discussion of weekend plans, the type of thing work colleagues mutter to each other as they walk out of the office.

But I was pretty sure it was a fucking code phrase.

For the past three years, I'd worked as Codex's resident computer nerd, using my skills to track down stolen manuscripts online. And the majority of that work consisted of using a website called Under the Rose. On its surface, it was a legal marketplace for private sellers and private buyers—they discussed gilded edges, conservation techniques, light restrictions for vellum pages. Using one of my many fake avatars, I witnessed sales of maps, books, letters, and illustrations.

Beneath the legal exterior was a murky world of thieves.

The world of antiquities was one of academic glamour and wealthy privilege. It was a world that operated on trust and handshakes and a shared passion for rarity. Which allowed a devious underworld to flourish, especially online. Identities could be hidden or forged, relationships were transactional, and bank accounts were difficult to trace.

Last year, I'd discovered a secret barrier on the Under the Rose site. A way for buyers and sellers to virtually *wink*.

Didn't I once meet you at Reichenbach Falls? It was a Sherlock Holmes reference and not a well-known one. If the person replied "*yes*" then they could be trusted with an item that had been stolen. If they said "*what the fuck is that?*" then you moved on. Victoria Whitney—who'd been caught red-handed by Henry and Delilah—had responded to that code. As had her frenemy, Bitzi Peterson, and their co-conspirator, Alistair Chance.

We believed Bernard Allerton to be the original purveyor of this code.

Except now, I was convinced I'd found another one.

The next level of crooks.

"Thought I'd catch you here."

Delilah slid into the chair next to mine, gripping a mug of steaming tea. She'd found me at the True Hearts coffee shop—my favorite place in Philly to enjoy a dog-eared book and Earl Grey tea on rainy days. Sunny days too.

"Officer Barrett," I teased. "Come to interrogate me?"

She shrugged an elegant shoulder, but her lips raised in a smile. "Figured you might like a little help on the summary you're working on for Abe. I'm curious about what kept you up all night."

I was comforted by her presence. Delilah was my best friend, my favorite stakeout buddy, and my daily hero. She was a beautiful badass—and watching her fall for Henry (and plan their wedding) had been too precious for words.

But I also liked having her analytical brain when I was throwing out theories, seeing what might stick.

"And you're not here to ask me about Samuel Byrne, right?"

"I mean, if he comes up."

I bit my lip, knew I couldn't avoid it. I'd left Codex a few hours ago—Sam had been deep in discussion with the rest of the team, and I was in desperate need of space. Everywhere I looked, his big, muscular body was crowding our tiny office. And every time I heard that gravelly voice, I kept tumbling back into memories I'd rather forget. Today was the third time I'd walked into a room and been shocked by the presence of Sam Byrne. It was some cosmic pattern I couldn't break. The first was day one at Princeton, when his arrogance, paired with his too-handsome-face, was immediately aggravating.

The second time was day one at Quantico. I was 25, and three years had passed since I'd last seen Byrne at our Princeton graduation. Most people intent on being accepted to the FBI's training academy spent a few years working in the field of criminal justice, which I'd done. And I knew about Sam's FBI aspirations, knew his father was a high-ranking official for the Bureau who expected his son to follow in his footsteps. I just didn't expect to walk into class and bump into Sam's giant chest.

"You've got to be *fucking* kidding me," he'd said with a full-on glare. I'd merely gawked, slack-jawed. Stunned into a rare silence. And then I was furious. Of course, there were only two seats left in the auditorium that day. Two seats next to each other. Which he and I had slunk into, heads down, then spent the entire class whisper-bickering with each other. As if those three years hadn't passed at all.

Delilah prodded me with her finger. "Earth to Frey."

I blinked, sighed. "If you let me babble on about my half-baked ideas, I'll let you ask one question about Codex's newest consultant."

"Deal," she said. She clinked our mugs together and settled back into her chair. "What's the hot gossip from Under the Rose?"

I turned my screen to face her—the website itself was innocuous. It operated like Craigslist for rare books, with subgroups and the ability to direct message buyers and sellers.

"Do the names Julian King or Birdie Barnes mean anything to you?" I asked.

She shook her head.

"I've been fucking around in these different subgroups, learning their language. Seeing if any trends appear that Codex should be aware of. Searching for patterns." I clicked, opening a screen where the discussion revolved around rare letters.

"Julian King and Birdie Barnes run King Barnes Rare Books in San Francisco. They're always on this site selling *extremely* rare first editions, usually signed. Big-ass price tags."

She cocked her head at that. "How much?"

"Half a million dollars. A million. Obviously, the transactions happen separately, but the price tags and the quality of the items sparked my attention."

"Legal though, right?"

I fiddled with my bun, pressing wayward strands back into formation. "I think so? They claim to have letters of authentication, but we both know that can be bullshit. The *thing* about these two is they're like...rock stars. The Beatles of rare books. They're being virtually fawned over left and right, although not a single picture of them exists online.

Nor permanent records, and I searched all night. Website and social media pages are bare of any identifying information, although they appear to be extremely active."

Delilah sipped her tea. "Sounds like something a criminal would do, doesn't it?"

I leaned forward. "That's what I'm thinking. These two are shady as hell, so I've been tracking who they're talking to, who they seem close to. Right now, it's a couple named Thomas and Cora Alexander."

"I *do* know them, actually," she said. "They've got an antiques collection that rivals Victoria's. Manhattanites with a penthouse overlooking Central Park. They're on Henry's shortlist of suspicious rich people that live on the East Coast."

"Wait, really?" I asked, the wheels of my brain spinning faster.

"Really," she promised. "The presence of the Alexanders plus shady booksellers is an interesting combination."

I shoved up the sleeves of my oversized sweater. Tapped on the screen. "This group right here, the ones chatting about rare letters, they're using code words when they speak to each other." I scrolled through for Del, pointing out all the times they'd sprinkled the phrase *house* and *empty house* throughout their frequent messages. "It's a subtle pattern but...I don't know, it's setting off alarm bells for me."

She hummed a little, eyes scanning the screen. "People talk about their houses. Sounds innocent, Frey. Right?"

"I don't think it is, actually," I said. "I need to tell Abe about it. See if I can't dig deeper and get to know the people in this group."

"Do it," Delilah said. "I trust you *and* your computer genius."

"Who's gonna make the office memes, if not me?"

"What you do is more than that, and you know it," she said softly—she was always calling me out over our mugs of tea. "I think you'll do great going undercover with Sam, should the occasion arise."

"Sneaky bitch," I smirked. "Is this your one question about our new consultant?"

I was almost grateful for the redirect. Admitting my fears and anxieties about going undercover wasn't something I was ready to do. Especially not to a woman who was so damn good at it.

She tapped her chin. "Actually, no. I want to know if Sam was the man that changed you."

"What are you talking about?"

Delilah set her mug down. "The night at the Copernicus exhibit, when I told you I had fallen in love with Henry, you told me you'd had an enemy at Quantico that you hated. That the feeling was so strong it changed you. Is that Sam?"

I sputtered through a startled laugh. "I must have been off my rocker, Del. Yes, Sam Byrne is the man I was talking about. But he didn't change me one bit. The only purpose that smug asshole serves on this planet is to compete with me constantly. And piss me off. Sam's a robot workaholic with no capacity for humor or joy. I'm not entirely sure why he's here in Philly, but the sooner he leaves, the better."

Her blue eyes danced with intrigue. "And you don't love him?"

"*Byrne?*"

She was silent, letting me dangle.

"Is this how you used to get people to confess, Officer?"

She smirked. "Okay, you do love him."

I balled up my napkin and threw it at her face.

She swatted it away with nimble reflexes. "And you *definitely* want to kiss him."

"Please." My palms were now sweating. "I'd rather French kiss a cactus."

She didn't need to know about the four straight months of late-night study sessions Sam and I had undertaken together. We were the top students at the FBI's training academy—which meant we were *always* the two students left in the library. Always alone. Competing constantly and under enormous stress. Bickering.

And it used to make me *stupid horny*.

When Sam wasn't looking, I'd stare at the lock of hair falling across his forehead, the stretch of his worn Princeton sweatshirt over those magnificent shoulders. I'd get caught in a looping fantasy—of shoving the notebooks and pens and highlighters off our long table and dragging Sam onto it. Wondering what would happen if I pushed my serious, honorable rival to take out his study stress on my very willing body.

"You're thinking about having sex with Sam right now, aren't you?" Delilah's voice was annoyingly smug.

I tapped my computer screen. "I'm thinking about our *thieves*, thank you very much."

Delilah Barrett crossed her arms with a secretive smile. "And you need to work on making your lies more convincing."

4

SAM

The faster I ran, the less I panicked.

Outside the windows of the gym, dawn was breaking over my Philadelphia hotel. This standard "fitness center" looked exactly like my gym back in Virginia. My hotel room felt less sterile than the white, unadorned walls of my apartment. When you lived your life in service to the Federal Bureau of Investigation, having a personal life was a luxury. Enjoying your own home was a luxury. Goddamn *sleep* was a luxury. After a twelve-hour day, my only cure for the heavy exhaustion was forcing my way through grueling workouts. More miles, more weights, more sweat. After, I enjoyed the briefest respite from the anxiety that had taken up permanent residence in my chest.

By morning, however, it inevitably roared back with the ferocity of a lion, suddenly uncaged. And that was only if I was lucky enough to sleep through the night.

I reached down and increased the speed on the treadmill.

I was heading into my second day at Codex and didn't need to bring the remnants of my incident into Abe's well-run operation. And I definitely didn't want *Freya* fucking *Evandale* to know about my newest vulnerability.

My cell phone rang, and I touched my earbuds, answering a call from the Deputy Director. I hadn't called him "dad" in a decade.

"OPR informed me that they've gathered everything they need to reach a decision on their investigation." My father's tone was clipped regardless of the hour of the day. He also hadn't formally greeted me in a decade either—that wasn't the parenting style of Andrew Byrne.

"Good to know, sir." I reluctantly slowed the treadmill to a stop, mopping my face with the end of my shirt.

"They informed me that you were very cooperative in talking about Gregory's crimes."

"Of course." I bit off the end of that sentence—*because I didn't do anything wrong*. When my ex-partner's crimes had been discovered, my father assured me he knew I hadn't participated in Gregory's years of deception. But the Deputy Director of the FBI couldn't tolerate an agent who'd been so easily misled. And he certainly couldn't endure the media frenzy of a son under investigation from the Office of Professional Responsibility.

Andrew Byrne had a perfect reputation to uphold—and knew a small private detective firm in Philadelphia where he could hide me from the spotlight.

Even though I knew I was innocent, his actions only fueled my veiled guilt.

"Do you know when they expect a decision?" I asked.

"As soon as possible. Until then, keep your head down. Abraham told me he'd keep you busy with minor cases. They're private detectives. It can't be that hard." There was a long pause, riddled with judgment. "You should have plenty of *free time* to fix this."

I winced, happy no one was around to see it. "Yes, sir."

The demand was a direct reference to the conversation we'd had after I'd been informed of my partner's nefarious crimes. He'd left me to sit in his office for an hour while news about Gregory broke and rumors about what had happened spread like wildfire. And when he'd returned, he still didn't face me as a father, concerned for his son.

He faced me like the Deputy Director.

Don't you ever feel this way? I'd said, desperate. Overwhelmed. *Don't you ever feel like the world is spinning out of your control?*

My father's face had remained expressionless. *If an agent feels anything other than pride when he walks through those doors, it is absolutely his fault. Fix yourself, Samuel. Before you embarrass yourself, and our family, even more than you already have.*

Fix yourself.

He had disconnected the call while I was lost in thought—the ensuing silence was his standard farewell. Working with Codex could be *more* than a punishment. If Abe trusted me with a case, and I closed it, it could go far in proving to my father that I was *fixed*. My father's opinions on Codex notwithstanding, it could go far in proving to the Bureau that my outburst was a freak mistake and not a symptom of an underlying issue.

I cranked the speed on the treadmill again—feet pounding hard. Arms moving, lungs expanding, sweat beading my brow.

I ran faster. And then faster still.

If we caught a case, it would be my best chance. I'd just have Freya as my partner while doing it. The only woman who'd *ever* gotten under my fucking skin. Yesterday she'd scowled at me like I'd lit a stack of her favorite paperbacks on fire. Angry, her green eyes flashed emerald. A fact I remembered from our countless arguments in class. And at the library. And during dinner. And walking down our dorm hallway.

I wished I'd forgotten how exquisite her eyes were, angry or not.

But that would be a fucking lie.

Her uniform hadn't changed in seven years either—giant glasses, messy bun, oversized sweater, and yoga pants. I'd always towered above her petite form, and I still did.

I increased the speed again. Faster.

I was sprinting now, burning through the spiky, hot energy that Freya always evoked. I hated that she smelled the same too, a nostalgic scent that knocked me for a fucking loop. Earl Grey. Cinnamon. Sugar. Freya smelled like her favorite things: tea, books, and cookies. She had when we were at Princeton. She had at Quantico.

My finger jammed down onto the button.

I ran like my career depended on it.

5

SAM

Two hours later and I was perched on the couch in Abe's office, watching my former instructor write the words *Antiquarian Book Festival* on a big whiteboard. Henry and Delilah sat nearby. Henry was whispering close to Delilah's ear, and even behind her hand, I could tell she was blushing.

Love, companionship, sex. They were also considered luxuries when you were dedicated to one job and one job only.

I glanced away, cleared my throat. Straightened my posture. Even when I was younger, I'd barely dated—a direct result of Freya's aggravating presence in my life. It required a lot of mental energy to stay one step ahead, one point better, one minute faster. She was compelling for too many reasons.

"Is Freya always late?" I asked, glancing at my watch.

A half-smile flitted across Abe's face as he wrote things down. "Every damn day. But she makes up for it by bringing all the food we could ever eat."

Not a moment later, the woman in question was bursting into the room like a ray of golden light—cracking a joke with Henry, making Delilah laugh, unpacking donuts and coffee and tea satchels from a bag that read #1 CAT MOM. She spun in a circle, noted the available seating, and flashed a defiant look my way.

"Byrne," she said.

"Evandale," I replied. "Take a seat."

Face rigid, body stiff, she plopped down cross-legged on the cushion next to me, careful to keep our bodies apart. The air filled with cinnamon and sugar. A strand of blonde hair brushed across her neck. Her lips were pink and plump and pursed in irritation. At me. While the rest of Codex talked around us, Freya prepared for battle.

"Didn't think you'd be back," she murmured. "Figured you'd be too intimidated."

"By you?" I asked. "That's never been the case."

"Spoken by the man I once knocked on his ass ten seconds into a sparring session."

I set my jaw, hid a smirk. Like most FBI agents, Freya and I had received extensive training in a hand-to-hand combat style called Krav Maga. Our sparring sessions were long and grueling because Freya never submitted. But neither did I. And the strange ability we'd always had to read each other's minds made it all the more challenging.

"I never back down, Evandale, you know that," I said, still refusing to look at her. "And if I remember correctly, you might have knocked me on my ass. But I was the one who pinned you to the ground."

Out of the corner of my eye, I caught her flush. A flare of her nostrils. Seven years later and here we were, seated next to each other, ready to take the other one down. So it was no surprise that I still felt the aching, illicit thrill of the fight. Of *her* fight.

Next to me, Freya shifted farther away. But not before muttering, "Pervert."

It startled a laugh, which I covered with my fist. Freya's mouth tipped up slightly.

When was the last time I'd done that?

Abe clapped his hands together. "Morning, everyone. Sam, happy to have you back."

"Morning, sir," I said. "I'm excited to get to work."

I didn't have to look at Freya to feel her rolling her eyes.

"We're talking strategies around the book festival," Abe said. "Freya's code words, any updates we can fill Sam in on."

"I've got good news on the code front," Freya said. "I think I've got these weirdo rich assholes figured out."

I was struggling to admit I was actually interested in this. The Art Theft unit was mired in bureaucracy, which meant I was levels removed from this kind of on-the-ground investigative work. If there were code words being discussed by my team back at the Bureau, I wasn't aware of them. But I wanted to be.

"Do go on," Abe was saying. "I want to make sure that we—"

But a rapping *knock* sliced through the room. Abe stopped.

"Are we expecting anyone?" Henry asked as he stood. Abe shook his head as Henry moved through the office. There was only quiet from Henry as the sounds of his footsteps reached the door.

"Who is it?" Delilah called over her shoulder.

"Well," Henry said slowly, "I believe it's Scarlett O'Riley."

A stunned silence echoed through the room.

"*The* Scarlett O'Riley?" Abe clarified.

"I think...yes. Yes, *the*."

"Well, for god's sake, let her *in*," Abe instructed. But we were already standing, crowding toward Henry. Who was, indeed, welcoming *the* Scarlett O'Riley into the Codex office. She was Hollywood's latest It Girl—the young, rebellious, pink-haired director the world was currently obsessed with. And she was standing in our doorway, nervously shifting on her feet.

"I'm looking for Abraham Royal?" The woman—Scarlett—said.

Smooth as ever, Abe stepped forward, shook her hand.

"I'm Abraham," he said. "Can we help you?"

In person, she was as bright and shiny as she'd been earlier that year when she'd become the youngest film director to win an Oscar. Her next project was already receiving a ton of attention, and it hadn't even started filming yet.

"I sincerely fucking hope so," she replied. "I'm Scarlett O'Riley, and I'm directing a film about the writer George Sand."

"We've heard of it," he promised. "And of course, we've heard of you."

She blew out a shaky breath. "George's love letters to the poet Alfred de Musset are a focal point of my biopic. The originals are being used on set, and we arranged to borrow them from the Franklin Museum and transport them to Los Angeles."

Understanding was starting to dawn on Abe's face.

"Early this morning, I met Francisco and his conservation team to oversee the preparation of the letters for transport. We'd agreed to meet at six to get an early start to the day. Two drivers were already in the parking lot, waiting to make the cross-country trip." Scarlett was flushed, disconcerted. “When Francisco let us into the storage room, they were gone.”

“All thirteen of them?” Henry looked physically pained.

“Yes,” she replied. “Sometime in the night, the letters were stolen. I don’t know, this is all very new to me and entirely unexpected. We *need* those letters to be on set, in Los Angeles, in four days. They cannot be lost or stolen or whatever the fuck happened to them.”

“Let me guess,” Abe mused. “Francisco sent you to us because of our discretion.”

“It’s the first thing he did,” she said. “No cops. No authorities. We just need the letters back and we need it done now.”

Freya’s emerald gaze found mine, and a frisson of adrenaline tangled between us. I should have felt more star-struck by Scarlett’s presence, but my fascination was reserved for another woman in the room.

“Thank you for letting me barge in here and demand help,” Scarlett was saying. “Francisco said you’d helped him about six months ago in a major way.”

Henry and Delilah exchanged a wry grin.

“One could say that,” Abe replied. “Come in, sit. Can we grab you anything to drink?”

Scarlett shook her head. The phone in her hand was going off constantly.

“Do you have staff with you? Assistants?” I asked.

“They’re back at the hotel,” she said. “I need to invent a convincing lie about what happened this morning. They can’t know either.” She sat down, and we all gathered around, Abe already beginning to pull out documents. Henry and Delilah snapped to attention, ready for action.

“Were the letters under extra security?” Abe asked.

“I don’t think so,” Scarlett said.

The underlying theme of antiquities theft was the complete and utter trust that prevented buyers and sellers from suspecting their extremely rare goods would be stolen. From what Abe had told me, Codex made its money on this vulnerability—and kept its pristine reputation by cloaking what they did in secrecy. Museums would pay an exorbitant sum to keep the theft of their antiques away from reputation-damaging press.

As would Hollywood directors.

"I'm guessing these letters have become extremely valuable since the news of your biopic broke," Abe said.

"These thirteen love letters are attractive enough on their own," Henry said. "If they were going to be featured in a highly anticipated film, you could expect to see their value double. Triple. We're talking millions at auction, easy. But they'd have to be dealing with other criminals and their private collections. These can't be featured at auction—they'd be too notorious."

"Who knew about the transport, Scarlett?" Abe asked.

"Everyone who worked at the museum," she said. "Francisco is on his way. He said he'd call you on the drive over to chat suspects."

"There's been lots of chatter about love letters on the websites I monitor," Freya said, pushing her glasses up her nose. "Antiques lovers follow trends. Believe it or not, the news of this biopic caused a renewed interest in letters like the ones you're planning on showcasing."

"Thieves follow the same trends," Delilah said. "Anyone chatting George Sand specifically?"

"Not specifically," Freya said, "but I don't think they would on a site like Under the Rose. Not unless it was encoded."

Abe's phone rang. "It's Francisco. Keep talking, all of you."

He strode out of the room, speaking low.

I turned to Scarlett. "And you're not reporting the theft to the police?

"No, I will not," she said. "Per Francisco's advice and guidance, he said that Codex could recover the letters without anyone knowing. Avoid the media spectacle." She looked tense. "The film company took out a large insurance policy on these letters. The amount we'd owe on a claim of stolen property of this value could bankrupt the project from the get-go. Tarnish my name, the film, and my company." She lifted a shoulder. "Oscar or not, my company is indie and new. We can't risk this so early on in our career."

Then you shouldn't have let the letters out of your damn sight.

Freya and I locked eyes. She was thinking the exact same thing.

"Ms. O'Riley," I started, "you should call the police. Right away."

"She'll do no such thing." It was Abe, strolling back in with a calm expression. "That was Francisco. Scarlett, he informed me that you'd like to formally hire my firm to recover all thirteen letters and return them to you untouched." He placed a warning hand on my shoulders. "The police are a last resort here at Codex. As you know."

"I understand it's a risk," Scarlett said. "But filming was set to begin on Tuesday morning. Can you have them in L.A. by then?"

"That's only four days from now," Freya said.

"Francisco said you could do it," Scarlett replied.

"Of course we can," Abe said.

"Can I suggest a team time-out?" Freya held up her finger.

"There's no time for further discussion," Abe said sharply. "Delilah and Henry, stay here and work with Scarlett on gathering additional information. Francisco is on his way. Freya, Sam—I need you in the field doing visual surveillance on a man named Jim Dahl. A photo of Dahl is on its way to your email, Freya. He's an intern working in special collections who did not arrive for work today. After six months of perfect attendance."

"What did Dahl have access to?" I asked, helpless not to pry.

"He was working as Francisco's assistant," Abe said, looking right at Henry. "Dahl was overseeing the conservation of the letters."

"So this...Dahl person was a librarian?" Scarlett asked.

"And possibly a criminal, too," Henry said. "This is a strange world, Ms. O'Riley. Hard to know who you can trust."

Abe handed Freya a slip of paper. The reality of this situation collided against me like a hard hit to the gut. Recovering an antique that was so high profile, and so urgent, was the perfect case for my current situation. But no *fucking* way could I do it with a woman who drove me up the goddamn wall.

"Uh...what..." I struggled. Focused. "What's the objective?"

"Just surveillance to gather intel. Do not spook him. Do not let him be made aware of your presence. Track everything he does. Right now, the element of surprise would be our strongest strategy. If he knows he's being followed by private investigators, we'll blow our chance to have him lead us to his hiding spot."

"Henry and Delilah are way better at that," Freya chimed in. "Send them. I'll stay here and order us tacos. Scarlett, you a carnitas girl?"

"My orders are for *you* and *Sam* to go." Abe's tone was icy —a tone he used on Quantico students when we were in his classes. It had the intended effect—we both straightened like disobedient schoolchildren. "Unless Dahl is waving the stolen letters around in public, which I highly doubt, *do not* involve the authorities."

Abe's voice held a note of caution only for me. My father's disdain for Abe—and Codex, in general—stemmed from the fact that private detectives didn't always utilize the proper channels. Justice, from my father's perspective, was a clear world of black and white, cause and effect. The only reason I'd been banished here was that he knew Abe would keep me busy on "cases" the FBI considered trivial and out of the spotlight.

This case, however, appeared to be neither of those things.

There was a flurry of fevered activity—the Codex team worked well under pressure—and all too quickly, Abe was shoving Freya and me toward the door. I glanced at the clock on the red brick wall. Barely an hour had passed since I'd arrived this morning for my first real day at Codex. Sixty minutes was all it had taken for Freya to become an intimate part of my life again. Would we ever escape each other?

"Be safe," Abe was saying. "Get the damn book back."

"Letters," Freya corrected. "And can I make one more complai—"

The Codex office door slammed in our faces—the sharp sound like a rebuke.

And suddenly we were alone—together—for the first time in seven years.

Freya stepped away from me. But her back connected with the wall, halting her exit.

Was she nervous to work this case because of our history? Or nervous to be in the field? Because Freya had been the most promising undercover agent at the Academy before she dropped out. *Nothing* made her nervous.

"That's it?" I said. "That's all the prep and information we've got?"

"Welcome to the wild west of private investigating. You'll get used to it," she said.

"I'm sure I will get used to it," I boasted. "Quickly too."

"You sure about that?" she asked, tilting her head to one side.

The action—and even the sentiment—was so fucking familiar my chest ached.

"Why are you staring at me?" she asked.

"I'm not staring at you."

Years of rigorous training were yanking at me, urging me to get in the car and speed away toward our suspect. Cases were won and lost in these spare moments. But the force of my history with Freya was stronger.

"You're still staring at me like a weirdo, and we need to go," she replied.

"I know we need to go." I cleared my throat. Cleared my head. "We'll take my car. You direct me to Dahl's location." I stormed down the narrow stairs, through the dusty bookstore, and out into the bright light of morning.

"How about we take *my* car, and *you* give me directions," Freya said.

"I've always been a better driver, and you know it," I growled back.

She snorted. "Seven years and your ego has only tripled in size, huh? Pretty soon, they'll be able to see it from space."

I stopped in the middle of the street, grabbing Freya by the elbow. She looked down at where our bodies met, startled. Shook her arm away.

"I didn't know you'd be here, okay?" I admitted. "You know how much I admire Abe. It's why I agreed to keep him informed of what the FBI was doing, help him when I could. When the opportunity came up to work with Codex on a few cases, I jumped at the chance. But I didn't know *you* worked here. If I had, I would have turned it down."

She eyed me warily. "Why are you here, Byrne? The FBI doesn't loan out its top agents for low-level private detective work."

Because I'm being punished.

"Because we...because we all want to crack down on antiquities theft. Helping Codex helps the Bureau. I can lend a different perspective, bring added resources." I tightened my cufflinks and avoided her sharp gaze.

"You're lying," she said.

"The last thing I want is to be your partner," I said. "You know that's not a lie."

Hurt sparked behind her gaze before vanishing. "Same here, buddy. I'd rather do that Quantico ropes course in a tutu than work with you. It'd be torture, but less torture than trying to get you to do things my way."

"I could do that ropes course in a tutu and *still* beat your time, Evandale. And we'll be doing things my way."

Freya's face brightened for a brief, beautiful second. "You in a tutu is an image I'm going to keep close to my heart. Better to laugh than to howl angrily into the void, right?"

We'd reached my car—as had been my intention. She was always easy to distract with bickering. Holding out the keys, I pressed the button and unlocked it.

"Oh, look. Here we are," I said evenly.

She glared at me.

"Get in the damn car," I said. "You want to solve this case or what?"

Annoyance radiated from her entire body, but she complied, sliding into the passenger seat and slamming the door. Because Evandale and I had one major thing in common.

A desire to win. No matter the cost.

6

FREYA

We sat in strained silence as Sam drove us toward Jim Dahl's apartment. The car was free of any identifying traits—no air fresheners or pre-tuned radio stations or books lying about. It was factory clean, devoid of personality—just like its owner.

Sam cleared his throat. "So. Anything you need to tell me from the last seven years?"

"Nope. You?"

"Nope."

"Take the next two right turns."

He did.

And the silence descended again. I could feel both of us trapped between our compulsive urge to fight and push and fight even more. But I was distracted by my own internal meltdown at being sent out in the field, back to a place where I felt neither strong nor confident.

And with Byrne, of all people.

One month before my graduation from the FBI's training academy, I told my supervisor I was dropping out, blowing up my life and the career trajectory I'd meticulously mapped out. The last time I'd seen Sam, I found him at our usual table in the library. Informed him I was quitting. The man I'd been aggressively competing against since eighteen merely sat there, impassive.

That's fine, he'd said, shrugging as if I'd told him the weather forecast. *You're making a big mistake though. You'll regret it.*

The snap judgment in his tone had me turning on my heel without so much as a chilly wave goodbye. And I'd never, ever admitted what I'd *actually* wanted to do. Which was press my face into his stupid superhero chest and cry.

I ached to admit how badly I'd been struggling. How alone I'd felt in my pervasive anxiety. Sam and I spent every single day with each other—bickering, sparring, studying, testing. Oddly enough, if I'd trusted anyone at that point in my life to hear my most secret fears, it would have been Sam.

That's fine. You'll regret it. My cold response to his bored tone wasn't completely his fault. He had no idea he'd voiced the exact words I was hearing in my head.

"This it?" he asked, breaking through my scattered memories.

"Sure is," I said, climbing out of his car before it had even fully stopped. We were on Second Street, in Philadelphia's Queen Village—an artsy, beautiful neighborhood with historic brick rowhomes and wide, tree-lined parks. At the far end of this block, Dahl's apartment was on the second floor over a store that sold fancy kitchen supplies.

Sam and I began pretending to window shop. His reflection was annoyingly competent: aviator glasses, black peacoat, broad shoulders. He all but screamed *government employee with a special set of skills that could kill you.*

"What's the plan?" Sam muttered.

I peered into the window, pretending to check the price tag on a framed picture. "Knock on the door. See if he's home."

"That's a terrible plan," he replied, side-stepping a pot of petunias.

I gave his reflection the middle finger. He rolled his eyes.

"That was a joke, Byrne."

"I'm trying to do our job here," he bit out. "I'm fine with staking out his apartment, per our orders. Attempting to blend in. Sound okay?"

I paused. "Yeah. Fine, whatever."

We were nearing Dahl's apartment. Sam and I had studied the picture of the museum intern that had arrived in my inbox: he was a bland-looking, youngish, blond man. Boring features that made it possible for him to blend in.

"Uh...how are things going at the FBI?" I finally said.

"Fine," Sam replied. His fingers were curled into fists at his side, but his face was completely stoic.

"Working art theft was your goal when we were at the academy." I pretended to wave to a shop's owner. "You must be happy there."

"We do important work," was all he said. We'd neared the kitchen supply store, and my senses sharpened.

Sam faced the window, so I watched the street. He assessed the sidewalk. I was prepared for Dahl. We had *never* been good partners. But we shared a strange intuitive connection. Even now, we couldn't help dropping into position like ballet performers who'd been dancing together for years.

"Didn't expect to find you being a private detective," he said quietly.

"Why not?" I asked. "Because I'm a dropout?"

His expression was an enigma behind those goddamn aviators. “No. I didn’t know what your plans were after you told me you were leaving. We never spoke again.”

“I’m doing a techy job,” I shrugged. “I’m mostly a behind-the-scenes girl.” My ears picked up a door opening and closing—a door overhead. Sam caught the sound too.

His hand landed heavily next to my head, bringing him much too close for my liking. The scent of pine trees on a winter’s night invaded my senses.

Sam’s smell.

“What are you doing?” I whispered. “If you pretend to kiss me right now, my knee is going to visit your balls.”

“I’m *not* pretending to kiss you,” he whispered back. “I’m guessing this door *right here* leads from the upstairs apartment to the street..”

I sniffed, turning my head back to the sidewalk. “I guess that’s semi-believable.”

“I’d prefer not to get a visit from your knee. I still have bruises from our sparring sessions.”

My cheeks flushed at the stray compliment. “Just because you’re bigger doesn’t mean I can’t kick your ass.”

“I actually think it’s the other way—” Sam stopped when the door opened with a loud squeal.

A man stepped onto the sidewalk, mere inches from us. He wasn’t walking quickly; he wasn’t acting like a suspect. But when I caught his profile, my gut said *Dahl*. Next to me, Sam was stiff, ready to spring. He touched his glasses, nodded once at me.

The man was meandering, walking toward a small parking lot.

“Remember,” I whispered. “Visual. Nothing else.”

“If that’s him,” Sam whispered back, “we should nab him now.”

"Sam, *no*—"

He was already off, walking quickly toward the man I assumed was Dahl. I had to jog to catch up, drawing attention to myself in direct violation of Abe's instructions.

"For someone who mocked my earlier plan, sure does feel like we're about to confront our suspect *plan-free*," I said, looping my hand through Sam's arm to force him to slow his pace. "Did you notice he's not carrying anything?"

"What did you think he'd have? A bag that says *Caution: Stolen letters inside*?"

"A bag or a crate marked with a skull and crossbones would be a nice touch, don't you think?" I yanked his arm, using all of my strength, and managed to stop him in his tracks. Dahl was still breezily strolling along.

"Visual," I prodded. "What do we see?" I was already using the tiny hidden camera in my watch face, secretly snapping pictures of Dahl with a flick of my wrist.

Sam sighed. "Potential suspect walking slowly. Nothing on his person indicates he's carrying letters, and he's not acting like he's on the run or under pressure."

"Could be a cool cucumber," I said. "Could be he's not our guy. What else?"

He watched Dahl for a minute while I cast my gaze to the balcony on his second-story apartment, searching for possible clues.

"What do you usually do when you're undercover?" Sam asked, careful to keep his voice quiet.

"I'm not usually undercover," I said. "I'm Delilah's stakeout partner when she needs extra help. But I haven't been in the field, truly, in a long time."

Six months earlier, I'd chased down Charles Kearney at a high-society event in Center City. He'd been holding a stolen copy of *Fahrenheit 451*. And with my usual threat of stiletto-induced groin violence, Kearney had given up the goods. I'd feigned confidence to Delilah and Abe—it was second nature at this point—but deep down, I'd been a hot mess of nerves.

Sam narrowed his eyes at my answer, sensing bullshit, but didn't press. "I don't like the way Dahl's walking toward the lot."

"You think his car is there?"

My hand was still wrapped around his elbow. Beneath my fingers, his muscles flexed with restrained motion.

"I think if we don't move now, we'll lose him."

"And if we spook him, we'll lose our chance altogether."

"What *chance*, Evandale?" he hissed, finally losing patience with me. "Also, fuck, *fuck*, he's getting in the car." He started to run—looking like an FBI hero in an action film, and *not* like a covert PI.

"Don't spook him," I called, louder than I intended. *Shit*. Of course, having a shouting match about *spooking people* caught the attention of the man we were surveilling. Dahl swiveled his head towards us. Then he jumped into the driver's seat of a silver car and revved the engine.

"Fuck-a-duck," I said, frozen in indecision. Sam was already grabbing me by the hand and half-dragging me.

"We're going after him. Come on," he said, breaking into a loping run.

"*What? No!*" I said, trying to keep pace. We rounded the corner, and Sam was out-and-out running down the side-walk now—arms pumping, back straight, stride perfect. Jesus *Christ,* could we draw any more attention to ourselves?

"Byrne," I barked, hitting the side of his car hard. "We need to stop and make an actual plan."

He shook his head, throwing open his car door and

revving his engine like Dahl. "Get in," he said through the window.

I was out of breath and pissed. I slid in next to him and grabbed his arm. "Listen. We can't just—"

There was a loud, bracing *squeal* of Sam's tires. A flash of silver right in front of us. The *tiniest* hint of a smile on Sam's face.

"That's him," he said. "Hold on tight."

The potential book thief's silver car was rounding a corner toward the I-95 on-ramp. Sam gunned it.

"Wait, wait, *wait*—"

But he was turning to me with an actual *grin* on his face. A grin that set my heart racing—and not from the hard sprint down the sidewalk.

"Relax, Evandale," he said. "It's a good old-fashioned car chase." We hit the on-ramp going twice the regular speed, Dahl's car only a bit ahead of us. Four lanes of highway traffic awaited us, and each lane seemed to have an inordinate number of silver cars.

I memorized Dahl's license plate and turned to my smug partner. "What are you *doing*?"

Sam wasn't smiling anymore—but he did seem oddly calm as he wove around cars, going faster than I would have liked. "You know what I'm doing. We did it in academy training a dozen times, at least."

The city skyline beckoned ahead, the glass shimmering golden in the autumn light, the river curving next to us.

"We're not federal agents. And this isn't a Colombian drug cartel with a kidnapping victim in the trunk. This is a guy who stole *love letters*," I said.

Sam appeared way too competent behind the wheel of a car going 85 miles an hour. Dahl, interestingly enough, was staying ahead of us. Which didn't bode well for his presumed innocence.

"I know it's not a Colombian drug cartel. Even though I'll remind you that I scored top marks in that simulation," Sam countered.

"Top *mark*," I corrected. "You scored one point higher than I did."

This time, he actually laughed under his breath.

"Is Mars in retrograde? I think I saw a smile earlier. *And* a laugh. Never known Special Agent Sam Byrne to express human emotion."

"Are you making jokes, Evandale? Or focusing on this case?"

"Oh my god, *shut up*—"

Dahl's car moved over three lanes, toward the exit to Center City.

"Shit," Sam grunted, executing a series of perfectly timed merges and gliding down the ramp, directly behind Dahl now. A trio of bicyclists came out of nowhere, blocking our passage as Dahl turned left down Broad Street.

"Come on, come on, come on," Sam chanted, fingers drumming on the steering wheel. "Are you watching Dahl?"

I was pressed far to my right, practically on the dashboard as I watched our suspect. "Broad. Middle lane. Crossing the street. Kimmel Center."

Squeal. I flew across the car as Sam took a sharp left once the cyclists had cleared the lane. I hit Sam's shoulder, which felt like hitting a brick wall.

"Hey, are you okay?" he asked. He looked uncharacteristically concerned.

"Yeah, whatever." I swallowed, tucked a strand of hair behind my ear. "You see him right there?"

Dahl was making another right turn, and we were all the

way in the left lane. The light changed. Dahl sped right, and we moved straight.

"God*dammit*," we cursed in unison. But I caught a flash of movement as we drove past.

"Wait," I said, tapping Sam's arm. "Wait, wait, I think he's parking down the alley."

With another curse, he swerved down a side alley and slammed on the breaks. We both jumped out, scanning the busiest street in Philadelphia. Tourists, people walking dogs, runners, food carts—it was the usual downtown chaos, and I was trying to spot a man I'd only seen once.

"What's the plan?" I asked. "Are we doing a foot chase after all? Or should we—"

I turned around to an empty spot where my partner should have been.

"Sam?" I called out, whirling around. But all I saw was the same chaos—people walking to work as the subway *whooshed* beneath my feet. "*Sam?*"

I leaned back against the hood of the car and tried to breathe through my fury. My *partner* had just committed a grave offense from an FBI standpoint. *Never leave your partner behind.*

But Sam wasn't my partner. Not really. He was the man who irked me to *no fucking end* and would until the end of time.

Out of the corner of my eye, I caught the fluttering of a white banner. Turned toward it, realizing immediately where we were. Every hair on my body stood on end, a pull low in my gut.

The Grand Dame hotel reared above me, dark brown and etched with Art Deco patterns and gargoyles flanking the upper-most floors. It was a renowned Jazz Era hotel—and every year it famously hosted one of the biggest book festivals in the entire world.

Dahl.

If I was a book thief, wouldn't I run with my stolen wares to the 60th Annual Antiquarian Book Festival?

7

SAM

I had missed the thrill of the hunt.

Nothing got my heart racing more than the pursuit. It was the adrenaline spike that zipped through my blood, that made me feel alive. As I raced down Broad Street, I was too distracted to think about how my former FBI partner had been actively breaking the law for years.

I was too distracted to think about how I *might* have had a complete mental breakdown in the Deputy Director's office, surrounded by his staff.

I couldn't think about my unending task list, the federal cases that never got closed, the work pressure that transformed me into an insomniac.

I was even too distracted to think about how I was disobeying direct orders—so intent was I to take Dahl to the ground. My brain only registered actions: *hunt, chase, pursue.*

Win.

"*Sam!*"

Freya's voice made me stumble, *of course*. She was my most distracting distraction. And in the split second it took for me to regain my footing, Dahl slipped deeper into the crowd. I ducked around groups of tourists snapping pictures and sprinted across a crosswalk to the sound of horns blaring. A trash truck roared in front of me, cutting off my line of sight.

I cursed. Slapped the truck on the side. Darted to the left, desperately searching for the same figure on the move.

Nothing.

I was facing an alley between an historic, fancy-looking hotel and a museum. I spotted movement at the very back, which had me sprinting toward the flash of color. Cornering Dahl in an alley would be a quick and painless way to best Freya. Yet the moment my palms met the back wall, I knew I'd made a mistake. I'd chosen the wrong path, trusted a false instinct.

Lost him.

"Fuck," I muttered, dragging a hand across my mouth. Loping back out to the street, I scanned the crowd. He could have grouped up with a crowd. Or he could be hiding in a bush right now with a knife, waiting to attack.

A sense of danger whispered against the back of my neck. Dahl? Another mad book thief? A bright blur of motion flickered in my periphery. My fists clenched, pulse spiking. A small body crashed into mine while shouting the word "*motherfucker.*"

Freya.

My chest and arms collided with her chest and arms, and she would have crashed to the sidewalk if I hadn't dropped down and caught her.

Our faces hovered an inch apart—close enough that I could see the hints of blue in her emerald eyes. Eyes that were wide with disbelief.

And then annoyance.

"I thought you were Dahl."

"I thought *you* were Dahl."

"This is the second time today you've tried to kiss me, by the way," she said. "Remember about the knee-meeting-balls thing."

I swallowed a smirk. Instead I stood quickly, yanking her with me.

"Interesting way of saying *thanks for catching me, Byrne*," I retorted.

Freya's hair had fallen from its bun, and her glasses sat askew on her nose. I went to fix them, then dropped my hands.

"What...what are you doing?" she asked, cagey.

"Nothing." I let my hands land on my tie, absently straightening it. "Dahl's gone, by the way."

"*Interesting way* of saying you lost our suspect, Byrne."

Tourists were clustered around us, cars speeding by. I took Freya by the elbow and headed toward the closest crosswalk. Like earlier, she shook me off, stalking ahead with her spine straight.

"A garbage truck cut me off," I hissed, easily matching her pace. "I followed him into an alley, and he disappeared."

She glanced over her shoulder once, pulling me into a darkened doorway of a hair salon. We were facing the hotel and museum where I'd chased Dahl down.

"That's the book festival Abe's been talking about all day," she said, pointing to the hotel. Now that I was paying attention, I noticed the long white banner stretched across its grandiose entrance: *The 60th Annual Antiquarian Book Festival*.

"Shit," I said.

"My thoughts exactly," she replied. "I ran inside, did a cursory search of the lobby and the first-floor rooms. The convention opens tomorrow morning, so the public spaces were all closed off. He could be in there, checked into a room. Or he could have run to that museum. Or he could have grabbed a cab and sped off to the airport. I couldn't keep a visual on him."

"Me neither," I admitted.

"You know what could have helped the situation? Having your partner there to help you. And not spooking him in the first place."

I scowled, walking quickly to the alley where we'd dumped my car. "Dahl took off. I followed. There isn't a law against it."

"Not a law," Freya said, tapping her chin. "But we don't leave partners behind, do we?"

She was absolutely right—but I didn't reply.

We slid into the car, both of us blowing out twin breaths of irritation. Her phone vibrated with a call from Abe—one glance at her face, and I knew she was as pissed off as I was.

I leaned in to listen, caught her sugar scent. Ignored my body's physical response to her nearness. Ignored the curve of her neck, the glittering gold studs along the curve of her ear. The studs were shaped like stars and planets. Freya Evandale had a veritable universe pierced in her skin.

"Update, please," came Abe's clipped voice as soon as she answered the call.

"Sam and I pursued who we assumed was Dahl all the way from Queen Village to Center City," she explained. "Unfortunately, we lost our visual."

Abe's silence was telling.

"We can't *confirm* where he ended up," I added. "But we believe he ran into The Grand Dame Hotel, sir."

"The book festival?" came his immediate response. Something electric sparked between Freya and me—

brighter than our combined frustration. I knew the unique sensation of this demand.

It was a lead. Abe felt it, too—because his next words were, "Come back to Codex immediately. We need a plan."

"I'm not usually one for brute force, but why don't we make it easy on ourselves and have Sam bust into the hotel with his FBI badge?" Freya said, shrugging. "Ask to see the guest list for the hotel?"

"That's not a good idea," Abe and I both said. Freya's eyes narrowed at me—an attempt to decipher what I hoped wasn't an obvious lie. Except she and I had been trained by the best human lie detectors in the world.

"Why not?" she asked. "Isn't that why we're using Byrne as a consultant?"

I was technically an FBI agent on administrative leave under internal investigation. I was denied FBI privileges at every level, had been stripped of my badge and gun. My privately-owned weapon was holstered at my back, but the weight of it felt off.

"Because I'd rather see Codex agents infiltrate undercover," Abe said. "It's smarter and raises less of a profile. Remember, Scarlett is paying us to be as discreet as possible. Not run into situations with guns blazing."

"That makes sense." Her tone toward her boss was conciliatory.

But the way she was staring at me betrayed her inner desire to call me on my bullshit.

"Let's regroup in twenty," he said. "I've got a signed contract in my hands. We've been hired by a famous Hollywood director for a case with a swift deadline. And the only people I want working it undercover are the two of you."

She rubbed her forehead, avoiding me. I stared at a spot on my windshield, doing the same.

"And not Henry and Del?" she asked. She was worrying at her bottom lip.

"I need their cover as the Thornhills to remain intact for a few pending cases," Abe said. "And I don't want them possibly blowing it to chase down Dahl surrounded by sources they've been cultivating for the past six months." There was a beat. "Are we clear?"

"Yeah, whatever," she muttered. Her body language was hunched, less pissed and more despondent.

"Good," Abe said. "So that means I better not hear that my field agents lost a *librarian intern* during a foot chase ever again. Also clear?"

This time, Freya's green gaze flew to mine, cheeks pink at his sharp tone. It could have been the Quantico classroom again, with Abraham Royal skewering the two of us for bickering during one of his lectures.

"Of course, sir," I said curtly. "Won't happen again."

He made a muffled grunt of assent before disconnecting.

"Looks like this partnership is off to a great start," I said grimly.

8

SAM

Freya and I jumped from the car at the same time, practically sprinting toward the Codex offices.

I hit the door a millisecond before she did, ignoring the whispered insults she muttered behind my back. An older woman with ivory hair sat behind a desk, face buried between the pages of a faded-looking mystery novel. She peeked from behind it, smiling when she saw Freya.

"Byrne, this is Bea," Freya said, giving the woman in question a side-hug. "She runs Marple's Home for Used and Abandoned Books and feeds my paperback addiction. She also doesn't ask too many questions about what we do *on the second floor*." She said this last part in a dramatic stage whisper, which made Bea giggle behind her novel.

"Allow an old woman to dream about book spies," she said. "And Abraham in that suit."

Freya made a *yuck* face. "He's basically my older, more annoying brother."

Bea snorted before turning her gaze to me. "And who is *this* now?"

I extended my hand and shook her hand. "Special Agent Samuel Byrne. A pleasure."

Bea's smile was awfully lascivious.

"Don't let his macho-man act fool you," Freya said, tugging me toward the door that led to Codex. "Byrne's a smug asshole."

"And Freya is the most irritating person I've ever known," I said easily. Bea laughed, thinking us joking, but as soon as the door slammed behind us, only cold fury remained.

"Evandale," I said, stopping her at the top of the stairs. "We just got assigned a case that's a huge fucking deal. I sure as *shit* can't fight with you the whole time."

She turned, arms crossed. Brows raised. "I'm not fighting with you, Bryne. I'm *disagreeing* with how we're handling things. If we're going to be partners, you need to trust that I know what I'm doing too."

"I have more undercover experience than you," I said softly. Pain creased her expression—a bit of those nerves she was failing in hiding. "I think Abe would say I had seniority because of it."

Freya stepped right to me, tips of our shoes touching. "This is how we got all of those fake people killed in our fake hostage crisis."

I almost winced—the memory was not a good one. Our second month at Quantico, Freya and I had been paired up in one of our classes on domestic terrorism. We'd led a team through Hogan's Alley—the fake town the FBI had constructed on the campus for real-life demonstrations. We'd been partners, led hostage negotiators on a simulation with a bomb threat in an office building with twenty hostages. Ten minutes in, we had buckled beneath the weight of our sniping and had failed across the board.

"We got those hostages fake killed because you're too stubborn to ever listen," I shot back. "That was the worst grade I'd ever received, and it was your fault."

Her brows shot even higher. She poked me in the middle of the chest. "If this is open feedback time, I'll remind you that you ran after our suspect and left me behind."

"Because you need to start thinking like an *agent*, Evandale."

"Oh my *god,* why are you the most infuriating man who ever *lived*?" She slapped a palm to her forehead. "We're private detectives, which means for once in the too-many years that I've known you, I have the upper hand. I should have seniority over *you*. And while we're on the topic, are you going to tell your partner why you lied about flashing your FBI badge?"

That stopped me dead in my tracks. The victory etched into her expression only irked me more. "I didn't lie."

"That's another lie," she said, hands on her hips.

"Maybe it's because I don't trust you." I said it harshly—and watched silly, free-spirited Freya Evandale become an ice sculpture. Frozen and stoic.

"Then we do have a problem," she muttered.

The door swung open, and Abraham stood there, face cool. "Once you're done fighting like children, would you like to come inside so we can talk about the most important case of our careers?"

My cheeks burned—I flashed a pissed-off look at Freya. Abe knew me as serious and hard-working and, above all, respectful of authority. There was no way you could grow up in my household and not understand deference. But I'd just let Freya tempt me into a pointless argument in front of one of the finest minds I'd ever known.

My father's words of advice echoed in the silence that followed Abe's instructions. *Fix yourself.*

I was beginning to fully understand the sentiment.

Freya and I both grumbled *sorry* and slid past Abe into the Codex office. Delilah and Henry stood at a table with their heads together, sifting through piles of paper and old books. A whiteboard stood in the middle of the room, and various laptops were running. I guessed they were all Freya's, based on the open programs. As an agent, I'd gone through intensive training in computer science. But what she could do was above and beyond my meager understanding.

Abe pressed two bags of what smelled like tacos into our hands. "Eat, then talk," he said. But as soon as I sat down, Freya was already typing frantically on one of the laptops, bag empty.

"What did you do, swallow them whole?" I eyed her guardedly.

She smirked, but her focus never left her screen.

"Talents, Byrne. I told you I got 'em." It was a subtle dig at our argument in the stairwell. But I'd known Freya long enough to know this new light tone was her way of waving a minuscule white flag—at least until we sorted out our plan.

"While Henry and Delilah work with Francisco on interviewing his other staff," Abe said, "I want Sam and Freya to work out how to get into that book festival. I don't like the coincidence of Dahl possibly fleeing there. My first thought is to send Freya and Sam in undercover, find the buyer, recover the letters."

Click-click-click went Freya's fingers across the keyboard. Distracted, I glanced at her over my shoulder, but her face was set in deep concentration.

"Let's walk this through." On the board, Abe wrote

undercover identities with a big question mark next to it. As much as I wanted to indulge in the bag of food, I wanted even more to prove to Abe that the favor he was doing for the Deputy Director wasn't a giant mistake.

So I jumped in. "Freya and I go undercover as booksellers. Invent an identity, put the word out that we're in the market for rare love letters. See what floats to the top."

"The book fair is sold out," she said from behind me. "They're not selling tickets at the door."

I tampered down my irritation. "That seems like a simple fix. Surely we can call and demand tickets if we convince them we're rich and powerful enough."

Abe said, "An intriguing idea. Unless you have a better one, Freya?"

The man was smart—and knew how to goad his most competitive students into brilliance.

"I do actually have an idea," she said. "Thanks to my expert sleuthing, I've learned that two of the guests that were expected to attend this weekend canceled unexpectedly because they're sick. Supposedly."

She popped a pen into her bun, expression hopeful. I knew this look—this was Freya at her most genius.

"Who canceled?" Henry asked.

"Julian King and Birdie Barnes." She wiggled her fingers through the air. "The rock stars of rare books."

9

FREYA

"I remember those names," Delilah said.

"What are you talking about?" Sam asked. My nemesis was perched on the edge of the table, still looking immaculate even after a foot pursuit and a car chase.

"Julian King and Birdie Barnes are two people I've been tracking on Under the Rose," I explained. Sam stood up, interest piqued, and walked toward me on the couch. I gave him a quick summary of what I'd told Delilah about—the secret patterns, the messages about letters, the names that kept appearing. "The first level of code words used is asking the question, 'didn't we once meet each other at Reichenbach Falls?'"

Sam actually sat down next to me on the couch, his body taking up more space than I wanted.

"It's a reference to a Sherlock Holmes story," Henry added. "The story where Holmes fakes his own death, although Doyle originally intended for the character to be killed off for good. But readers were so incensed he was forced to bring him back to life in the next story."

"But I believe there's another code phrase, another level of thievery and deception," I continued. "This group of people is always talking about their *empty houses*."

Henry seemed intrigued but stayed silent.

"Julian and Birdie are beloved," I said. "Trusted. May already be into shady shit, given their big price tags. I think it'd be a straightforward identity to assume with the largest pay-off."

"Assuming the identity of *real* people is a much greater risk," Sam rumbled next to me. The back of my neck prickled, reacting to his nearness.

I turned to him, palms up. "Sure, being Julian and Birdie is a risk, but the reward is a faster way to earn trust. I've been low-key stalking these two for the last couple of days. No photos of them exist online. They use their bookstore logos as avatars on the site. Their social media pages are only two years old. Just posts about the store, nothing identifying."

"I think we can assume Julian and Birdie are using aliases," Delilah chimed in. "Which makes it less risky, since you can become anyone with that kind of identity."

"Unless we meet someone there who's met the real Julian and Birdie in person," Sam said.

That insight thudded into our debate.

Abe rubbed his jaw, glancing out the window. "Do you have a sense of how much Dahl saw you during your car chase?"

Sam's mouth pinched in the middle. "That could be an issue. If he's in attendance, he could make us as the ones who tried to run him down." Disappointment sloped along his shoulders.

"Counterpoint," I said, "Dahl won't be there. Let's be honest. It's likely that dude was the go-between. Responsible for the drop and nothing else. What happened this morning was *unfortunate* but probably didn't hurt our chances that badly."

Sam appeared surprised at the life preserver I'd tossed him. Almost as surprised as I was that I'd thrown it to him.

"What would your plan be if your cover was blown?" Abe asked.

"Throw a drink in their face like a woman on *Real Housewives*," I said. "Run away as fast as I can."

"Not bad," he said dryly. "Sam, I'd like to hear your response from a Bureau perspective."

"Honestly, there wouldn't be much *to* do," Sam said. "I've never had my cover blown before. But FBI procedure would direct us to inform the person they were mistaken"—Sam cleared his throat—"and get out of there alive."

Abe nodded, face grave. "The longer you'd be undercover as Julian and Birdie, the more dangerous it will become. Our ticking clock is fast on this one for a number of reasons. The festival is three days long. We have four days—max—to recover these letters. And your cover could be blown, easily, at any second."

Next to me, Sam leaned forward onto his knees. "All due respect, sir, I think we'd be playing with fire. Agents at the Bureau could find these letters faster than we can."

"Not based on my experience," Abe said, voice chilly. "It'll take them four days just to get their act together. The letters will have disappeared. I guarantee it."

Sam's hands clenched into fists, tendons standing out in his forearms. If anyone drank the FBI Kool-Aid, it was Sam. But Codex had been Abe's counterargument against the Bureau's sluggish bureaucracy. Given our impressive success rate, I tended to side with Abe on that matter.

"I think Sam and I were born to play Julian and Birdie," I continued. "They're already interested in rare letters. That's an access point we can manipulate. If we assume new identities, there's no telling if we could infiltrate this next level during the course of this festival."

"We'd draw less attention to ourselves if the identities were our own," Sam interjected. "Which, according to the contract, is what our client wishes. Seems like that should take precedence over following a tenuous code word that might not even exist."

"Oh, it exists," I shot back.

"Your proof is circumstantial, at best."

"I've been working these contacts for three years. I know a pattern when I see one."

"And I know a sloppy plan when I hear one," Sam said.

"We'll go with Freya," Abe said, cutting our argument off cold. Sam and I were still glaring at each other, assuming our favorite adversarial positions—and Abe's decision shocked us both.

"What?" Sam said.

"Um...what?" I echoed.

Abe was writing *Julian King and Birdie Barnes* on the board. "Freya, you'll be working your first undercover case as Birdie Barnes. Sam will be Julian King. Spend tonight and tomorrow morning developing your cover stories so that you can successfully uncover where Jim Dahl is, where those letters are, and who the hell has them. Once we have that information, we can make an extraction plan."

Delilah and Henry were already jumping into familiar action—but I was still frozen in place.

"Freya?" Abe said. "Do you have any issues with this?"

I had about a metric fuck-ton of issues with it—but with my irritating rival sitting next to me, I decided that a smug, "That sounds grand," was my best next play.

Internally, I was screaming like a banshee. I'd let my

need to *win* against Byrne convince my boss to send me undercover on a high-profile case with a hard deadline and Sam as my partner.

Debating with Sam in class had been my favorite thing to do—pressing on the vulnerabilities in his arguments. Exposing the flaws. He did the same to me in the most aggravating way possible. It was our version of a relaxing Sunday morning brunch.

I'd let Byrne yank me into an argument I accidentally won. And now my most annoying enemy would have a front-row seat to all the reasons why I couldn't hack it as an FBI agent.

"Sam?" Abe arched a brow his way.

"We'll make it work, sir," he replied.

Abe tapped the whiteboard. "Well done, Freya. Seems like your behind-the-scenes work was exactly what we needed to put you undercover."

I nodded meekly—an action Delilah didn't miss. She glanced at me, her face kind.

"What if I helped you and Sam prep tonight?" she said. "We can run through scenarios for your characters, get the two of you on the same page."

"I'd love that, actually. Should I call for more emergency tacos?" But when I stood to give my friend a grateful hug, the room slanted violently, and I pitched forward, vision gray.

"Hey, careful," came Sam's voice, sounding uncharacteristically gentle. But his hands were locked tight around my arms, cradling me. I blinked. His face swam back into view. "Are you okay?"

"Of course," I said, uneasy. Adrenaline had tricked my body into staying awake for almost two days straight.

"When was the last time you slept?" Sam asked, eyes narrowed.

"I'm going to guess Monday," Abe said. Delilah was already pressing a glass of cold water into my hands.

"I get a little *fainty* when I'm not sleeping," I explained. With control, Sam edged me upright. I was wobbly, but able to drink the water. While trying not to notice the heat of his reassuring palm low on my back.

"I know. This used to happen at Princeton during finals," he said. "I once caught her before she fell down a flight of stairs at the library."

The glass paused at my mouth. "Wait. You did?"

"You forgot my act of dramatic heroism?" he asked, voice dry.

The memory flared to life, buried beneath a hundred others. We'd been at the top of the fourth-floor staircase at Princeton's library. It was late, past 1:00 in the morning. I'd been teasing Sam, being silly—my flirtatiousness a by-product of having slept a combined six hours in three days. One moment, I'd been trying to get him to laugh—a pointless endeavor. The next, I was tumbling down the stairs.

And Sam had caught me. When my eyes opened, I'd been clutching at his worn black sweater, fingers grazing the hard planes of his chest. He'd looked terribly frightened. And I'd wondered what would happen if I leaned in and kissed his throat.

"I...remember it now." My voice was shaky. "Your heroism did not go unnoticed. Thank you."

"You don't look right," he continued—looking like he had that day, holding me in the stairwell. Although he had the nerve to look *hotter*.

"I am, I promise." My smile at Sam was truly sincere,

which brought color to his cheeks. "Anyway, where do you want to chat, Del?"

"Not a chance," Abe said, nodding at Sam, who was already gently escorting me toward the door. "Delilah will drive you home."

I inhaled to argue, but a vicious yawn stopped me in my tracks. Exhaustion settled over my bones, threatening to drag me under.

"The next seventy-two hours are going to be stressful," Abe said quietly. "I won't have my agents going into a high-pressure situation on no sleep."

"But I need to prep, Abe. I've never gone undercover like this for Codex before." My anxiety was duking it out for dominance over my exhaustion. "Don't I need—"

"You need sleep," Sam said. "I'll work with Delilah for a couple of hours and then I'll pick you up at your house in the morning. We can reconvene and head to the hotel in the morning to register."

The thought of my giant warm bed and a cup of tea felt so fucking amazing I almost fainted again out of sheer need. "Maybe you're right."

"They're right," Delilah murmured next to me. "I wouldn't let these guys send you home if they were wrong." She draped my jacket over me and squeezed my shoulders.

"Hey, Frey?" We all turned to Henry, looking every bit the dapper librarian, surrounded by open books and scribbled notes. "I'm pretty damn sure you're right about that code."

"House?" I asked. "Empty house? Thirteenth house?"

"Empty house," he said confidently. "It's a Sherlock Holmes reference."

Sam turned to openly gawk at me.

"Sherlock Holmes fakes his own death in the story *The*

Final Problem. In the next story, Sherlock re-appears to Dr. Watson. Alive and very well, much to Watson's surprise. They're investigating the case of a colonial governor killed by a gunshot to the temple. The mystery being the man was in a room that locked from the inside, and the only escape would have been through a window with a twenty-foot drop. And not a single person heard the sound of a shot."

Ever the FBI agent, Sam asked, "How did the murderer get away with it?"

"If I remember correctly, it was a sniper with an air rifle. When Sherlock Holmes reveals himself to John Watson, he's disguised as an elderly bookseller." Henry paused, adjusted his glasses. "The story was called *The Adventure of The Empty House*."

10

FREYA

It was 6:59 a.m., and Sam's boring car was pulling in front of my rowhouse.

I peered through the pink curtains in my bedroom, watching him step out of the driver's side and scan the street —presumably for criminals. His suit today was a dark blue. As usual, his hair was perfect, face clean-shaven.

I didn't know what Julian King looked like in real life, but I figured it was a safe bet that Sam Byrne would give him a run for his money in the looks department.

I glanced at my own reflection in my floor-length mirror. The night of uninterrupted sleep had eradicated the haze in my brain. But the sight of Sam—and the knowledge of what we were about to do—lit a fire beneath my nerves, sending them cartwheeling. I pressed a hand to my stomach to quell the twitchiness.

My cat, Minerva, meowed from the doorway.

"How do I look?" I asked her, striking a dramatic pose. For the first time in my entire life, I was wearing a *tight* sweater—black—instead of my usual extra-large sweater. Black pants, red high-heels I'd found in the back of my closet. Lipstick to match and a set of dusty (fake) pearls I'd once worn on Halloween when I'd gone dressed as *Vogue*-era Madonna. Even my trademark bun was neat and tidy.

To the mirror, I said, "You are Birdie Barnes. Rare bookseller. Rock star among thieves."

But when I pressed a stray strand of hair back into position, my fingers were trembling.

Sam's sharp knock sent Minerva fleeing down the stairs, and I was quick to follow her. When I opened the door, Sam stared at me quizzically. "You look different."

"You look the same," I said. I pulled him into my hallway and closed the door. His imposing shape dominated the narrow space, and his jaw worked, expression a mystery, as he examined the framed art on the wall. I'd never even seen inside his dorm room—not at Princeton. Certainly not at Quantico. Seeing him now, in my actual home, made me feel naked.

"Do you want, um...a cup of tea?" I asked, backing away from his broad shoulders.

He nodded, casually looking around as I led him through my tiny sitting room with the window seat—perfect for rainy-day reading—and into my kitchen. He pulled out a kitchen stool. Minerva jumped onto the counter and tried to climb his shoulders. As I put the kettle on, I chanced a glance when Sam wasn't looking—it was such an oddly domestic moment, I wanted to pinch myself.

"Who's this?" he asked.

"Minerva," I said. "A stray the animal rescue found living behind Bauman's Rare Books in Old City. She looked feral when I adopted her but adapted overnight to being an indoor love-bug."

I poured steaming water into two blue mugs with Earl

Grey teabags and caught Sam tapping Minerva lightly on the nose.

"Minerva, as in McGonagall?" he asked. "Harry Potter, right?"

I tilted my head. "How would you know about that? You told me at Quantico that you never read for pleasure."

It had been a random anecdote he had shared with me one day, pestering me as I dog-eared a worn paperback before a sparring session. My little nerd-girl heart had wilted at his admission.

He lifted a shoulder. "I read."

"Yeah?"

"I read those books, anyway."

"*You* read Harry Potter?"

"After you told me about them." He looked a little uncomfortable.

"Oh," I said, completely shocked. "Did you enjoy them?"

"Yeah. I read them all in a week." Sam didn't smile, but he did hold my gaze while sipping his tea. Minerva butted her head against his shoulder. Picturing him in bed reading my favorite books made me feel fizzy, like a shaken-up can of soda.

"I finally understand why you used to call me your *personal Malfoy*." His tone was dry, mouth curved like a comma.

I hid a smirk. "I never could figure out the spell to shut you up."

He raised his mug at me in cheers. "Same."

I scratched my bun, pretended to be interested in my tea. Sam touched a fingertip to his mug, which had a picture of a vintage Nintendo controller. The text beneath read *Self-Rescuing Princess*.

"You had this at Quantico," he said.

"Well, I've been nailing my personal brand for years," I shrugged. Our gazes met for a feverish second. Dropped immediately.

"So you're probably a Gryffindor," I said.

"Extremely brave and incredibly strong? Of course."

I tapped my lip. "And yet you weren't valedictorian of our class at Princeton, were you?"

He didn't reply, but his nostrils flared. Slipping back to our constant back-and-forth felt as soft and comfortable as a favorite sweatshirt. Sam's eyes, however, lacked any sense of *comfort*. Instead, they flashed dark blue and hungry.

I took a step back—startled—and bumped into the counter.

"We should prepare," he said. "Delilah dropped a few things off at my hotel room this morning." He slid two driver's licenses my way—there were our wallet-sized pictures and the address of King Barnes Rare Books. Mine falsely identified me as *Birdie Barnes*.

"The things the kids can do these days," I remarked. "Who did Delilah use?"

"A gentleman she referred to as *Grim*."

"The less an FBI agent knows about him, the better," I said. "Grim enjoys strolling through the legal gray-area, same as Codex."

"I got that impression. He make IDs for you often?"

I shrugged, pocketing the fake ID. "Depends on how deep we're going. Usually we're not undercover for long. But for an event like this, I'm sure they'll require identification."

He held a dangling chain out across the counter. "Delilah also gave me this watch and this necklace for you."

"Spy shit," I cheered, slipping the necklace from Sam's outstretched fingers. I dropped it over my head, the gold bauble landing right below my breasts. "There's a tiny camera in here."

"Did Grim make these for you?"

"Please," I said. "You can get this at Best Buy."

Another almost-smile from my rival. He showed me the watch on his wrist. "Camera inside here too."

I nodded. "Without a warrant, I'm guessing you're bound to private investigator rules. That means we can legally take pictures of anything we see that's shady. But we can't record voices or conversations."

"Got it."

"What else did you and Del review last night?

"Playing up the notoriety angle. Letting our fans fawn over us. Inciting a sense of trust by allowing them to feel close to us."

"I like it."

"We don't speak unless spoken to," he continued. I knew this lesson, but my nerves clamored to hear it again. "Listen and watch everything. Let everyone else do the talking. Allow for silences. No promises, no commitments."

"Birdie and Julian are sexy thieves, I think," I said.

"This is based on evidence?"

"You don't think we're sexy?" I kept our eyes locked as I drank, saw Sam's flick down my body for a nanosecond.

"Sure." His voice was thick. Clearing his throat, he said, "My sense is that Julian and Birdie are extremely wealthy. Smart and savvy. Elegant."

I snorted. "I'll have to work hard to nail down *elegant*."

"You won't," he said.

I touched my hair, unsure of what to do with that. "So... sexy thieves with adoring fans who are elegant and filthy rich. Got it."

Sam stared down at his mug, turning it left and right.

"Codex has been working more intimately with book dealers than the agents in the Art Theft department. In your opinion, how would Julian and Birdie be running an illegal operation through their legal bookstore in San Francisco?"

I clicked my nails on my mug. "We could have connections to libraries and museums. A shady contact who steals the books. We give them a cut, turn around and sell it for a significant profit. Masquerade as a legitimate bookstore, but underneath we're illegal as hell."

"At a place like the book festival..."

"We'd be looking to acquire illegal books. And legal ones, of course, to maintain the façade. Solidify the relationships we have to build trust. Close the circle and keep it tight."

His expression brightened. "That's our angle. Sexy thieves looking for illegal wares while maintaining our allegiances."

"I think that's absolutely what Julian and Birdie would do. At least the Julian and Birdie we're going to be," I said. "And I can't believe I got you to say *sexy thieves*."

His gaze lingered on my lips. "I can't believe we had a fairly civil conversation that ended on agreement."

"I'm sure a pig will fly past this window any second," I replied. We *almost* smirked at each other.

"I like your kitchen," he finally said. "Do you have books hidden in your pantry?"

Cheeks warm, I hooked my index finger on the pantry latch. Tugged it open to reveal five shelves full of paperback books instead of the requisite cans of soup.

"You know me so well, Byrne."

"I do though," he said.

"Oh, um..." I mumbled. "I guess that's true."

Sam looked about as awkward as I felt. He went to stand

by a wall I'd painted bright yellow and decorated with framed vintage book covers. From the top of a bookshelf, he picked up a blue frame. I knew the picture well—wished, suddenly, that I'd hidden it from view before he arrived.

"You and your mom?" he asked. I stepped closer, careful not to let our shoulders touch. As embarrassed as I felt, the picture still brought me happy sparks of joy.

"That was my fifth grade Halloween costume," I explained. In the picture, I was wearing a short red wig and rocking a pantsuit like a powerful woman in a sitcom. My mom wore a suit and a long pea coat, her hair tucked into a men's wig. "We went as Agent Mulder and Scully from *The X-Files,* of course. My mom was so obsessed with David Duchovny, she volunteered to be him *immediately*."

Sam looked more wistful than anything. "You always said she was nerdier than you."

"She raised me right," I said proudly. "Also, all night I got to flash a fake FBI badge and say things like *Mulder, that's just not plausible*. And she'd say, *The truth is out there, Scully*. It was my favorite Halloween, actually."

His throat worked as he continued to stare at the faded picture.

"Did your mom dress up with you at Halloween?" I asked cautiously. His mother had died when he was twelve. In all the years that I'd known him, he'd only spoken of her a handful of times. He always looked like he wanted to say more.

Now, he nodded his head and said, "She loved anything that felt like magic."

In the remaining silence, our shoulders had drifted closer, barely brushing. I took a step back from his natural magnetism—only to find him pinning me with a discerning look.

"What?" I asked.

"You always did want to be an FBI agent, didn't you?"

Regret slid down my spine. *Why hadn't I hidden this damn picture*?

"I did," I said, raising my chin on instinct. Steeling my voice. "But dreams don't always work out."

He flashed me a strange look. Then put the frame back —gently. But as I moved past Sam toward the hallway, he reached out. Caught my wrist and held me still.

"Are we sparring, Agent Byrne?" My voice fluttered. His thumb swiped once across my pulse point before he let go.

"Are we avoiding talking about our fight in the stairwell? The one from yesterday?"

"Oh, that," I said flatly. I tugged at the sleeves of my sweater, avoided looking directly at him. "Listen. You and I have a long...history together."

"Correct," he said. "And?"

"You've made it clear that, given the choice, you wouldn't want to be my partner. And I don't want to be your partner either." The words flew out quickly, but I didn't enjoy the feeling they left in their wake. "Four days is all we've got. Then I'm sure your dad will pull you back to the FBI, right?"

His throat worked. "I could be consulting a bit after."

I shrugged. "My point is that our situation is temporary. Extremely temporary. If we're going to be successful, we should keep our heads down and get it over with."

The faster we found those love letters, the faster I could be back where I belonged—behind a computer screen. And Sam could go back to being a distant, aggravating memory.

"Fine by me," he grunted.

"You're not going to tell me what this *consultant* position is actually about, are you?" I asked softly, crossing my arms.

"I'll be returning to the FBI either way," he replied.

"That wasn't an answer."

"That's all the answer I can give you."

The thought of Sam hiding the truth made my chest tighten uncomfortably.

"Partners..." I cleared my throat. "Partners need to be honest with each other."

"Then tell me why you're nervous to go undercover."

"I'm not nervous," I lied.

He took a step closer to me. "If you want us to be *real* partners, even for a few days, you can't demand honesty from me and not return it. Does it have anything to do with why you left Quantico? Because you can tell me why you quit."

"Do you truly care?" I asked.

Sam rubbed his neck. "More than you think."

A lingering silence stretched between us. What would it be like to give in to that persistent urge to press my cheek to Sam's chest and let him hug me?

"I know you care. I know, Byrne." My tone was conciliatory, and when our eyes met, I touched his arm. Briefly. I considered saying more but stopped myself. All that time trapped in arguments, we had cultivated a false intimacy. But sharing my health struggles with him felt too vulnerable, too authentically intimate. I wasn't sure if I could bare my soul to a man I felt this strongly about. Too strongly to ever admit to weakness.

"Tell me why you're nervous," he said.

My nostrils flared. It was always *push* for *push* with this man. "Tell me what's really going on with your job."

He took another step, foot sliding between mine. "One day in and you're already more frustrating than my actual fucking partner, and he's—"

His mouth clamped shut. He stepped back from me and strode toward the front door.

"Let's go."

"Wait, wait," I said. "Your partner was...what? Your partner at Art Theft, you mean?"

"Gregory," Sam finally said. "When I go back, I'll have a new partner."

He was leaving that gap of information for me to fill in with assumptions. And my assumption was that he and his former partner were being split apart intentionally.

"Was he not good?"

"Not honest."

A not-honest partner. A consultant position that didn't seem completely on the level. And a weariness etched into his face when he forgot to school his expression.

I stepped right back up to him. "I'll tell you the truth when you tell me the truth. How's that for a deal?"

His tone was dry. "And for a moment there, I thought we were getting along."

My lips twitched. "We're in a tenuous truce at best."

"Our professors at Quantico would be proud."

"Our professors at Quantico would be failing us right now because we're about to be late on our first day."

He cursed under his breath. "Goddammit. Get in the car."

"After you, Julian."

Sam stalked out my front door and down my front steps—walking angrily, as he often did when he was around me.

Except this time, I was more focused on the phantom feeling of his fingers on my wrist.

Equal parts strength and plea.

I liked it.

11

SAM

"Dreams do come true," Freya said, head falling all the way back as she took in the lobby at The Grand Dame hotel.

It was, admittedly, a paradise for a book-nerd like her. The domed ceiling was carved with Art Deco designs—hanging from the center was a banner welcoming people to the 60th Annual Antiquarian Book Festival. Two curving staircases dominated the room, draped with a blood-red carpet. The massive fireplace against the right-side wall was decorated with classical-looking portraits and colonial-era lanterns.

And the room was packed with booksellers. Cart after cart moved past us, all of them covered in tarps and canvasses to protect the antiquities inside. Two distinguished-looking men with handlebar mustaches brushed past, talking excitedly about scientific advancements in gilded edge analysis. A tall woman wore a hat plumed with peacock feathers. In front of us, the line crawled toward the registration area—and behind that, two doors opened into a cavernous room filled with even more people.

A quick inventory of my physical reactions revealed a surprise.

I actually felt *excited*.

Nervous, of course—but that was par for the course when you were about to assume an undercover identity. But mostly I could sense wonder. Intuition and genuine interest. A strong desire to find those love letters pulling me toward the cave-like room ahead of us.

So different from my reactions at Art Theft when a case landed in my lap. Even before I'd been made aware of Gregory's betrayal, I was engaged in a daily battle with exhaustion, entwined with sheer panic. It was the oddest dual sensation I'd ever experienced, the urge to crawl under my desk and sleep for a hundred years. And the urge to crawl under my desk to hide my frenzied stress.

"Let me do most of the talking when we get to the front," I muttered, straightening my tie one last time.

"Sure thing, Julian," Freya said. Her smile was cheeky until she bit her bottom lip. A tell that indicated she was afraid.

"You acquiesced to that request more easily than I anticipated," I said, noting her nerves.

"I'm a woman full of surprises," she replied. "Plus, I believe business acquaintances probably don't bicker like we do."

We moved close to the front—only one person away from registering. Freya's green eyes flicked toward mine, snapping our roles into place just like that.

I didn't want to acknowledge the other reason why this case was exciting.

Freya Evandale was the epitome of *sexy thief*.

And it pissed me the hell off.

Back in her kitchen, I kept spiraling between arousal

and anger so fast my head spun. I'd never seen her in anything even remotely form-fitting. Not that it mattered—Freya-in-big-sweaters was who she was and I liked that. A lot actually.

But Freya in a tight, low-cut black sweater and fitted black pants was an extra diversion I didn't fucking need right now. She was nothing but graceful lines and glimpses of pale flesh, red lips and vibrant eyes behind her glasses. This morning, I'd craved her trust as much as I'd craved her fighting back.

Both cravings had me longing to pin her to the wall and kiss her throat.

"Welcome to the Book Festival," the ticket lady said, beaming at us with a friendly expression. "Last names, please."

"King," I said. "Julian King. And this is Birdie Barnes. We're representing the King Barnes bookstore out of San Francisco."

The woman brightened even further. "Oh! Oh, we're so glad to hear you recovered from your flu. You sounded horrible when we spoke on the phone yesterday."

On cue, Freya coughed into her elbow. "The miracles of Tamiflu, prescribed just in time."

The woman's fingers flew over her keyboard. "Of course, of course. And luckily your hotel room is still booked under your names. Room 211. Shall we check your bags? Your books?"

"Airline lost everything, if you can believe it." I managed. Leaning in, I dropped my voice. "We've arrived with nothing."

"They lost your books?" The woman looked horrified. As she should be. If we *were* rare book dealers, a loss like that would be financially and personally devastating.

"Delayed," I clarified. "Stuck in the Phoenix airport. We've been assured they're locked away for safekeeping."

"Wonderful news. IDs, please?"

I gave her a tight nod as I removed my fake license.

"Thank you. Security is a concern of ours this weekend, Mr. King," the woman said. "I'll need to copy these for our file." She returned a second later with our IDs and badges to wear.

"Any particular reason why you're concerned?" Freya asked, tone light.

The woman leaned across the table. "No idea. But Dr. Ward has us on strict rules for identification."

"Makes sense," Freya said. "Things have certainly been dicey in this field recently."

"That they have." Her walkie-talkie squawked next to her. "Ah, I forgot. The Alexanders will be quite happy to hear of your miraculous recovery."

This time, Freya stiffened next to me.

Glancing at the white registration binder, I dropped my voice again. "Has Jim Dahl checked in yet?" We might as well *know* if we were going to bump into a man who might recognize us as frauds.

Frowning, the woman flipped through. Shook her head. "Mr. Dahl isn't listed as being in attendance. Has there been a mistake?"

"No, ma'am," Freya said smoothly. "We thought he might change his mind at the last minute. Seems like we were right."

Not a moment later, as we shuffled past the check-in table and into a very crowded hallway, a booming voice called out to us.

"*As I live and breathe.*" An older white couple, dressed in expensive-looking clothing, came striding through the crowd with outstretched hands. "Julian King and Birdie Barnes."

The woman had red-hair, porcelain skin, and an alluring expression aimed right at me. The man was much shorter, with a gray mustache and wire-rimmed glasses. They appeared star-struck, surprised—and deeply pleased.

We were the rock stars of rare books.

Before we could prepare, Freya and I were having our hands shaken by the pair. Their badges identified them as *Thomas Alexander* and *Cora Alexander*. I could see the gears of Freya's mind working.

"Thomas and Cora," she said, "what an honor to finally meet you in person."

"What an honor to meet the convention's most *notable* guests," Thomas exclaimed "Come, come. He's about to give his opening remarks, but he'll be very happy to hear you've made it. When we'd learned you'd been struck down by illness, we were simply *aghast*."

Thomas and Cora were already on the move through the crowd, heading toward a machine I was very familiar with.

Beep-beep went the metal detector.

"We've been anticipating meeting you as well," I said. "This event is one we look forward to every year."

A quizzical look from Cora. "But this is your first year attending though. Isn't it?"

"Absolutely," Freya jumped in. "What Julian means is that we've always looked forward to it even though we could never attend. It's a dream come true for us."

The flash of concern across Thomas's face mirrored my own. This was why I hadn't wanted to *be* Julian and Birdie. Too easy to make mistakes when you had no clue about the relationships you held.

"Is that so?" Thomas asked. But his tone had a crisp edge to it. Freya heard it, fiddling with the pearls at her neck.

"As you know, Julian and I have had an empty house for a week now. We're looking forward to...meeting everyone." Freya said this in a low voice, holding eye contact with the couple.

Empty house. It was the code word she had unearthed online. The one I'd given her a ton of shit about. Yet as soon as the words left her mouth, it was like a switch had been thrown.

Thomas and Cora exchanged tiny smiles. They both took a step closer to us.

Maybe Freya had been right. Not that I'd ever say that to her face.

"We as well," Thomas replied. "And if you're concerned about keeping in touch, rest assured we made sure to book the hotel room next to yours. You won't be able to escape us this weekend. And I think you'll be truly impressed with the festivities. Most first-timers usually are."

"Wonderful," Freya said. I gave a nod. We were six feet from the metal detector now.

"I'm afraid everyone needs to go through these blasted things," Thomas said. "Cora and I will be waiting for the two of you inside. Dr. Ward's remarks begin in ten minutes."

"Great," Freya and I answered in unison. The very second the couple was out of earshot, Freya and I spun toward each other.

"I told you we were sexy thieves with a code word," she whispered.

"We have bigger issues right now," I whispered back. *Beep. Beep.* "Seems unlikely that a rare bookseller would be carrying a weapon, right?"

Freya fake-laughed and hissed. “Oh my god, *you brought your gun* inside with you?”

I fake-laughed in response. “Oh my god, *you didn’t?*”

“We’re chasing after stolen letters, you nit-wit.”

“You’d know this if you hadn’t dropped out of Quantico, but the world of antiquities theft is pretty cozy with violent crime. Safety should be our priority.”

Her eyes scorched the brightest green I’d ever seen.

“Right this way, sir,” the security guard interrupted, waving us through. I froze, mind searching for a way out.

All of a sudden, Freya was shoving me out of the line. “We’ll be right back,” she said to the guard. She dragged me down a narrow hallway and pushed open a swinging door with one shoulder.

The men’s bathroom, thankfully empty.

“Not a bad move,” I admitted, searching for a hiding space.

“Especially for a dropout like me, huh?” She didn’t turn around, but hurt creased the words.

Which made me feel like shit for once.

Freya kicked open a stall, hands searching. She opened trashcans and the toilet tank. I glanced up, saw the paneled ceiling. I stood on the toilet, reached behind me, and removed my gun from its holster. Ejected the magazine. Pushed the panel above me and carefully slid everything inside before sliding the panel back.

Freya was leaning against the bathroom door with her arms crossed.

“Evandale.” Her eyebrows rose in response. “Listen, I feel—”

The bathroom door opened with a loud *creak*. Freya’s feet would be visible from beneath the stall if we didn’t move fast. I crouched down, hoping whoever entered hadn’t seen me placing a gun into the ceiling. I spun, lifted Freya by the waist, and deposited her where I'd been, her legs up on the seat and out of sight. Hair flew from her bun, her expression one of shock.

My hand covered her mouth. The other flushed the toilet to mask the sounds of our movement. Rushing water filled the tight space. The other man was washing his hands, drying them. Freya's mouth was warm beneath my palm, her breath tickling my fingers. A surge of dominance hit me low in the gut—a sensation that only happened when I was around Freya. My weakest moments around this woman were when I allowed my sexual attraction to edge past my irritation. It was the way she uncovered my secret buttons and gleefully pushed them—I yearned for the sweetness of her submission.

I dropped my palm. Forced that yearning back to the darkest recesses of my brain.

"I'm sorry," I mouthed, aware of the footsteps moving along the tiles.

She tapped her ear. The faucet flipped on again—I leaned down, mouth against her skin. "I'm sorry for what I said about Quantico," I whispered.

She pointed to my chest. "You are a dick," she mouthed.

My lips twitched. I shrugged. "I know," I mouthed back. The door swung open, and the man left. Freya and I let out twin sighs of relief.

"You never apologized for being a dick at the academy. Or Princeton. You must be evolving as a person."

"When was I ever a dick at the academy?"

"Literally every second."

"You have an awfully subjective memory."

"All human beings do. Oh, wait, you're a robot, I forgot —" She was swinging the door open, smirking at me, when she walked right into a man with a top hat and a purple cravat.

"*Oof.*" She bounced off him, and I reached forward, steadying her while pulling her against my side. The man was clearly startled to see the two of us coming out of the men's bathroom.

"He's terrified of toilets," she explained. "Strange phobia, I know."

Jesus Christ.

I smiled weakly at the man before yanking Freya by the elbow toward the metal detector. "Was that necessary?" I growled.

"Toilet phobia is very real."

We re-approached the beeping machine, and even though I'd hidden my contraband, I bristled with nerves. We couldn't be discovered so soon into our undercover roles —it'd be the worst kind of failure. I certainly couldn't look the Deputy Director—my father— in the eye and tell him I'd failed again.

"Step through, miss," the security guard said. He waved his wand over Freya then beckoned to me. I stepped through.

Silence.

"You're clear to go," the guard said. I nodded, joined Freya at the end of the hallway. Two large white doors swung open into an exhibit hall filled with hundreds of people; booths with black tablecloths, stacks and stacks of books, and a lit stage. I searched for our suspect who, at this point, could have been anywhere.

"Julian. Birdie. You made it through." Thomas and Cora Alexander stood in front of us, arms linked. I assessed them as glamorous high society—the kind with waitstaff and a service elevator and vacation homes in luxury destinations.

And for reasons I didn't yet know, we were part of a shared world that was a complete and utter mystery to me.

"We did," I said. "We're looking forward to the festivities."

Thomas nodded his head at us. "Let's get you two settled in, shall we? And welcome to the 60th Annual Antiquarian Book Festival, my dear friends."

12

FREYA

It was barely past breakfast on the first day of an antiquarian book festival. And Thomas and Cora Alexander were dressed like they were about to board the *Titanic.*

Cora's red hair was immaculately coiffed, her eyes sharp, missing nothing. This woman knew me as Birdie Barnes. But *I* knew her as one of the members of this *empty house* club that I'd been spying on through the Under the Rose website. From my basic sleuthing, Cora and Thomas Alexander had married young and consolidated their money and empires. Thomas made his money in big oil; Cora was an heiress and low-level British aristocracy by blood. The Manhattanites had made a name for themselves by being sophisticated antiques-lovers. Even the *New York Times* had many flattering articles about their collection of art and rare manuscripts.

"You've made it just in time," Cora mused. "The booths are opening now. But, of course, the two of you will have access to whatever your heart's desire."

Like stolen love letters?

"Our hearts desire quite a bit," Sam replied. He slipped his hands into his pockets, looking like the dashing book thief he was pretending to be. The soft light from the chandeliers bounced off his blond hair. Cora reached for his chest, pinched something between her fingers.

"Lint on this beautiful suit," she murmured. But her fingers lingered.

"Cora's heart desires quite a bit as well," Thomas said. Cora's lips pursed in response, but she didn't back away from Sam.

Sam kept his face impassive. Merely nodded and said, "We're just feeling grateful that our flu passed. Although the airline did lose our luggage and merchandise."

"How ghastly," Thomas said.

"We're flying our assistant out to Phoenix as we speak. They'll retrieve the books and return them to the store immediately."

Thomas and Cora exchanged a look. "You won't be providing any of your orders?" Thomas asked.

"Sadly, no." Sam looked apologetic. "We'll have to make other arrangements." I wondered if Julian and Birdie were bringing stolen goods to the convention. Would we have angry customers this weekend?

The ballroom ceiling curved overhead, and gold curtains draped down nine-foot-tall windows. The booths stretched around us in organized rows, like a planned village of book dealers. Or thieves. Most were draped with white cloths, heightening the mystery. The mood was jovial —people were meeting, shaking hands, speaking in low tones. It was reminiscent of many of the events Delilah and I had crashed as private detectives—the antiquities community was one of highly educated, elegant wealth. Champagne and caviar and manuscripts that went for millions of dollars at auction.

It was a world of extravagant money and secret handshakes.

"Who are these people?"

A tall man stood in front of us with a barely disguised sneer. He was thin as a reed, wearing a navy blue suit and a flashy gold ring.

"Roy," Thomas said, "*this* is Julian King and Birdie Barnes."

"I thought you had the flu?" Roy said to me.

I gave another tiny cough. "Last minute decision to tough it out. And some miraculous medicine from our doctor."

Roy looked young—and wealthy, of course. But he had none of the Alexanders' moneyed confidence. He was fidgety, like the suit he wore was uncomfortably tight. His skin could only be described as *pasty*.

"I went to visit your bookstore last month when I was in San Francisco," Roy said.

Sam placed a hand on my shoulder and squeezed. Our undercover training had focused extensively on the art of staying quiet. *Human beings despise an awkward silence. The more space you leave for them to talk, the more they'll fill it with incriminating information.*

"And you weren't there?" Roy prodded, exasperated.

"Ah, yes," Sam replied. "We weren't there."

"I wasn't happy about it, as you remember," he said.

"For Christ's sake, Roy, when was the last time you were ever happy?" Thomas sighed.

Roy scowled in his direction. "I'll be happy when I get what I came here for," he said.

"That's not up for him to decide this morning, now is it?"

Cora asked, voice hushed. "And can't you tell that he's *preoccupied*?"

The audience hushed, turning as one toward a man on the stage.

"There he is," Cora said next to me. "He was nervous, what with all the recent news, but I doubt anyone will suspect a thing."

The chandeliers dimmed. The hotel staff tugged those golden curtains closed. A candle-lit darkness draped the exhibition room. We were in the middle of a bustling city, on a Friday morning, and yet the still, dramatic atmosphere said otherwise.

Sam's heavy hand squeezed my shoulder. He appeared calm, confident. My archnemesis had been an FBI agent for seven years. The arrogant young man I'd fought with was now a broad-shouldered, square-jawed, highly competent special agent.

It was both comforting and irritating.

I rolled my shoulder, dislodging his hand.

Sam looked away, sliding his hands back into his pockets.

The man on stage stepped into a golden spotlight. Like every other man here, he was dressed in a suit. He was white, burly, with a trimmed red beard. *Unlike* every other man here, he wore an Indiana Jones-style fedora. When he unleashed a crooked smile on the crowd, I heard a few sighs of adoration.

"Good morning, ladies and gents," he said, with a slightly Southern drawl. "My name is Dr. Bradley Ward, and I am honored to be the keynote speaker and president of the East Coast's chapter of the Antiquarian Book Festival."

Recognition shivered through me. Roy Edwards. Dr.

Bradley Ward. I knew those names. They were the other names from the *empty house* group.

Dr. Ward gripped the podium and let his gaze roam across the large, silent room. "I've never been a man to beat around the bush. As many of you know." There were a few chuckles. "So I'm going to come right out and say it. The coyotes are at the door. Our community is being threatened at every level. Rare book theft is occurring at a rate never seen before. Forgeries, counterfeits, whole collections slipping through our fingers. Thieves are everywhere."

Thomas and Cora wore matching martyred expressions. Roy appeared disinterested, scrolling through his phone.

"We have built this community of history buffs from the ground up. But that means we must be vigilant with who we trust. Vigilant with who we let into our stores and into our booths. Second-guess everything and trust nothing that you can't personally verify. The great masterpieces of our time are being traded on the black market like playing cards. That's on us. Which means it's all on us to stop it. My hope this weekend is that coming together will be a rallying cry against the liars and the cheats in our midst."

Maybe this would be easier than we thought. Maybe all we needed to do was tell this Bradley guy that we were hunting the George Sand letters, and he'd haul the perpetrator out of hiding for us.

"Y'all know I'm a cowboy. I might live in a penthouse instead of a ranch, but I'm of rancher's blood. Growing up, my father used to drag me out of bed before dawn and tell me to load my shotgun."

Sam's hand landed back on my shoulder again.

The liars and the cheats in our midst. This time I didn't move it.

"Because we had coyotes too. Sneaky, deceptive things.

They attacked us every night, stealing our chickens. Our cows. Ruining the land we grew our crops on. They were a threat to our livelihood—just like these thieves are a threat to our way of life. And I think y'all know what my father and I did to our coyotes." Bradley let a long, dramatic pause linger before leaning into the microphone. "We shot 'em."

"Jesus," Sam muttered beneath his breath. The audience reacted with stilted applause. I caught a few nervous glances. The Alexanders looked even more smug as they clapped enthusiastically. Maybe these 'empty house' people weren't thieves at all? Maybe they were gun-toting book vigilantes?

Thomas turned around and winked at me.

Was *Birdie* a gun-toting book vigilante?

"We must redefine our values as antiquarian experts; redefine our boundaries and expectations of our relationships with each other. I hate having to work with the *authorities* as much as any other book dealer. Having police meddling in our personal business feels invasive, I know. But they'll continue to be sniffing in our business if we don't crack down on black market theft. This weekend should be a celebration of all that is antique and beautiful in this world. Let's keep it that way. I refuse to lead a community that is more well-known for its shady underbelly than its pure and golden heart. Because that's not what we're about, now is it?"

A chorus of *no*'s throughout the room, plus stomping and clapping.

"Let's make the next three days an antiquarian celebration, filled with hope for our future." Bradley lowered his voice, cultivating the drama of this hushed, candle-lit room. "And I meant what I said about those damn coyotes."

13

SAM

An awkward, heavy silence followed in the wake of Dr. Ward's speech. People whispered to each other, shifting back and forth on their feet. A polite murmur became a soft clap, punctuated with cheers that grew louder. Dr. Ward seemed unfazed by the confusing reaction to his veiled threats of violence in the middle of a goddamn book festival. I watched the Alexanders with a careful eye—they clapped for the man with a dignified air.

Roy, however, glared like he held a personal vendetta against Ward.

Dr. Ward bowed and exited the stage—immediately, the booths surrounding us sprang to life. The curtains were pulled back, light streaming in. A visible wave of relief moved through me, dislodging the tension I hadn't realized I'd been holding during the speech.

"The three of us need to talk to Bradley for a moment," Cora said to Freya and me. "But we'd be honored to host the two of you for brunch on The Grand Dame balcony. Say twenty minutes?"

"We can continue our conversation from the other day," Thomas chimed in.

"We'd be the honored ones." Freya's hand landed on her chest. "Come find us when you're ready. Julian and I will browse the goods."

The Alexanders bid their farewells, dragging Roy behind them like a toddler.

"I don't like that guy," I said, eyes narrowed.

"Dr. Ward?"

"No," I said. "The trust fund dick."

"That's what *I* thought about him too," she replied. "But he seems both spineless *and* harmless to me."

I rubbed the back of my neck, unsure.

"What first, partner?" Freya adjusted her pearls. "And we already have much to discuss."

"That we do," I agreed. This would have been a lot fucking easier with a gun and a warrant and a badge. Being a special agent for the FBI was harder than I'd ever expected it to be. Not that I'd ever share that with my father or even Freya. Being a private detective, in many ways, seemed just as hard—high stakes but diminished resources.

"We should wander, wait for Thomas and Cora," I said quietly. She nodded, immediately turning toward the first row of tables, covered in dusty books. Filtering through was the quiet hum of antiques talk and a few sideways glances when people spotted our *Julian* and *Birdie* nametags.

"Tell me more about these letters," I said to Freya, one eye scanning the room for Dahl or other suspicious activity. "Why would criminals give a shit about George Sand and this poet? Or Hollywood directors?"

"Spoken like a true romantic," she said.

"I don't think I've ever given that false impression."

"I'm sure your girlfriends *love* you." She stopped to pick up a book by Emily Bronte, admiring the back cover.

"Birdie Barnes," she said to the bookseller. "How lovely to meet you." The man wore a pork-pie hat and suspenders. He beamed at Freya like she'd told him he'd won the lottery. A golden cage held a dignified-looking parrot at the end of the table. When Freya stuck her finger into the cage, the bird squawked at her.

"I know you," the man said. Freya and I both went completely still. "I purchased a first edition of Milton's *Paradise Lost* from your store a few months ago. See? Surprised you didn't recognize it."

There, in a glass case, was a small book with a maroon cover and a golden crest of two lions protecting a shield.

"The gilded edges are as divine as the words inscribed on them," the man continued. "I have no idea how the two of you came into this gem, but I won't question it."

That sentiment was the reason why the Art Theft unit existed.

"Julian and I love seeing these antiques in person," Freya beamed. "But I also thought we'd once met each other at Reichenbach Falls?"

The man looked puzzled—but delighted. But who wouldn't be delighted by a smiling Freya?

"I'm sorry, where?" he asked.

She slid her big glasses up her nose. "Never mind. Just someplace I thought I knew you from. Thank you again for showing us our precious Milton."

The bookseller grasped Freya's hand, holding it between his own. "I cannot thank *you* enough."

We moved along slowly, Freya trailing her fingers along books and maps, bending down to peer at a first edition of *The Velveteen Rabbit.*

I rapped my knuckles hard on a table as we passed it. "Keep telling me about the letters."

"George Sand was a rebellious French novelist in the 1830s and '40s," she said. "She didn't conform to societal pressures. She wore men's clothes and smoked cigars. She loved who she loved. She was even more popular than her contemporary, Victor Hugo. And she had a reputation for writing especially seductive letters. George was obsessed with Alfred de Musset, who was a poet and playwright. At least until she wasn't." Freya glanced over at me, sly. "Have *you* ever written a love letter before?"

I thought about the piece of paper I'd scrawled on the night Freya left Quantico. I'd trashed it, too embarrassed to even read the mangled version of it the next day.

"Never," I replied.

"Heart of stone, huh?"

"Focused on my career," I corrected. "And what about you? How many hearts have you broken, Birdie? Leave a string of sobbing computer nerds in your wake?"

She covered her mouth and stifled a snort. "That's a typical Tuesday for me."

She was deflecting with humor—her usual M.O. But at Princeton, she'd certainly had boyfriends. Freya always appeared happy and silly with them. Carefree, even.

Not like she was with me—angry and stubborn and viciously competitive.

We stood in front of a table showcasing a first edition of *The Adventures of Huckleberry Finn*. She was enchanted. There was no need for her to fake Birdie's fascination.

"So you don't have a boyfriend?" I managed. "It's, uh, best if we know the full extent of each other's romantic attachments. Could be a vulnerability." Sure, that sounded good.

"I don't, actually," Freya said. "You're not jealous, are you?"

"Hardly," I bit out. We passed another row of antiques—long, scrolling maps bearing the names of countries that no longer existed.

"Were you serious about what you said earlier?" she asked, voice a whisper. I bent my head to be near hers, our fingers moving close on a glass case. "About the violence? Being concerned for our safety?"

I cleared my throat. "Yes. Six months ago, the Bureau lost an agent while breaking up an illegal art theft ring. It's not as bloodless as we used to think."

Freya touched her bun, straightened her pearls. "Okay. I get it. And I'm so sorry for your agent."

It was another tenuous truce. But instead of strengthening my trust, it only made me feel muddled.

"Thomas and Cora are ready to dine with you." A voice slashed through our whispered conversation. Roy, the creepy trust fund kid.

We both startled—Freya knocked a book to the floor with her flying arms. She immediately dropped down, grabbed the book, and smacked the top of her head on the table.

"Ow, *fuck me,*" she squeaked. I stilled her by the shoulders. My thumb stroked the curve of her hairline as she watched me, looking grateful. She appeared to be in physical pain, which I'd never seen before. Sparring on the mats was one thing. Freya actually hurting herself was another thing entirely. It made me want to crack the table in two, throw it in the garbage.

"Uh, hello?" Roy said impatiently.

"Apologies from Birdie," I said, turning to face him.

Freya stood on wobbly legs. "She's easily startled. Did you say the Alexanders are ready for us?"

"Yeah." Then he gave Freya a look of open admiration—trolling his gaze down her body. The action had me reaching for a gun that was no longer in my holster.

"I think your fly is down," she said. He blushed furiously—saw that his fly was, indeed, open. He made a toddler-like sound of frustration. And when Freya met my gaze with a tiny smirk, I gave her a nod of approval.

"*Anyway*," he continued, "Thomas and Cora wish to see you on the balcony."

"How was Dr. Ward?" Freya asked, following him through the crowd of booklovers. "His speech sure was passionate."

"You know how he is," Roy spit out. "Needs to make everything into a fucking show. It's why I have to wait until Saturday night to get what I came here for. But I have *money* and I want it now."

"What a jerk," she said.

"He's a pompous ass," he added.

We followed Roy through a small dark hallway lit with gas-lamps, although it was barely 9:30 in the morning. The schedule Freya and I had found online had listed a continental breakfast and mingling hour that I assumed would be awkward and brightly-lit with coffee and stale bagels. I'd attended more criminal justice conferences than most. The 'breakfast networking hour' was always terrible.

We stepped into an ornate, high-ceilinged room with a long table piled high with food. One wall was filled with open doors that led to a balcony terrace and a view of the city of Philadelphia.

Thomas and Cora, looking even more polished than they had twenty minutes ago, waved us over.

"Thank you for waiting while we attended to business," Thomas said, eyes darting around. "Please, join us."

Freya and I perched on chairs at their table next to the ledge of the terrace. The morning skyline glittered behind us. Large pots filled with roses and evergreen bushes provided a feel of privacy.

While the server took our orders, I studied our companions. Big, shiny diamond ring on Cora's left finger. Matching diamonds in her ears. Most likely in her fifties but Botox-ed. Her clipped, mid-Atlantic accent spoke of boarding schools and elocution classes. Thomas appeared similarly sophisticated, dressed like a wealthy New York City oil tycoon.

Roy, meanwhile, twitched like a weasel, shifting like he expected a goon squad at any second. As the server asked for my breakfast order, Roy took a call and stalked off with a harried expression.

Thomas and Cora visibly relaxed with his absence.

Thomas leaned over our small cups of coffee. "I trust you'll be ready for our festivities. I remember being nervous my first year. But you'll do great."

"Of course," I said. "We'll be attending with the two of you?"

"How else would you get there?" he asked, quizzical.

"Just verifying," I said.

Breakfast was served, but Freya and I didn't touch our food.

"We appreciated what Dr. Ward said about trust," Freya said, once the server left. "I know how highly you value that among your friends. It's a hot commodity these days, it appears."

Cora sipped coffee from a fine china cup. "That attitude is why we believe the four of us are going to be the best of friends this weekend. Don't we, Thomas?"

"We do." His gaze on mine was sharp, searching. This man might be pretending to admire us, but he was certainly wary.

I glanced at Freya, nudged my knee against hers. "Birdie and I are on the hunt for several items this weekend. I thought I might see if you knew their status."

"Oh?" Thomas asked.

Freya nudged my knee back. "Love letters."

Cora smiled mysteriously. "We know of several dealers selling one-of-a-kind antique letters this weekend."

Freya traced a finger along the rim of her cup. Dragged the moment out. "Lucky number thirteen. We heard they arrived yesterday."

This glimpse of Freya—teasing out our suspect—snapped me back to the past so fast I felt dizzy. She *was* nervous to go undercover again. That much was clear to me. I could read all of her cues—touching her hair, biting her lip, trying to joke instead of answering a question. She did those things around *me*.

But in class, during our undercover drills, I'd watched this woman come alive with the thrill of it. She had been a naturally talented undercover agent—a fact that my father had made sure I'd been well aware of. I wasn't the only member of my family to be disappointed at the loss of Freya Evandale.

Thomas glanced at Cora, who gave a discreet shake of her head. "Everything went as planned, as you well know. But has he been talking to you, Birdie?"

Under the table, Freya pressed her knee hard to mine. Pressed and left it there, making my skin burn.

"That's a secret, now, isn't it?" she said.

Cora looked mildly irritated at that. Thomas looked confused.

"We'd love to see them," I said, forging ahead. "As soon as possible."

Freya dropped her spoon with a *clink.* Moved her knee.

"Patience," Thomas warned. "You're not the only interested parties. You know this must wait until the final night."

"Who else wants them?" I asked.

His face went cold. "You know I can't talk about that here."

"We're very excited," Freya said quietly. "We tend to be homebodies back in San Francisco. Don't get out like this. Sometimes interacting with other human beings is challenging for us."

She was vibrating a little. Irritated with me, I guessed. But I was pissed too. We needed to *push* here, and Freya was pulling back. Maybe I needed to lean forward, identify who I was in a menacing whisper, and take those letters back. Under pressure, I bet Thomas and Cora would sing like canaries.

"We're all aware of the other person who *might* be interested in letters that *might* be here," Thomas said. "I'm sure you can already see what the issue is, given recent developments."

"We do see the issue." Freya sipped her coffee with her pinkie up. "You promise we'll have the opportunity to see what we'd like to see at the festivities?"

"That is what we discussed," Cora said. A line formed between her brows. She was confused by us. We were veering past the ability to merely listen and nod.

"Julian and I can be patient. Why don't you tell us a little bit about this gorgeous hotel? We're first-timers in awe of this magnificent location."

I shrugged a shoulder, grateful for the topic change. "I

would have assumed the biggest antiquarian book festival on the East Coast would be held in a convention center."

"Convention centers are pointless and boring," Thomas said. "Dr. Ward would never allow anything that pedestrian. He's a man of unique tastes. He chose The Grand Dame because of its storied past."

"Bootlegging," Cora added. "There was a speakeasy here in the 1920s, although you'd never know it now. The basement once masqueraded as a perfumery. Exotic scents from around the world for the wealthiest of this city's upper echelon."

"Perfume bottles make an interesting hiding place for liquor," Thomas said. "By day, the shop was filled with society women. By night, the shop was filled with an utterly different clientele. Jazz, escorts, drugs, alcohol. All happened in the rooms that exist beneath this street. The confluence of the Schuykill and Delaware rivers made Philadelphia a bustling city of underground bootleggers. Although The Grand Dame was never raided—historians believe the owner had so many police officers on the take they were able to keep out of legal trouble." Thomas looked me square in the eye. "For eons, criminals and those who have been trained to catch them have often worked in concert."

Just like Gregory.

"I seem to know more crooked cops than straight these days," I said, holding his gaze. The sentiment went against my core values—but he wasn't wrong about the devious connections between cop and criminal.

"You'll have to regale us with those tales during our festivities," Cora said. "We're always interested in gathering certain information."

Thomas glanced at his silver watch. "We should be off

soon, my dear. Before we go, can you tell dear Cora what you were telling me the other night, Birdie? You promised we could continue our conversation."

Freya went completely pale. "You'll have to remind me."

Thomas let us hang for a fraught few seconds. "I understand. We do have a lot of conversations. This was about those letters you were referring to. I've been trying to explain the cryptography to Cora for days, but she doesn't understand."

Cora blinked innocently. His speech sounded too practiced, and I wouldn't be surprised if this was another test. One of the informal codes they used to confirm loyalties on the fly.

Beneath the table, Freya was shaking her stilettoed foot, knuckles white where they gripped her coffee cup. Her knee landed back against mine—a signal, I was sure—but I didn't know shit about cryptography.

"Maybe another time," she hedged. "We should probably be off too. Right, Julian?"

"Ri—"

"Oh, please," Thomas said. "Cora's been asking me for days. Surely you can explain it again for us here?"

Freya swallowed hard. "You're sure you can't explain it, Thomas? A brilliant man like you? I seem to remember you understanding the code-cracking immediately when I told you."

It wasn't a half-bad deflection.

"And yet I'd prefer if *you* told her," he said, the knife-edge of his voice lifting the hairs on the back of my neck. "Right now."

14

FREYA

This is what happened when computer nerds were forced into high-stakes undercover roles.

Every investigative instinct I'd ever had seized up. Where Delilah would have been nimble on her feet, I felt clumsy and slow. Worse, my partner and I seemed to be on totally different wavelengths *as usual.*

"Trust," Thomas was saying, "certainly is a hot commodity, as you said, Ms. Barnes."

But before either of us could answer, my phone rang. I'd forgotten to turn it off, but thankfully the shrillest ring tone shattered through the elegant terrace.

Which was a good enough distraction for me.

"Yes, um, hello?" I said frantically.

"Freya. I'm so glad I caught you." It was Henry. "Listen, I forgot to mention something about those love letters. George wrote them using a cryptographic code, a detail that might—"

"Oh my *god,*" I wailed into the phone. "This is terrible. *Terrible.*" I hung up on Henry and grasped Sam by the hand. "I'm truly sorry, Thomas and Cora, but I've had the most dreadful news. I need my partner. We shall be in touch, I'm sure."

Before they could answer, I forcibly dragged Sam past people whispering and pointing at us, back through the fancy, high-ceilinged dining room and into the dark, narrow hallway. The gas lanterns lent a dreary air to the space, even though it was a bright and sunny summer morning. This hotel's nefarious past seemed more obvious with Sam and I squeezed together next to fluttering candlelight.

"We're *fucked*," I said.

"I think we should arrest them," he hissed back.

"Are you serious?" I asked. "With your fake warrant and fake evidence?"

His jaw clenched so hard I thought it'd break. "Our cover's blown. They probably know who has the love letters. A little bit of pressure, and we can get what we need and get the hell out of here."

A door opened about fifteen feet from us—the back terrace. We exchanged a terrified look.

"We need to have this conversation elsewhere." Walking as quickly as we could without outright running, Sam and I strode back out into the glamorous lobby where I did the first thing I could think of.

Pulled Sam back into the damn men's bathroom. Locked the door this time.

We huddled into the stall where his contraband gun was hidden. He looked debonair and handsome, even jammed into a men's bathroom stall. "We're floundering out there, and they're onto us," he hissed.

"They were on to us when you pushed them too fast. What did we learn at Quantico? These relationships take time." My hands went to my hips, blocking his exit.

"I'm good at my job. I know how to handle people like

Thomas and Cora. You need to be more aggressive with them."

"Hard to do when they're asking me the tough questions, and *you're* sitting there, watching me suffer."

"At a certain point, force is necessary." Sam pushed past me, out into the bathroom and back onto the lobby floor. I was seeing red, tamping down the urge to tear my fucking hair out. He stopped dead in his tracks, and I smashed into his back.

"I just saw the elevator close on the Alexanders," Sam said. "Didn't they say they'd booked the room next to ours?"

"They did. Though I'm surprised they didn't have security called on us yet," I said, rubbing my forehead. "Also, why is your back like a brick wall?"

In an instant, Sam was shoving open the door marked *stairway* and sprinting up the stairs. But he wasn't in fucking stilettos. Or carrying a bag with a small laptop in it. Grumbling, I stopped to slip off my heels and loop them around my wrist. Then I took off after Sam Byrne with a fury.

"When did you get faster than me?" I panted.

"I was always faster than you," he shot back.

We hit the second story doorway a second apart. But Sam still had time to flash me the *smuggest grin* before yanking it open. We needed to stop. Plan. Not run recklessly down the hallway like a pair of cops without an identity or an alibi or a warrant or cause to be here. I wanted this case to be over just as much as Sam did. But Abe had *trusted* that we could do this, and Sam was about to destroy everything.

The door to room 213 clicked shut as we rounded the corner. Sam was already slipping our room key from his pocket—211. There was a *beep*, a click, and Birdie and Julian's hotel room was revealed. The room was huge—luxurious. In the middle was a four-poster bed with too many pillows, everything in crimson and hunter-green. An antique-looking fireplace dominated one wall, and a small gold chandelier hung from the ceiling.

Interestingly, there was only one bed for Julian and Birdie.

I pressed a finger to my lips as Sam paced. "*Shhh.* They're right next door." My voice was barely above a whisper.

He strode right up to me. My back hit the wall, but I kept my chin raised.

"We are out of options. The faster we get those letters, the faster we never have to see each other again," he said.

The coldness of that hit me harder than I expected. I mean, of *course* I wanted the same thing. But it still stung. "I agree that I'd prefer to be done working together. Thomas and Cora seem too savvy to back down due to pressure. Especially since they've done nothing wrong. Literally nothing. Even if you had them investigated for using the code word I stumbled onto, none of their conversations online are even mildly illegal. I can usually get away with quick blackmail when they're holding the stolen book in their hand. These two? We have nothing except that they've alluded the stolen letters *might* be here. But they could be alluding to any love letters. We don't know enough."

Sam rubbed the back of his neck and broke eye contact. I could see his teeth grinding. With my head pressed to the wall, I could just hear the sounds of conversation from next door. Tilting my head, I pressed my ear there.

We should listen, I mouthed, pointing to the wall. Sam looked unimpressed. With an eye-roll, I moved past him and toward the middle of the room—a small space between the dresser and a wing-backed chair.

I slid down, hugging my knees to my chest and laying

my laptop and phone nearby. Shot off a quick text to Henry asking him to send me the information on the cryptography in the letters. Ear to the wall, I tried to capture the threads of conversation.

Going to be a problem...filtered through. *Must have been why she ran*...

I pressed my ear as hard as I could.

Letters...thirteen... more murmuring that was indecipherable. I pressed my ear so hard it actually stung a little. And when Sam tapped me on the shoulder, I jumped out of my fucking skin.

He was holding a glass. "Would this help?" he whispered.

"Very old-school," I whispered. I crooked a finger. "Come listen." I dug through my bag and found a pen and loose paper. Sam joined me, but it was a tiny space, and it took us an awkward minute to arrange our limbs so that they weren't touching. In the end, I was pressed to the wall, and Sam sat next to me, my ankles against his thigh.

Our faces, when we set the glass to the wall, were barely a foot apart.

"This must have been the reason why she ran," Cora was saying—and I heard it, clear as a bell, amplified by the glass. Sam's face brightened.

"It's a nightmare. You see this happening at stores like *Walmart*"—Cora said *Walmart* like it was disgusting—"but certainly not a place like Kensley's. This is a crisis, Thomas."

Kensley's? he mouthed at me. I shrugged. It was the largest auction house in the country, but I didn't know what they were referring to.

"They also could have been running because they're not who they say they are." That was Thomas.

"They knew the code. They have IDs, for Christ's sake. You can stop being paranoid. You harassed that poor girl."

"I don't believe she's a poor anything, my darling. With all that's going on, we cannot trust as easily as we once could."

I pointed to my laptop on the floor. He grabbed it, placed it in my lap. I typed *Kensley's* in the search bar and waited to see what news would pop up.

"Besides, we have bigger problems."

"Bernard?"

I got so excited I acted without thinking. Grabbed Sam's hand, squeezed it. He shifted, and the left side of my body lined up with the right side of his body. My heart was a steady *thud* in my chest. His tantalizing nearness and the name *Bernard* were equally intoxicating. More words were said, mumbles, indistinct chatter.

Sam shook his head at me. *What are they saying now*?

Don't know, I mouthed back.

But then I was just left holding Sam's hand. I dropped it, stared at the collar of his shirt instead of his annoyingly attractive face.

There was a rustle. Silence. Thomas and Cora weren't speaking. I took the opportunity to peek at my laptop. The first article said *Kensley's Announces Wide-Scale Data Breach; Thousands of Customers' Information Leaked*.

My little hacker's heart leapt.

It was a clue.

"It was a mistake to ever involve him. It's blackmail, plain and simple." Thomas said.

"Blackmail," Cora replied. "In this day and age. It used to be we were all civil."

Boots. High-heels, stepping away. Thomas and Cora

were still talking but had moved to the door—which we heard open and close.

"They're gone," I whispered. I put the glass down.

"And we learned nothing," Sam said.

I held up a finger. "Not necessarily." I turned my screen around to show my reluctant partner. "I'm going to hack Birdie and Julian."

15

SAM

Freya sat barefoot and cross-legged next to me, pen in her mouth. Her tidy Birdie bun had grown loose, strands tumbling out. I blinked—saw Freya at 25, in sweatpants and a giant sweatshirt, pestering me to share notes from our counter-terrorism class.

"Watch me work my magic," she was saying now, voice muffled by the pen. "This is where computer nerds shine."

"How are you going to hack Julian and Birdie?" I asked. She truly had excelled in all things tech at Quantico—a fact she'd yell at my retreating back whenever I passed her on the running track.

"Well, it's only a hunch right now. Give me one second, and I'm going to blow your ever-loving *mind*."

"Just like in the fake bomb threat hostage situation," I said mildly.

She snorted, which felt like a different kind of victory. I studied her profile as she typed. My rival had the audacity to look achingly beautiful in this quiet moment.

"Hell *yes*," she suddenly cheered, giving herself a high-five. I hid a smile, tried to read over her shoulder.

"Tell me," I said.

"You have to admit first that I'm the most incredible person who's ever lived."

"Bold request, Evandale."

"You've known me since I was eighteen years old. You've had enough evidence to support my completely objective claim."

A low laugh rumbled in my throat—slipped out before I could stop it. A lightness was breaking through my chest.

"You're the most incredible person who's ever lived." I paused. "Next to me."

"Oh, you've got jokes now?"

"I have a sense of humor."

"Spoken like a true robot." But she was smiling. Dancing in her seat. Whatever was on that screen had made her giddy.

"Show your robot partner what's on that screen."

She brushed strands of hair from her face. Our knees touched, but she didn't retreat. "How do you feel about things that are morally...gray?"

"I'm opposed to them. Obviously."

"Give it time. I'll corrupt you."

"You've been saying that since Princeton and it's never happened," I said. "What was that dance you used to try and get me to go to? The Valentine's Day one but for super nerds?"

"Black Hearts Ball," Freya said, spreading her hands through the air like she could see the words on a marquee. "And it wasn't for general nerds. It was for bookworms and creative writers who were too dark and too moody to celebrate a holiday as cheerful and commercially manipulative as Valentine's Day. We read depressing poetry and did shots named after classic books. Like Tequila Mockingbird."

"Like you ever did shots," I said.

"Like *you* ever did shots," she shot back.

"I've...partied." I was lying through my teeth. "You and I wouldn't have partied together at Princeton anyway. You always had those writer boyfriends who took up all of your time. And alcohol was banned at Quantico."

"You had girlfriends, Byrne," she said. "Brittany, right? She was class president and captain of the volleyball team... sorority girl too?"

I shrugged. "She was very ambitious and hard-working. We were a good fit."

What we were together was *boring*—but god help me if Freya ever uncovered that tidbit of information.

"So who are you dating now?" she asked. "Prove you're not a robot."

My hand actually lifted an inch off the floor, compelled to tuck a tendril of hair behind her ear. But at the last second, reality halted me.

What was I *doing*?

My rival had always been a whip-smart, funny blonde with full lips and emerald eyes. The hard truth of Freya's stunning beauty hadn't changed. I simply seemed to be more susceptible to it.

"Byrne?"

"Um...oh, no," I said. "Not dating. Haven't for a while. Work."

She held my gaze for a second before shaking herself free. "See? Robot. Anyway. I think I caught us a break. Kensley's just announced a data breach, meaning their customers' login and financial information has been stolen and made public. It happens all the time, but it's big news because they work with extremely private and wealthy clientele. As you can imagine, hackers have already created a site on the dark web where they've posted the information."

"That's illegal."

"Absolutely," she said firmly. "And I'd never steal Birdie and Julian's financial information. But I thought it was worth a search for their login details. If people like the Alexanders had their accounts leaked, it's likely that Birdie and Julian could be in the same boat."

I rubbed the back of my neck, thinking. "You can get on the dark web?"

"Believe me, it's not a place I go often," she explained. "A year ago, we thought we could track down rare book thieves there. Plenty of criminal activity happens on the dark web, and I hoped there was an even shadier version of Under the Rose that I could find. Get the books back faster if the thieves didn't have to speak in codes." She shrugged. "I couldn't find it. Although I only waded in the *shallowest* waters of the dark web. It's honestly too gross to go much deeper."

Freya clicked a few buttons on her laptop, showing me a browser called Tor. "This is what I use to access it. There's a different search engine and everything. Some sites that list leaked data charge you for access, using Bitcoin. But I know of one that allows you to commit criminal acts for free."

After a few more seconds of searching, up popped a black box with white lettering. *Julian King* it said at the top. Beneath that, a login and a password.

"Why would a Kensley's customer need a login and password?"

"They have an interactive site where you can post prelim bids before items are officially for sale. It looks like Julian and Birdie *both* had accounts on this site. If I take Julian's username and password," she paused, "I might be able to log us into his Under the Rose account."

"Okay, so *that's* also illegal."

"I prefer *ethical gray area*. Besides, I'm just logging in to a website to look at their private messages about letters they might have stolen. PIs are allowed to dig through a suspect's garbage to find information. You're telling me if Thomas and Cora had written this information on a piece of paper and thrown it in a trashcan, you'd leave it be?"

"You're spying."

"I am," she said.

I cracked my knuckles, pondering. Of *course,* I'd nab it from a trashcan. But what she was suggesting was not entirely aboveboard either.

"What are you waiting for?" I asked.

"We're partners." She bit her lip. "We do it together or not at all."

Her expression dared me to deny that we were partners. She still owed me honesty, and I still owed her honesty. Yet maybe this was a first step.

"Fine," I sighed. "Do it. And remind me to never let you near my trashcan."

"Please. I've been reading your emails for years. What do I need a trashcan for?"

She pulled up the Under the Rose website.

My back was starting to ache, but I wasn't about to suggest sitting on that bed. With Freya.

"The likelihood they use the same password is low though, right?" I said.

"Hacking pro tip—the majority of people *never* change their passwords, even though they're supposed to. I mean, you can barely call that hacking."

"Even two rare book thieves operating under an assumed alias?"

"You're a trained special agent with the Federal Bureau of Investigation," she shot back. "When did you last change your non-work passwords?"

I thought for a second. "That's classified."

She smirked. "Watch and learn, Agent Byrne." She waggled her eyebrows at me, voice low and throaty. "Three...two...one...*sweet, beautiful victory!*"

She raised her arms to cheer. Then went red in the face. "Oh, wait. Fuck."

I grabbed the laptop before she could stop me. *Username or password incorrect. Please try again.*

"Hacking pro tip—try having the right login info," I said.

"Fuck-a-*duck,*" Freya swore, chewing on a nail. "We still have my girl Birdie's info."

"I'm going to call Abe. Get his support on busting into their room—"

She spun her screen around with a triumphant, cheeky grin. "Don't say I never did nothing for ya."

Welcome Birdie Barnes, the screen read. *You have three (3) new messages.*

And right there, in the middle of the screen, was a blinking message from one Thomas fucking Alexander.

This might sound bizarre, my dear friend. But are you in Philadelphia right now?

"Holy shit," I said. "You hacked Birdie."

16

FREYA

"Nerd girls for the win," I cheered.

Sam actually looked impressed with me.

"*This* is where I belong," I added, pointing at the screen.

Sam narrowed his eyes. "You don't believe you belong in the field?"

"This is where I *excel*. I can do more from here."

I'd wanted to be an FBI agent for as long as I could remember, even before my Dana Scully Halloween costume. Yet by the end of that first week of training, I knew I couldn't hack it. In the end, Sam *had* won. He'd won it all. Graduated as a special agent with the respect and glowing reputation that came with that.

I'd flown too close to the sun and still had the singed wings to prove it.

"Is that why you're nervous?" His voice was flat—because he wasn't asking.

I ignored him and scrolled through the rest of Birdie's messages on the screen.

"For what it's worth, I thought you did extraordinary work out there, Evandale."

"I royally screwed things up with the Alexanders. Didn't think fast enough and almost blew our goddamn cover." *Fuck*. I shook my head. "I mean, anyway, back to—"

"We were presented with a situation we couldn't have planned for. You think that makes you unqualified?"

I leveled a sure gaze at my partner. "Your father would say I was a massive fuck-up."

His jaw worked. "My father isn't always right," he said, each word sounding forced.

The subject of Sam's father was the most personally contentious topic we'd fought over. He'd expected perfection from his only son ever since Sam's mother had passed away suddenly when he was twelve years old. At Quantico, the Deputy Director was always around, spying on his son, measuring him in degrees of excellence. Since Sam was a human who made mistakes, he always, always fell short. *He's just a bully in a suit*, I used to tell Sam, which pissed him off to no end.

"That's the nicest thing you've ever said to me." I reached forward, touched his hand.

"Evandale, come on."

I shook my head. "Sam, I'm being serious. In all the years I've known you, you've only ever agreed with that man. I meant what I said."

The use of his first name had his eyes burning into mine. His fingers clenched and unclenched on the floor, moving beneath my feather-light touch.

"Not to ruin this Hallmark moment, but we're going to have a problem with those messages if we don't react soon." His voice scraped through the silence.

"Right," I whispered. Cleared my throat. Sam pointed to the message blinking from Thomas. Thomas had sent it twenty minutes ago, probably when he first started suspecting we weren't who we claimed to be. There was an icon that said *message not seen*.

I opened the message. Typed out *I'm sure you are confused. Yes, Julian and I are here. Yes, we just ate breakfast together. I'm sorry about what you asked me to do. With the jet-lag and the flu medication, I'm not feeling like myself. Combined with the news of Kensley's, Julian and I were quite shaken up.*

I glanced at Sam.

"Wait." He grabbed my wrist, then quickly dropped it. "Um...add a line with that code. Something about trust. They've been going on and on about it since we got here."

I swallowed my own irritation. I should have thought of that. *With our house being empty, we're glad to be in your company. Trust is paramount. Thank you for your dedication.*

Sam nodded his approval. I hit send.

And deleted Thomas's original message.

"Okay," I exhaled, "Real Birdie, recovering from her flu, logs in and sees no new messages. But that means I need to stay on top of this constantly. Let me see if I can't link the notifications to my phone."

I worked through their settings until I found what I needed. My laptop pinged.

Thomas again.

My deepest apologies for my boorish behavior. You know I've been under great stress with this curse.

"*Curse*?" Sam and I said in unison. "What the hell is he talking about?"

Ping. Another message.

You know where we're heading this evening. We will escort you.

"What the hell?" I murmured.

"But how does this help us find the love letters?" Sam pressed. "Do you think Dahl was their criminal contact?"

I turned my head and almost collided with his.

"Sorry." His eyes lingered on my mouth before he dragged them back to meet mine. "We're still lost here."

"I know," I admitted. "Let's start with reading the backlog of Birdie's messages. And usually this is the time where a partner might offer ideas."

He stood and began to pace again. He removed his jacket, rolling up his shirtsleeves in a movement that made his forearms flex. And flex. Loosened his tie to expose an inch of golden skin at the base of his throat. Even slightly mussed, Sam Byrne was the picture of serious. Unflappable. Controlled. It was why I enjoyed teasing the man—poking at the bear was fun. I wanted to see Sam's wild side, the unbridled side that was merely *yearning* and *urges*.

Between my legs, a seductive pulse began to drum. The sight of the luxurious, four-poster bed wasn't helping.

Down girl, damn.

"What's the code that Henry sent?" Sam asked. "The one that George used in her love letters? Might contain a clue."

I scrolled through the long email that Henry sent me. Cross-checked it against the most recent messages on Under the Rose.

"This is where you say *great idea, partner,*" Sam added.

"What now?" I said, smirking. *Poke, poke*. "I think I've got something."

I stood, back aching, and plopped onto the bed. I wiggled my butt, got comfortable. Sam immediately moved to the other side of the room. He leaned against the antique dresser with his arms crossed sternly in front of his chest.

"According to our in-house librarian, George Sand used basic cryptography to hide secret messages to Alfred within the letters." I scanned a website with pictures of the letters and digital circles around the code. I started reading out loud, desperate to find a connection.

"It is possible to note hidden messages in 10 of the 13 letters that George and Alfred exchanged during their tumultuous, but passionate, relationship. They fought often but the ardor of these letters indicates a wild love affair regardless of their arguments."

I glanced at Sam and found him staring at me. I dropped back to the page. *"The first letter of every word on the left-hand side of the page spells a message. 'Our love will never die' was written into several. 'The moon and stars are forever as is my love for you.'"*

"Any of those connect to this case at all?" he interjected.

"Not that I can tell," I said, hopes deflating. "*'You are my supreme beauty' Alfred encoded into one short note.* Seems like a nice guy. You ever tell Brittany she was a supreme beauty?"

"No," he grunted. "What do the letters say? Anything vital here, Evandale?"

I scanned and scanned. "Um…*'Night after night I dream of you and you alone; of that place between your legs where my mouth wants to—'*" I stopped. Blushed. Looked up to find Sam still staring at me. "Very, uh, descriptive."

"Anything else?" His voice was pure silk.

"*'Our bodies are one. Our hearts are one. You gasping my name as we couple together is the only divine prayer I need, the only god I choose to worship.'*"

This lush, adorned room seemed to shrink the longer I read. A bead of sweat rolled between my shoulder blades.

"These are certainly a little different than '*Do you like me, circle yes or no*,'" I said lightly. "I mean, that's the only letter I've ever gotten."

"You had all those writer boyfriends, and none of those nerds ever wrote you a damn letter?" Sam sounded pissed.

"Girls like me don't usually inspire grand romantic gestures through the written word."

"Girls like you?" he asked.

"You wouldn't know," I said. "I'm guessing high school was pretty easy for a six foot three, broad-shouldered jock with perfect grades."

"You don't know shit about what my life was like in high school," he muttered.

"Right back at'cha, Agent Byrne."

By the time I'd arrived at Princeton, my only goal was to be the smartest person in the room. And to black out every fucking memory of the bullying I'd experienced back home. Finding a *burn book* specifically about me and my many faults was not the most enjoyable way to celebrate my high school graduation. Every friendship I thought I had was a cruel deception. I'd been a joke to my classmates the whole time.

The *only* thing I had left to be proud of was my genius—which I coveted and protected until Sam Byrne swaggered into criminology club and proved himself to be my academic equal.

"You really did keep a lot of things from me, didn't you?" The ghost of something melancholy flitted across Sam's face.

"What? You mean at Quantico?" I asked. "We weren't *friends*. And we certainly weren't friends at Princeton. Rivals don't bond over high school memories."

"You're right. How could I have forgotten." His tone was chilly. Unforgiving.

"Should I…keep reading?" I finally asked.

"Is it going to actually help us?"

I sighed, irritated. "Here's a thought. We figure out what

event Thomas and Cora want us to attend with them tonight. Work our magic as Julian and Birdie, reinforced by this secret weapon we have here." I pointed to the Under the Rose messages. "Try to pin down who has the letters. Thomas and Cora made it seem like they were a hot ticket item and we'd have competition. Find the competition. Find the letters."

"Here's my better idea," he replied. "Find this Dr. Ward guy, who seems to be in charge. Threaten him with calling the FBI. Get the letters."

"Does he have them though?" I asked.

"Someone has them, Evandale," Sam said wearily. "I know this is how private detectives work, but I *genuinely* think these trust-building exercises over martinis and pearl-clad gossip will fuck us in the end. It's time to move. We have less than three days. Abe would agree."

"I've worked with Abe for three years now," I shot back. "He'd want us to keep infiltrating. Play at being thieves, even if we lose a day. It's worth it in the end."

"And I'm a goddamn FBI agent," he growled. "I know more about these situations than you."

Fury blurred my vision. Every fucking *time*. One measly inch forward, one mile hurtled back. Sam unrolled his sleeves, donned his jacket, and strode toward the door with angered purpose.

I darted ahead. Got there first—my back against the door, hands on my hips. He stopped short, bringing us literally toe-to-toe.

"Evandale."

"Byrne."

Another irritated sigh. "I'm calling Abe, and I'm making a move whether you like it or not. We're partners—which means you should be coming with me," he said.

"Tell me what to do one more time, and you'll experience my knees back in your groin again."

His lips twitched. The look on his face was one I recognized from our countless times sparring. Sam and I always walked into those classes bickering. And ended them with one of us pinning the other to the mat.

Every time we'd fight, these *flickers* of sexual hunger would transform his otherwise stoic expression. And not necessarily when he won.

No. He'd stare at me like this when *I* won.

Sam Byrne always liked a challenge. And I was his greatest challenge.

"It's the hostage simulation again," he insisted. "If you won't listen to reason, shit's going to blow up again. And this time, we have more at stake than fake bystanders."

"I know what we have at stake," I said. "I've worked this job for three years. Worked it *passionately,* I might add. Because I believe in what we do. A thief is going to make off with rare love letters because you're too proud to admit that the *actual* private detective knows what she's doing."

He took a step closer, big hands landing on either side of my head. Both of us were breathing heavily—glaring with the full force of years of frustration.

I dream of that place between your legs where my mouth wants to—

My mind flooded with fragments of that written fantasy—my naked legs spread on that gorgeous bed, Sam's blond head between them, my fingers messing the perfectly tidy strands of his hair.

"Why do you always do this?" he asked, mouth dangerously close to mine. "Since the first day we met, no other *woman* has ever been so *irritating.*"

Poke poke poke.

We had a ticking clock on an important case, and yet I *still* needed to do it.

"If I'm so irritating," I said, "why does it look like you want to kiss me?"

17

SAM

"I don't want to kiss you," I said. "I want you to *acknowledge* that I'm right and come with me."

Freya sized up her opponent. "You're lying through your teeth, Agent Byrne."

She wasn't wrong.

It was taking every remaining shred of my willpower not to claim her lips with my own. They were so full, the bottom lip so plump, and the red of her lipstick was luring me in like a siren song. I could read the twists and turns of her mind. I knew she was remembering how we used to spar. Our sweat-slicked bodies pressed tight, muscles alive, chests heaving as we panted.

I used to pick a stupid fight with her right before a training session just to work us both up. There was no better release than going toe-to-toe with your equal—the woman who pushed you more than any other.

Gripping the wall with my fingers, my gaze dropped *all* the way down her body. I drank her in like I'd never allowed myself to do before. This, too, had been a compulsion I crushed like every other emotional weakness. I'd had to remind myself, always, what not to do.

Don't look at Freya's body.

Don't stare at her hair.

Don't notice the sound of her laughter.

The more we fought at school, the hotter my nightly fantasies became. Even I couldn't control my secret desires when I fucked my own fist—those fraught, vulnerable moments when I was merely a man, lusting after a woman who had not a goddamn *clue* how she affected me. We'd fight, and I'd win. We'd fight, and she'd win. And every time I'd end up back at my dorm room, door locked, picturing a naked Freya sprawled on my bed, begging to come.

And in those fantasies, I made my beautiful rival come. I made her come over and over, in as many ways as my feverish brain knew how.

"Cat got your tongue?" she asked, all temptress now.

Don't enjoy Freya flirting with you.

"If I did want to kiss you," I said, "would it even change anything?"

"Oh. I see this game," she breathed. "Trying to dismantle my defenses with reverse psychology so that we do things your way."

"It's no game."

Was it? Or wasn't it?

Freya pushed onto her tiptoes and hovered her red lips over mine. Our breath danced, mingled. It was a warning shot—she was ripping my fake white flag to shreds.

"Kissing me would change everything," she whispered.

"And why is that?"

Her soft mouth *just* brushed mine, demolishing my best barricades. "Because if you kissed me, *really* kissed me, you wouldn't be able to stop."

Just the hint of her mouth so close to mine had my nails digging into the wall by her head. The rote sex I'd been half-heartedly enjoying with previous women was exposed for the cold, brutal lie it'd always been. Freya's kiss was my true craving.

"You want full honesty from your partner?" I said.

"Please." It was almost a goddamn plea.

"Yes," I growled against her mouth. "Kissing you is all I want. And *yes,* I wouldn't stop there."

We'd finally touched the forbidden third rail of our relationship.

I'd never told Freya why Brittany had broken up with me. *All you do is talk about Freya and think about Freya and ask me questions about Freya*, Brittany had said. *You say you hate her, but I think that's a big old lie.*

I despised that memory. It was *confusing*. Because Brittany's accusations had been correct. Every action in my life had a Freya-inspired reaction. We were moths drunk on the same flame.

Freya's hands spanned my ribcage, fingers slipping beneath my shirt to press against my bare abdomen. I hit the wall with my fist, needing to release the sheer ecstasy of skin on skin. Her fingers were trembling, *Freya* was trembling. And her expression was shifting from haughty tease to vulnerable beauty.

I needed the haughty tease—the haughty tease I could handle. Her aching vulnerability would make me fall for her.

"I want you to kiss me," she said quietly.

She was giving me a precious weakness in her armor. It wasn't the full story I suspected she was hiding from me, but she *was* revealing a secret. Maybe not the best-kept secret—we both knew we'd been trying not to kiss each other for years.

I allowed myself the tiniest paradise—pressing my lips to the fluttering pulse-point at the base of her throat. Sugar—her skin smelled and tasted of it. Her shaky exhale threatened to crack me wide open.

"Wanting to kiss each other is certainly something we can agree on," I murmured against her skin. She laughed, very quietly. "Let me go. Come with me. And let's go solve this case. We'll do it together."

She shook her head—stubborn as ever. "I'm not picking a fight with you, I promise."

"And neither am I."

"Your plan is a mistake. I can feel it, Byrne. Stay with me. Please."

I lifted my head and we stared at each other—our expressions rippling between arousal and anger. Freya slipped her hands from my waist and crossed her arms.

"We're partners who can't even agree on the right course of action," she said.

I didn't reply—it was another truth.

But I did take a step back from her, my hand already on the doorknob.

"You're actually going?" Her voice had gone flat, the charged moment disintegrating.

"I'm going to go get those damn letters." It came out harsher than I intended and hurt flared in her green eyes. I didn't have to give voice to the elephant in the room—that separating went against our training and was usually the foolish thing to do.

She stepped away from the door, posture defiant. "We'll see about that, won't we?"

"We will."

It wasn't an unusual way for us to end an argument, but

as I clicked the door shut behind me and stalked toward the elevator, I didn't feel my usual blend of smug victory or bristling irritation.

It felt strange, even wrong, acting without her by my side. But all I had were my own internal instincts about this case, and they were pointing me like a bloodhound in the direction of Dr. Ward. If I'd learned anything from Gregory's betrayal, it was that partners didn't always have your back. And they didn't always care about justice.

The doors *binged* open, and I stepped into a long, carpeted hallway. I was in the hotel basement.

Goddammit. I'd let Freya and the almost-kiss distract me so much I'd hit the wrong button. Wasn't this where the speakeasy had been?

It didn't look like a typical basement—one wall opened up into a large circular area, where a stage or bar would have been. White tablecloths draped over the shapes of tables and chairs, and a dirty-looking chandelier hung in the middle. I knocked my fingers against the left wall—hollow. Probably covered by construction crews after the cops had raided the place one too many times in the '20s. Gas lanterns still graced the hallway. Black and white photographs hung in evenly spaced rows with gold plaques inscribed beneath. They appeared to be of Philadelphia high society of the era—jazz singers, local politicians, heirs, and heiresses. The wealthy and elite of one of America's oldest cities.

Why was every room in this hotel dark as a dungeon? I peered closer at one inscription. *Dutch Luciano and Charles Lansky, well-known bootleggers, dance with Viola Stark at The Grand Dame's annual New Year's Eve ball.*

The fact that this hotel displayed pictures of known criminals made me itchy. I felt drawn to faces in the photo I was staring at—smug, smirking. These people embraced being criminals and enjoyed getting away with it. It pissed me the hell off.

My ringing cell forced me back into the present moment.

"Byr—hello?" *Fucking distracted.*

"Samuel." It was my father. Glancing past my shoulder, I stepped into the closest shallow corner, lowering my voice.

"Yes, hello, sir."

"Abraham has debriefed me on the details on this case. I trust you're on your way to solving it?"

I hesitated, examined the empty hallway. "I am, sir."

"Close it faster," he said. "It will go far in instilling my confidence in your abilities as an agent again."

The elevator doors slid open, revealing Dr. Bradley Ward, hat and all. I stepped back into the alcove but felt fully exposed. The man was whistling like it was a fine spring morning.

"Yes, I understand," I said.

Dr. Ward tipped his hat to me before continuing down the hallway.

What the hell was he doing in the *basement*?

"Listen," my father said, "I fully anticipate a positive result from the internal investigation. And I fully expect you to be back here at the FBI's offices shortly thereafter, with Abraham giving me a glowing review. Is that clear?"

"Positive result?" I asked. "You're sure?"

What did that mean for Gregory? And what did that mean for my reputation?

"People do what I say, Samuel. That's the deal."

"Thank you for the update. It's appreciated," I replied.

"I trust you are taking care of your *issues* while in Philadelphia?"

I rubbed my forehead, wishing Freya was here. "Of course. Won't happen again, sir."

He barked to a subordinate in the background. Then ended the call with, "I'll be in touch."

Not since the death of my mother had he shown me the slightest affection or love or kindness in the traditional sense. That had always been her parental purview. My mother had been affectionate and joyful, and my twelve years with her were the best of my life. But I knew, deep down, what being an FBI agent meant to my father. It made him unequivocally proud to serve the Bureau. My following in his footsteps made him just as proud. And that was all the love I needed.

"You have the look of a man talking to a notoriously difficult father." Dr. Ward appeared by my side, tipping his hat again before lowering it.

"Dr. Ward," I said, "it's a pleasure to meet you in person. I'm Julian King."

He smiled crookedly—looking like a sunburned rancher even though his suit was more expensive than my rent.

"Same here. When Thomas and Cora informed me that you overcame your illness, I was delighted. We have much to discuss, after all."

"I'm looking forward to it," I replied. On instinct, I turned to Freya, who of course wasn't there. "I, uh...Birdie will be jealous I got to meet you first."

"Fine woman, your business partner," he said.

"Birdie is the finest," I agreed. "And that *was* my father on the phone. He could be described as *demanding*."

Dr. Ward nodded sagely. "I recognize the sound of a son seeking the approval of the only man he's ever cared about. Had the same relationship with my father before he passed away five years ago." He grasped the sides of his jacket, tugging it close. "He was a mean old bastard. And he thought what I did was *hoity-toity*. Sure is tough to be a rancher's boy when your true calling is archeology. All that formal schooling I went through, I paid for myself. Never got a damn dime of support. I have two younger brothers who were all too happy to step into his shoes. But I remained a disappointment to him until the bitter end."

Dr. Ward reached out and touched one of the pictures on the wall—two women were smiling, holding bottles of perfume. "My father's world was the size of his ranch and no bigger. I've gotten to see everything, Mr. King. Tombs, pyramids, ancient relics, the ruins of our oldest civilizations... that's what a man needs. To reach out and touch history, regardless of the cost."

"I couldn't agree more," I said. "I appreciated your speech this morning. We're in truly hazardous times."

"That we are," he nodded, then stepped closer and dropped his voice. "A member of our community was arrested six months ago. I wouldn't be surprised if we were being spied on as we speak."

Was he talking about Alistair? Victoria?

"I've thought a lot about what you've said, Julian," he continued in a soft voice. "About our circles of trust, tightening them. Making them as small as possible until the threats are sniffed out. I've had no luck locating my missing item."

"I'm truly sorry to hear that," I said.

"When I find the person responsible, I'm going to kill 'em."

The words left his mouth so casually I yearned for the gun I no longer had. I couldn't be sure whether they were truth or posturing. My first analysis was that Dr. Ward merely played at being a stately gentleman with a keen mind. Beneath that expensive suit was a man with a rash temper.

Which made him even more dangerous.

"What happened to you was a disgrace," I said. "It's like we..." I pictured Freya next to me, tried to anticipate what she'd say. "It's not like we choose empty houses without intention. We trust that we're protected."

A look of understanding appeared on his distinguished face. "Very true. If it is, indeed, a member of our inner circle, it will be a real betrayal. The kind that cuts deep. And I haven't informed our leader."

"Your secret is safe with me," I promised.

"Good man," Dr. Ward said. "I was merely down here to find a few minutes of peace before this weekend's scheduled chaos." He knocked his knuckles against the same hollow spot. "Are you ready for tomorrow night?"

"Ye-yes," I hedged.

"I've always loved this old hotel," he continued. "Such a grand history of subverting the laws of the land. Capitalism thrives on a system of supply and demand. Even Prohibition couldn't halt the flow of buyers and sellers, purveyors and consumers. It's a travesty to deny a man a stiff drink. And it's a travesty to deny him other things as well. Nothing, however, can be denied if you have money. And even the authorities"—his voice dripped with disdain—"haven't figured out how to make money less powerful."

I swallowed a rising tide of irritation. Of all the criminals I'd had the privilege of investigating, it was those like Dr. Ward who pissed me off the most. *I steal because it is my right*. If I had my way, I'd be tossing Ward in a grimy jail cell.

"Do not be late tonight," he commanded. "My room is on the thirteenth floor. 1303. Nine p.m. sharp."

"Absolutely," I replied. "Although it's odd for a hotel to build a thirteenth floor, isn't it? Bad luck?"

"There's no such thing as luck, Julian," he said, placing a hand on my arm before turning to leave. "There is only opportunity. The men who bought this hotel knew that, as do I. As do you, if memory serves."

I nodded but remained silent. *You should have stayed with Freya and read more of those messages.*

"I do remember," I said. Safe enough. "I'll let you get back to your preparations."

But as I turned to go, he called my name again. The low lighting gave him a devilish air.

"It's black tie. This whole weekend, as you well recall." He gave my standard government suit a slightly aghast once-over.

"I do recall. The airline lost my luggage..." I shrugged, backing slowly away.

"Yes, I heard," Dr. Ward said. "The two of you have been plagued with troubles since you arrived."

"We have," I said, stepping backward into the elevator. "But things are finally looking up."

18

FREYA

I texted Delilah. *Can you bring me a fancy and un-Freya-like dress to wear to a top-secret thing tonight?*

She replied immediately that she'd be right by. I'd spent the better part of the afternoon scouring through Birdie's messages on the Under the Rose site. Every sentence seemed encoded, or too general to arouse suspicion, but based on context, Julian and Birdie were beloved. There were hundreds of messages from happy customers —"*Received your valuable packages, thank you for your discretion and timely action*"—and a high volume of daily activity. But their *exact* relationship to the Alexanders, Roy, and Dr. Ward was still shrouded in mystery.

Not every puzzle piece fit together. From what I could gather, Birdie had deleted whole swaths of messages—and I still hadn't been able to crack Julian's password. I didn't like missing such a huge chunk of information. It was going to make pretending to be them significantly harder.

I re-read a selection of messages between Birdie and Thomas. The man truly believed he was the victim of an honest-to-god curse. *Bad things follow me now, Birdie,* he'd written. *I'm as sure of it as anything.*

My phone buzzed with another text from Delilah. *How's Sam doing? Does he need anything?*

I drummed my fingers against the side of my phone. Fidgeted on the bed. *He's a-okay*, I typed back, uncomfortable with the lie. Although he *could* be "a-okay." I just had no fucking clue where he was right now.

Sam couldn't have known that not trusting my investigative instincts cut deeper than our usual competitiveness. He *couldn't* have known how often I agonized that dropping out of Quantico meant I couldn't handle the pressure of being a real federal agent. That I would never, ever be good enough.

And he could never know what our almost-kiss had cost me.

His admission had sent hope rippling through my body. Too much hope. I'd felt positively buoyant, ready to float into the clouds. His muscular body towering over mine had my head spinning and my hands curling against his bare, ridged abdomen. My archnemesis was a man who did things right the *first* time. Perfection was his goal in all aspects of his life, and I'd bet George Sand's love letters that he aspired to that goal when it came to sex. There had always been a dance-like quality to the intensity of our sparring sessions. It was our peculiar ability to anticipate each other's moves, to read each other's bodies, the unique twists and turns. The two of us, naked, in bed together?

I'd probably *explode.*

I'm here outside the hotel came Delilah's text. I placed my laptop in the hotel room safe and headed for the bank of elevators. I wished there was a way I could find these letters without having to go directly undercover again. I'd demanded Sam do it my way, but without a partner on my arm, nerves were settling in. Online sleuthing from the comfort of a hotel bed was my happy place.

Going undercover with a bunch of fancy book thieves—sans a partner—was my idea of a nightmare. But the alternative was telling Sam I needed his help, which would never happen in a million years.

The elevator doors opened on Roy Edwards, looking especially weasel-y in the hotel lobby. He slouched toward me.

"What are you doing here?" he asked. "Shouldn't you be getting ready for Ward's thing?"

Neither Birdie nor Julian had had recent contact with Roy—only a flurry of exchanges around the time he wanted to meet them in person. Their reticence had been telling. Maybe Birdie and Julian didn't trust Roy Edwards.

"I'm about to get ready," I said brightly. "Julian and I were lucky enough to acquire a couple rare finds this afternoon at the convention. You might see them in our store the next time you come out that way."

He took a step closer to me—subtly menacing even in this crowded lobby. I held his gaze, but my palms were sweating.

"Next time, I'd be happier if the two of you didn't blow off our agreed upon meeting. I didn't wanna make a big thing in front of the Alexanders, but we both know what happened."

Think think think.

The messages had stopped abruptly after this supposedly botched meeting. But before that, Birdie had been promising him something *extremely unique and valuable.*

"I know you were upset, Roy," I said softly. "We promised you something very unique."

"Unique is good. I can make a lot of money with *unique*," he said.

"Listen, Roy, can I tell you a secret?" I asked. His face lit up—he was probably a man who accumulated secrets the way he accumulated wealth.

"Do the Alexanders know this secret?"

"Not even Julian knows I'm telling you this."

He looked around, covert. "I'm a keeper of confidences. You know that, Birdie."

Bullshit.

"Julian and I were too embarrassed to see you that day. We'd made this big promise and..." I paused, seeing if I could get a read on him.

"And what?"

"The shipment disappeared. The shipment of what we promised you." I made a show of glancing at the people milling around us, the public space.

"Why?"

"I don't..." I fake-stumbled, dropped my voice to a whisper. "I don't know, Roy. You're a man of this world, well-regarded in this community. You know all the ways these transactions can fail."

He lifted his head at that—looking like such a trust fund douchebag I wanted to smack him. "Thank you. There are *some* in our circle who don't see me that way."

"I've always seen the real you, Roy." I touched his arm. "And I can't say what truly happened except that our shipment was interrupted."

"Interrupted how?"

I hardened my tone. "Stolen."

Roy was shaking his head. "Thieves among thieves. Who can you trust anymore?"

"I couldn't agree more," I said. "If we seemed *hesitant* after our failed drop-off, it stemmed purely from embarrassment. We take our reputation seriously at King Barnes Rare Books. I'm sure a man of your stature would understand."

He preened like a peacock. "I like knowing things that others don't, Birdie. And I don't enjoy being disrespected."

"I'm well aware," I said. "And tonight? Just remind me of where the festivities are?"

He narrowed those devious eyes again. "You received the information, didn't you?"

"Yes, and promptly forgot. It's been a *day*. I'm too ashamed to ask Thomas."

Roy's distrust was replaced with eagerness. "Room 1303. Ward's room. 9:00 pm. And don't forget you're in my debt now, Birdie. Twice."

And then he slithered away like a swamp lizard. I fought a shudder. But at least I had the room information, and a possible in with Roy. And if the letters were one and the same...

It was a small victory, but I'd done it on my own. As Birdie. Without Sam's help or Delilah's or Abe's.

Standing right outside with a few fancy options. See you in a minute?

Delilah's text was still blinking on my phone. I'd received it just as Roy stopped me. Tucking a strand of hair behind my ear, I took a quick breath, straightened my sweater, and started to stride as confidently as I was able to through the lobby.

I'm Birdie Barnes, motherfucker.

That is until I spotted a familiar, elegantly dressed, white-haired woman walking out the doors and toward the sidewalk.

A woman who could totally *not* see Delilah Barrett—because Delilah and Henry had technically stolen a book right from under her and gotten her arrested in the process.

Victoria Whitney.

19

FREYA

"*Victoria,*" I trilled. "*Yoo-hoo.*"

I was halfway across the lobby, and Victoria was frozen between two sets of double doors, seconds away from stepping out onto the sidewalk where Delilah was standing. I dialed Delilah's number and heard her say, "Frey, is that you?"

I kept the line open as I skidded to a breathless stop in front of Victoria.

She turned fully and took me in with a cool assessment. Victoria was dressed in all black, with heavy pearls and her white hair swept into a low bun.

"Did you just *yoo-hoo* me?" she asked. One hand clutched her purse, the other, the door.

"Apologies," I said humbly, "I'm still a bit jet-lagged from our flight out of San Francisco. I'm discombobulated."

"And you are?" she asked.

"Birdie. Birdie Barnes," I said.

A lightness came over her features.

"I've heard whispers about you and your partner,

Julian," she said. "And yet I don't know you. How is that possible?"

I fluttered my hand to my chest. "We must rectify that immediately. I'm assuming you're a lover of antiques?"

Victoria's smile was inscrutable. "One could say I have a penchant for them, yes. You've surely heard of my collection?"

"Everyone knows your collection," I replied. "If you're ever in need of anything, anything at all, let Julian and me know. We often come into items you can't always find in regular rare book stores."

A slight tilt to her brow. "Ah. I see. We are of the same ilk."

"You could say that."

She was eagle-eyed, examining me like a rare first-edition she wanted to steal.

"I have a feeling about you and your Julian," Victoria said. "You are the blood of the next generation. Young, attractive, wealthy." She dropped her tone. "And understanding of the many *complexities* of what we do to acquire what we love."

"What an honor *and* a compliment I will treasure," I said. "Are you enjoying the convention? Do you attend every year?"

"Of course," she said. "The book festival is the most notable rare book gathering in the country. And I've been homebound for quite a long while." She laid a hand on my arm. "I'm redoing my kitchen, and it has been *ghastly*. I tell you, you can't find good contractors these days to save your life."

"One of the tragedies of our time," I sighed. *Redoing my kitchen* was an interesting interpretation of *I was placed on house arrest by the FBI*.

Victoria peered out the door, waving at a black limousine that was pulling up to the curb. "I'll be returning tomorrow, but I have dinner guests arriving, and someone needs to oversee the cleaning of the portraits. Let's discuss more at a later date, Birdie, shall we?"

"We shall," I said. My heart was crammed into my throat —unsure if I'd given Delilah enough notice. But Victoria sailed through the doors and floated out to her waiting limousine with not a single care in the world. I was secretly pleased to see that house arrest couldn't stop Victoria from being, well, *Victoria*.

As soon as she was out of view, I stepped outside, scanning the sidewalk for Delilah. I expected to find her crouched behind a telephone pole, wearing an ill-fitting fake mustache and glasses.

"*Frey. Psst. In here.*"

I turned around. She was in the narrow alley between The Grand Dame and the museum right next to it.

"Close call," I said. "Did you get my signal?"

"I did. But don't worry, I was already hiding. I figured at least *some* of our contacts might wonder what Delilah Thornhill was doing here," she said, referring to the fake-married-name she'd used when first partnered with Henry. "I didn't expect it to be Victoria though."

"Of course," I said, exhaling. "You always think ahead."

"How's it going in there?" she asked.

I glanced back toward the street, made sure no one was lurking. I gave her a quick rundown of what we'd uncovered but left out my fight with Sam.

Delilah listened, eyes widening at appropriate times. "Nice work. Even though it's terrifying at times, it's kind of fun, right?"

"I'm pretty sure I'm failing miserably," I said. "I'm only

about twenty-five percent sure about what we should be doing, or how we're ever going to get those letters back."

"You're doing what a private detective does," she countered. "Following a trail of clues. You might end up with nothing. You might end up with everything. Who's to say?" She leaned in. "More fun than stakeouts though."

I scratched my bun. "I like our stakeouts. We get to eat French fries, and you let me give you dramatic reenactments of the books I'm reading."

Delilah waited—like any good detective. I sighed. "Okay, *yes,* it's fun. Doesn't mean I'm any good though."

Her cell phone rang, and she gave me a quizzical look before answering it. *Abe,* she mouthed. I could hear his voice but not what he was saying. Delilah's forehead creased as she listened.

"Of course," she said. "She's right here. One sec."

"Are you missing me in the office?" I said, trying to hide my sudden nervousness.

"Not in the least," Abe drawled. "Listen. I'm calling with a complication."

My senses itched with dread.

"Scarlett was just approached directly by another private detective firm. They were following a source that informed them they know exactly where the letters were taken after the robbery. According to Scarlett, they're on their way to recover them now."

"Let me guess, they're not here." I kicked the wall of The Grand Dame.

"Freya." Abe's tone held shades of an apology. "Our contract's in jeopardy. This other firm says they're being stored at a location in New York City. They expect to have them by midnight."

Midnight. I leaned against the brick, letting my head

fall back. "Okay. This is what I have thus far. I spent all afternoon memorizing online exchanges from Under the Rose and trying to decipher patterns. We've befriended a shady rich couple named Thomas and Cora Alexander, who have heavily implied stolen letters are here. Somewhere."

I gave Abe a summary of our breakfast, the messages, and the intriguing things we'd heard through the hotel wall. "And Thomas referred to these letters as being encrypted with a code. George and Alfred used a code in their letters."

"But without a visual or some other confirmation, this could all be coincidence," he said. "There are other rare letters that use coded language."

"I think it's too coincidental *not* to be them," I argued. "Especially given the timing. We'll all be ecstatic if the real letters are found, regardless of who finds them. But my instinct says they're here in the hotel."

"I hear you, I do," he said slowly. "Unfortunately the evidence this other firm has must be strong—and tempting—for them to directly approach her."

I let out a long sigh. "I know," I conceded. "You're right. I'm working as fast as I can. If we only have until midnight, I'll make it work."

A pause on the other end. "Where's Sam been in all of this?"

I bit my lip. I couldn't say *I don't know* but I didn't really know. "He didn't call you?"

"No."

Interesting. He'd been all talk four hours ago about going in guns blazing.

"Sam is...has been working the convention floor. Getting a sense of what rare books are available, who's selling, who's buying."

"Freya," Abe said, "is there a personal reason why you and Sam aren't standing right next to each other right now?"

"Not at all. We just thought it'd be fun to separate. You know, work the room, make friends, influence people." I kept my tone carefree.

"Don't," he said sharply. "I'm serious. This is your first big case in the field, and you need to stick with Sam. Partners are smarter together. And safer. You need to get out from behind that computer and get your sources to trust you. Get them to take you and Sam to those letters. Because if that other firm comes up empty, we still have a contract and a fast timeline."

"That's a tall order, boss."

"I gave this case to you because I know for sure you can handle it," he said.

It was a sincere compliment that I no longer felt I deserved.

"I understand, I do," I managed. "We'll get it done."

"And, Freya?"

"Yes?"

"There's no stronger pairing than the two of you together. Whatever is pissing you off about your partner, I highly recommend you get over it."

He hung up.

"Remember when you asked me if this was fun?" I sighed, handing Delilah her phone.

"Abe pissed?"

"Pressure's on," I said. "Scarlett has a competing offer from an agency that swears we're chasing our own tails."

"Maybe this will help." She reached down into a plastic bag she was gripping, revealing a white carton of noodles from my favorite Thai restaurant.

My hands flew to my chest in a swoon. "Girl, you didn't."

She shrugged, looking innocent. "You've brought me a lot of noodles when I've been undercover. Can't I return the favor?"

I leaned against the wall, digging in with a pair of chopsticks she passed to me. My stomach grumbled—we'd been running around, and I'd barely eaten. "Thank you. You are the Hermione to my Ron."

"Meaning?"

"You're my soulmate."

Delilah grinned. "Don't tell Henry." She let me eat in peace for a moment, which I appreciated. I needed to figure out what the hell Sam and I were going to do. We had an invitation to an "event" tonight at Dr. Ward's room, but I wasn't even sure where Sam was.

When I glanced up from my guilty reverie, Delilah was assessing me just as Victoria had done.

"Noodle coming out of my nose?"

She smirked. "Wondering when you first started thinking you couldn't handle this side of our job."

I coughed on the spicy sauce. "Warn a girl before you take a direct hit, detective."

She crossed her arms. "And don't act like you'd ever let me talk down about myself or my abilities. You're my number one cheerleader. Why can't I be yours?"

"You *are*," I promised. "But it's okay to admit what your strengths and weaknesses are. Charming book thieves into giving me the information I need has never been my strength. I've never..." I looked down at my noodles, trying—and failing—to suppress a memory of the panic I'd felt during my undercover training. Sam was always alert and calm next to me, while I had to hide my sweating palms and labored breathing. It was hard to go from smartest person in the room to person most likely to fail. "I've never been good, Delilah. That's your job. Sam's job."

"When Abe hired me, he told me my partner was going to be the smartest undercover operative he'd ever met," Delilah said. "Why do you think he reached out to hire you, and you alone? He didn't call Sam. He called you."

"He knew I was probably looking for a job. Most Quantico washouts are."

"*Leaving* Quantico isn't the same as not being skilled."

I shoved my glasses into my hair, rubbing my eyes. "I disagree."

"I'm merely repeating unbiased information that I've learned," she said kindly. "Do with it what you will. But it's intriguing evidence, don't you think?"

"You and Henry ever roleplay sexy cops and robbers?"

She snorted. "Master evasion. Point to Evandale."

"That's Birdie Barnes, to you." I hugged her. "Thank you for the noodles. And the cheerleading."

"Keep us in the loop and be careful tonight," she said. "I'm serious. You got duct-tape and zip-ties?"

"I'm always packing that kind of heat."

"And where is Sam, by the way? I could hear Abe asking about him."

Never be best friends with a former police detective. They forget *nothing*.

"Investigating," I shrugged. "We were able to get into Birdie and Julian's hotel room, which is conveniently located next to Thomas and Cora's. We've both been using it as unofficial headquarters all day."

"So you've split up?"

"Uh, we're working different leads."

"I'm sure Abe already told you to work together with your partner, right?"

"Yes, ma'am," I said.

"If you don't kill each other, or kiss each other, you'll do just fine," she said.

"Who said anything about kissing?"

"Who said you two were subtle? And I'm still waiting on you to tell me the full story."

I had to suppress a laugh. "Okay, okay, I have to *go*. Important detecting business that requires me to don a cocktail gown and put on even more makeup." I unzipped the black garment bag she was holding, peeked inside. It was a long, shimmery, gold-sequined number. Definitely un-Freya-like. "You put the yoga pants on under this, right?"

"Birdie Barnes probably owns a single pair of yoga pants. And they're the kind repped by Gwyneth Paltrow."

"Good character note," I said. "I'm going to slip out. I'll be—*we'll* be—at this shindig by 9:00. We'll radio in after that. Hopefully with the letters or a way to get the letters. Midnight or bust, I guess."

"Go get 'em," Delilah said. "Remember what I said. You've got this under control."

But as I slipped out of the alley and back into the lobby, teeming with booksellers and thieves alike, I didn't believe I had *anything* under control.

Especially without Sam.

20

SAM

I'd found a tuxedo at a bridal shop down the street and mingled through the book convention for hours. There were no jarring realizations, except that rare booksellers were a chatty and eccentric lot, and they'd talk to you about gilded edges without interruption. As Julian King, I questioned dozens of people about the George Sand letters.

But learned not a single thing I could sink my teeth into. They were only aware that the letters were going to be featured in the new Sand biopic. A few times, I tossed out Freya's code word—*Reichenbach Falls*—but if they answered in the affirmative, I was lost on what to do next.

Suffice it to say, I was fucking frustrated.

I refused to acknowledge why I hadn't threatened Dr. Ward like I swore to Freya that I'd do. Tonight, I'd ply the man with gin and tonics and scare him into handing over those damn letters. Then I was getting the fuck back to Virginia.

With fifteen minutes to go before our mysterious meet-up with Ward, I stalked down the carpeted hallways leading to Julian and Birdie's hotel room. The door opened, and there stood my irritatingly stubborn rival.

"Sa-*Julian*, there you are," Freya stuttered, as startled to see me as I was.

Cora and Thomas are in there she mouthed, pointing to the room adjacent. I nodded my quick understanding and swallowed a massive sigh of relief. I'd been *worried* about Freya—yet another distraction.

I took in her extraordinary appearance—golden hair in a sleek bun, dark lipstick, and a long, shimmering gold dress that clung to every illicit curve of her body. My frustration now competed with a scorching arousal—a dark desire in my veins, a temptation to take her by the wrist and drag her back to that hotel bed, letters be damned. She was slight, delicately curved, skin glowing from the reflection of those sequins. With her glasses on, Freya had officially achieved Hot Glamorous Librarian status, and it was fucking with my willpower.

"I've been looking for you, Birdie," I said, gaze steady on hers. "Are you ready?"

"Ready as I'll ever be." There was an obvious shake to her voice. One ear listening for movement next door, I stepped close until our faces were inches apart.

"Are you okay?" I asked, concerned.

"Yeah," she whispered. "I'm okay. How about you?"

"Fine. I was doing my own thing."

"Same here."

My jaw clenched. "Did you achieve anything?"

Freya glanced down the hall before pulling me behind the door, propping it open an inch. She crooked her finger, and I lowered my head so she could whisper at my ear. "The Alexanders messaged Birdie on the website, confirming that we need to go together to whatever this event is in Ward's room. They'll be here any minute. We don't have much time."

Her soft mouth at my ear was wreaking a special kind of havoc on my nervous system.

"Abe called," she whispered. "Another firm approached Scarlett because a source told them the Sand letters were being stored at a location in New York. If they're right, they'll have visual confirmation by midnight."

"*What?*" I asked. "That's not possible. They're *here*. I feel it in my gut."

She pursed her lips. "I told Abe the same thing."

"This is bullshit," I said. "That other firm is following a false lead. We're this-close to finding them. They can't compete with our brilliance."

Her expression was disbelieving. "Are you sure? Because I think our professors at Quantico would give our work thus far a C-plus at best."

"Nothing wrong with a C-plus," I lied—and she knew it.

"For *you,* maybe. I never got below an A-minus."

"And neither did I," I said, smiling a little despite the mounting stress of the moment. Freya straightened the gold strap gracing her collarbone, fingers lingering. I tore my eyes away from the delicate hollow, only to catch the light pink flush in her cheeks.

"So. Midnight," I said, shaking the daze from my voice. "We'll know who won."

"And we've still got a ticking clock regardless," she said. "The letters need to be back in L.A. by Tuesday. If they're wrong..."

"We're right," I said. Her lips curved, competition sparkling in her expression. "Let's compare what we learned this afternoon before they arrive."

She nodded. "I spent the afternoon reading past

exchanges between Birdie, Julian, and other people in their inner circle. Messages between Thomas and Cora show a deep friendship between the four of us, although messages were deleted, and the remaining ones seemed coded."

"They're fucking smart."

"Very," she said. "Thomas legit thinks he's cursed. He only speaks to Birdie about it."

Our faces were close—too close—ostensibly to whisper. But it meant I was surrounded with her scent of tea and cookies and much too tempted by the heat of her skin. Skin I had finally tasted.

"I talked to Roy," Freya continued. "He's still pissed Julian and Birdie blew him off that one time he wanted to meet. I told him it was because the shipment was stolen." She pushed onto her tiptoes to reach my ear—she wobbled, and I wrapped an arm around her lower back to steady her. She didn't move away. I didn't let go. Her breasts pressed against my chest, and my mouth dipped dangerously close to the curve of her neck.

"Roy's a fucking creep."

"I agree," she said. "What did you learn?"

She peeked through the one-inch door gap. Voices were growing louder through the walls. The second my lips landed at her ear again, she shivered—I felt it, felt her body's response to my body's nearness. I wanted to scrape my teeth and lick her throat and taste the curve of her neck.

"I talked to Ward," I whispered. "Someone's stolen a book from him—he believes it's a member from their 'inner circle.' He said he'd kill the person who did it."

"It's all swagger," she murmured. "Right? The man's an *archaeology professor*."

"Roy has secrets, and no one seems to trust him. Ward's

on the hunt for someone who betrayed him. And Thomas is 'cursed,'" I summarized. "What the hell is going on?"

Her eyes were a kaleidoscope of changing greens. "I don't know. But maybe"—she bit her lip—"maybe we could try this funny thing called *working together.* And I'm only suggesting it because Abe's pissed. He expected us to be together when he called, not gallivanting about on our own."

Abe was the magic word for me—but even as I was compelled to follow orders, I was also compelled to do things my way. It was like a boxing match happening right in my gut.

"We'd have to agree on a plan though, and we can't seem to do that," I said.

"It might be our only option," Freya replied. "You did a good job. With Ward and all. Gaining his trust is vital."

"You look like you're trying to swallow nails."

"It's not every day I give you a real compliment." Her brow lifted. "Okay, now you. Quick before they get here."

"That's good info on Roy. And good info from the website. You're an expert computer-whiz."

And incredibly beautiful.

"Okay." She blew out a breath. "Failing on this case isn't an option for me. Is it for you?"

"Failure has never been an option for me," I said. "You know that."

Her face softened. "I do. Maybe this whole *partner* thing ain't half bad. We can bicker in our off hours. You know, unwind a little. Drink a glass of wine. Piss each other off."

"But you love bickering with me."

"I don't *love it*, you *make me* bicker with you," she retorted.

"That was a joke. You should try them."

Her answering smile was a slow, breathtaking reveal—it was silly Freya, the side I rarely got to see. "Another joke? That's your second one today. What's next...having *fun*?"

"This isn't fun?" I said.

"You know it's not."

"Don't forget I also know when you're lying to me," I replied, giving her the *tiniest* grin. Her breath hitched, as if I'd surprised her too.

"Running after a suspect down an alley and chasing them in a car did bring up a few nice Quantico memories," she whispered. "It was practically a Norman Rockwell painting."

"We have nice memories."

"Yeah, like *three*."

"And I cherish all of them."

Another silly smile from her—bigger this time. Dazzling.

But just like that, it dimmed. Replaced with a look that was half-seductive, half-nervous. "Is our almost kiss one of those memories?"

Freya had no idea how desperately I wanted her, how fiercely I craved her body against mine. Even now, with suspects six feet down the hall, I was inclined to fall to my knees in front of my gorgeous rival. Slide all those sequins up, up, up her thighs. Let my feverish fantasies direct every caress, every lick.

"We finally agree," I said. "Our almost-kiss is the very best one."

21

SAM

This was a hazy distraction from the intensity waiting for us right down the hall. But Freya's beauty and that skin and her scent were a temptation I was struggling to resist. I was sure that my father would categorize wild, uninhibited sexual attraction as an emotion as *useless* as stress, anxiety, and panic. If a man wasn't crushing his weaknesses—*feelings*—then he was beholden to them. This was a common refrain in the Byrne household—and so very different from my mother's free-spirited approach to life.

"You have your clutch? Your shawl?" Thomas Alexander's voice echoed in the carpeted hallway, screeching through the intimacy of this strange, dream-like moment between the two of us. We were still half-wrapped together, faces too close. I coughed into my palm, stepped back, smoothed my lapels.

Tried to force away my erection.

"Yes, darling, I have everything. Oh, is that Birdie and Julian I see?" Cora trilled.

"Oh, yes, hello," Freya called out, disguising the tremble

in her voice.

We can do it, I mouthed. She nodded at me, exhaled. Winked.

"We're ready to go." Freya opened the door wide, unleashing a megawatt grin on the couple.

"Please let me apologize again," Thomas said, taking Freya's hand. "Our fear reduces us to blathering fools in times of great unrest."

Freya demurred, but I didn't fully buy his new nice-distinguished-guy act. Every action thus far indicated he was quick to distrust and quick to throw his weight around. But if Freya could rely on whatever connection they'd developed online, maybe she'd keep his confidence.

"It's truly fine. We're all on high alert. And very glad to be in a community of our peers," she said.

The elevator doors slid open. Inside stood Roy Edwards and six other older, wealthy-looking people in tuxes and gowns. Three men even wore top hats and tails. They all greeted Thomas and Cora—and even Freya and me—with good cheer and a kind of buzzing excitement.

Only Roy looked creepy and ill at ease.

"I know where we're all going," Cora mused as we stepped inside. "Prepare yourselves."

She pressed the button for floor number thirteen.

I squeezed into the very back corner, Freya standing directly in front of me. Every time she swayed, the curve of her perfect ass brushed across my still-hard cock. I gritted my teeth, tried to think of anything—*anything*—that didn't involve me going mad with lust.

But if we were alone, just the two of us, I would have told her to wear what she felt comfortable in. That was how I always saw her. That was how I liked her.

"I can tell you're thinking about it," Cora said, turning

around. The packed elevator did the same, heads revolving as one. Freya stepped back until her shoulder blades brushed my chest.

"Thinking about what?" I asked, steeling my tone.

"Don't be scared," Cora said. "I was, my first time. But I promise—it's not nearly as scary as it seems."

Ding.

The elevator doors opened, and Freya managed a sideways glance that said *what the fuck*.

I bit down hard, stomach in knots. I wanted to beat the hell out of the stubborn side of my brain that had pushed me to storm out of our hotel room this afternoon instead of planning for tonight. *A lack of foresight betrays an impetuous mind,* my father would have said.

We arrived at the door to the penthouse hotel suite. And in front of that door was an extremely large guard that I recognized—he'd been the hulk working the metal detector.

"If you'd please wait in an orderly line, Dr. Ward will see you one person or couple at a time," the guard instructed.

Our elevator companions stepped neatly to the side, as if scripted, silently awaiting their turn. Individuals and couples slipped inside every time the guard called *next*. The line moved rapidly as I tried to settle my racing thoughts.

Cora touched Freya's arm with a white-gloved hand. "This isn't even the scary part," she said, voice lowered. "But it's only a few questions, and the two of you have prepared for this. If you don't play the game, you can't get what you want."

"*Next*," the guard said softly, escorting Thomas and Cora in. He stayed put, which meant Freya and I had an audience.

She turned fully toward me, eyes wide behind her

glasses. I felt the same encroaching fear, but if we didn't restrain our nerves, we'd be in worse trouble. I reached for the first comforting memory that popped into my head—one I played on loop whenever I needed to feel happy.

"You know what I was thinking about today, Birdie?" I said, one eye on the guard behind her. "The cafe in the hotel lobby reminds me of that time you brought me coffee to our shop. Coffee and that chocolate-chip cookie the size of my face."

Freya gazed at me quizzically—until comprehension dawned. "Your father had just been for a visit. I remember. I can't remember what you two spoke about, but you'd been upset with the results."

I'd been more than upset. I'd done poorly on a counter-terrorism assessment, and my father had been there to witness it. He'd admonished me after class—like I was a 10-year-old schoolboy, not a 25-year-old man about to become an agent. Halfway through his lecture, I saw Freya, framed by the open door, her face filled with true sympathy.

Thirty minutes later, my father was gone—and she slipped quietly into the seat next to me with my favorite coffee and that goddamn cookie.

If it helps, she'd said, *I think you performed better than I did. Your dad can suck it.* It had stunned a grateful laugh from me—a rare moment of frivolity between two competitors. And a rare reminder Freya had known me for a long time. Longer than any of my friends, in fact.

"I'm not sure why I'm remembering it so strongly now," I continued, "except that I'm not sure I ever thanked you for it. It was a hard day."

"No thanks necessary, Julian," she replied. "You would do the same for me."

She began straightening the bowtie I'd purchased mere hours earlier. Smoothed her hands down my shirt, palm pausing directly over my heart. I'd been trying to protect her with a sweet memory, and now she was trying to protect me.

"Mr. King? Ms. Barnes? Dr. Ward will see you now."

22

FREYA

Dr. Ward will see you now.

My heart leapt in my throat.

The need to have Sam—my partner—by my side for whatever was about to happen next was abundantly clear. How *silly* and fucking shortsighted we'd been to separate like that. Abe's voice on the phone had not only been disappointed but gravely concerned. Because we weren't undercover as two imagined people. Sam and I had assumed the identities of *real people,* which meant our cover was stronger—but not as likely to hold up to questioning.

We could give award-winning performances as sexy thieves, but all it would take was one person who'd met Julian and Birdie in real life to point out that we weren't them. The threat was very real. The threat could be waiting for us inside this penthouse.

The hulking guard stepped aside as we opened the door to Ward's suite. A small foyer with dark, rose-patterned wallpaper and sconces on the wall awaited us. Dr. Ward sat on a chair in the middle, one leg crossed gracefully over the other. His tuxedo jacket gleamed in the candlelight—but I caught a hint of a leather holster, right hip. The man was high-class with a literal finger on the trigger.

Sam's palm rested on the small of my back, his fingers sliding beneath the edges of the sequined fabric. Birdie and Julian were business acquaintances who probably didn't touch like this, but Sam must have known I couldn't face this man without it.

"Our newcomers have arrived," Ward drawled, nodding at the two of us.

"Thank you for having us," Sam said, deep voice calm.

"I can sense your nerves from here," Ward said. "Though this room would make anyone nervous. In Prohibition days, those suspected of treachery were dragged into rooms like this, hidden within the penthouse suites. A party could be going on right outside"—at this, Ward knocked on the door behind him—"and no one could hear the interrogations happening within these four walls."

What the actual fuck.

"How lovely," I mused. "I love that kind of violent history."

"Yes, I'm sure you do, Birdie," Ward said. "The two of you have been the talk of our little circle for some time now. You can imagine my guests have anticipated your arrival."

"We aim to please our customers," I said. "Julian and I are proud of our role. We take that responsibility seriously. As your guests can attest, it's meaningful to provide them with their specific desires. Especially those that are the hardest to come by."

"Indeed," he replied. "You are quite the pair of heroes. And I like heroes. I don't, however, like liars."

Goosebumps raked along my spine. Sam's palm shifted —gliding up to my shoulder blades and back down again.

"We despise liars," Sam said. "How can you not?"

"So you understand what this game is about," Dr. Ward said. "It's vital to test loyalty at every step of the way. Thomas and Cora spoke plainly to me of your authenticity, but you really can never be sure." He straightened his glasses, cleared his throat. "We've met once before, of course. Tell me where."

Sam stiffened next to me, and I could only guess his instinct was to demand the letters and get us out of here. But between Ward and the burly guard behind us, that felt like a risky shoot-out we couldn't afford to provoke. Before he could act, I blurted out, "Reichenbach Falls."

Sam's fingers flexed on my skin.

Dr. Ward nodded his approval.

It'd been a big leap on my part—he could have met Julian and Birdie for a Slurpee at the goddamn 7-Eleven. But I knew what these book thieves were all about. They liked the spy shit.

"I approached your empty house once before," Ward said. "You probably didn't recognize me, however."

Was that a question? I remembered what Henry had said about the origin behind the *empty house* code word. "You made a fine...bookseller," I stammered. His eyes narrowed, and I injected steel into my tone. "A bookseller in disguise. Quite the shock but welcomed nonetheless."

Ward's lips twitched. Sam was vibrating.

"Indeed," Ward said. "Just one more question. What's the quietest way to assassinate a foe?"

The answer bloomed in my mind. Hadn't Henry given us this juicy tidbit yesterday?

"Not you," Ward said. "Julian will answer."

Sam's face blanched slightly before he let me go, slipping his hands into his pockets. He rocked back on his heels.

Stalling, I guessed, but to an onlooker, he looked handsome and in control.

"Simple," Sam said. "I'd hire a sniper and give him an air rifle."

Dr. Ward smiled. Chuckled a little. "That is my favorite part of that story."

"You can learn a lot from Sherlock Holmes," Sam said.

Ward leaned forward. "I don't play favorites, but if anyone was to secure those letters, I'd like it to be the two of you. Not that fucking weasel. You best come prepared for a fight. Do you understand?"

I shivered at the hard glint in his eye.

"We do," Sam said.

"We'll be leaving shortly. Go have a drink. And you're not claustrophobic, are you?"

I *was* claustrophobic. Very.

Sam's fingers stroked back along my skin. I hated crawling through those tunnels on the practice field at Quantico. Sam used to crawl next to me and pick an argument about a test score. It aggravated me to no end. Although now I wondered if he'd done that on purpose to help me. A distraction.

"Of course, we're not," Sam said.

"Good on ya," Ward said. "I could never tolerate that kind of weakness."

I watched Sam's jaw set. For all I knew, Sam could have been terrified of small spaces as a child. But if he was, his father would have forced him to suppress his fear.

Ward opened the door and revealed the most glamorous hotel suite I'd ever seen. Wall-to-wall windows let in the glittering skyline, but the room itself had the same turn-of-the-century feel that Julian and Birdie's hotel room had. A gleaming, mahogany bar took up one part of the room, a bright chandelier bathed the room in twinkling light. I felt truly transported in time—if Ward's guests had turned around in flapper dresses, with long, skinny cigarette holders, I wouldn't have been surprised. Nine people were arranged elegantly on crimson fainting couches and high-backed, ornate chairs. Thomas and Cora. Roy. A few faces I recognized from the convention—all booksellers.

Were they *all* thieves?

Thomas and Cora were waving to us from their fainting couch. But I made a beeline for the shiny bar top, Sam on my heels.

"Two gin martinis, please," I asked the bartender. As he prepared our cocktails, I touched my bun. Released a shaky breath. Technically, Sam and I shouldn't be touching a drop of alcohol while on the job, but I needed a drink to come down from whatever the hell had just happened in there.

"I'm guessing *that weasel* Ward's referring to is Roy?" Sam murmured, careful to keep his voice low and our faces close.

"Mm-hmm," I hummed. "Apparently we have competition for what we want."

My nemesis caught—and held—my gaze. "Interesting that you think you can't do this job. You were incredible back there."

My cheeks went hot. Everything went hot. Maybe compliments from Sam were now turning me on more strongly than fighting with him.

I made another play at straightening his bowtie and kept staring into his steely-blue eyes. "Thank you. You have a perfect memory, as usual. Nice save."

"A-plus work—what do you think?"

The bartender handed us our martinis. I clinked my glass against his. "I agree."

Ward walked into the room, and the conversation immediately tapered off. He placed his hat on top of his head and nodded our way. "Would The Empty House please welcome our newcomers, Julian King and Birdie Barnes."

Polite applause rang out as Sam and I flashed stilted smiles. What was next? Rich person fight club? Strip poker with diamonds on the line?

Ward moved to the center of the room. Roy scowled at him. Cora beamed like a student. Thomas pulled at the collar of this shirt.

"Tomorrow night is often the highlight for most of us during the convention. A chance to bid on the items you *actually* came here to see." Ward turned in a circle smugly, loving the attention. "A chance to own a piece of history that you wouldn't normally get a crack at. Julian and Birdie, you've been warned. This crowd can be quite bloodthirsty."

Light amusement rippled through the room. It set my teeth on edge.

"There's a reason why we wear masks," Ward added.

Masks?

"But our benefactor likes to see all of us dine together the evening before. To cement the bonds of trust that make what we do so special. I've loved antiques since my first archeology class in college. But I've never had the privilege to be with this many like-minded people until our circle was formed. It's not about old wounds or previous misconceptions. You can act on that tomorrow night. Tonight is about civility and celebrating our values."

I gulped half of my martini by accident, coughing at the burn. The sound rang out in the hushed room.

Ward stared at me like a vulture.

"Sorry," I said weakly.

The man strode confidently to the scarlet-red door in the far corner of the room. As he opened it, I caught a glimpse of utter darkness just as the bodyguard appeared. In his hand was a tray of lit candles.

"Philadelphia is a city filled with secrets. Like the bootleggers, we of The Empty House understand that laws are meant to be..." He paused here, to a few nervous giggles. "Stretched and manipulated to fit our liking. Like the bootleggers, we are the tributaries between the auction houses and the black market. We are the navigators of murky waters, my friends. And yet who here isn't afraid to get a little murky once in a while?" He gave a charming wink to Cora, who flushed like a princess. "Tonight we descend beneath the streets to travel the paths criminals traveled before us. And tonight we dine and celebrate the rare and the antique in a building that is sublimely rare and antique."

The guard passed him a candle, which painted his face in a ghoulish light. He was going to take us into that dark room, and I was already not okay. Two sets of candles were passed our way. Sam took one, I took the other. The room was rustling as the nine others began gathering their things while balancing their candles.

Sam dipped his head to my ear.

"Tight spaces still make you nervous?"

"Yes," I whispered back. So he *had* known. He nodded but didn't say another word.

"Come, come," Ward waved us over. The guard followed closely—a lurking presence at our back. Thomas and Cora were in front of us, Roy nearby. Once we were in a tight circle, Ward stepped to the very front and led us through the red door. A narrow hallway led to a steep flight of stairs.

"Watch your step, Birdie," Sam said. And then he threaded his fingers through mine. His grip was firm. His thumb stroked the inside of my palm as I silently freaked out. I didn't like dark spaces in general. As a kid, my mother would keep our tiny house blazing with light to eliminate the shadows. My mother was claustrophobic too and understood the fear of tight spaces. *Find something good to focus on,* she used to tell me. Now I tethered myself to the sensation of Sam's hand in my own—callouses on his fingers, the short hairs on his wrist. The way he'd sought to comfort me immediately.

Maybe we could be partners, after all.

There was more nervous laughter from the front as we descended into the darkness. But I was only aware of the blood rushing in my ears and the guard behind me. I was so distracted I almost didn't notice when the floor leveled out, the low tunnel stretching far ahead. It was cool, almost cold, and I could hear water dripping all around us. I squeezed Sam's hand, and he squeezed back, pressing the sides of our bodies together.

Everyone stopped. All I could see was Dr. Bradley Ward illuminated in the center, smiling in the flickering candlelight.

"Have no fear, Julian and Birdie," Ward said. "Everyone struggles with the path we take to our annual dinner the first time they do it. But it's not to invoke a threat, I promise."

The low grunt I heard from Sam matched my own assessment. Which was *bullshit, it's not a threat*. Dr. Ward was in control of this show—from the bodyguard to this creepy tunnel trail. And he wanted you to know it.

"Where..." I coughed again, throat dry, "Where are we?"

"We are in the bootleggers' tunnels that stretch beneath The Grand Dame and several notable historic buildings in

Philadelphia." Ward knocked on the stone with a look of pride. "Only the true criminals are lucky enough to walk them."

Sam squeezed my hand one more time. "Must make us true criminals, then."

23

SAM

I wanted to arrest the hell out of every person in this fucking tunnel.

Their brazenness alone had me grinding my teeth to stay in character. The real intention behind Dr. Ward's speech was becoming clear. It *wasn't* calling out those who had the audacity to tarnish this community's reputation with their illegal actions. The real message had been tucked inside his bombastic words—*the coyotes are at our door.*

The man despised liars and cheats, was concerned about recent arrests and his own stolen property. His actual fury had been directed at the threats he perceived toward The Empty House. Those *deceptive coyotes* were a code for law enforcement or anyone else getting in their way.

Which made being trapped in this tunnel with him a lot more dangerous.

Freya shivered. I shook off my jacket, draped it over her shoulders, then rejoined our hands.

I also wanted to punch Ward right in his face for forcing her to be inside a place I knew she was afraid of.

"The history of these tunnels is as notorious as the bootleggers who built them," Ward said, voice echoing in the dark.

Freya cupped her fingers around the flame of her candle, drawing the light source closer.

"The woman who ran the perfumery in The Grand Dame basement was named Viola Stark, a fine woman in the history of our darker traditions. She paid off the police to keep them willfully ignorant of the speakeasy. She paid off the bootleggers using the money she made from selling liquor to high-society women in their perfume bottles. And she became rich herself off one of the most popular speakeasies in this region. Men and women used to travel from miles around to slip into that basement and indulge in something forbidden but no less virtuous."

An insidious fury pumped through my veins. First a trickle, and then a roar that dominated my attention. *Gregory*. A man I'd trusted with my life—literally—had been a thieving piece of shit for our entire partnership. His crimes had started long before we were partners in Art Theft—he was twenty years older—but I still felt completely responsible for missing the abundance of warning signs. Warning signs, my father had accused, I *wouldn't* have missed if I wasn't preoccupied with my own issues.

My gaze slid to Freya, head high and bravely putting one step in front of the other. The candlelight exposed the variations of blond in her hair—light and dark blending together. Here I was, responsible for a high-profile case and preoccupied with my most distracting distraction. Almost kissing her with a suspect just down the hall. Holding her hand as a source of comfort—and getting an illicit thrill from the romantic gesture.

"It's not hard to take advantage of the authorities, my

friends," Ward was saying. The ground beneath us was slick and smelled of mildew. "Viola did it. They're not immune to money."

I flashed to my father the day of my incident. The rage in his eyes, the disappointment. *And you had no idea he was tipping off suspects for a monetary reward this whole time?* Gregory was not immune to money, that was certainly true. Which had only made me feel sicker that day—not only that my anxiety had made me ignorant of his betrayal, but that he had gone against the core values of the Bureau. Like these book thieves, he had bent the laws to suit his selfish needs.

"When the shipments came in from the river, a gin-loving academic would let them into Philosopher's Hall. They would descend into these tunnels, carrying crates of liquor. Viola's guards manned the entrance from these tunnels to the basement of The Grand Dame."

"And the staircase we just used?" I asked.

"For parties," Ward said. "A way to sneak contraband from the tunnels to the penthouse without being seen. Or judged."

Freya was openly shivering now, even with my jacket on. And I didn't blame her—the tunnels were hushed and pitch black, with the exception of the tiny flames. Everyone ahead was somber and serious, like a band of monks walking the halls of a monastery.

I could *feel* the guard behind us—a powerful warning amid a sea of unending shade.

I wrapped my arm around Freya's shaking shoulders, holding her as tightly as I could. We came to a stop at what appeared to be a door, and Ward fiddled with a large ring of keys. My lips moved across her hair, fingers firm as I pulled her close.

"Almost done," I whispered. "We're almost done."

She nodded.

I racked my brain for a banal, funny memory that wouldn't blow our cover. Seeing her afraid felt like taking a sledgehammer to the chest. "Remember last week when we were going on a run near that big open field right next to the bookstore?"

Cora turned her head slightly. I caught the gesture—she was clearly listening. In the tunnel, whispers echoed.

Freya nodded but stayed quiet. I was trying to project an image of the track we used to race on at Quantico—the length of a football field, surrounded by nothing but flat, open space and blue Virginia skies. Not a dungeon-like tunnel.

"I bet if we go running tomorrow before breakfast, you'd beat me."

"I know I'd beat you. Because I always let you win," she said.

I squeezed her tighter, lips moving across the top of her head. It was a bald-faced lie—I was a faster runner—but I let her have it.

"Come in, friends. I believe dinner will be served shortly. Watch yourselves on these steps," Ward called back. It was interesting that the man didn't volunteer to hang back behind his guests.

Maybe Freya wasn't the only one who felt uncomfortable in the dark.

We were squeezed again into an even narrower passage, which split Freya and me apart. I moved her directly in front of me, keeping my hands on her shoulders, thumbs stroking her neck. The flame of her candle shook with her tremors. This was classic Freya—I'd watched her take on equally as frightening simulations at Quantico, and she executed them with aplomb.

These tremors though—I recognized them. Not just when we used to crawl through field tunnels on our elbows and knees. The feel of them beneath my fingers was sparking a memory of touching her shoulder once after a test. And realizing she was pale and shaking.

The light around exploded from pitch black to golden. Two waiters in white jackets stood with trays of champagne, bowing slightly as we entered a grand room with a dramatic-looking table. There were thirteen high-backed chairs, and in front of each were silver plates and silver utensils. Everything was lit by wall sconces and chandeliers. The hunter-green walls were hung with portraits of men I didn't recognize. Two arched hallways appeared to the right and left of a giant fireplace, leading to other rooms.

Ward posed like a showman, removing his hat and placing it on the chair at the head of the table. The action caused a slight ripple of reactions from the people in front of us. "Welcome to Philosopher's Hall, one of the oldest buildings in all of Philadelphia. Built in 1745 and maintained by scholars and academics alike. We are quite lucky that Thomas and Cora are the main financial sponsors of this historic building. It's the reason why we've been able to host this dinner for years. Money hushes wagging tongues. And, as usual, the waitstaff we've hired have been sworn to secrecy." The waitstaff in question were already passing out drinks with neutral expressions. "But I don't need to remind any of you that refraining from using details is a priority in these strange times."

The fireplace crackled to life—although it was a warm summer evening, the room was cold. The other guests took drinks and began to cluster together, speaking in low tones.

Freya slid my jacket from her shoulders and handed it back to me with a sheepish expression.

"Thank you," she whispered. Her smile was tiny but warm.

I gave her a short nod. In the rich light of this dining room, the intensity of this case came screaming back into my subconscious. Draping my arm around Freya's shoulder, letting my lips linger on her soft hair, were dark, secret urges that belonged in dark, secret places.

Maybe this was why Freya and I always fought against being partners. It meant not bickering or competing. Which left only one thing.

Temptation.

24

SAM

"I saw how nervous you were," Cora said, pushing a drink into Freya's hand. "I was the same way my first time. Which was more than ten years ago now."

Thomas appeared, lips in a grim line. His eyes kept shifting around the room, his hands fluttering around every few seconds.

"I fibbed a little when I told Dr. Ward I wasn't claustrophobic," Freya said apologetically.

"It's best to keep your vulnerabilities to yourself," Thomas said, voice low. "Especially at a time like this."

"That's good advice," I said.

"I've been pondering our community's recent fascination with George Sand and her numerous love letters," Cora mused. My hand tightened on the stem of my champagne glass.

"It's a unique interest, to be sure," Freya said.

"Well, and we have you two to thank for it," Cora continued. "You've led the charge in the rebirth of antique letters and the fascination with handwriting and signatures. Not reproductions, but truly owning a piece of *personal* history.

It's incredible. The intimacy you glimpse, between family members, lovers, friends. There's nothing like it—because I do feel we are more honest through the written word."

Freya wasn't shaking anymore. In fact, she was growing stronger by the second. "It was truly a delight to acquire those Alexander Hamilton letters for your private collection."

Cora touched the diamonds at her ear. Shot Thomas a knowing look. "Those letters will certainly acquire an untold value over the next ten years. And for now, I do enjoy knowing that we have them and no one else."

"You understand why we've been persistent about the letters we've come here to purchase," Freya continued.

"I can see how two *business partners* can identify with letters of a more passionate nature," Cora said. "That must be it for the two of you, yes?"

"Birdie and I enjoy showcasing rare works that provide an intimate look into human nature," I said.

"Such as?" Cora asked.

"Seduction," Freya jumped in. "I believe our community is fascinated with George Sand because she was an expert seductress through the written word. A lost art these days between"—Freya danced her hands about—"text messages and emails. George and Alfred bled their most ardent secrets onto that page. It's thrilling to read, especially knowing how dramatically George would then end their affair. And how dramatically they fought."

"Mmmm," Cora nodded. "We have a real interest in couples of a tempestuous nature. Bickering one second, proclaiming their love the next."

Freya's throat worked. "It's no wonder they broke up. A couple that disagrees that much couldn't possibly last."

"Oh, come now, Birdie," Thomas piped in. "Hating a

person requires as much feeling as loving them. Both are a form of obsession. George and Alfred understood that—the woman used a *code* to inscribe her romantic feelings towards the man *within* her romantic letters. She might have fought with him non-stop, but they must have expertly walked that thin line."

Thomas's body language toward Freya—Birdie—was warm, personal. Lots of leaning in close with teasing notes in his tone. I knew he and Birdie talked often on that website. But I figured it safe to assume that Thomas didn't expect his thief contact to be a woman as gorgeous as Freya.

He stepped closer to her.

So did I. Thomas caught the action, nostrils flaring when he made eye contact with me.

"Maybe," I interjected. "Or maybe there was never any hope for them at all. Hatred is more consuming than love."

He glanced between the two of us. "You must disagree often? I mean, running a business together as friends—"

"Colleagues," Freya interjected.

"Colleagues," he corrected, "can't be easy. How often do the two of you argue?"

"Never," I said, as Freya blurted out, "All the time."

Thomas and Cora looked happily stunned. I ran a hand through my hair and moved away from my partner. Colleagues didn't touch each other the way I'd been allowing myself to touch her. Especially colleagues that argued *all the time*.

"We even argue about how often we argue," Freya finished smoothly. "Which is why Julian can safely say there's only true disagreement behind that line. Not passion."

"Our interest in the letters," I said, dropping my tone, "is purely professional. Especially given their..." I glanced over my shoulder, pretending to look behind me. "Especially given their recent popularity."

Thomas and Cora exchanged a look—but remained frustratingly silent.

They were close though, had to be. I could feel it. And Freya and I were going to get these two to break by the end of the fucking night. Now that we were in this room, fully undercover as Julian and Birdie, that curiosity was coming back, filling in all the dark spaces that my stress at the FBI had eaten away. Because every closed case I had under my belt at Art Theft was colored by Gregory's crimes—did I only ever close a case when Gregory decided not to tip off suspects?

If Freya and I tricked this inner circle into thinking we were just like them *and* recovered the letters, that victory would be 100 percent *mine*.

Mine and Freya's. My pulse tripled happily at the thought.

"Have either of you ever written a love letter?" Cora asked. "Received one?"

"I should add that Cora has received several," Thomas said. "From me."

Freya made a sound of amusement, but Cora gave me an extremely suggestive wink over her champagne flute.

"I've never received a love letter," Freya said. There was a note of real sadness in her voice—disguised if you hadn't known her as long as I had.

"I've written one, a long time ago," I said.

Freya's emerald eyes widened behind her glasses. "Is that true, Julian?"

I held her gaze, swallowed hard. "It is so."

Pink flushed her cheeks, and her full lips parted. "Who was it for?"

My most distracting distraction had a hold on me now. Even Thomas and Cora faded to the far edge of my vision. I was captivated by the bespectacled beauty in front of me. Could a gold sequin dress have magical powers? Freya would know.

"It was for a woman I knew who was leaving. I was never going to see her again." My voice was rough.

"Oh?" Cora pressed.

"I wanted..." I cleared my throat, pausing to share a smile with our two suspects. "You see, I wanted her to stay with me. We don't always realize how much we'll miss someone until we're forced to reconcile that reality."

"Missing someone desperately," Cora said, sipping her drink. "Now that's passion. Such yearning."

"Maybe that's why our community is desperate for original love letters right now," Freya said—eyes still on mine. "Maybe we're looking for that thrill. Of passion that's been restrained."

Our bodies on the mat. Sweat dripping. Breathing heavy. Wrists pinned.

I knew why I was struggling to resist her seductive beauty. At Quantico, we'd had a physical outlet, a way to suppress our blistering attraction by doing what we did best—fight each other into submission.

But it had been too long—I was understanding that fully now. Seven years without an outlet meant that every additional minute I spent next to her felt like I was being suffocated with pent-up sexual arousal. *And while undercover at that.*

My father would be furious. *I* was furious. So furious I could have slammed Freya against the closest wall and fucked away our mounting tension. The last time I'd let myself unleash my messy, uncontrolled sexual appetite was…

Never.

Thomas grabbed Freya's elbow. "Listen, after dinner, I need to speak with the two of you. It's not about the money, it's about the pride—"

"Thomas, be *quiet*." Cora glared at him.

I felt glued to Thomas's fingers, tightening on Freya's skin. She had told me multiple times that she hated "that macho shit"—her words—and I knew her to be extremely capable of kicking his ass.

But I still took a big step forward, crowding Thomas's space.

"Cora's right," I said. "This is our first dinner, but I'm guessing cocktail hour is a bit conspicuous, don't you think?"

With grace, Freya twisted her arm and disengaged from his hold—like she'd been trained to do. "You're on edge, I understand," she said. She was trying to connect with him, getting on his side. "Your bad luck?"

"My curse," he said quietly. He touched his ear, glanced behind his shoulder. "No one believes me. Not even Cora."

Cora gave an exasperated sigh.

"The garage in our Nantucket summer home flooded. Our car was stolen two weeks ago. I sprained my knee on the golf course. In the past few weeks, we've had multiple flights canceled, we've both been ill twice, and there was a fire in our orchards at our house in Vermont. And it *all* started happening…"

Cora's hand lashed out and landed squarely in his chest. "It's time to be seated," she commanded. "Come. We must find our seats. Thomas, you need another drink."

She dragged him to the table. They were whispering to

each other, fraught body language destroying their elegant illusion.

"Another drink, Julian?" Freya asked. We weren't actually drinking, but it was an excuse to steal a minute's time.

"Of course." The server appeared just as Dr. Ward waved us over.

Two seats, right next to him.

We had been tossed into the lion's den, and now we were seated next to the goddamn lion.

I stepped as close to Freya as I could, one eye on the table to watch everyone's reactions to us. "Don't leave my side. This whole night feels dangerous."

"I can't go back through that tunnel," she whispered back.

"Okay," I said. "I'll make sure we leave out the front door. I promise."

"I'll bake you chocolate chip cookies for a month," she said.

"That's—" I started, brow furrowed, surprised at her olive branch. "You know that's not necessary."

She lifted her slender shoulders. "I'd like to though."

There it was again—that heat crackling between us. Surrounded by rich book thieves, there was no room to bicker or fight or even compete. And now I wanted to slide my fingers into that blonde hair and kiss her breathless.

"Julian? Birdie?"

Ward stood at the foot of the table, face a mask of regal self-righteousness. Freya and I quickly mirrored the poses of those around us—who all stood nobly, hands clasped to their chairs.

I knew Ward's type—humble beginnings he used for show, and a life spent perfecting his social performances. "The formal dinner is about to begin. Welcome to Philosopher's Hall, which has dutifully housed The Empty House for fifteen years. Our inner circle has certainly changed, but there are always thirteen of us—thirteen who have met at Reichenbach Falls and still believe in a man's word above all else." He rocked back on his feet, looking briefly like the humble rancher he styled himself as. "Hell, I'm not sure there's anyone I trust more than the twelve people standing in this room right now."

"Eleven."

It was Roy, looking smug and seedy at the very end of the table, directly across from Thomas and Cora. His presence tonight felt off to me, like an out-of-focus picture. Even I could tell he didn't bear the same seriousness, the affinity for elegance and cloak-and-dagger bullshit.

"What did you say, Roy?" Ward's voice was sharp.

He circled his finger around the room. "There's eleven of us here." He pointed to the chair right next to Freya, which looked slightly more ornate than the rest. "When are you going to tell us where the hell Bernard is?"

25

FREYA

Just as Roy gave a ferret-like sniff and asked about Bernard, I felt my phone buzz in my clutch.

A long buzz, which meant an alert.

Buzz. Buzz. Buzz.

It was vibrating against my hands. And even though I was riveted by whatever the *fuck* was happening at this table, I was also riveted by an alarming thought.

Birdie Barnes could be getting messages on the Under the Rose site.

"I'm sorry, what was that?" Ward asked.

The waitstaff stood at the ready, silent in the corners of the room. Food smells wafted in, blended with the birchwood fire. The room actually *felt* like history—from the 18th-century designs carved into the ceiling to the rows of academic texts that lined the walls. I would have been nerding out over the antique portraits if Sam and I weren't currently pinned between Ward and Roy. And a missing *Bernard*.

"We can count, Ward. Where's Bernard?"

Ward's face was already flushing red. I was almost scared he would shoot Roy on the spot.

"Let's sit," Ward said—sharper this time. "Dinner is served."

I watched them glare at each other, watched Roy finally look away, back down. Ward's face became pleasant again, but the slick tension remained. Without music, only the pop and crackle from the fire served as background ambiance.

I wobbled a bit on my heels before lowering into my chair, pasting a fake smile on my face for Ward. The empty space between us felt even more conspicuous.

"What happens tomorrow evening?" Sam asked Ward. Anticipating my thoughts, as usual. In his tuxedo and perfectly neat blond hair, Sam looked like a classically handsome spy from the 1940s.

"You'll see," Ward said, placing his napkin on his lap. "The actual specifics are not up for discussion this evening, certainly not in such an accessible place as this."

"Why does The Empty House choose Philosopher's Hall to host this exquisite dinner?" I asked, switching subjects.

"Because they do a lot more than just host the dinner," Ward said. He swirled amber whiskey, sipped it. "You see, the Philosophers see the value of what we do with The Empty House. Ensuring access to pieces of history—a democracy free from the oppressive hold of museums and libraries."

"Isn't this a museum?" Sam asked.

"It is not," Ward replied. "But the equipment and facilities are still here. Which we're grateful for, as you'll soon discover."

Buzz. Buzz.

My foot started to shake beneath the table. Nervous habit. The tremors worked their way to my knee. There was no way I could check this phone here, with the head of a secret society bearing down on me with a charming grin and a gun at his hip.

"Philosophers, academics, archaeologists," Sam said, nodding at Ward. "Birdie and I have always found their sympathies lie with our own."

"You know why that is, don't you?" Ward asked. He leaned in closer—he smelled of whiskey and leather, reeked of ostentatious wealth.

Buzz. Buzz.

My whole leg was shaking now, fluttering the cream-colored tablecloth that draped across our laps.

"Please tell us," Sam said. Casually, he placed his arm on my leg—elbow on my thigh, fingers gripping my knee. His arm was heavy, strong, skin hot through his jacket. His fingers squeezed firmly, quieting my nerves.

"Because we're invested in the same profession. A profession that brushes up against the great works of history—art, manuscripts, maps. Do you know what it's like to uncover a sixteenth-century tapestry and know that you're the first to behold it in five hundred years? The first to touch it, to know the power that connects a modern-day explorer to a Renaissance master?" Ward's face filled with greed. "It is an enchantment of the highest order."

I could feel Sam's touch and silently wished there wasn't a barrier of fabric there. The slit in the dress rose above my knee—the side of his thumb was *just* brushing where bare skin met sequins. I was laser-focused on it.

"Do you believe an artifact can bewitch a person?" I asked.

"Like what, my dear?" Ward asked, enjoying himself.

"Like love letters," I replied. "Do words of passion gain

magical properties because of their history? Would two people reading those words fall in love?"

You gasping my name as we couple together is the only divine prayer I need.

"Is that why you're fascinated with letters right now?" he asked.

My hands closed tightly around my fork and knife. *Just tell me you fucking have them.*

I looked at Ward, then down at Sam's arm. Then back at the table, where half of the guests were openly listening to our conversation and staring at Sam touching me.

"Julian and I are available for bewitching," I said.

Ward chuckled, looking between the two of us. "You know," he said, "I once worked with an order of monks in Athens. Old monastery, magnificent. And they had the most beautiful Grecian artifacts I'd ever had the privilege to see. I was there on a mission for the university, studying religious art with a group of my archeology students."

Sam's thumb slipped beneath the fabric and caressed the side of my knee. Skin on skin. It was comforting and arousing all at once.

"And wouldn't you know, Ms. Barnes," Ward continued, "all of that art had been stolen."

Sam's thumb stopped.

"Stolen?" he asked, voice hard.

"Who would suspect monks?" Ward replied.

"Who would suspect an archaeologist?" I added.

Another chuckle from Ward. "The two of you are not what I expected. No wonder everyone is staring."

Sam and I smiled, but his tone wasn't entirely friendly. Jealousy?

Or suspicion?

Buzz. Buzz.

Sam's thumb began working his magic again.

"But do we believe the antiquities in our private collections are imbued with a spirit?" Cora asked from the far end. "Could an artifact carry a curse instead of love?"

"Sure, it can," Ward drawled. "There are tales that will set your hair on end about people stealing or disturbing an object that has cursed them. They might be superstitious folks, but I'm liable to believe them."

"Why some objects and not others?" Thomas asked, face still red.

"Maybe the object isn't theirs," Ward replied. Embers in the fireplace *popped,* and I jumped in my seat.

"In that case," Sam said, "wouldn't we all be cursed?"

I admired Sam's strong profile in the candlelight. When I used to feel panicky during undercover practice days at the academy, I would watch him take on the role of another person perfectly, like he was inhabiting their brain. It was like witnessing a concert pianist place their fingers on the ivory keys—that heady anticipation of genius.

Ward sipped his whiskey. Held Sam's gaze for a tense five seconds. "Except the antiques in our collections want to be owned, Mr. King."

Our plates were cleared, replaced with chocolate mousse and cordials and tiny cups of coffee. The staff carefully placed slips of thick paper and pens next to our chairs.

"You and I spoke of this in the basement just this afternoon," Ward continued. He had lowered his voice but was undoubtedly aware the table was watching him. "But there are cracks in our little secret circle. My first edition of *Don Quixote* was stolen three months ago. Right from under my nose. A manuscript so rare it would fetch tens of millions at auction."

Sam's hand slipped beneath the material of my dress, his fingers closing around my knee.

"How could I forget?" he asked. "A true tragedy."

"I guarantee you," Ward said mildly. "The thief who took that damn book is probably up to his ears in curses right now."

Sam squeezed my knee—still arousing, but there was a message there I read loud and clear.

Thomas. Who was sipping his cordial and chatting lightly with Cora—but I could see his jaw clench.

Buzz. Buzz.

I disengaged my leg from the comfort of Sam's palm. "Be right back," I murmured to him, hand on his shoulder. Slipped away from the table and asked the server in the corner where the bathroom was.

The minute I was out of that ornate dining room, I walked quickly, fingers already fumbling for my phone. The bathroom was on the second floor, up a wide staircase. I slipped out of my heels and ran those stairs, thankful the carpeting hid the sound. The second floor opened up into smaller sitting rooms filled with books and manuscripts in glass cases. One door I passed read *Do Not Enter.* The final door was the restroom. I sat on the toilet, propped my shoes on the edge of the sink, and scrolled through the ten alerts I'd received.

Two from Abe. *Send any updates. Also, are you and Sam safe?*

I sent a rapid chain of messages to my boss. *George Sand love letters might be available tomorrow. Nothing confirmed, and not sure yet what "tomorrow" is. An auction maybe? The letters are definitely being talked about. Lots of interest.*

I moved quickly, pulling up Birdie's messages, trying to put out as many fires as possible.

She had five of them.

Palms sweating, I opened the first message. Another text from Abe popped up, blocking my view of the screen. *Are you and Sam safe though?*

The bathroom door creaked open, and I jumped out of my skin.

"Sam—" I started to say, hand on my chest, wheezing. "I was just—"

But it wasn't Sam.

It was Thomas. "We need to figure out what we're going to do," he said. "Now."

And then he locked us in.

26

FREYA

"Th-Thomas," I stumbled. "What are you doing here?" *And did he hear me use the name 'Sam'?*

I hid my phone and stood, placing as much space between us as I could. But it was a minuscule bathroom with 18th-century dimensions. His presence triggered another burst of claustrophobia.

"I'm sorry to follow you like this. I'm not at my most dignified," he said urgently. "But this whole thing is falling apart. The man *knows*, Birdie. He knows I took that Cervantes, and he knows I'm being punished for it."

Holy shit. Had Birdie and Julian helped Thomas steal an incredibly valuable book *from the man downstairs with the gun?*

"Calm down," I said, more for myself than him. "You know Ward. He loves a good show. Ignore him and focus on your plan."

His nostrils flared. "Birdie, darling, *you're* supposed to have the plan. That's what we discussed."

My stomach bottomed out. All those deleted messages, the gaps in the conversations. Birdie was a smart woman.

"Right," I said, shifting on my bare feet. Without my heels, I was much smaller than Thomas. "Right, I know that. Things are tense down there. I'm a little...discombobulated."

"Did you know he wasn't going to show this weekend?" he asked. "We're only in this mess because of him."

"Who?"

His eyes narrowed. "What do you mean, who?"

Realization dawned on me.

"Bernard, you mean?"

"Yes, Bernard," he hissed. "He wanted that Cervantes and he wanted those goddamn letters, and both put Cora and me in an extremely perilous situation. We could very easily take the fall for a lot of our leader's misdeeds. This is why Roy's blackmail threat cannot possibly be ignored."

Blackmail. Cora and Thomas had been whispering frantically about it through the wall. What had Thomas said in the dining room?

It's not about the money. It's about the pride. Roy was *blackmailing* Thomas with the knowledge that he'd stolen Ward's book. Loyalties in The Empty House shifted like sand on a windy beach. Who the hell could keep up?

"You're absolutely right. Roy is a problem," I said. "Maybe we should pay him off."

"So you're changing your mind then?" He took a step closer, a reckless gleam in his eye. There was no room to slide past him.

"We, uh, shouldn't talk about this here. The guests will be wondering where we are." I nodded at the door. "Let's go."

"Not until we figure this out. If we pay off that miscreant, he'll never stop. He'll drain us dry."

He wasn't wrong. Roy didn't seem like a reasonable blackmailer.

"Bernard will know what to do once we inform him of the issue," I said. "But he's not here, therefore we can't keep talking, Thomas."

I tried to move around him, but he blocked my exit.

I stepped back again. Attempted a long exhale as my pulse fluttered. The walls were pressing closer. And closer. Goosebumps shivered along my skin.

I went for the doorknob. He grabbed it first.

"You and Julian could be in just as much trouble if Roy follows through on his threat," he said. "Bernard cannot know about this. That's what we discussed. We'll only appear weak." Thomas's face was red. And growing redder.

"I know you're upset," I said slowly, "but you need to let me out of this bathroom, or I'm going to yell for help."

He blinked rapidly, shuddered. He passed a hand over his gray hair and stepped to the side immediately. He looked utterly distraught. "Christ, Birdie, you must think I have no control over my actions."

Yes, I fucking did.

"I'm sorry," he continued. "Truly, truly sorry."

"Don't let it happen again. I *will speak with you* but at a more opportune time." I kept my chin raised, spine straight.

He nodded, chastised.

And when he swung the bathroom door open, Sam Byrne stood there like a tuxedo-clad wrecking ball. His gaze burned ice-blue, his fingers flexed at his sides.

"Ju...Julian," Thomas stuttered.

"Why were you trapping my colleague in a bathroom?" Sam asked, tone nonchalant but posture rigid.

"We were having a serious discussion, and I didn't realize I was crowding her. I'm very upset."

"And yet she expressed her discomfort multiple times."

"How long were you standing outside?"

"Long enough."

The man nodded. Gulped audibly. "I apologize again. It was not my intention to frighten you. Surely my wife is wondering where I've gone off to."

Sam moved nary an inch, forcing Thomas to confront their six inches in height difference. Sam's expression was murderous—like he wouldn't hesitate to throw Thomas down the stairs and wanted to ensure he damn well knew it. Thomas practically ran down the echoing hallway, then down the carpeted staircase.

Sam gazed at me like I was long-lost treasure, finally discovered.

Long-lost treasure he was kind of pissed at.

"Will you feel comfortable if I close this door?" he asked.

"Yeah," I nodded. "Yeah, I'm okay. I'm not as claustrophobic when you're around."

Sam clicked it closed, and I twisted the tap on, drowning out our voices with running water.

"I need another minute here to delete messages that Birdie's getting on the site," I whispered. "Can you cover for me down there?"

"I can," he said somberly. A muscle ticked in his jaw.

"Thomas told me that *Bernard* had him and Cora steal Ward's book. *And* he said that Bernard demanded they steal the letters. That man is playing a mind game I can't figure out."

He nodded again.

"And what the *fuck* is up with the *vibe* down there, right?" I blew out a breath, shaking my head. Sam's massive body in this small space was starting to make me nervous. But not like Thomas had. "You and I will need to make a plan before midnight. Also, let's admit it, the food was delicious. Those thieves know how to cater an event, am I right?"

"I told you not to leave my side." His hands wouldn't stop flexing—although his face was carved with worry. Had Byrne been *worried* about me?

"Hey," I said, placing my hands lightly on his fists. "I'm okay. Thomas is a weirdo, but I would have kicked his ass from here to Sunday."

"We're in a dangerous situation, and you left my sight."

"Our cover could have been blown, and I needed a safe place to make sure that didn't happen," I murmured. "I'm sorry I left you, but I didn't have another option."

"I thought you were *hurt*, Freya."

Whatever space was left in that bathroom fell away, the outside world drowned out by running water and the blood roaring in my ears. The last thing Sam needed to be doing was saying my first name in a house filled with gun-carrying book thieves.

But the syllables sounded like pure, perfect magic on his lips.

"I'm sorry," I said. "I really am. I was only trying to keep us safe. We're partners now. I'll always protect you. You'll always protect me." I touched his arm again. "That's the deal."

He stared at my mouth with a look bordering on fury. I could see the effort it was taking for him to restrain himself from acting—on what, I wasn't sure. Until he closed the remaining distance between us. Gripped my face with those strong fingers.

"You are fucking *infuriating*," he whispered fiercely.

And then Sam Byrne kissed me.

27

FREYA

Sam Byrne—my arch-nemesis, my reluctant partner, my competition—had me weak-kneed within seconds.

His lips moved over mine with a fine precision. There was no equivocation, only a devouring. My enemy had always been too *tempting.* Who wouldn't want to be kissed by a man who looked like Captain America and had a brilliant mind and stared at you like you were the only thing that mattered?

I nipped his bottom lip, and he tilted my head back farther, our tongues meeting. My hands fisted in his expensive tuxedo jacket, wrinkling it as his fingers destroyed my hair. But, *oh,* that felt good—his nails scratching along my scalp as I submitted to his skillful worship.

This assault of lips, this battle for breath, was the natural conclusion to all those sparring sessions on the mat. *This* is what those fights were actually about—a primal hunger that went deeper than petty bickering. Sam was my equal. Sam was my challenge.

And I let him know that with another brutal bite.

He growled against my mouth and lifted me high, dragging me along his hard body. When my legs wrapped around his waist, he gripped my ass and held me there. We were panting into each other's mouths, tearing at each other's hair. Sam opened his mouth and cut his teeth at my jawline, savored my neck, every kiss as rough as it was seductive. This wasn't the poetic intimacy of love letters—this was seven years of pent-up sexual frustration unleashed through a *kiss.*

And for all those years I'd spent angrily fantasizing about his cock, the thick, iron-hard reality pressed against my sex fully answered my questions. Sam was big. *Big.* And Byrne unshackled from his tight, stoic control was a snarling beast whose sinful mouth kissed my hair, my ears, the crook of my neck. I arched as much as I could and felt him bury his face against my exposed cleavage, shuddering. There was too much fabric between the two of us, too many damn *sequins.*

I reluctantly separated our mouths—but only to take in gulps of breath. My eyes fluttered open, and his face was transformed. It sent a delicious shiver along my spine, knowing I was responsible for the man in front of me with swollen lips and disheveled hair.

Sam Byrne was fucking *beautiful.* I had not a single iota left of willpower to deny it. He was beautiful, always had been, and we'd been restraining ourselves for far too long.

"So..." I panted, "so you *did* want to kiss me."

He turned, pinned me to the wall and speared his fingers into my hair. Tipped my head with firm direction and kissed my throat. No teeth this time, although each caress ached like a bite. He kept his mouth focused, each kiss a long, deliberate lingering that had me squirming and twisting.

"*Freya*," he whispered. "Let's stop the bullshit. I told you what I wanted in our hotel room."

"Told me or implied?"

It was more fun to bicker with Sam when his cock was between my legs.

He dragged his mouth to mine, held my gaze. "If we weren't in public, surrounded by *people*, I'd tear this in two." To prove his point, his fingers slipped beneath my dress and twisted in the fabric of my underwear. "I'd take you against the fucking wall, and you'd love every second of it."

I gave him a bruise of a kiss, evoking a soft growl from low in his throat. "I'm pretty sure the two of us could fuck right here with no one the wiser." I rolled my hips, a full-on tease now, and his body went *rigid*.

"Will you ever stop *pushing me*?"

"Never," I gasped.

Sam hoisted me higher, until my breasts were pressed to his face. He nudged the strap of my dress down my shoulder—nudged until it dropped, exposing my bare right breast. Eyes locked on mine, he flattened his tongue against the nipple, sending a piercing pleasure through my body. He kept our eyes locked, forcing me to watch his slow, languorous, licking, the flicking of his tongue, the edge of his teeth, the devotion, the totality of his worship. When he finally stopped—after what felt like a year of tortuous sensation—he stared at my nipple, wet with his saliva. Stared at it with a possessiveness I'd never seen before. This had gone from two stressed-out, sexually-frustrated partners kissing in a bathroom to an intensely erotic *dream*. An unreal vision with bright, fractured edges.

"You forget," Sam whispered, breath hot on my skin, "that every time you push, I push back."

There was a burst of conversation from downstairs loud

enough to break through the curtain of rushing water. The sound even broke our bodies apart. And let reality fill the space between us.

"Sam," I whispered, chest heaving. "*Sam.*"

We were both shaking like leaves in the wind. Beneath our feet were ten book thieves wondering what the hell we were doing up here.

This was what could blow our cover.

He let out a rough exhale, pressed his forehead to mine. "I'm sorry. Fuck, I'm sorry. We're going to get found the hell out, and it'll be because I kissed you."

"I wanted it," I said. "We're both at fault."

"This is reckless," Sam said. "We need to stop."

But whether he was aware of it or not, he kept dragging his mouth along my neck again. And I kept arching against his thick cock. Finally emboldened, our hands were relentless in their exploration.

"I agree," I sighed, as he bit my earlobe. Tugging it. Soothing it with his tongue.

"I'm going to let you down now," he said against my ear. "But don't think for a second I wouldn't be doing things differently."

I nodded, too turned on for coherent speech. I slid easily down his body, which meant I got to experience the feel of his erection again. With respectful fingers, he straightened the straps of my dress as I attempted to brush away the wrinkles on his tuxedo jacket. He dipped his head, and I unmessed his messed-up hair, smoothing down the strands.

"I never thought I'd see the day when your hair wasn't perfectly in place," I mused.

"This is the first time it's ever been out of place." His gaze was flirtatious, a smile tugging at his lips.

"Another point for me, I guess," I said.

He turned off the water.

Are you okay? I mouthed.

Sam nodded. He pressed his palm to my cheek, a river of unspoken sentiments flowing between us. We needed to get back to this *case*. But the urge to sit and spill my secrets to this man was unbearably tempting.

Instead, I straightened my glasses—the final piece out of order.

"I'll be one more minute," I whispered.

He left a sweet kiss on my cheek and slipped back out of the bathroom.

I immediately dropped onto the toilet, with only the *drip-drip-drip* of the faucet to distract me from my racing, lust-fueled thoughts. I knew what I needed to do, but I also needed twenty seconds. Twenty seconds to slow my heartbeat. Twenty seconds to catch my breath.

Beneath my dress, my nipples were hard and aching against the tight material. I knew without a shadow of a doubt that if Sam and I weren't in the middle of an historic building while deep undercover, he would have fucked me on this bathroom sink. Probably would have ripped the whole thing right off the wall with the force of his powerful thrusts. His ass flexing with every motion, my bare legs wrapped around his trim waist, one hand over my mouth to keep our tryst secret.

Oh, *god,* I wanted that.

My forehead dropped to my hands. The sensations were too strong. He had incited an arousal that was too distracting and much too persuasive. But the fantasies kept coming—Sam and I staring at each other in the mirror as he fucked me from behind, dress around my waist. Sam on his knees with his head between my thighs.

Me on my knees. Staring at Sam with his cock hard and ready for my lips.

I turned the faucet back on and splashed icy cold water on my face until I shocked myself back into the present moment. I looked *drunk*. Wild and winded. I forced myself to go through Birdie's messages. All from "friends" who'd seen me at the convention. Every single one was marked *unseen*.

Thank god.

I fired off general replies to maintain their trust, but then I deleted them all. Either Birdie and Julian had the flu of the century…

…or there was another, more insidious reason why they weren't here this weekend.

They might have been the rising rock stars in the world of book theft. But now it seemed like they were up to their ears in scalding-hot water.

Are you safe?

Abe's text came through again.

Safe. Just a lot going on, I sent back.

A beat later: *That other firm is still saying they'll have visual confirmation to Scarlett by midnight. Thoughts?*

That was an hour from now. And every investigative instinct I had was screaming that the letters were *here*. Sam and I were on the right trail. Had to be. And pitting us against another firm was like setting a match to a trail of gasoline. If we weren't busy competing with each *other*, competing with someone else was even better.

I knew exactly what to write back.

We'll have the letters within the hour.

28

SAM

When I walked into the dining room, every single person swiveled around to stare.

It would have felt threatening if the atmosphere hadn't turned jovial while I'd been upstairs. More drinks had been served, and a few people had clustered off, laughing in corners and admiring the historical details in the room. Even Ward was joking around with Cora, who waved me over excitedly.

"We're about to do the final piece of The Empty House dinner," Ward said. "I knew you two wouldn't want to miss it. And Birdie is all right?"

"We've had a lot of calls from customers regarding the shipment that was delayed at the airport," I said, holding my hands out apologetically. "It's been a real headache. Birdie was responding to two extremely irate customers."

"Such a shame," Cora said. "I can't imagine you leave many customers unhappy with all the good that you do."

"Our customer's happiness is always our first priority."

"Excuse me one second," Ward said. He went striding

toward Thomas—Cora looked extremely concerned before schooling her features into a demure smile.

"You didn't share my letters with Birdie, did you?" she asked. "All that talk about passion and thrill-seeking she was going on about. It made me worried."

"No, of course not," I said. "Your secret is safe with me."

"Having you as a confidante has been lovely. Although I wished I'd known that you look like, well, *this*," she said, running her nail up the side of my jacket.

I coughed into my fist but stood still. "How did you think I looked?"

She tipped her head to the sprightly man in his eighties a few feet away. "Like that."

"I just look like me."

"I'll say." Cora sipped her martini with cool elegance. "Thomas wouldn't even be bothered except that both men won't stop sending letters to the house. He doesn't mind what affairs I indulge in, in my own time, but he feels like I'm 'boasting about.'" Another eye roll. "Of course, this is part of what he sees as his *curse*."

I watched Thomas and Ward from over her shoulder. Ward was telling some story in his booming voice about sheep herding. A ploy to make Thomas feel comfortable? Or did he honestly not suspect it was the Alexanders who'd stolen his valuable first edition?

"I guess that'll serve me right for carrying on with two men at the same time. Two men with a flair for the dramatic and a love of the written word," Cora mused.

I coughed into my fist again, concealing my surprise. "A lesson for next time, I suppose."

She tapped her nail on her glass. "May I ask a personal question?"

"Of course."

"Did you love that woman you wrote that letter to?"

"Love?" I repeated because Freya was walking back into the room and I had to remind myself to breathe.

In the flickering candlelight, in this lavish room, Freya was more beautiful than any antique. She held my gaze for a lasting moment, framed by the doorway, and I knew she was recalling our kiss.

That kiss. Was kissing Freya what living life uninhibited felt like? If life wasn't crushing anxiety and exhausting dread and forcing down any inclination toward *joy*...then did life feel like Freya's lips? Could life feel like something you wanted to take *more* of? To savor and indulge?

For the very first time, I'd acted on hungry impulse. I hadn't weighed the consequences beforehand, hadn't suppressed my feelings for duty or honor. In fact, what I'd done in that bathroom was dangerous, reckless and stupid.

The ends of Freya's soft lips quirked up.

It was fucking worth it.

"It was years ago," I said to Cora. "I don't even remember what I wrote."

Yes, you do.

"How very cute," Cora said.

"Come now, friends," Ward suddenly boomed, looking ruddy-faced from liquor. "The hour grows late, and we have one last tradition to perform before tomorrow's delights. Birdie and Julian, I trust that your masks are probably still stuck in the Phoenix airport?"

Freya was back by my side. I swore I could feel her body heat.

"They are," she said. "If anyone has masks we could borrow, Julian and I would appreciate it."

"I'm sure Thomas and Cora can oblige this request," Ward said.

"I always bring extras," Cora promised. "I can't ever decide. You're welcome to take your pick."

A slight wind had picked up outside, rustling the branches against the window. The room felt darker, quieter —*fraught.* The fireplace and the candles and everyone's black-tie dress made the room feel released from time. I eyed the secret door we'd come through warily, wondering if bootleggers were scheduled to arrive.

"Now, everyone, pick up those pens and the slips of parchment paper," Ward said. "This is a silly game, a game of competition, to get the blood stirring before tomorrow. The items we'll be bidding on are not available to the general public. They do not come with the proper *paperwork.* They come with strings, notoriety, and a grave responsibility. This is your chance. One chance for a piece of rarity you cannot live without."

Freya stepped close to me, and our arms brushed together.

"On this slip of paper, truly decide what it is you crave. And be honest with how much you are willing to spend on it."

Ward nodded at us to go—the guests were scribbling frantically as if they'd known for weeks what they wanted.

"What should it be, Birdie?" I asked quietly.

Freya took the slip of paper and the pen. She scrawled *The Love Letters of George Sand and Alfred de Musset.* I nodded my agreement.

"And how much?" she asked lightly.

One of the last cases Gregory and I had worked together had been busting an illegal art auction in an old shipping container in Brooklyn. It had held absolutely none of the flair of this Empty House circle—it was merely interested buyers who didn't give a shit about authentication papers. It was motivated by greed, less by the desire to own a piece of history. The prices, however, had been staggeringly high.

I took the pen, wrote *$1 million* underneath.

"A paltry amount," Freya mused.

I winked at her—which I'd never done in my entire life. She flushed.

Ward flipped his hat around. "In here now."

We folded our slips, dropped them inside. The other guests were brazenly staring at me as they dropped their slips in. Thomas wouldn't meet my eye. Roy dropped multiple pieces of paper, even though the directions had only been for one.

"Do you want to know what I wrote on mine?" he asked, sidling over to us. He looked bleary-eyed and flushed.

"Why not?" Freya shrugged.

"I wrote down *where the fuck is Bernard?*"

Freya's eyes flew to mine. "Bold choice, Roy."

"Just because he's the leader doesn't mean he controls us," he said. "That's what I *most desire.*" His words dripped with disdain. "If that man has been caught, I think it's only appropriate to let us know so we don't all go to fucking prison."

Roy's voice was slightly raised now, and the other guests were definitely listening. Ward was methodically opening each slip of paper, but I caught his lip curl at Roy's words.

"How very interesting," Ward cut in. "You all want the same item."

"We all want you to tell us where Bernard is?" Roy asked sarcastically.

Ward chuckled darkly. "Oh, Roy. Any rancher can tell you there are strong members of a pack of animals. And weak members. Guess what happens to the weak ones?"

Roy, swaying a little, mumbled into his drink but kept quiet.

"Now," Ward said sharply, "as I was *saying*, every single person in this room is vying for the same item. An item with a lot of attention right now." He shuffled through the slips of paper and began reading. "*$4 million, $875,000, $1 million, $1.5 million, $6 million, $550,000*." Another chuckle. "Your pre-bids are all over the map, ladies and gentlemen."

I could see the point of this exercise now—if you were truly serious about bidding on a rare manuscript, would you hear the highest bid and try to out-bid it? Were the highest bids only mind games? Was Ward even reading the correct numbers or lying?

Which brought up an even more persistent question—who was the new seller and who stood to profit?

"Six million is preposterous," a man grumbled from the corner.

Ward merely grinned. "That's what everyone said last year. And yet I remember the highest bid for the rarest item standing at ten million."

There were murmurs in the room, a few smug glances, some anxious posturing.

"Remember this is merely information to help you decide how far you're willing to go tomorrow night. We won't be the only ones there. Masks will be on. Lips will be sealed. Trust is the priority. Sleep on it, my friends, and come tomorrow prepared to pay for what you want."

The waitstaff were rapidly cleaning up. Time was up in Philosopher's Hall. It was already almost 11:00 p.m.

"We'll give these folks another few minutes, and then we'll all be exiting together."

The guard opened the secret door, back into the tunnel,

and I remembered what Freya had told me. *I can't go down there again.*

"Give me a second," I whispered in her ear.

I walked confidently to Ward, body language open, palms out and open. "I'm sure you're curious to know how things will shake out tomorrow."

"It's always interesting to pit people against one another," he replied. "You should know that very well, Mr. King."

I slid my hands into my pockets. "I do. And Birdie and I intend to win."

"Good man," he said. "With a father like yours, how could you not go for victory?"

Only losers quit, Samuel. Have you ever seen me quit?

"Very true," I managed. I looked behind me at Freya, studying the bookshelves with a familiar gleam in her eye. "Can I ask you a favor?"

Ward nodded, turned closer to me.

"Birdie didn't want to share this earlier, because she's nervous about this being our first time and all. But she's deathly afraid of cramped spaces. Her claustrophobia is, well, it's quite serious. She almost fainted on the walk over here in those tunnels."

"I see."

"Is there any harm with the two of us exiting out the front?"

"Of course there's harm," he said. "With the exception of our secret contact, no one knows we're here. No one is supposed to be here. You can't be seen coming out of this house."

I looked at Freya, remembered how badly she'd trembled down there in the dark. Knew that it would terrify her again. Also knew that she'd do it—because she was brave.

"How is the waitstaff exiting?"

"The tunnels as well."

I swallowed a growl of frustration. Glanced around the room. "Is there a side window?"

"You're mad."

"Is it crazier than using secret underground tunnels?"

Ward's smile grew across his face. "I sure do like your style, Mr. King."

"I know it's a risk," I said, dropping my voice. "And I think you're aware of the many rare items Birdie and I can get our hands on. Items that don't need to be offered to the public when they can be offered to one man."

His gaze sharpened, sensing opportunity. "How much?"

"Please. It would be our treat."

He let me sit for a few seconds before responding. "Leave now. There's a first-story window on the east side of the building, behind two very large oak trees. You should be fairly hidden."

"Much obliged."

Freya had wandered down the hallway. Neck craned, she was staring at the paintings, tracing her fingers along the displayed rare manuscripts. A small table at the front door to the hall had business cards, brochures, information about the building's historic nature.

"Follow me," I whispered, taking her arm. "Ward said we can leave through a side window. But it's on the first floor, so not a big jump."

"This is the weirdest fucking night of my life," she whispered. "And we haven't even gotten to the masks."

"I think we've agreed with each other more tonight than all of our years at Princeton and Quantico combined." I glanced behind me, saw no one. Sounds filtered in from that back room—people moving around, chairs scraping floors, plates being cleared.

We approached the only window facing east. It was an 18th-century building, which meant windows were limited. There was one, and it wasn't modernized. It slid up, no screen, and locked from the inside. I pushed it open, letting in the humid night air.

"I can go first and catch you," I offered.

"No way," she said, shaking her head. "It's fine. *I'll* go first and catch *you*."

With a sly grin, I slid out the window and let myself fall to the ground. My feet landed on soft, wet grass. "Not if I get there first."

She was peering down at me from the window. "I'm getting a Rapunzel vibe."

"Come on," I said.

"Don't you dare catch me."

"I *won't*," I said. "Come on."

She slipped one leg out, then the other, dangling for a moment before she let go. Every impulse in my body demanded that I catch her.

So I did. My arms wrapped around her waist, stopping her mid-drop.

"*Ooof*," she said, giggling. She kicked her legs. "This feels like you catching me."

"Sorry," I said, sliding her down my body—an action that immediately evoked what we'd done in the bathroom. We stood there for a second, breathing in the darkness, utterly silent. Just staring at each other.

"I kinda liked it."

"Admitting you were wrong? Another first," I said.

The window slammed shut behind us—probably a server closing it. Freya and I broke apart, and I searched for a suitable hiding place. She pulled me toward a small back building that was probably a shed or a garage. We were on

Pine Street, in Old City, with a graveyard on one side and another historic building on the other. Across the street was a long stretch of brick rowhomes, gas lanterns flickering by their front doors.

"Thank you for getting me out of walking through that dank-smelling murder tunnel." Freya shivered audibly.

"You don't have to thank me," I said. "I was happy to do it."

With a nod, she whipped out her phone to show me the messages from Abe. I read them quickly in the darkness. Rubbed my forehead, tried to think. "At the earliest, we're looking at having access to the letters tomorrow night for whatever this masked event is that we're going to."

"I know, I know," she said, worrying at her bottom lip. "But whoever this other firm is, they suck big, hairy donkey balls. Right?"

I laughed—and she slapped a hand over my mouth, giggling. "*Shhh.* Don't start getting my jokes now, Byrne. You're going to get us caught."

"Sorry. It's been a night. Of course, they suck..."

"Donkey balls."

"Donkey balls. *And* I think their source is wrong. Has to be. Those people can't all want letters that aren't available to them."

She propped her hand on her hips. Glared daggers at Philosopher's Hall, rising before us. "I have a wild idea."

"I already hate it."

"Remember when I told you I'd corrupt you?"

The bathroom came to mind—I couldn't help it. The kiss and the things I'd wanted to do with my tongue. My hands. My mouth.

"Byrne." Freya snapped her fingers. "Do you want to find these letters or what?"

"I hate not winning," I growled. "I hate failing."

My father will never let me live it down if I do.

"So what do two super-competitive people do when they're competing with another team?" She pointed at the Hall with a big smile. "They break into the building where they're keeping the evidence."

29

FREYA

"No."

"Hear me out."

"*Evandale.*"

Sam and I were whisper-arguing behind an old tool shed while trying to stay hidden and away from the prying eyes of nosy Philly residents. I pulled him deeper into the shadows until I could barely make out his handsome face.

"Listen to me," I pleaded. "Ward said a number of times that the philosophers are their most sympathetic partners. He said this hall was *not* a museum, but luckily *acted* like one. And he also said that they did *more for us than you could ever know*."

"What's the connection?"

"What if the items being auctioned off tomorrow night are *here*. In this house. Stored here. Talk about a needle in a haystack—their sympathetic contact could store rare books surrounded by their own collection of rare books. I passed rooms with glass cases and private storage areas. Those letters could be in there."

I caught the turn of his head but couldn't read his darkened expression. "We're running this out like a scenario," he said.

"Goddammit, Byrne."

"First," he said, using his serious *I'm an FBI agent* tone, "say we break in and find nothing."

"The other firm *could* be right. Or they're wrong, and we have to wait another twenty-four hours to *maybe* get to the letters at the auction."

"And we lose the hours we could have used to, say, search Ward's hotel room for them," he countered.

"That's not a bad instinct," I said, "but Ward's too smart to store recently stolen books on his person. He *is* smart enough to have someone else do it for him." I nodded back at the hall behind us.

"Fair point," he said. "We break in there, find nothing, and get caught by the police. It's not like private detectives are above the law."

"Scenario three. We break in there, find the letters, and *don't* get caught by the police," I said. "Or scenario four—we get caught by the police, surrounded by stolen goods, and help bring down The Empty House because we're sitting on so much actual evidence."

"Everything we've overheard is circumstantial at best," Sam said. "We can't record them without their permission. And we have no photographic proof. They could turn around just as easily and say that *we'd* stolen the letters."

But he was looking up at Philosopher's Hall like a mountaineer about to scale Everest. Like he respected it for the challenge even though danger lurked ahead.

"Other option is we fail," I said.

He shifted, and a slice of moonlight illuminated his face. His lips were tipped into a slight smile. "You sure Abe isn't tricking us into working together?"

I opened my mouth to argue. "Well, *shit*, that's actually a good point."

Sam continued to stare ahead.

"What's your plan, partner?" I asked.

He let out a big sigh. "What's Abe's stance on breaking and entering?"

"I'm going to guess negative."

"The only other option is failure," he repeated.

"And the worst that can happen is we go to jail."

Sam dragged a hand down his face. "It's possible you've gotten weirder since Quantico."

"It's possible you've gotten even more *lame*."

"Are we even telling Abe? Henry? Delilah?"

"We can tell them if we succeed," I said. I chewed on my lip. I hated keeping things from Del. But she and Henry had also gone against Abe's direct orders on the first case they'd worked together. At the time, I would have told her not to do it.

And yet it was the only way they could have succeeded.

"Think of it as a funny story. *Hey. So wild, but guess what we did last night.*"

"We can't let those letters slip away," Sam finally said.

"I'm trying to keep it light here, but"—I touched his arm—"you know I wouldn't suggest anything this intense if I didn't have a good hunch."

"Your hunches were legendary at the academy."

"No, they weren't." I waved my hand through the air.

"Yes, they were," he said. "As much as it pains me to admit this, if you think they might be in there, they might be."

"It's a big deal. This is like the hacking thing. We do it as partners or we don't do it," I said.

One last glance into the sky, as if the moon held the

answers. Then he muttered, "Fuck it," under his breath. Crouched down like a cat burglar, pulling me with him.

"Here's the thing," he whispered, "I didn't hear that waiter latch the window after he closed it. Did you?"

I shook my head. "Nope."

"Could be an access point."

"Let's do it."

Sam stood up. "Wait. You're not going to argue with me?"

"This is your area of expertise," I replied. "I hacked us into the site. You break us into this building."

"FBI agents don't go around breaking into buildings."

"Don't they?" I said. "You and I had to conduct like twenty simulated rescues out of buildings like this one. I always wanted to go in from the roof, and you always told me to quote *fuck off* unquote."

"I have *never*, in my life, said the words *fuck off* to you."

"Okay, fine," I admitted. "You said something like 'your plan lacks legitimate resources and is basically implausible.'"

We were whispering to each other urgently, low and sliding through the grass. I'd kicked off my heels, and my feet were wet from dew, hem of my dress already dirty. Our hands hit the wall, and we both peered at the window from where we'd launched ourselves. All the lights in the building were off—not a sound came from inside.

"You're sure he said the catering staff was leaving through the tunnels?"

Sam nodded. Held his hand out. "I'll boost you up. See if you can slide the window open from the outside."

A dog barked, and I almost fell over. Sam grabbed my arms, kept me standing, finger pressed to his lips. Some rustling—wind again—another barking dog. But we were blanketed in darkness as a stream of clouds floated across the moon.

He cupped his hands, and I placed my foot there. One hand on his shoulder, one on the building. I desperately tried to ignore the sensation of Sam's face this fucking close to my breasts. Every time he exhaled, I could feel his breath, caressing my collarbone.

"Ready, partner?" I whispered.

"Ready. And please be careful."

He scooped me up—it wasn't far, just the first story. I was able to place my fingertips on the window and apply the lightest pressure. Pushed.

It slid open.

"Holy shit," I breathed. With deliberate care, I pushed the window up gently, looking behind me to make sure no one was catching our first B and E. Once the window opened an inch, I listened. No staff. No movement inside.

Slid the window all the way up and rolled inside, landing quietly. Popped my head out and waved Sam in. We were near the table I'd been glancing at earlier—staff business cards, brochures about the history of Philosopher's Hall.

Sam hoisted himself with all the grace of a Crossfit enthusiast. He'd shed his jacket, and I could make out the muscles of those massive shoulders shifting beneath his white shirt. He dropped to the floor. Handed me my shoes.

"Did we do it?" he asked, standing to his full height.

"I think so," I said. I lightly punched him in the shoulder. "Suck it, *other firm*."

He looked around. Let out a relieved breath. "Okay. Okay we need to focus. Think. We won't have much—"

"*Shit*," I hissed. "Shit, fuck, shit."

Sam whirled around—expecting an attacker, I'm sure.

But all I could do was grab his arm and point to the red blinking lights flaring to life on the ceiling. *Blink blink blink.* Two small, white security cameras were pointed directly at our faces.

"The security alarm," I said. "Byrne, we tripped the—"

But I didn't need to say more.

Because those red lights exploded into a wailing siren.

30

FREYA

The security alarm at Philosopher's Hall was the loudest thing I'd ever heard. It was a screaming banshee of sound, and all Sam and I could do was gape at each other as those red lights blinked faster and faster.

That dog was barking again—more dogs, a pack of fucking dogs, all reacting to the same high-pitched frequency. Quickly, Sam slid the window shut and dragged me to the ground.

"Remember that time you said the worst thing that could happen was we'd go to jail?" Sam hissed. "Looks like your dream's about to come true."

"Trying to see me in an orange jumpsuit, eh?" I shot back, army-crawling across the floor until I reached a black box with white lettering. *Vesper Systems.* I grabbed my phone.

"What are you doing?"

"Activating my nerd girl powers," I said. I crawled back to him, both of us sitting against the wall.

"We need to get out of here," he said. "Slip out that same

window and run. There's time. Maybe the security cameras didn't catch our faces."

I held up a finger. Searched for *Vesper Systems* customer service line. Dialed it.

"We need to *go*," he urged.

Another sound now—farther in the distance.

Police sirens.

"Thank you for calling Vesper. Is this regarding a problem with your security system?" A woman's chipper voice came over the phone. I pinched a business card between my fingers. *Shannon James, Director of Operations*. I'd grabbed it earlier, before we'd gone out that window the first time.

"Hi, yes, this is Shannon James." I injected as much authority into my voice as I could manage. "I needed to get back into Philosopher's Hall to grab some files and tripped the alarm. It's blaring so loudly I can't hear myself think, let alone remember what our alarm code is."

I army-crawled back to that box. Felt along the edge until my fingernail caught the end of a piece of plastic. Flipped it open to reveal a keypad. I pressed the phone hard to my ear.

"Of course, happy to help, Ms. James." There was a familiar *click* of nails on a keyboard. "I see you are the primary account holder for Philosopher's Hall. We can supply the code, but we'll need your four-digit password to authorize."

Dammit.

Of course, they did. The police sirens wailed closer, and I swore I saw flashing lights reflected on the far wall. Sam was watching me intently—he was either impressed or pissed as fuck. Or both.

"Yes, of course," I said, stalling. Picked up the brochure

from the table. *Philosopher's Hall was constructed in 1743, the first of its kind in Philadelphia...* "Our password to authorize is 1-7-4-3."

"*Evandale,*" Sam whispered. He was less than a foot away from me. I slapped a hand over his mouth. Shook my head. The siren felt like a hammer between my temples.

"Ma'am?" The woman said impatiently.

"Um, what?" I strained to hear her.

"Ma'am, I said your passcode is 1-7-9-7." I slid quickly across the floor and typed *1797*.

It stopped.

The alarm fucking *stopped*. It left a tangible hush in its wake, like stepping into a quiet forest after a busy day in the city. Sam and I stared at each other with gaping mouths.

"Ma'am? Hello?"

"Oh, yes...um, it worked, thank you," I said.

"While I have you, do you still want the security cameras disabled for the weekend? I can reactivate them if needed."

Relief collapsed me against the wall. My guess was that Ward had put that into action—no camera footage, no tape, no record of the thieves who'd just dined here.

"Nope, keep the cameras off as discussed," I said firmly. "And thank you." I ended the call.

"You did it," Sam said hoarsely.

"I did do it," I said. That had felt *good. Really* good. I beamed at up at my nemesis. "Not too shabby, eh?"

He took one giant step and brought our lips together. It was a rough and dirty kiss, a hard kiss. It felt way more than *good*.

It was hot as hell. The demanding feel of his hands in my hair, holding me still, had me jelly-kneed in an instant. I liked this feeling of being taken by Sam Byrne. Actually more than liked—this was becoming my new craving. I'd always liked slamming Sam down onto his back with a knee to the chest. It was undeniably gratifying to best a superhero. But now, as his tongue stroked against mine, I remembered Sam pinning my wrists, holding *me* down. The deep trust we had as sparring partners mirrored our intimacy as rivals—as much as we argued, you couldn't spar with someone you didn't trust not to hurt you.

Sam's thumbs stroked across my cheekbones, and I whimpered. He pulled back. We were panting in the still-sudden quiet. "Sorry."

"You don't need to apologize every time you kiss me," I whispered.

"I miss..." He cleared his throat. "I've missed watching you kick ass, Evandale."

I'd spent all those weeks at Quantico secretly watching Sam succeed—had he also been watching me? But if he had, wouldn't he have *seen* how every little thing sent me into a nervous tailspin?

Police sirens sliced through the softness. Sam shoved us both back against the far wall, and our necks craned to stare at the front door.

"Excuse me, is everything okay in there?" *Knock knock knock.* "It's Glen, from across the street? Just wondering if you need the police?"

Sam straightened his bowtie and adjusted his cufflinks. *Winked* at me again. And walked confidently to the door.

No one had ever told me that your annoyingly smug enemy could wink at you and turn your bones to mush. If they had, I would have been better prepared for my body's aroused response.

"Glen?" Sam's deep voice was assured. Calm. *Always use their names* had been a little psychological trick our instructors used to tell us. "Is that you?"

I could hear a man sputtering, surprised. "Oh! I didn't…I mean, is everything okay? Also, who are you?"

"Julian King," Sam said. "I'm the new director here at Philosopher's Hall. We had a private event this evening, and I'm tidying up. Tripped the damn alarm while I was securing the windows, I'm afraid."

The whine of the police sirens was definitely on our block now. The red-and-blue lights rippled across the walls of books across from me. But their engine wasn't slowing down.

"Oh, it's fine, it's fine," said Glen, who was clearly the block busybody. "I only wanted to make sure you weren't a murderer or a thief or a common vagrant."

"No thieves here, I can assure you," Sam said. "And we've always appreciated the care you show. Shannon has spoken highly of you during our meetings."

More surprised sputtering from Glen. "Oh my goodness, Shannon said that? Shannon's a dear. Happy to be of service. And glad everything's all right. You have a nice night."

"Same to you, Glen," Sam replied.

I marked Glen's footsteps back down the front stairs. And then the cop car sliding right past us, off to chase down another crime.

"Nicely done," I breathed, letting out the world's biggest exhale.

Sam nodded, glancing behind him. "Okay. Alarm off. Cameras off. Cops gone."

I propped my hands on my hips. "Let's go find those love letters."

31

SAM

My job hadn't been this exciting in years. My job had been tedious and panic-inducing. Depressing. Working for Codex was actually having fun. It was *different* and intriguing and satisfying all at once.

I glanced sideways at the gorgeous firecracker standing next to me.

She was certainly not the reason I was enjoying hunting down criminals again.

Although Freya *was* the reason I'd acted against my better judgment—or *any* judgment—twice. I could count on one hand the number of times I'd seen her full smile—the one that made her so very *Freya*. The one she'd flash to her favorite professors or friends or those boyfriends I'd hated. It was wide, cheeky, dimpled. It was carefree and silly.

And she'd pointed it right at me with precision.

What choice did I have except to steal one more kiss?

"If you were nineteenth-century love letters encoded with perverted messages—where would you hide?" she asked, straightening her glasses.

"Where were those rooms you saw that had the glass cases?" I asked.

Freya glanced at her phone. "Good call. And we've got a deadline. We'll know in sixty minutes if we've been on the right track."

"Staying here longer than an hour anyway is risky. We need to move," I agreed. "The longer we're here, the more likely we'll be discovered."

She brushed past me, waving her hand. "Second floor. Race ya to the top of the stairs."

I rolled my eyes. "Not everything has to be a—"

But she'd already scooped up the ends of her dress and was sprinting up the carpeted staircase. I shook my head and took off, too compelled to win.

"Cheating already, Evandale," I said, flying past her on the steps.

"Cheating would be tripping you," she panted back.

I hit the top of the step and turned around with hands raised in victory. She finished a second behind me, bent over at the waist, laughing softly.

"Point to Byrne." I smirked. "What are the total points so far for this case?"

"Can't recall, I'm afraid," she said breezily.

"Four-three. I can recall. I'm winning."

She knocked her knuckles against a door marked *Private*. "You'll get another point if you can break us into this door."

I shook my head with a grin, reaching into my back pocket for the lock-picking tool I'd hidden.

"Ha," Freya said. "I knew you'd bring it."

"How many laws are we going to break tonight?"

"Until you're fully corrupted," she said. Strands of golden hair were starting to fall from her bun, framing her face. "Don't think I'd forgotten you were the best lock-pick at Quantico. Next to me, of course."

"Tell me that purse is filled with zip-ties."

She snapped it open to reveal strips of duct tape and zip-ties. A trick our professors had taught us if you were caught in a dangerous situation but forced to carry light. Subdue them. Zip-tie their wrists. Slap a strip of tape over their mouths. They'd also taught us how to pick locks—which came in handy for an agent more than most law-abiding folks realized.

She used her phone flashlight to light the tiny keyhole. I dropped to one knee, wiggled the tool inside. Twisted, ear to the door. Twisted. Twisted one more time.

Click.

"Got it." I turned the knob and slowly opened it, prepared for hidden danger. We'd heard not a peep this whole time, but those Empty House assholes seemed to lurk in every corner. The thin beam of her flashlight revealed a storage room filled with boxes and files.

Freya flicked the light switch.

"That's a lot of boxes," she breathed.

"Yep." It was. More than any two people could conceivably get through in an hour.

"This is what the letters look like." She found pictures from the internet on her phone and propped it on the closest flat surface. "They're obviously hella old, and Henry told me they'd need to be stored in packaging that protected them from touch and damage. I think we'd recognize something like that. They're not in a file folder, you know?"

"Yeah. I think so too." I ran a hand through my hair, wondering what the hell we'd just gotten ourselves into. "We'll work each room together to make sure neither of us misses anything. We'll start here, then move to that room with the glass cases."

She walked to the bathroom and came back with a handful of tissues. "Use these to wipe down prints. And we'll need to be careful not to upset anything. Everything has to go back the way we found it."

"Good call, Evandale."

"I aim to please, Agent Byrne." She gave me a sassy salute and set to work yanking open drawers.

Like our academy days, we fell back into a focused silence—the way we used to sit for hours when studying or test-taking. We moved through the small space, both muttering to ourselves as the minutes ticked by. I ran my hands along the baseboards, stood on a chair and examined the ceiling for false panels. She knocked on walls and listened for hollow spots.

Nothing.

The room with the historical documents seemed more promising as we swept in, both of us examining the 300-year-old documents put forth by Philadelphia's political philosophers and great thinkers of the time. I checked my watch.

Twenty minutes down, forty to go.

"Cora Alexander is having an affair. Or affairs," I said. "That's what she and I were speaking about when you were in the bathroom." I stumbled, forced away memories of what we'd done in there.

"What now?" Freya said, face impressed. "*Affairs?*"

"Julian is her confidante. Her two *lovers*—her word—have been sending her letters to their house. It's probably one of the reasons why she's also been fascinated with the George Sand letters. She's living that life."

"And Thomas...?"

"Is okay with it, apparently," I said.

She shook her head as she slid her fingers through old books, shaking them out. "Thomas believes he's cursed because Bernard had him steal an extremely valuable first-edition of *Don Quixote.* And Cora's over here bangin' two dudes and getting love letters about it."

I studied her for a moment. "What did you mean back in the hotel room? You said"—I worked to keep my tone light—"you said you weren't the kind of girl who ever got love letters?"

She turned, surprised. "Oh. I forgot I'd said that."

I didn't push. Instead I went back to examining the two small closets in this room. Waited. A second later, she joined me, sliding into the tight space, already anticipating I'd need the extra eye.

"I didn't have a lot of friends in middle school or high school," she began. She avoided eye contact, but her body never stopped brushing against mine—her hips, her shoulders, her fingers. "You know I was—still am—close to my mom. Extremely close. I was never, ever raised to think my nerdy interests or hobbies were weird or wrong. They weren't mainstream at the time, but fourteen-year-old me didn't give a shit."

She had one bookcase shoved aside in the closet and was running her fingers along the wood paneling. I dropped to my knees to help her, putting us on eye-level.

"I cared about books and the characters in those books. I cared about my mom and our cats. And I cared about being smart. More than smart. Brilliant. When I first started being bullied my sophomore year, it seemed so *juvenile* I told myself it didn't matter. Who cares if you're smart? And why is that a reason to make fun of someone?"

"Teenagers think differently," I said. "But why would anyone make fun of you?"

"What do you mean?" she asked.

"You're..." I shrugged, my fingers accidentally brushing against hers on the spine of a book. "You know."

"I'm what?"

"Funny," I said begrudgingly. "And happy. And nice. At Quantico, everyone always wanted to be around you and laugh at your jokes."

Freya's expression opened up dramatically. "I always thought they wanted to be around you."

"I don't think many people feel the need to be around me," I said. "Which is fine, since I have no time to be around people."

She bit her lip. I ignored the response that incited in my body. "You're smart and thoughtful and believe in honor and duty. You're basically a real-life Superman. Trust me. Our classmates wanted to be around you."

I ran a hand through my hair, unsure of how to answer that.

"Did kids make fun of you for being too smart?" she asked.

"I thought you said there was no way I could have had a shitty high school experience?" I was teasing, but she winced.

"I'm sorry I assumed that," she admitted, poking her head around from the bookshelf. She was barefoot, hair a mess, glasses askew.

Adorable.

"It's okay. Truly, it is."

"No, but I am, Byrne. I can't imagine..." She shrugged. "I can't imagine living with your father when you were a teenager was *enjoyable*."

"Having a strict father meant that if kids at school *were* making fun of me, I never knew," I said. "I was always head down, studying. Serious. Extracurriculars, like football, were only to improve my transcript."

"When did you enjoy being a kid?"

"When my mom was alive."

Stupid. It was stupid to say things like that, especially in front of Freya.

She stood quickly as if perceiving a threat.

"Did you hear something?" I asked, looking up at her from the ground.

"That's fucking sad."

I couldn't look at her emerald eyes, shimmering with empathy.

"Not really," I mumbled.

"I'm so sorry you experienced that," she said.

"It's nothing," I said firmly. "Tell me about why you didn't get love letters."

Freya shook her head. She was standing over me, and this position of powerful submission was destroying the remaining shreds of my self-control. Her hand moved across my forehead, brushing a strand of hair back into order. When she did it a second time, I grabbed her wrist. Put my lips there. Her throat worked as we stared at each other.

"Tell me about the love letters," I said, voice thick. She nodded but left the closet to examine the room at large. She grabbed one side of the giant red rug in the middle of the floor. I got up, left the closet, grabbed the other side. We lifted, rolling it away.

"Anything?" she asked.

I was on my hands and knees, searching for hidden latches or trap doors. "*Goddammit*. No."

Frustration mounted the more we searched and the less we found.

"Let's move on to the next place," she said. We did, pulling apart the bathroom and another room of books. I waited until we'd gotten to another natural conversational point to push her again—but she'd already started speaking.

"My senior year, I suddenly had these two friends. Courtney and Jessica. And they were popular friends. The instances of bullying I had been experiencing stopped because of them. No more mean whispers or weird rumors." She paused. "It changed everything. Friends in books are one thing. Friends in real life felt like finding secret treasure, felt like..." She trailed off and looked heartbroken.

Having never truly explored *feelings* before, I didn't know what the fuck to do with what was happening inside my body.

"Are you okay?" Freya asked. "You look like you're about to punch this table into two pieces, Hulk-style."

"Just listening," I managed. "What happened with these friends?"

"They weren't friends." She sighed. "For the whole year, they kept this notebook they shared with their elite circle of teenaged jackals, who shared it with the whole school. The notebook kept track of things I'd done that were embarrassing. They wrote down secrets I'd shared in there. Crushes." Her cheeks flushed at that, lip curled. "Every boy I'd ever even thought about, they told. Transcribed notes I'd written them. And they gave it to me on the day we graduated, after I'd given the valedictorian speech."

"You were valedictorian in high school too?"

"Fuck, yeah," she said, giving a real tiny smile. I was grateful to see it. "I was truly *happy* on that stage. My mom and I had planned a trip to Prince Edward Island, where we were going to do an *Anne of Green Gables* tour."

"Your first favorite book," I said.

She cocked her head at me. "What?"

"*Anne of Green Gables* was your first favorite book." I shrugged, tried to appear nonchalant. "You told me that once, probably at Princeton."

There it was again—her toothy, charming grin, aimed right at my heart. It was the definition of *enchanting*.

I rocked back and forth on my heels. "You were saying?"

Her gaze lingered on mine before she launched back into her story. "That day, on that stage, I'd achieved a goal I'd worked hard for and truly believed in. Even then, I knew it was the first step to becoming an FBI agent. But we all know how that turned out." She said it sardonically, but there was no mistaking the note of pain hidden beneath. "I didn't think I'd care, *really* thought I was mature and beyond something so childish. But I loved having friends."

She didn't have to say more—full devastation was splashed across her face. For only a moment, but I caught it. Understood it.

"I was the joke of my school. Had been the entire time. Every dinner and sleepover and study session that year had been an elaborate fake. Looking back on it, it was *extremely obvious*. I mean, these were seventeen-year-olds, they weren't exactly subtle. But I think all of us are pretty adept at ignoring the obvious when we don't want to admit something painful, don't you?"

I remembered my ex-partner, Gregory, cheerfully showing off a new car I *knew* he couldn't afford on a special agent's salary. I thought about how good it had felt to smack my hand against that full mug of coffee, staining a stack of case notes I was never, ever going to finish—because that was exactly the way my job was structured. *Never ahead, always behind. Always a disappointment.* In high school and college, I'd been able to force my high academic course load into submission to garner my father's stilted approval. Being a special agent was the first time in my life when I couldn't overwork my way to success. Because I was already officially overworked and—according to my father—failing across the board.

"It's hard for people to recognize what's been true all along," I said.

"That was definitely the case for me," Freya admitted. "So, yes, that's why I was never a girl who got love letters. Even if I had received one, it probably would have been a joke."

I had to blink away a surge of anger. "And all those nerdy, writer boyfriends? They never—"

"It wasn't like that in college, Byrne," she said.

"Like what?"

She pushed her glasses up her nose. "Passionate. Earth-shattering. Whatever it was that George felt for Alfred that compelled them to put it down on the page. It wasn't seduction or hunger or compulsion. They were just boyfriends, I guess. It wasn't like they were under my skin. It wasn't like I couldn't stop thinking about them, day and night. Dreaming about them." She swallowed hard and avoided my gaze. "Craving them."

I knew *craving* well. Especially the kind you bury deep enough to deny for years. The kind that makes you promise a woman you'd tear her underwear in two and fuck her without mercy against a wall in a bathroom, surrounded by book thieves.

"They should have written them for you," I said, coming to join her on the landing.

She looked startled at that—so startled that I immediately regretted saying it.

"I'm sorry I was pissed at you after you snagged the valedictorian spot at Princeton," I admitted. I'd been an asshole when she'd told me—walked off without congratulating her and glared at her whenever I had the opportunity.

"Oh, that's right," she said, lips tipping up. "You wouldn't speak to me. And I'd thought we weren't ever going to see each other again anyway until..."

"Quantico happened," I finished.

"We were bloodthirsty back then, Byrne. I launched a smear campaign against you for the honor of being president of a twenty-person college club. Those were dark days."

"Still," I pressed. "You deserved the top spot. I was a shithead."

Freya blushed a little, fiddling with the strap of her gold dress. "Well, you don't have to apologize. We were twenty-two years old. We were *all* shitheads at that age."

We took the stairs down—walked this time—and immediately began searching the lower part of the house.

"Also, time check." she glanced at her watch. "Twenty-five minutes left."

"Son of a bitch," I swore. "Is there a basement? An attic?"

"No attic, not that we found. Maybe a basement?" But as we moved through the lower half of the hall, we found nothing. It wasn't a huge building, and the easily accessible hiding spots revealed no box of rare letters. We searched as fast as we could while careful not to leave a noticeable mess.

We were officially empty-handed.

"Time check," I asked wearily, knowing we were fucked.

"Eight minutes."

She was sliding a couch back to its original spot, having discovered no trap doors or secret pages taped to the bottom. I rolled my head from side to side, getting the kinks out. Wincing.

Pissed.

"We don't have to leave in an hour," Freya said, sensing my irritation. "If the other private detectives are wrong, we should keep looking."

I shook my head, already envisioning the conversation I'd be having with my father. *Private detective for three days and I already fucked up*. This was supposed to be *easy*—at least in the words of my father. But I'd promised to get my head on straight and instead all I'd done so far was lose it around Freya.

Thud.

"What was that?" I hissed, both of us freezing in our tracks.

Thud. Thud.

Fucking boot steps. A heavy tread outside the front door. Muffled voices. Dragging.

And a doorknob, starting to turn.

32

FREYA

Sam and I didn't even have a second to consider a coherent thought. My shocked, terrified expression was enough to have Sam grabbing my hand and pulling me toward that window. I scooped up my purse, my heels, and the tux jacket as Sam slid the window open.

The front door opened at the exact same time—the *creak* loud in the quiet room.

"Go, go, go," Sam whispered, practically shoving me out. I dropped to the grass easily, and he followed right behind. We didn't even bother closing the window—just ran across the front grass and down the sidewalk.

"My car's close," he whisper-shouted over his shoulder, booking it through yellow pools of streetlamp light. He reached the stop sign at the end of the street, turned around.

Noticed I was far behind.

It was my *heels*. Breaking, entering, and fleeing into the night was horrendously challenging when tottering along in stilettos. I ripped them off and tried to run in my bare feet. But the sidewalk was rough and rocky, littered with glass. He was on me in an instant, bending down and scooping me against his chest. I let out a sound that was half laughter, half frustration.

"Byrne," I whispered, "I do not need to be carried."

"I will admit to your prowess on the track if you let me carry you to the car. You slicing open your foot on broken glass—or breaking an ankle trying to run in heels—is only going to further jeopardize this case. I'm being a good partner."

"What was that about prowess again?" I mused. I should have been more jostled in his arms—he was running fast—but his hold on me was tight, arms strong, chest broad and perfect for me to rest my cheek on. He only ran for one more city block, passing groups of people out on the town. Ran until we hit Broad Street. A normal person would have been out of breath, but Sam appeared only slightly winded as he placed me gently on the ground. I kept my hand on his arm as I slipped my devilish heels back on.

"You *are* Superman," I said.

"I wouldn't ever let you get hurt," he said.

"I know that," I said, "and I appreciate it. Next time I'll strap you to my back, okay? Make it even."

His eyes twinkled before he nodded at the parking garage where we'd parked his car that morning. Glancing behind us, we jogged down the aisles until coming to his car and climbing inside.

My phone rang the minute we locked the doors. *Abe.*

It was fifteen minutes past midnight. I put it on speaker while staring at Sam across the console.

"Good news or bad?" I said by way of greeting.

"Bad," Abe said. "Unless you have those letters in your hands?"

Sam exhaled an angry-sounding breath. "No, sir," he said.

Silence, and then—"Scarlett and I just had a long conversation. She said this other firm walked into Francisco's office at the Franklin Museum with the George Sand love letters. All thirteen of them, in pristine condition."

"Fuck me," Sam swore.

"Abe, that's not possible," I said. "We just spent a very strange night with these weird-ass rich people, and they couldn't *stop* talking about the letters. We all had to write down what we were bidding on at this auction tomorrow night. Or tonight, rather."

"What's happening tonight?" Abe asked.

Sam and I exchanged a look.

"We don't quite know, sir," Sam said. "A kind of underground auction, I believe. Evandale wrote down that we were most interested in purchasing the George Sand letters. Nine other people were there. Dr. Ward read the slips and announced that all of us were interested in the same exact item."

"The letters," I said.

"Ward could have been lying, or it could have been a trick," Abe said. "They could have forged copies."

"That firm could have forged copies," I said.

"I suggested the very same thing. They are, of course, going about authenticating them. But until then, consider our contract canceled and the case finished," Abe said.

Sam slapped the steering wheel with his hand. Glared out the window. The finality of it hurt more than I anticipated, especially considering how badly I'd wanted *off* this case from the beginning.

"Sometimes we try our hardest and we still fail," Abe said.

"This is a mistake," I said. "Believe me, I'm the last

person to ever suggest this, but I think we need to keep our cover. Go to that auction. The letters are there."

"They can't be in the hands of the museum *and* at this auction," Abe said shortly.

"Sir," Sam said, "I agree with Freya."

We shared a tentative smile.

"Unless you can gather concrete proof, I can't authorize the two of you moving forward," Abe said. "Risky and expensive are the two things I try and avoid the most, as you well know. The two of you have worked non-stop for the past forty-eight hours. Go home. Sleep. We can debrief in the morning and see if the authentication comes back in our favor." He shifted his tone. "I'll even bring you donuts."

"That actually doesn't seem appetizing right now," I said, rubbing my forehead.

There was a pause until he said, "I know you're disappointed."

Sam was about to tear the steering wheel in two.

"It's fine," I said and knew I sounded pissed. But I was. "We'll see you at Codex in the morning."

Abe hung up the phone, and I let it drop onto the console.

"Those letters *can't* be real," I said.

"I cannot believe we're not going to close this *case*," Sam growled. "I should have threatened Ward in the basement when I had the chance."

"Do you disagree with the decisions we made as partners?" I asked, tone icy.

"You made decisions," he shot back. "And I made decisions. We made barely any decisions together as partners."

"That's not true," I said. "We actually worked *well* together tonight. At least I thought we had."

"Negative, Evandale," he said. "If we lost this case, it's because you're too stubborn to *listen* to anyone but yourself."

"Says the most stubborn person I know."

Sam turned to face me fully in the car. I was struck with the massive size of him. He'd tossed his jacket in the backseat, and the white shirt could barely fit the breadth of his shoulders. He'd been tugging at his bowtie, which was now open, revealing an inch of bare chest. One hand was in his hair, one hand was wrapped around the back of the seat like it was tethering him down.

"I think it was true at Quantico and it's true now," Sam said quietly—but fiercely. "We don't work well together. We lost this case because of it. The two of us together are a distraction. *You* are a distraction to me. I can't focus around you."

"I'm a distraction to you?" I asked. "*You* kissed me in the *bathroom*. That's pretty fucking distracting."

"I hoped that would remove the temptation," he growled. "Because we'd know what it was like." His voice was growing rougher and rougher.

"If you liked our kiss that much, are you pissed at me? Or pissed at yourself for making us even more distracted?"

We were glaring at each other now, the space between us shrinking with our combined irritation.

"I'll give you real honesty since you won't give it to me," I continued. "I think you're picking a pointless fight because you're more comfortable arguing than you are expressing your feelings. You forget that we share the same personality attributes, *unfortunately*. Which means I hate failing as much as you do. I know how shitty it feels."

I swallowed against a very real hesitation to be vulnerable in front of my nemesis. But he was staring at my mouth.

I liked being stared at like that—like I was rare and delicious.

"I hate failing," I repeated. "And I've wanted to kiss you since the day we met."

His nostrils flared at that, but he didn't say a word.

"Is that what you wanted too?" I asked.

He closed his eyes like he was in pain. His breath was coming fast, heavy. I worried that he'd flex his muscles and rip the car in half—he was that tightly wound.

"I have never kissed a woman like that before," he said. "I've never *needed* to touch a woman like that before."

Now I was panting, rubbing my thighs together to try and ease the persistent ache that appeared whenever we argued.

"So, yeah, I fucking wanted it," he said harshly. "But wanting to fuck each other is exactly the reason why we failed."

My jaw dropped open. "That's that, then? We lose this case, you go back to the FBI, and we end things the way they began? Fighting with each other and never talking about what's actually going on between us?"

Sam shrugged like it was no big deal. Even though I could *tell*. Could tell there were things he wanted to *say* and things he wanted *to do*. But he was holding himself back like he always did, tamping down any inclination for messy emotions.

"This was inevitable," he said. "Our failure was inevitable. If you weren't the most stubborn and irritating woman I'd ever known—"

"And if you weren't the most *arrogant* and *frustrating* man I'd ever met—"

But I didn't even finish the sentence. I grabbed his white

shirt and dragged his upper body across the console at the same time as he crashed our lips together in a bruising kiss.

He wrapped his arm around my waist and pulled me across his lap.

It was our first real kiss in semi-private, and I didn't hold back. I moaned, I sighed, I ripped his shirt, sending buttons flying, and scratched my nails down his perfect superhero chest. When I latched onto his lower lip and bit, Sam Byrne snarled like an animal. Speared his fingers into my hair and captured my mouth, groaning every time my nails bit into his skin.

"You wouldn't be such a fucking distraction if you weren't this goddamn *beautiful*," he hissed, ripping the strap of my dress clean off my body. The fabric fell from my breasts, and he descended upon them with ravenous intent. "You used to sit next to me in class and slide that *pen* in and out of your fucking *mouth.* Are you kidding me, Evandale?" He yanked me higher, one palm spread between my shoulder blades, face pressed to my sternum as he sucked my nipples into tight peaks.

"What a little perv you were," I gasped, yanking at his thick hair. "Must have been subconscious on my part."

"You're too smart for that." He scraped his teeth across my rib cage, and I shivered. His thumb was stroking across my lower lip. I sucked it, felt his body tremble with restraint.

"Maybe I wanted to tease the hot guy next to me," I said, arching again into his mouth, which was currently doing extraordinary things to my nipples.

"Which guy?" he demanded.

I picked his head up, kissed him hard. "*You*, you jerk."

Our kiss this time lacked finesse but made up for it in passion. I was practically climbing him, and he was shifting away the fabric of my gold dress. When his palms landed on my ass, he squeezed *hard*. It felt amazing, to be handled roughly, to have serious, controlled Sam unraveling right in front of me.

"You wouldn't be such a fucking distraction if you hadn't strutted around half-naked and wet every night in our Quantico dorms," I whispered, nipping his throat.

His chuckle was dark, arrogant. "Must have been subconscious on my part."

He moved me with firm hands, laying me across his lap in the car. The windows were slowly starting to steam. And the sounds we were making were nothing like our previous sparring sessions—there was nothing to describe the guttural, biological release of Sam and me slamming together like this, of devouring each other in the front seat of a car because we'd always expressed things better physically anyway.

"Spread your legs."

"Don't tell me what to do," I said—but who was I kidding? They were spreading of their own accord, my body already seeking the pleasure that awaited me. I'd known Sam for a long, long time. And what I knew was that his ambition and tireless drive made him very, very *good* at everything he did.

It turned out that finger-fucking me in a sequined dress while in the front seat of a car was no exception.

33

SAM

Freya was beautiful, adorable, pliable in my lap. Her glasses were torn off, hair tangled, breasts bare and perfect. Nothing could stop me from making this woman say my name and beg for more. She deserved *exquisite* pleasure. Nothing less.

My hand smoothed along her toned legs, fingers stopping at the seam of her underwear, already wet. I stroked up and down along it—and Freya slammed our mouths together. Pulled hard on the strands of my hair as I stroked. Stroked. Her hips were rolling not a second later, seeking a deeper friction.

"Is making your partner come a distraction?" I whispered against her lips.

"Yes," she sighed. "Yes. Oh, it's the *best kind*."

I slipped past the material, touched the folds of her sex for the first time. She was hot, wet, perfect. "Is this right?"

I slipped a finger inside her. She was gripping my face, out of control.

"That's fucking perfect," she gasped. "I'd be furious with you if you weren't so goddamn good at this."

"Say that again." I fucked her in slow, smooth strokes, slipping in and out of her body with ease. Teasing her inner walls with the pad of my finger.

"You're good at this, Sam," she breathed. I slipped another finger in, and her face broke out in a satisfied, teasing smile. "Really fucking good."

My name on her lips sent a bolt of possessive lust coursing through me. How could sex feel this vital this immediately? An entire career spent within the confines of a hierarchical bureaucracy meant suppressing my inner desires was as natural as breathing to me. And now here was Freya—spread on my lap with my hand beneath her dress—and I already never wanted it to end. It was a wicked action with no grander intent behind it. No outcomes, no close rates, no higher-ups to impress with your ability to toe the line. This—this slick, seeking discovery—was unplanned and spontaneous.

She writhed as I buried my mouth against her ear, inhaling the sugar-scent of her hair. "I should have done this for you while studying for finals," I said. "Helped you with stress relief."

"What a way to learn." She moaned loudly, head back. "*Oh, god,* we'd never have made it to graduation. And keep moving your fingers just...just like that."

"Now who's bossy?" I couldn't stop licking her nipples, sucking her breasts into my mouth, biting her neck. There was so much beauty suddenly available for my enjoyment, and my head spun with the intensity of it all.

"Oh, god," she sighed, "oh, god, *oh, god.*" She was starting to flutter around my fingers. I let my palm graze her clit, and her toes curled on the dashboard. "*Please fuck me.*"

I didn't stop my fingers, but I pulled back, staring at her. "What did you say?"

"Fuck me," she said. "*Please.*"

Eyes heavy-lidded, lips parted—Freya the temptress had me utterly enthralled. If I'd had a pen and paper, I would have written her a hundred letters, secret codes and all.

With a groan, I slipped my fingers free and dragged her up until she was straddling me, our faces barely an inch apart.

"Freya."

"Sam."

I stroked the hair from her face until her eyes opened and met mine. Arousal and trust burned bright in all that green. "I want you to drag me into the back of this car and fuck me senseless, Agent Byrne."

I didn't need to be told twice.

I lifted her off my lap, then she was crawling into the backseat—breasts bare, dress torn, hair wild. She crooked her finger at me, and I was on her in an instant, palm to her chest and shoving her back down. She reared up, kissing me roughly while I unzipped my suit pants. Freed my cock and stroked it as she leaned back on her elbow, breasts heaving. Hoisted her legs high on my back and lined my cock up at her entrance, our eyes locked in a dance of challenge and submission.

"Wait, wait," I said.

"No, no, *don't stop.*"

"Condom," I panted out. "I don't have a condom."

Freya yanked me down by the collar until our mouths met. "I trust you to save my life out there. I trust you with this. I'm clean and protected. You?"

I nodded, feeling a tightness in my throat I couldn't source. "You trust me out there?" We couldn't stop kissing, every sentence fraught with heavy breaths, our lips like magnets, unable to stay apart.

"You'd protect my life, wouldn't you?"

"Always," I said. It was what partners were *supposed* to do. Even when disagreeing. Even when arguing. There was no doubt in my mind.

"Fuck me bare," she said.

I kept our lips close, hovering. And I slid my cock inch by sweet inch inside her.

Immediately we cried out together, muffling the cry with our mouths—she was tight, wet, hot, *everything*. She fell back against the seat—one leg on my shoulder, the other held down by my hand for leverage. I flexed my hips and fucked back into her. And she arched, fingers scrambling for purchase. I thrust hard, and her answering wail almost set off my own climax. It was hot and ragged and desperate and real. The sound was stripped of our bickering and competition—it was purely *her*.

"I don't want to hold back with you," I bit out. Gave her a brutal rock that flicked a devilish smile across her face.

"Then don't," she whispered, breasts bouncing with every thrust.

My hand left her leg to close lightly around her throat, thumb tugging at her chin. Her expression dared me to refuse her demand. Every hard and fast thrust was met by her body, arching to meet mine.

I gave into the years of restrained sexual frustration and fucked Freya Evandale like I was more beast than man. The car rocked with our movements, and we weren't silent, no. She moaned, and I grunted. She scratched, and I bit. She pushed, and I pushed back. I sat up on the seat, pulling her with me, and guided her back down over my cock. Pistoned her fast on my lap and took her breasts back into my mouth. It was the messiest, sweatiest sex of my life. And the orgasm waiting at the base of my spine was going to destroy me. I tried to linger, tried to slow us down with soft kisses and deliberate rolls of my hips.

But she and I had never played things slow.

"Sam, Sam, *yes, Sam*," she chanted, head thrown back.

"Don't you dare quit saying my name," I growled, leaving a bite on her throat. "And when you come, you say it."

"Make me come," she shot back, before sighing into my mouth again. Freya was part princess, part viper, and I needed all of her. I wrapped the golden strands of her liberated hair around one hand. Kept her head still and plundered her mouth. Reached between our bodies and found her clit with my thumb.

She screamed against my mouth. Screamed *my name*. She rode me hard, rhythm uncontrolled, and I kept my thumb right on that bundle of nerves. Freya was gorgeous in her wild ecstasy, and I didn't wait a second longer. Was surprised I'd held out as long as I did. Freya pressed my face to her chest as I groaned out the longest, most intense orgasm of my life. My mouth opened against her sweat-slicked skin, inhaling her. I was panting hard, arms shaking from holding her tight. She was positioned the same, running her fingers through my hair, soothing me.

We were silent for a long, long time. There was no trainer calling *time*. No fellow recruits laughing around us. Nothing to cut through the intensity of our bodies touching.

I felt it all. I felt it change me.

"I'd protect your life too," Freya said softly—so soft I almost missed it.

"I know," I panted. "I know you would."

I kissed her gently along the collarbone. Her jaw. Brushed our lips together as our eyes met. The windows were fogged, clothes torn, marks all over our bodies. We were still tangled as one, a storm of intensity rippling between our shared gaze.

"Sometimes..." I started. Gathered my courage. "Sometimes I'm still angry with you because you left. You left me."

Her lips parted. "Angry? About Quantico, you mean?"

I nodded, running my nose along her skin. She smelled so *good*.

"Oh, Sam," she said quietly. "I didn't think you'd care. We were competitors. We fought constantly. I thought you'd be happy not to have me in the way of the number one spot anymore."

I tucked a strand of hair behind her ear. "Competitors can still be friends. Friends tell each other things."

She assessed me for a minute, worrying her bottom lip between her teeth. If our electric attraction to each other was the third rail of our relationship, the concept of *friendship* was truly taboo.

"You're right," she finally said. "Friends do tell each other things."

"You were set to graduate with top honors," I said. "My father told me you were the most promising new recruit they'd seen in years. That's high praise, coming from him."

Freya closed her eyes, like what I'd said was hurtful. "I couldn't do it."

"What?"

"I couldn't handle it," she said, eyes opening. Shining with tears. "From the first day I arrived until I officially left, I suffered from *severe* anxiety and panic attacks. Racing thoughts, night terrors that led to insomnia. I spent every second nervous, upset, and so tightly wound I couldn't think straight."

I thought about that feeling I had in my chest all the time at the FBI—like my sternum was being crushed by a herd of elephants. And I'd never, ever withstand the weight. *Freya* felt that way too?

"You were in pain?" I asked.

"A lot of pain. All the time," she said. "I hid it very well."

My arms tightened around her back, pulling her even closer. I couldn't stop staring at her, as if the act alone could undo her suffering.

"You and I shared a similar dream," she said. "I *knew* I'd be an extraordinary agent. I was too smart and too analytical and too focused not to be. But even if you're *good* at something, and even if you might have wanted it before, it doesn't always mean it's the right fit. The right fit or the healthy fit."

That sentiment short-circuited my brain waves. It went against every aspect of my father's strict perfectionism.

"You could have told me," I said, wrestling the emotion from my voice.

Freya's thumbs stroked across my cheeks. She seemed as surprised at the anguish in my tone as I was.

"I hid it from everyone, Sam. Except my mother, who came for a weekend visit and could tell right away I wasn't feeling like myself. Special Agents have extremely high-pressure jobs, as you well know. If I felt like I was panicking every single second while *training*, imagine what it would have felt like throughout a thirty-year career?"

"It would have felt like a responsibility," I said firmly. "It's the highest duty to serve as a federal agent. There's a lot of honor in the Bureau."

"Honor had nothing to do with it," she said sadly. "I prioritized my health over the needs of the Bureau, as much as it hurt. As much as it *still*—" She stopped. Shook her head. "It was a tough decision, but it was a failure of the best kind. I quit for the right reasons."

That nervousness was coming back into her gaze

though. Was this the source of her anxiety on this case? Did Freya feel like *not enough*?

"Did I make it worse?" I asked, brow furrowing. "Always *pushing* you and competing? Always making you feel—"

"No," she said. "No, not at all. I've been a competitive overachiever since the day I got my first A. If I wasn't competing against you, it would have been another student. And I was always, always competing against myself."

Freya settled more firmly on my lap, brushing a strand of hair from my forehead.

"I'm sorry. You told me at the library, and I didn't expect to feel…" I thought back to that day, the feelings that had compelled me to put a pen to paper and write my first—and only—love letter. "Sad. I'd gotten used to kicking your butt in class."

Her smile lit up the dark car.

"I was so sad," I repeated—seriously this time. "I never, ever let myself admit it. But I missed you so much, Evandale. And I'm very sorry that the last thing I said to you was that you were making a mistake."

"Yeah, real dick move," she said, smile growing. "But you couldn't have known. I didn't tell a soul."

I pressed a kiss between her breasts, rested my head there.

"I missed you so much too," she whispered. "When I told you I was leaving, I almost begged you for a hug."

"Why?" I asked, even as I squeezed her tighter.

"Because part of me knew you were put on this earth to protect me."

Words froze in the back of my throat. I didn't feel worthy to receive these secrets of hers, these feelings. And she must have sensed my hesitation because she giggled against my ear. "Although let's be honest. If you and I had hugged it out, we would have definitely had sex on one of the tables in the library."

That startled a husky laugh from me. "Did you also... want that?"

"To fuck you in the library? Hell, *yeah*."

I was growing hard again—and not because the gorgeous blonde on my lap was slowly, slowly grinding against me. The dam had broken, and now we couldn't stop touching and talking.

"There was this one study room on the fifth floor," I rasped, staring at her. "I used to fantasize about fucking you in it."

"The soundproof one?" she teased.

My palms danced along her rib cage, fanning across her breasts. She bit her lip, twisted her hips.

"You know the one?"

"I might have the same fantasies."

She was flirting with me now, her joy filling up the small, dark space. I fluttered my fingers down her side, and she shrieked, head thrown back. I took advantage of her distraction to flip her onto her back, settling between her spread thighs.

"Sam?" she said, sighing a little as I kissed her throat.

"Hm?"

"Do you ever feel that way at your job now? The way I felt at the academy?"

I stilled.

Freya the Mind Reader.

And I wasn't going to be able to hold back the truth much longer—if she hadn't already figured it out. Especially not tangled together like this. The intimacy was softening the edges of my own secrets.

"I have extremely high stress levels, per what's expected of me." *Such a robot.*

"Your health is more important than the Bureau. No matter how vital your job is."

Strands of her hair kept brushing against my skin. "I wish my father felt that way."

Stupid again. She was chipping away at the lies I held dear.

She kissed my cheek. Wrapped her arms around me and held on tight. "I wish he did too, Sam. I really do."

A fast buzzing sound erupted from Freya's purse in the front seat. She made a frustrated noise, turning toward it. "Should I get it?"

"Could be Abe."

I sat up reluctantly, releasing her to grab her phone. I reached into my gym bag where I kept a clean change of clothes. "Do you want my, uh...sweatshirt?"

She looked down at her chest with a cheeky grin. "You don't like this look on me?"

"I love that look on you," I said.

"This is Delilah's dress, by the way. Looks like you'll be buying her a new one." She took the sweatshirt, pulling it over her head. It was gigantic on her, but it said *Quantico* across the front, and the look of her in it had my heart pounding.

"I'll buy her ten new ones," I promised.

Freya slid her glasses back on and pulled her hair into a bun.

"Oh shit," she said.

"What?"

"Birdie's getting messages on the Under the Rose site."

That same anger and disappointment rose in me again.

Closing this case will go far in helping me trust you again, Samuel.

"Can I see?"

She showed me. The first one was from Thomas. *Where are you two? We've been knocking on your hotel room door for hours.*

She glanced sideways at me, as if seeking permission. "Abe said no."

Then her fingers flew across the keyboard. *We're truly sorry. Julian and I need to shore up some reserves for tomorrow. Pre-bids were higher than we anticipated for the Sand letters.*

"You're just going to call it out?" I asked. But I was more intrigued than I realized—even going against orders.

"What's the harm now?" she replied.

We need to make sure Roy doesn't get them, Thomas pinged back. *And we have not finished our conversation about our plan of attack.*

"I hedged heavily during this conversation because I didn't want to corner us into a situation we couldn't get out of," Freya explained. "Things are *tense*. I think Roy's blackmailing Thomas because he knows Thomas stole Ward's *Don Quixote*. But Thomas doesn't want to pay. And he doesn't want Bernard to know about Roy's threat. And no one seems to want Roy to purchase those letters tomorrow."

"Maybe *this* is a distraction," I said. "This secret society is in a fucking crisis. If they spend the night battling it out over money and alliances, you and I could sneak off with the letters."

She tapped her chin. "That's not a bad plan, partner. In fact, I'd say that's the kind of plan an expert private detective would come up with."

"You think so?"

She nodded. "We might lack Bureau resources, but we're

nimble as hell. We get close to people. Getting close to people opens avenues of justice I never thought possible before. I know the FBI feels like the only true way to fight crime, but Codex does a damn good job too."

That buzzing in my veins was back and heightened—a combination of adrenaline, sleeplessness, and wild, back-seat sex. We *were* close to our suspects—faster and more intimate than I'd ever gotten while working in Art Theft. There was a thrill to it I hadn't expected. It felt personal. It felt fucking real.

"I concede your point," I said slowly. "Codex has done excellent work."

"I know we have." She smirked. "My point is that *you* would make a damn fine PI."

My hands gripped her hips, shifting her closer on my lap. "That *might* be true. But I've got a legacy to uphold at the Bureau and a father who'd like nothing more than to see me become Deputy Director when the time's right."

Her fingers sifted through my hair again. "I know it. I also believe that without the burden of Andrew Byrne's legacy, your genius and talent could shine even brighter. No external pressure, just *your* motivation and drive. No one else's."

I wasn't quite sure what to do with that revelation. The FBI might be the primary source of my emotional pain, but the thought of leaping from the nest—and disappointing my father—was too scary to contemplate.

But before I could overanalyze Freya's words, my beautiful rival wrapped her arms around me and held on tight. A big, bold hug that melded our chests together and allowed her to rest her head on my shoulder. It was a hug of friendship, and compassion, and tenderness—a hug from a woman who truly *saw me*.

Maybe taking a leap with Freya by my side would make things *less* scary. Maybe I didn't need the FBI after all.

I grazed my lips along the column of her throat. Licked deeply into her mouth for a lingering kiss that left us both breathless.

"Thank you for that," I said. "For believing in me."

"What are partners for?" she said.

"But let's focus on those letters first, potentially life-changing decisions second," I replied. "And we'd need Abe's approval to go back undercover."

"*Do* we?" She pouted.

I ghosted our lips together. "You know we do."

"You can't just kiss me to get me to agree with you, Agent Byrne," she said dreamily. "But I agree with you."

"Then we need coffee and sandwiches," I said. "And to go find Abe. Is he at the Codex offices, you think?"

She shook her head. "It's way too early for that. I think we need to surprise Abraham Royal at home. He'll *love* it."

34

SAM

Abe lived in a sleek-looking loft near Philadelphia's City Hall. The lofts looked out of place jammed between two historic-looking brick buildings that Freya told me had been constructed before the American Revolution.

"Those gym shorts fit okay?" I asked, turning to Freya in the seat next to me. She'd tossed her ravaged dress and was shimmying into my clothing.

"They reach past my knees." She laughed. "But I'll roll them up twelve thousand times, and they'll fit just right. I appreciate the outfit change, by the way. You look a little less sexed-up than me."

I checked my bowtie in the mirror one last time, hoping Abe wouldn't notice the missing buttons from my shirt. "Are you wearing those heels or do you want a ride to the door?" I asked, shutting off the car.

"Ride, please."

I came around the car and opened her door. "Hop on my back," I said, kneeling.

She wrapped her arms around me, and I hoisted her legs onto my waist. Stood and shut the door.

"Is this what it feels like to be superhero tall?"

"Why do you keep referring to me as a superhero?" I asked, secretly pleased.

"It's your whole vibe, Byrne," she said. "You're telling me that if our planet was in dire peril from a mysterious archvillain, you wouldn't suit up and save the world?"

"Of course," I replied.

"See? That's what I mean," she said. We reached Abe's front door—it was 3:00 in the morning, and the summer sky was still dark. We'd had coffee and sandwiches and giant bottles of water, and I felt buzzy and exhausted all at the same time. I knelt, depositing Freya on the ground. As soon as I saw her fully beneath Abe's doorway light, I realized her throat had two mouth-sized hickeys.

I touched one with my fingertip. "I marked you."

Her lip curled. "You did."

"Should Abe..."

Her eyes widened, and she yanked down her bun, pulling her hair to one side to cover the bruises. *Good catch*, she mouthed. She peeked into the side window with her hands cupped around her face.

"We're in luck," she said. "As usual, Abe Royal is burning the midnight oil."

She pressed her finger to the buzzer. Abe had the door opened not five seconds later. Dressed in a pressed suit, of course.

"Did you ever stop and think there was a reason I never told my employees where I lived?" he remarked.

"Don't hire a computer nerd if you don't wanna get found." Freya grinned. "And let the record show that Abe Royal *does* sleep in a suit."

"Dear god, please tell me you didn't wear basketball shorts as an undercover operative?" he asked coolly. He looked tired though—even the suit couldn't hide it. "And where are your shoes?"

"I won't lie to you and say I didn't dress this way," she said. "And you can't ask me to wear stilettos with this outfit."

Abe's lips twitched at the ends, but he stepped back, opening the door wider.

"I have a feeling the two of you are here to argue with me."

I nodded my head at him as we stepped inside. "Evening, sir. Or morning. Thank you for seeing us on short notice."

Abe settled back on a low gray couch next to a glass table. He sat easily, one leg crossed over the other, sipping coffee. "Short notice? I've just been surprised by the two of you during a normal person's sleeping hours."

"Right," I said, sheepish. "Thank you for opening the door."

"Sit," he said. "Tell me what's happening and why the two of you *aren't* sleeping, per my express orders."

"Because Sam and I believe we should be at this underground auction tonight. Undercover, as Julian King and Birdie Barnes. Thomas has been messaging Birdie all evening. I've referred to the letters multiple times—the *Sand love letters*—and he's made it as clear that they'll be there."

She showed Abe the messages.

He took the phone, scrolled through. "Very interesting." He looked at us. "Except the authentication of the other letters is already underway. They appear to be real."

"The last forgery cases I worked were so realistic they had to authenticate it twice to spot the inconsistencies," I told him. "In the years since you've left Art Theft, the forgers are getting better. Smarter. It's not unlikely that they could have a very, very good forgery on their hands."

"I don't disagree," he said. "But we have no contract, no money to do this."

"If we get the real letters back, we'll get the money," Freya said.

"From your updates, this group of individuals is a powder keg—guns, tempers, and a tendency to get their way no matter what. That's a volatile situation I'll not have my agents walking into."

"Sam can retrieve his gun from the bathroom where we stored it," she said.

"A gun which can be taken from him," Abe countered.

"Abe," she pressed, "these people are working closely with Bernard within an organization that illegally sells rare books and art. And your two agents have been invited to participate. Maybe we don't find the letters, but we've got open cases and still-missing books that could be sold tonight. It could still be a win. Or depending on how much access we get, we take a ton of pictures and report all of these fuckers to the police." She patted Abe's knee. "We both know you love a good arrest."

"I do love getting people arrested." Abe sighed almost wistfully.

"So? Huh? We're in?" Freya nudged him, winking at me. As usual, she was joking through her own talent—putting forth a concrete argument for action even though she'd admitted in the car that she was unable to handle high-pressure situations. I wondered if she ever realized that even though the Bureau wasn't the right fit, she shined here at Codex.

I didn't wink back at her, but I smiled genuinely until her cheeks flushed.

Meanwhile, Abe was facing away, lost in thought.

"What's the worst that can happen?" she said. "The two of us are killed by a secret society or whatever?"

"If I say no, you will merely do it anyway and go against my orders," he said.

"That's *very* Henry and Delilah." She smirked. "And yes."

Abe looked directly at me. "We've got big problems though."

"Name 'em," she said.

"*If* you are to go undercover and bid on these letters, you'll need access to millions of dollars. What I know of shady black-market auctions is that you can't just walk in, bid, and walk out whistling. They expect you to give up your offshore bank account as soon as you're inside. And they'll expect a wire transfer immediately between the accounts."

"Okay," Freya said cheerfully. "Can Codex float like ten million?"

"You know we can't," Abe said. But he was still staring at me. My nerves started to hum, sensing his thought pattern.

"And we'd need better tech than we have," he continued. "A team that could go in and rescue the two of you if you needed it."

I rubbed the back of my neck, looking away from Abe. A few hours ago, sitting in the back seat of my car, I'd started to feel the very beginnings of freedom from the Bureau. The smallest sense that maybe, just maybe, I could do this on my own.

No, please don't say it.

"Sam, I think you know what we need to do."

"Wait, what?" Freya asked, looking between the two of us.

The silence dragged until she nudged me.

I sighed. "You honestly think it's necessary?"

"I wouldn't suggest it if I didn't," Abe said.

"Won't involving them void our contract? Scarlett wanted no authorities involved, no splashy press."

"She's already voided the contract," he countered. "Now it's about getting the damn letters back. It's about justice."

Freya rubbed her hands together, expression excited. "*That's* the spirit, old chap. Now what the fuck are you two talking about?"

Abe glanced at his watch. "And if I remember your father's work habits, he's already in the office terrorizing his staff."

"Oh, goddammit." Her head fell back against the couch. "Not that asshole."

I pulled out my phone. Asking my father's help right now felt like the worst possible thing I could do. Would this help him trust me again? Or would this only prove his point that I was now too *soft* to do the job of a real agent?

It's about justice.

Except Abe was right. A *win* for this case could only come with the help of the FBI. There wasn't another option. But maybe it could still be my and Freya's win. A case that we'd close together, as partners. And I'd do anything to make her smile at me again the way she had today. Like her smile was a gift, and I was the luckiest bastard in the world to receive it.

"Abe's right." My tone was grim but determined. "We need the Bureau."

35

FREYA

Abe left the room to call and wake Henry and Delilah. And Sam, with a curt nod, slipped into the back bedroom to call the Deputy Director of the FBI.

I lasted all of a second before I went to stand outside, giving Sam a tiny wave as he put the phone to his ear. Call it a consequence of our earth-shattering sex, but I was feeling extra-protective of my partner.

And I knew firsthand the effect his father had on him.

Our eyes locked in the dawn light, and my heart sparkled with feeling. Sam was the first sexual partner I'd ever been that unrestrained with. There was no shame or discomfort, no hesitation. I took what I wanted, and Sam *let* me. I had a sneaking suspicion I was the first woman to truly see Byrne unleash his inner sex-beast. The man had fucked me with the single-minded determination to *get me off*. And when he had come—when quiet, stoic Sam let out a hoarse, gratified groan against my breasts—I'd nearly climaxed again. I'd loved every fucking second. And then I'd gone and spilled my secrets.

I'd loved every second of that too.

Never—not in a million, billion years—could I have anticipated that Sam and I would give in to our angry sexual frustration. Then end up sweetly holding each other while unveiling our personal mysteries. *I missed you, Freya. I missed you so much.* It was a bittersweet ache, acknowledging all that we'd denied each other over the years—attraction, intimacy, romance.

Friendship.

I leaned against the door, arms crossed, and listened to him request an exorbitant amount of Bureau resources on the fastest deadline imaginable. It couldn't have been comfortable to be that vulnerable to a man I knew was an egotistical, smarmy shithead. And as I watched my partner pace back and forth, his body language screamed *tension*. His only verbal contribution was "Yes, sir." or "No, sir," in a clipped, respectful tone. I wanted Sam to tell me what was going on with his ex-partner, with his job, with his mental health. But his walls remained high and guarded.

Sam ended the call, slapping it against his palm before joining me in the hallway.

"He'll do it," he said. "He wants all of us on a video call in an hour."

I blew out a breath. "That was fast, huh?"

"He pulls the strings," he said. "Plus, you know he has a unique way of getting people to do his bidding."

"I remember." I took his hand in mine. "But we're still the ones kicking ass. Not him."

He ran a hand through his hair. "I'm expected back in Virginia to meet my new partner tomorrow morning."

"Oh," I said awkwardly. "I mean, right. I guess I thought you were going to be our consultant for a few weeks?"

"Me too," he said quietly. "But it appears as if my consultant role is being terminated early by my father."

I bobbed my head, tried to keep my tone casual. "Sure, sure. Sounds good."

This was the real complication of our hot, angry fucking. This warmth in my chest had finally been given room to breathe, to blossom. Which was bad news, since Sam was heading back to the FBI after this anyway.

His expression was etched with concern. But before he could say a word, Henry and Delilah burst through Abe's front door with more coffee and swift questions. We spent an hour getting everyone up to speed and tossing out strategies and ideas. The hour flew, and before I knew it, Abe was casting his computer screen onto the large white wall in his living room.

The face of Andrew Byrne appeared. I hadn't seen him in seven years, but he hadn't aged. His hair was still short and silver, expression still sharp and critical despite the early hour. The minute the call began, I watched Sam shrink into himself—the action was minute, subtle. But I *knew* Sam.

I wished Andrew Byrne were here in person. I'd slap him in the fucking face.

Henry, Delilah, and I were squished onto the couch. Abe was sitting in his high-backed chair like a king. Sam stood ramrod straight.

"It's nice to see you, Andrew," Abe said mildly, one finger at his temple.

"You as well," Andrew replied.

They were both obviously lying.

Abe introduced Henry and Delilah—but stopped when he got to me. The Deputy Director concealed his reaction to seeing me well. I remembered what Sam had said in the car —*my father said you were the brightest trainee he'd seen in a long time.*

"Ms. Evandale," Andrew said. "You appear well."

"Sir," I said shortly.

Abe arched his brow at me.

"Thank you for helping us," I said through gritted teeth.

"The FBI's help is obviously needed," Andrew said, eyes cast off to the side as he read a document. "You were right to call me, Samuel."

Sam was silent.

"You're welcome for gaining entry to an elite secret society the Bureau's been trying to access for years," Abe said dryly.

I cough-laughed into my fist.

"Come now, Abraham. We would have gotten there eventually. Pity you got there and can't move forward without our help."

"The clock is ticking, gentleman," Delilah cut in. "Surely we can continue fighting over jurisdiction *after* we prepare our agents to go deep undercover. What can the Bureau do for us?"

I nudged Delilah's shoulder with mine. "You're a bad bitch," I muttered.

"I would just prefer if you *didn't* get shot tonight."

"Same, girl," I replied.

Andrew sighed audibly. Put the document down and stared at us from his office at Quantico. "The Bureau is intrigued by the names that Samuel brought forth. Dr. Bradley Ward and the Alexanders have high status and an extreme amount of privilege. The fact that you believe they may be connected to Bernard Allerton is additionally intriguing."

Intriguing was surely Andrew's codeword for *we're shitting ourselves*.

"And Roy Edwards certainly has some cache," I added.

"Trust fund brat with a penchant for attention-seeking tabloid exploits. I'm sure he wasn't on a short list of potential criminals."

Andrew's mouth thinned. "Also intriguing. Of course, all of this could end up being hearsay. This auction could be perfectly legal and above board. And if that happens, I will blame the resulting waste of time and resources entirely on all of you."

That knife-sharp gaze landed on Sam, who seemed to accept it gratefully.

"And yet, if the Bureau truly thought there was much risk, they wouldn't be this *intrigued,* nor would they be allocating any of their precious resources," Abe replied. "The truth of the matter is that Samuel and Freya have managed to uncover a tight-knit circle of criminals who claim Bernard Allerton as their leader. We all know the man wouldn't deign to show his face this evening. But a capture of *any* of these suspects could lead to Bernard's future arrest."

Andrew pursed his lips. "And your little firm will get money."

"A sinful amount, yes," Abe replied immediately. "You see, it's a win-win."

Andrew's sneer was full of vitriol. "I do see," he said. "The Bureau will provide agents on the ground that will be listening in along with the Codex team. If Samuel or Freya are in apparent danger, we will send them in. The goal, of course, would be to arrest everyone in attendance on sight."

My pulse spiked with pure excitement. Sam slid his gaze toward mine, nodded.

"Freya and Sam will be provided with earpieces that are on their way to being delivered as we speak. I understand Sam will have his weapon?"

"Yes, sir," Sam said.

"Evandale?" Andrew looked at me. I held up my palms.

"My hands are considered weapons, sir."

Sam shot me an uncharacteristically wolfish grin.

His father continued as if I hadn't spoken. "The teams will wait in unmarked cars parked within a two-block radius of the location of the auction. Do you believe it's in the hotel?"

"That's our best guess," Sam said. "But I can make sure Freya or I give clues throughout the night."

Sam's father waved his hand on screen, and an assistant delivered a slip of paper. "My staff is setting up a bank account for Julian King. I've located fifteen million dollars."

Henry let out a low whistle as I said, "Well, fuck *me*."

Andrew looked directly at his son. "Samuel, fifteen million is the maximum amount I can get in that account. Will you be doing the bidding for the Sand letters?"

"I will," Sam said.

"Bid smart. I'll need a visual confirmation that it is, in fact, the George Sand love letters. Once your hands are on those letters, my agent on the ground will give the team the call to move."

A heaviness settled throughout the room—an acceptance of what we were all about to do tonight.

"Do we know anything about their capacity for violence?" Andrew asked.

Sam and I exchanged a glance. "I think they *could* be a violent bunch, yes. But for the most part, it's all talk. No action," he said.

"Your getting wounded would be a nuisance," Andrew said. "Please don't."

"Your concern is truly endearing," Abe said.

Andrew ignored him. "I need to get to a meeting, but my

staff will be calling shortly to coordinate. Do we need anything else?"

"No, sir," Sam said.

Andrew nodded, then disconnected without saying goodbye. And I had to physically fight the urge to get up and wrap my partner in a hug.

"That's your father?" Henry asked.

"He has a unique communication style," Sam said. He slipped his hands into his pockets, affecting a relaxed stance.

"Sam's father and I disagreed often," Abe said. "If you couldn't tell."

Delilah hummed next to me. "He must have been pissed when you started Codex."

Abe tugged on his cufflinks, but his lips were tipped into the tiniest smile. "Words were said, yes."

Delilah squeezed my hand. "I'll run point with the Bureau agents, get you set up with the earpieces. Henry can pull together information on any open cases we have. If the letters aren't there, we should be on the lookout for anything hot and currently missing."

Henry pushed his glasses up his nose. "I'll pull together a list of any books we *weren't* able to recover. We can even do a little light Sherlock Holmes studying, get you prepped for any additional code words."

"Speaking of," Delilah interjected, "we need a verbal code if the two of you are in direct danger and need rescuing."

"What about *help, we're in danger*?" I suggested.

"Something a little less obvious."

"Mention the Copernicus," Henry said. Delilah squeezed his knee—it was a reference to the manuscript they'd recovered from Victoria Whitney's mansion.

Sam was nodding along. "*Is that a Copernicus*?" he tossed out. "Wouldn't set off any alarm bells necessarily."

"I like it," I said. "Although I very much doubt we'll be in danger. We need to bid, get the letters, have the money wired from the Bureau's fake account, and get the hell out of there."

"Without blowing our cover," Sam added.

"You can do it," Abe said firmly. "I meant what I said to the Deputy Director. They're pretending like they're doing us a favor. But they don't have two agents with access like you two have created. You're helping *them*."

I let out a massive sigh, resting my elbows on my knees. My nerves sparked like little fireworks in my belly—a sensation that felt more like excitement than fear. Flush with sex-confidence and Sam's newly garnered trust, I'd barreled in here and demanded Abe pull the trigger on this plan. A month ago, I might have *wanted* to be the undercover badass, but I would have tamped it down. Now?

Sam stood next to me, and when I looked at him, I recognized what Abe had been trying to show us all along. We were stronger together.

We could accomplish anything—*together*.

Next to me, Delilah and Henry were already a blur of motion—talking through tasks in a verbal shorthand that betrayed the many levels of their intimacy. Abe crossed his legs, leaning back in that regal-looking chair. Our boss and former instructor pinned Sam and me with an intense stare.

"You were the most brilliant students I'd ever had the pleasure of teaching at Quantico," he said seriously. "Even if one might have not *completed* the training in the traditional sense, there's a reason why the two of you are right for this job. And right together."

"Yes, sir," Sam said hoarsely.

"Thank you, Abe," I said softly.

"Do *not* let him get hurt," Abe said to me.

He glared at Sam. "Do *not* let Freya get hurt. I want the two of you to sleep here for a few hours. Henry and Delilah can handle working with the Bureau. Is there anything else I need to know before tonight?"

I held up one finger. "Sam and I might have broken into Philosopher's Hall."

He sighed. "If I wasn't impressed, I'd be pissed. Now go sleep."

36

FREYA

Sam and I were back at The Grand Dame hotel. Fifteen hours had passed—hours in which we'd both napped, fitfully. Prepped and strategized with Henry and Delilah until my brain felt overflowing with tactics. I knew every random factoid about Sherlock Holmes I could manage, had elite technology placed into my ears, and knew the floor plans of this hotel inside and out. All day, we'd monitored the Under the Rose site, but the only messages Birdie received were from Thomas, confirming tonight's details. *Meet us at our hotel room at 8:00 pm. We have your masks.*

We strolled through the lobby beneath the long, white banner declaring the 60th Annual Antiquarian Book Festival. Past the lobby, I could see booksellers dismantling their booths and packing their historic tomes. How strange that Sam and I were about to enter a world where those same books were bartered illegally. The difference between the two was like night and day—the conference room blazed with light and good-humored chatter.

Sam and I were descending into a world much, much darker.

The ornate elevator doors *dinged* open, and we slipped inside. The doors closed, and we turned to face each other —our first minutes alone since we'd had hot sex in the back seat of his car. Sam had the audacity to wear a white tuxedo jacket, black bowtie, black pants. Hair slicked back, jaw clean-shaven, eyes midnight blue. He looked like a superhero dressed for the opera.

I wanted to ravage him in this fucking elevator.

"Can you hear me, Frey?" Delilah's voice—tinny on the earpiece.

"Loud and clear," I answered. Surprisingly, my voice shook not a bit.

Sam touched his ear, head tilting subtly. "I can hear you," he repeated. Henry was in his ear.

"We're listening in on you both," Delilah said. "Me, Henry, and Abe. The other agents." There was a flurry of *here, here, testing* from the ten agents scattered in unmarked cars near the hotel.

Her voice was light, but I'd known Delilah for two years now. Her subtext was *don't say anything you don't want our boss to hear*.

I let out a grateful sigh. "Thank you. Knowing the three of you are close makes me feel like I've got magic powers."

"Of course," Delilah said. "We're Codex. It's what we do. And *you* are going to be amazing. You don't even need magic."

"We are amazing," I said, smiling at Sam. His expression was impassive.

The elevator *dinged* as it neared our destination on the second floor.

"Time check," Sam said loudly, glancing at his watch. "We'll be at the Alexanders' door in two minutes."

"Got it," Delilah said. "We're going quiet now. But we're on and listening. I'll see you on the other side. With donuts."

I was left with a low hum in my ear but no more voices. Even still, Delilah's hidden presence provided the final piece of confidence I needed. Smoothing my hands down my gown, I exhaled. Looked up. Caught Sam staring at me with blatant lust. With a sardonic smirk, he pressed his finger to his lips. Pointed to his ear.

I shrugged. Gave him a funny twirl in my gown. It had come from Delilah's never-ending closet of gorgeous eveningwear. The black, clingy dress was cut low, my hair in a bun to ensure no one could spot the earpieces.

Sam took a giant step toward me. Paused the elevator right below the second floor. We came to a grinding halt.

"Time check—ninety seconds," he said.

But he wasn't looking at his watch. He was still staring at me.

Sam's knuckle landed right on my sternum, bared by the dress. It dragged up the valley between my breasts. Slowly, slowly along the front of my throat, raising my chin. Our breathing was whisper-quiet. We couldn't say a word but didn't need to. For the first time in years, we couldn't hide our truest desires beneath the armor of endless bickering. He dipped his head, coasting his lips over mine. Sweetly. Tenderly.

I pressed onto my toes, deepening the kiss. My arms wrapped around his neck, and his hands glided lazily down my spine. Our tongues met, mouths urgent, everything *quiet*. Instead of sexual frustration, this kiss betrayed our other, even more secretive desires. Not the sexual ones. It was every memory of the two of us filled with kindness, awareness, late-night jokes. It was caring, protection, real trust. It was the intimacy of knowing someone since you were eighteen years old, watching them grow into their honor, grow into their brilliance.

I remembered how young and boyish Sam had looked the day I brought him that cookie. We were just babies, barely twenty-five, but as he sat there, surprised at my gesture, I hadn't wanted to fight with him *or* kiss him angrily. I'd wanted to stroke his hair, hold his hand, curl up on a couch and watch movies as I snuggled my head against his chest. This pure romantic yearning had stuck with me like a sharp thorn—a reminder that if I let Sam Byrne into my heart, there was no going back for me.

I clung to my partner, shuddering as we broke apart. He swallowed hard, ghosted his lips along my temple.

He hit the elevator button again. With a jerk, we started moving.

"Thirty seconds," he said, stepping clear of me. His voice was still professional, but he kept our hands entwined until the doors slid open on the second floor. We stepped out, strode down the carpeted hallway. My heart beat wildly in my chest—even more so when Sam gave me one last wink before knocking on the hotel door.

Cora Alexander—resplendent in a silver gown—opened her hotel door immediately. At the sight of us, her hands flew to her mouth.

"Well, don't you two look like *royalty*," she squealed. Over her shoulder, she called out, "Darling, Birdie and Julian are here."

To us, she dropped to a stage whisper. "And your masks are simply divine."

Sam and I smiled at each other as Julian King and Birdie

Barnes—rare book thieves, members of a secret society, undercover private detectives with federal agents listening in our ears.

"Oh, I can't *wait*," I said.

37

SAM

"Come in, you must be nervous," Cora said, opening their hotel room door wider. Their room was even more ornate than ours, and they were both already dressed in their black-tie attire.

"We're sorry about leaving so dramatically last night," I said, catching Freya's eye. "Dr. Ward was kind enough to let us slip out a side window. Birdie couldn't go through the tunnels again."

"Completely understandable considering your claustrophobia," Cora said, waving her hand in the air.

"I trust you've ascertained the funding needed for tonight?" Thomas asked.

Freya and I nodded. "We are ready and prepared to take those letters home with us," I replied.

Cora was busying herself with two masquerade-style masks. She brought a black and gold mask over to me, patting the edge of the bed. Amused, I sat, and she tied it around my face, covering the top half but leaving my nose and mouth visible.

Freya watched with barely disguised humor.

"How do I look?" I asked.

"Like the Phantom of the Opera but handsomer," she said. "Tell us all about tonight's festivities. Julian and I have been talking about it for ages. I can't believe it's finally here, and we're actually about to attend."

"Well, this evening is an opportunity for members of The Empty House to mingle with others who have interests that lie outside of societal norms," Cora said. "The core eleven of us will be in attendance for the auction, of course. But rest assured, if you and Birdie have come looking for things that are more *exotic*, that will be available for purchase as well."

I heard nothing but a low hum in my ear—pictured all of Codex and the team of agents listening intently.

"As you know, not everyone understands what we do or why we do it. But money is power, and we have both money *and* power. There should be no limitations to the breadth of your passions and desires. If you are wealthy enough to afford the rarest artifacts in the world, tonight is where you are allowed to purchase them."

"Not enjoy them in a museum," Freya said.

"Who enjoys antiques more? Antique-lovers or a bunch of snot-nosed children on a school trip?" Thomas sneered. "Our collection is legendary. Leaders and royalty from around the world salivate over the items of history we own."

"It's true," Cora said. She presented Freya with her mask—black lace with a plume of black feathers off one side. "Can you see without your glasses on?"

"Not even a little bit," Freya said.

"Pity." Cora narrowed her eyes. "I guess I'll have to tie it around your head with your glasses on."

Freya made a non-committal sound but subjected herself to Cora's ministrations.

"The masks are a symbol of our privacy and trust," Cora continued. "In fact, the whole system is based on trust. We agree to protect each other's identities, but if there's a weak link, that system shatters. We've brought you into this circle. If you do anything to betray that trust, *we* will be in danger as well. It was initially described to us as a sort of mutually assured destruction. One member exposing another exposes us all."

"Naturally," I said, as calmly as possible.

"It's important to know that you might recognize people here this evening, even with the masks on. Very powerful and wealthy people. Do not acknowledge them. Do not use their names. Do *not* use your own names."

"Of course not," I promised.

The black rims of Freya's glasses only added to the intricate lace and beadwork of her mask. Her eyes were brilliantly emerald, lips a deep red, gown elegant and scandalous in equal measure. She fractured my focus even while standing in a hotel room with two known thieves—she was that striking. This woman had clung to me in an elevator—shuddering, sighing—not ten minutes earlier, and I'd been sorely tempted to keep kissing her. Keep undressing her, keep revealing the mysteries of her naked body. She possessed a seductive comfort, drawing me in, making me feel strong.

Which was the exact opposite of the conversation I'd had with the Deputy Director. *How many times must I bail you out, Samuel?* He'd made it clear that being under investigation usually made what I was requesting *goddamn impossible*.

But, he'd said, *I've had them make an exception for you. I'm not sure how much more leeway I'll be able to provide after this.*

Abe had seen the situation differently, oddly enough.

His view positioned Codex as the hero, positioned Freya and me as valuable assets doing what the agency wasn't able to do—gaining vital, intimate access. Abe wasn't wrong. And I didn't know *what* that meant for my father. Or my future.

"I know I wasn't making it clear last night at our dinner," Freya said to Thomas, "but I really do understand the true cost of Roy's threat of blackmail. For the four of us and for The Empty House. And I agree that we keep this information from Bernard. It only makes all of us look unreliable."

Thomas glanced at me and visibly swallowed. "Yes, well, I'm still truly sorry for the way I behaved. I'm short-tempered at the moment."

I gave him a respectful nod. But if he made my partner feel uncomfortable again, I wouldn't hesitate to protect her.

"You wouldn't be short-tempered if you hadn't gone and *told* Roy that you'd stolen the Cervantes," Cora snapped. All the air rushed from the room. Freya and I stayed silent, cautious of the couple's unraveling. Tempers were always risky. But outbursts often led to gems of truth.

Thomas looked apologetic and then incensed. "A night of too much liquor and too much confidence I'm still paying for, I know." He cast a sideways look at Freya. "The curse was already in full effect, however, before I even told Roy I'd stolen the Cervantes. Birdie knows that."

"Roy's blackmail is part of the curse," Freya said soberly.

With an exasperated sigh, Cora swept into the walk-in closet and slammed the door. Grimacing, Thomas tugged on his bowtie. "I'll admit I made a mistake spilling what I'd done to a trust-fund brat deep in gambling debt. But The Empty House made an even bigger mistake allowing him entrance into our club."

Gambling debt *did* fit Roy's personality—high risk, high wealth, high drama.

"To Roy, trust is a bargaining chip," Thomas continued. "He'll sell it to the highest bidder. Or use it against you, in the case of his threat. If Ward found out I stole his book *or* if Bernard found out we were being blackmailed, all four of us could be in real trouble."

"We agree," I said. "After the auction, we'll need to make a decision about Roy immediately."

"We'll *go* with the plan that Birdie came up with," Thomas replied.

"Of course, we will," Freya said.

Cora strode back into the room, wrapping a cream-colored shawl around her shoulders with an irritated expression. "When we first accepted Roy, we were wary of his new money. His family connections were shallow and couldn't hold a candle to the rest of us. But his other, more nefarious interests allow him to move within circles where many things we covet are more accessible."

"Which *did* make him a trusted asset," Thomas said defensively.

"Until he became our largest liability," she argued. "I know our leader doesn't care a whit about who wins those letters this evening. But it *must not be Roy*."

Freya caught my eye, before shifting her focus back to the Alexanders. "Truthfully, I'm still astonished Roy can afford to bid on this item given his debts."

"That's because what he'll pay for the letters is a mere drop in the bucket of what he owes," Thomas grumbled. "I wouldn't be surprised if he traveled with private security to this event. Last I heard, Roy Edwards had pissed off a lot of dangerous people."

Heading into a mystery location with this chaotic secret society was feeling less safe by the minute.

"At the end of the day, he's not the kind of person we

want owning such a conspicuous item," I said, starting to understand the threads of their rationale. "He can't help drawing attention to himself."

Cora pursed her lips. "And we know it's even worse than that. He's already bragged that his *'connections'* will pay triple the price to own these letters."

"But he can't sell right away," Freya said. "That's idiotic. He'll only..."

"Bring the entire Empty House down with him?" Cora smirked. "Our thoughts exactly."

They were truly backed into a corner. The *mutually assured destruction* aspect was clearer now. Once you allowed someone into this elite club, you were bound to each other through your shared criminal acts.

"Remind me, what deadline did Roy give you to pay him so he doesn't tell Ward?" I asked.

"Sunday night," Cora answered. "Roy believes he'll be leaving this city in possession of those letters and five million dollars richer."

I could see the effort it took for Freya to keep her expression neutral.

"We'll make sure we bid high enough," I said firmly. "They're ours. We have the money."

"How much?" Thomas asked.

"We've made fifteen million available," I said.

Thomas didn't bat an eye. "Should be enough. Ward sure did enjoy pushing everyone's buttons last night. He's always loved putting on a show."

"He sure does," Freya said.

"Oh! We almost forgot the final piece." Cora unlocked the hotel room safe and removed four small silver items. Handed two to Thomas and presented them to us. "The speakeasies had their membership cards, of course," she explained. "For tonight, the members of The Empty House wear these pins—to make sure you're recognizable beneath the masks. Recognized and trusted."

It was an intricately detailed red rose, about one inch long. Freya's lips curved when she recognized the symbolism.

"This is very special, Cora. Thank you. We understand it's a noble responsibility." Freya touched Cora's shoulder before putting hers on. She reached for mine, meeting my gaze as she slipped the sharp point through my lapel. Like last night, she placed her palm over my heart—warm, soothing. A caress I felt deeply.

"How does it look?" I asked, voice gruff.

"Incredible," she replied.

I could see the pulse fluttering at the hollow of her throat. What she'd told me about leaving Quantico painted a more accurate picture of her nerves in the field. I knew Freya had made the right choice, for herself and for her health. But I sensed something deep down she *didn't* care to admit—Freya believed the reason she'd struggled during training was that she wasn't actually talented. She downplayed her skills continually, never seeing her true value.

"This *is* very special," I said to Cora, but eyes still on Freya. She flushed a little before disengaging, turning back to face our elegantly dressed thieves.

Cora tipped her head. "Do you know what the two of them look like, Thomas?"

He was red-faced, still distracted. "No. What?"

She seemed truly thrilled. "The next leaders of The Empty House."

38

SAM

"We must be heading back into the tunnels?" I asked. A few people had come and gone on the elevators as we'd descended—but if our elegant attire and garish masquerade masks intrigued them, they didn't say.

"Definitely not," Thomas said. "Ward didn't tell you? It's a whole affair. Takes him weeks to pull together—longer because it all has to be done in secret."

The doors opened at the basement level—the old speakeasy Cora had told us about. The place where I'd bumped into Ward that one time. He'd been *getting things ready*.

"Oh. We're in the basement," I said for the agents listening in. There was no one in the hallways, but the space *felt* crowded with a low noise, shuffling feet and muted conversation. The hair on the back of my neck stood straight up.

Cora stepped over to the hollow wall I'd tapped on. Knocked four times. She was clearly enjoying herself. Freya kept her hand looped around my arm.

A knock came back.

Cora knocked three more times.

And then the hollow brick wall transformed into a door, opening up six inches. Freya's hand tightened as a large guard waved us inside. Dr. Ward stood next to him, surrounded on both sides by golden sconces, flickering with candlelight. He wore his Indiana Jones hat with his tuxedo, and I could see the gun holstered on his hip. It had a pearl handle. Freya must have seen the same thing—her hand left my arm and very lightly touched the small of my back. Abe had loaned me his gun.

"Welcome to the auction," Ward said with a grin. "The night you've been waiting for. I trust that the two of you have come prepared to bid. To bid and to win."

"Yes, sir," I said.

The guard peered at us suspiciously—the mask blocked my peripheral vision, which was spiking my adrenaline. I didn't like having one of my senses compromised when I was about to walk into a dark, secret basement with a bunch of people I couldn't trust. The guard was gigantic, and his uniform read *Dresden Security*. He scowled like he'd made it his mission to scare the shit out of us. His eyes hardened when they landed on mine, and I didn't dare back down.

"I greet each attendee personally to ensure discretion and secrecy are of the highest order," Ward continued. "Do not use names or say anything that identifies the people in this room. Your phones and identification will be removed from you and stored in this safe. Pictures and recordings are absolutely prohibited. Do not mention what happens this evening to any other person in your life. Spots available for this auction are extremely limited. The general public has never—and will never—know about it."

Freya and I nodded as we removed our wallets—

stripped of anything identifying other than our fake IDs. We'd been smart enough to leave our phones back with Codex.

"I'll need to pat you down for weapons and hidden cameras," the guard grunted.

"Are weapons common at this event?" Freya asked, staring pointedly at Ward's gun.

"Don't you worry your pretty little head," Ward said. "I'm never not carrying a gun. But I'm the president. Which means everyone else needs to drop their weapons here for safe-keeping."

Her fingers dug into my arm. "This *pretty little head* isn't even a bit worried."

I looked at the guard. At Ward. At Thomas and Cora watching us expectedly. Which action would earn us more trust?

With my palms up, I stepped away from Freya and faced Ward and the bodyguard. "I have a gun holstered at my back. I'm going to reach for it and place it on the desk."

The other man went for his own weapon, but Ward stopped him. "Wait." Ward stared openly at me. "Although I'm surprised to find you carrying a gun."

"My father is an excellent marksman," I said. Which wasn't a lie. "The shooting range is the only place where we've ever connected."

His expression shifted. "Ah, I know this well."

"I've had a license to carry for years." I was reaching behind me as I said this, unclipping my gun. I showed it to Ward, flipped the safety. Removed the magazine. "But this is my baby. Take good care of it."

The guard didn't answer, merely took the weapon and deposited it in a locked safe. We submitted to another pat-down, ensuring we didn't have cameras taped to our bodies.

Thanks to the Bureau's fancy tech, our earpieces weren't detected.

A bald, bespectacled man appeared behind Ward. "He'll take your account information and prep the wire transfer," Ward explained. "If you do, indeed, win, the transfer will happen as soon as the item is in your hand."

"Wonderful," I smiled. Reached into my pocket and handed over the account information the FBI had created for this very moment. With a nod, the man left—preparing to move millions of dollars if we were lucky enough to get those letters.

"It's amazing that the basement at The Grand Dame can be transformed like this," Freya said. "The book convention is happening —"

"Only two floors away," Ward said. "Amazing, isn't it? We live in a world where lies are buried inside deeper lies, where everything's a smoke screen. Nothing is real. For every law-abiding book convention in this world you'll find, well..." He spread his arms and indicated the hallway behind him, "You'll find this."

It was a large, low-ceilinged room with dark, paneled walls and flickering candlelight. Jazz music floated in on speakers I couldn't see, and my eyes were drawn to the backlit stage at the far end. A long, low bar glittered with glasses and liquor, and the space was filled with men and women adorned in masks. Feathered, beaded, sequined—it was disorienting. As an FBI agent, I was used to scanning faces, recognizing suspects, and categorizing them instantly. Instead I faced a sea of people who were unfamiliar, all dressed in confusing garb.

"Absinthe?" asked a hostess.

Freya selected an oddly shaped glass from the tray. "Perfume bottles?"

"A nice touch, don't you think?" Ward said.

"I should have worn a flapper dress," she exclaimed. "I had no idea."

"It's high time this kind of circumventing of the law was celebrated in our society, and not scorned," he said.

"And the hotel staff...?" she ventured.

Ward slipped his hands into his pockets. "As it is so awfully true in the history of this world, you can do anything if you pay people off."

"How quaint," she said.

A man and a woman in elaborately feathered masks grabbed the attention of Cora and Thomas, which left us alone with Dr. Ward.

"When does bidding start?" I asked.

Ward stepped closer to me, as if sharing a secret. I dipped my head in anticipation.

"I don't know who you think you are, but god help me if you bring a weapon into my house again." Then he clapped me hard on the shoulder before nodding and walking away.

A reckless man with the only gun in the room—besides the armed guard—was not an ideal situation. Especially one who'd been pissed—rather than pleased—at the presence of a perceived threat.

Freya was at my side in an instant. She tilted her head, listening. A beat later, I heard Henry in my ear. *Abe wants to know if you're safe. If not, get out of there now.*

"How are you feeling?" Freya asked. "Excited or...?"

"Excited," I said firmly, watching her reaction. She nodded. "It's a lot to take in, but I feel confident about our plan to bid."

Me too, she mouthed.

Please be careful, Henry said urgently in my ear. I tracked Ward's movements—he was glad-handing around the crowd like a local politician. Thomas was eyeing Ward covertly, sulking. Unpredictable.

There was movement at the stage—long tables covered in velvet tablecloths being rolled out. Freya and I moved through the back as couples laughed and the jazz music swelled. One of the side rooms was open. In the center was a red curtain. I was intrigued by the scuffling sounds coming from behind.

"I'm curious to know who will take this beauty home tonight." It was Roy, suddenly next to us with a scowl on his face. He looked out of place surrounded by soft conversation and jazz. I realized he wasn't wearing a mask of any kind. I touched mine, shifting it.

There was a sound like thunder from behind the curtain —a roar that rattled my bones.

Freya jumped a foot in the air, hand on her chest. "Jesus *fucking* Christ, what was that?"

Roy's scowl deepened. "Wouldn't you like to know?"

My partner sized up Roy and clearly found him lacking. "Where's your mask?"

"I'm not afraid of anyone in here," he grumbled into his drink. Although his jittery fingers and cagey gaze betrayed his lie. "Any word on who this mystery bidder is going to be tonight?"

"Bidder on what?" she asked, stroking her nail down the perfume bottle.

"The only thing here everyone wants."

"Couldn't it be everyone in this room?" she asked.

"Funny, because word on the street is that it's you," Roy said sardonically. "And you forget that you owe me. Twice. So if I were you, I'd reconsider your plan."

His eyes flicked over Freya's head to meet mine. I glared at him until he took a step back, tugging at his collar.

"We were told members became bloodthirsty on the night of the auction," she sighed.

"We had a *deal*," he whispered urgently. "No one in this room understands the situation that I'm in."

I wasn't afraid of Roy—he was an annoying pissant I could knock unconscious in a millisecond—but those shifting loyalties were alive and well tonight. The confined space, the low ceilings, the way the masks concealed facial expressions...everything felt much, much more dangerous.

"I don't recall making any such deal with you. I know what I want," Freya said. "And I'll be taking it." She extended her hand for him to shake. "May the best woman win."

Roy walked away with a sneer.

I would let Freya Evandale take *me* however she wanted.

"Interesting conversations we're having this evening," she said quietly.

"I don't trust him," I said quietly. "Not one bit. Especially after what we learned back upstairs."

She grimaced. "We're in agreement."

We watched as Roy slithered through the crowd, drawing stares at his unadorned face. The seats by the stage were starting to fill. The auction was about to begin. And the scuffling behind the curtain had grown louder.

"What's behind it?" I asked again, desperately curious.

Freya twitched the material back an inch and froze in abject terror. I was by her side in two strides, grabbing it from her fingers.

It was a giant, rattling cage. Inside was a full-grown white tiger, snarling like we were his next meal.

39

FREYA

"Oh my god, *what the fuck*," I wheezed, leaping a foot back from the wild carnivore prowling in a cage much too small. "I didn't know they'd be auctioning off exotic animals tonight. I've always wanted to see a white tiger, I guess."

Exotic animals, stolen rare books, it's a lot of the same people, Delilah whispered. I nodded, touching my throat. I knew this rationally, but being confronted with the strange, creeping tension of this evening was unsettling.

"As much as I want to keep hanging out with this tiger, I think we need to be seated," Sam murmured.

"Let's do this," I replied.

After a furtive glance over his shoulder, he kissed my palm, the tips of my fingers, the inside of my wrist. I needed the reminder we were in this together.

Thank you, I mouthed to him, cupping his face for all of a second. We slipped back into the auction room. The old bar was carved with art deco designs and lit up with lightbulbs. The bartender could have stepped right out of the Prohibition era. The jazz music, the masks, the pearls and bowties, the absinthe in perfume bottles. Dr. Ward was a showman, and tonight was certainly *his show*.

"Your bid paddle, sir," one of the attendants said, passing us a paddle with *#13* in the center.

"Some would call that number unlucky," I said.

"Not Ward." Sam studied the man on the stage. "Ward doesn't believe in luck. Only opportunity."

Ward motioned for the two of us to sit in the very front row. Sam and I sat in the two seats on the left side, next to the narrow aisle. The stage was short—barely six inches in height—which brought Ward directly in front of us.

Sven stood guard by the only exit. He was employed by the "morally gray" security firm that Victoria Whitney had hired to protect the manuscript she'd stolen. Sven had shot at Henry and Delilah as they ran from her house. The firm was beloved by the rich and fucking shady, and their sole motivation was money.

And Sven had taken Sam's gun.

Roy swooped into the empty seat to my left. "Remember our deal," he whispered in my ear. I turned up my nose and didn't reply. All we had to do was get our hands on those letters, transfer the funds, and let the FBI do the rest.

As long as Ward didn't feed Sam and me to that tiger first.

"Let us begin," Ward said. "Once an item is presented, I will open the bidding. Once the winner is selected, they will be escorted to the back room to pay immediately, securing their ownership. All of you will be provided with letters of authentication as well as letters confirming the legal sale of this item. Keep these in your records should you ever have any problems."

Sam glanced at me sideways. How could they provide those letters for items that were stolen?

"Up first for the animal lovers in our audience." Ward smirked with glee, and the audience tittered. The prowling, caged tiger was rolled across the stage, and I felt utterly heartbroken for it. My mind spun with the implications—implications that Delilah and Abe had been talking about for the past year. The criminal underworld bled across boundaries and barriers, and thieves like Victoria Whitney were common. But that meant thieves like Ward and Bernard were common too.

The bid paddles flew up rapidly, winnowing down to two bidders who were furious with each other by the time the winning $2 million bid was announced. I schooled my features, trying to watch with a neutral expression. And when they won—a glamorous-looking couple that dripped wealth—the woman wiggled her fingers at the bars like the tiger was a kitten at a shelter.

The big cat growled at her.

"Don't worry. We have more exciting things to come," Ward said, clapping his hands. Two attendants wheeled out a very large, instantly recognizable tome in a glass case.

"A classic," he said. "*The* classic. A manuscript that only grows in value, my friends. If you're looking to add to your collection, a Gutenberg Bible will do it. You'll recognize this copy from our good peers at the University of Texas in Austin."

Sam knew it. I knew it. Two years ago, the University of Texas had its Gutenberg Bible stolen in a robbery that had flooded the news. It was worth millions of dollars.

Even more, it was one of the most vital pieces of cultural history in the entire world.

And it was sitting right in front of us.

The bidding battle for that Bible stretched on and on. Sam and I watched as casually as we could—even Thomas and Cora threw in a few million when they had a chance. But it was another man who finally won, triumphant with a bid of $20 million. People clapped as he strode down the aisle.

Henry is having an absolute meltdown, Delilah said in my ear. I could believe it.

Ward rubbed his hands together as the next item was wheeled out, concealed in the same type of glass case that I knew meant whatever was in there was fucking old. "Who here in the audience is a fan of Edgar Allen Poe?"

The audience murmured their assent.

"A heart beneath the floorboards," he said. "A man buried behind a stone wall. A grave filled with live souls, not the dead. He is one of the most celebrated writers, and what I have here for you tonight is his book of poetry, of which there are only fifty left in the world. *Tamerlane and Other Poems* was written by Poe but published as *anonymous*. It was recently released by the McMaster's Library at Oxford in England."

Holy shit, came Delilah's voice. Sam winced, touched his ear. I guessed Henry was shouting.

"All of you here are familiar with our very close connection to the librarians at the McMaster's Library," Ward said, face sly.

He was referring to Bernard Allerton. When Henry had confronted the man about it, Bernard had shown Henry a letter with Henry's forged signature, declaring the book officially released. When, in actuality, Bernard had stolen it.

Watch who gets that fucking book, Delilah said—though she knew I didn't need to be told twice. The battle for the *Tamerlane* was fierce—$16 million was the grand total. I didn't recognize the woman who won. But she stepped into the back room, and I kept my eye on her. She needed to *stay.* Stay and be arrested by the FBI when they got here.

Two tables were wheeled out—propped up on one was a selection of old letters. The second table was placed close to the edge of the stage. It held two antique letter-openers.

"Call it a theme," Ward said. "To the left, two letter-openers owned by a high-ranking officer in George Washington's army and used during the American Revolution."

Ward's eyes twinkled as they landed directly on Sam and me.

"And to my right, the love letters between the controversial author George Sand and the poet Alfred de Musset." Ward spread his hands open and winked. "Now who would like to start the bidding off?"

40

FREYA

"Are you ready to bid?" I asked, struggling to keep my tone steady.

"I am," Sam said roughly.

I was happy to see that my partner appeared excited but still calm. Levelheaded. His rigorous training was shining through. Drop Sam Byrne into a room of bloodthirsty book thieves, and he'd complete the task in front of him with a quiet honor.

"We all know fascination with George Sand's passionate and tempestuous love letters is at an all-time high right now, especially given the anticipated biopic set to begin filming next week," Ward said. "These letters were to be a dynamic set piece for the film. For obvious reasons, whoever takes ownership of them this evening will be screened to ensure their absolute ability to keep their presence and location a secret until the media has died down. And we'll start the bidding off at one million."

Sam snapped his bid paddle up a full three seconds before Roy could. Several women were eyeing Sam like a piece of prime rib.

"Thank you for the first bid, number thirteen," Ward said, careful not to reveal identities. "Do I see one point five million?"

Roy parried, raised his paddle. Smirked at us. Sam cleared his throat and set his jaw. And immediately responded to the request for $2 million. Their bid battle felt interminable, when in reality, I don't think more than three minutes went by. Other attendees competed as well, increasing the bid increments quickly. We'd been so focused on Roy, we'd forgetten the other players in the room.

Everyone wanted these fucking letters. Paddles flew up, then down, in a blur of white numbers. To say the room was hushed was an understatement. Even the music had stopped. To Sam's credit, he didn't break a sweat, merely met each competing bid with a small, confident smile.

Roy was sweating at $3 million. Scowling at $6 million. By the time Sam had pushed things to $11 million, Roy was red as a tomato, and the remaining competitors had dropped out.

Breathe, breathe, breathe, I chanted. But it didn't help. My heart was going to beat out of my chest and land on the floor.

Ward pushed the bids to $15 million with the look of a symphony conductor holding the climactic note. It was our absolute max—the cap of our spending limit. Sam's paddle in the air didn't even tremble—my partner was pure poise.

"I see a $15 million bid," Ward declared, scanning the crowd. "Going once."

A beat.

"Going twice." Next to me, Roy was growling like the tiger. His fingers twitched on the paddle, and for a devastating second, I thought he was going to lift it.

"*Sold* to bidder number thirteen."

The audience actually clapped—and Sam had the good sense to stand and take a short bow. He was impressive in that tux, strong and sure of his abilities. I found myself clapping without thinking about it, cheering his performance.

"Thank you, sir," Ward said. "Would you like to step—"

"Why is an FBI agent here?"

There was a single second of silence—until the audience reacted with shocked whispers and the scrape of chairs moving.

"I'm sorry, what?" Ward demanded. "Who said that?"

It was an older man in the far back I didn't recognize at all. But even with the mask on, I could *see* the moment Sam recognized whoever that person was.

Fear erupted across my nerve endings. *This can't be happening.*

"That bidder is an FBI agent. I'm guessing he shouldn't be here," the man repeated.

The next five seconds would forever remain a blur in my memory. I blinked, and Sam was turning toward me in slow motion. Blinked again, and I was yanked up and pinned by a strong arm, wrapped around my windpipe. As soon as my hands moved to defend myself, the letter-opener was pressed to my throat. You'd think a blade from the 18th century would be dull—but I only knew the sharp point against my skin. Screams and cries from a very surprised audience thundered around me.

Roy's voice was slimy in my ear. "You stay the *fuck* still."

I barely had time to panic—because my partner had sprung into confident action. With one brutal kick, Sam knocked Dr. Ward to the ground with a *thud*. Reached for the man's pearl-handled gun. And had it pointed right at Roy's face not a millisecond later.

It was like a dangerous ballet of calculated movements.

Sam maintained a perfect stance, arms straight, gaze laser-focused on the man with the knife at my throat.

Meanwhile, Ward was trying to scrabble off the ground like a crab. Sam kept his eyes and gun trained on Roy—and pressed his foot against Ward's windpipe. Ward went still, palms coming to surrender.

"Nobody move," Sam said calmly. "Roy, put that knife down right now, and nothing bad will happen."

"You're a *fucking FBI agent*?" Roy seethed. The movement pressed the knife harder against my throat, and I winced.

Sven appeared with his own gun raised—right at me.

I gazed into Sam's eyes, where I could read the years of intensive training mapping his decision-making. Even now, with a knife at my throat and a gun trained on my head, my heart rate began to slow, pulse steady. Sam and I had partnered on this simulation at the Academy countless times. I knew what I needed to do. Knew I could do it. Because the *only* person in our class with better aim than me was Sam. And the person I trusted to save my life was Sam.

"Drop the gun, hotshot," Sven snarled from the side. Ward whimpered from the ground.

"Not a chance," Sam said.

Sven took a step closer to me, weapon up.

"Sven," Sam said evenly, "take your gun off my partner right this goddamn second or your boss isn't going to like what I do to his fucking throat."

"Do it," Ward cried from the ground. "Just—just do it."

With a glare, Sven took a step back, gun at his side. I sensed people sneaking out the side door, bodies on the move. The tiger roared from the back.

"Is she an FBI agent too?" Roy asked.

"No, she is not," Sam said. "Drop that knife."

"Of *course* this is happening," Roy spit out. "Everyone

here thinks they're so *smart,* but you're all stealing from each other and lying to each other, and *this* happens. An FBI agent tricks all of us into trusting him."

Roy pressed the knife *hard*, breaking the skin. "I need those letters and I need money. So why don't you drop that gun and give me the letters, and I'll let this bitch go."

Fury was building in Sam's face. Beneath the calm, I could sense my partner about to snap.

"No," Sam repeated. "I can't let you do that."

Roy yanked me tighter against his body. I forced back the encroaching fear. Fear muddied your thinking—and my partner wasn't afraid. He was focused and prepared for anything.

"Are you here because of Bernard?" Roy babbled. "Did he turn us all in?"

"Put down the knife," Sam said.

"Put down *your gun*," Roy yelled.

The action shifted him forward, over my shoulder. Which gave my elbows the three inches they needed to slam back into his stomach with every ounce of strength I had.

Roy cried out in pain, and I dropped to the ground just as Sam's gun went off. Roy flew backward, clutching his right shoulder. The letter-opener fell to the ground, and Sam was on Roy immediately. In the ensuing few seconds, my ears flooded with a dull ring as everything slipped back into slow motion.

Sam, flying past me to subdue Roy.

Ward, standing up and rubbing his throat. Reaching into his boot and retrieving a small pistol. Raising the gun at Sam.

Sven, running toward us. And doing the same thing.

And Sam, completely unaware of any of it.

41

SAM

I was only able to breathe when Freya was safely out of harm, dropped to the ground and away from Roy.

Then I shot that asshole in the shoulder.

It was a flesh wound, intended to stop him in his tracks, but I wasn't taking chances. I had nothing to restrain him except for my body weight. Which was why, as I flipped him and pinned his arms down, I was unaware of the tableau unfolding behind me.

Until I looked up.

Ward's arm was rising, hand holding another gun. The barrel was pointed right above my heart. I had not a single second to act. But my partner had things under control.

Freya Evandale tore off her mask and strode up to Ward like a vengeful angel. Her hand lashed like a lightning strike, shoving his hand to the right and punching him square in the fucking nose. She twisted his wrist, released his gun, and knocked him back down to the ground.

"You've got Sven, right, Byrne?" she called over her shoulder, gun on Ward, stiletto to his chest.

"He's not going anywhere," I said.

Of course, I had him. I'd known the moment I saw the flash of Ward's weapon what I needed to do. What *we* needed to do. My knee was jammed hard between Roy's shoulder blades, and my gun was trained squarely on a very pissed off Sven.

I heard gasps, bodies moving, chairs hitting the floor. Then the very recognizable sound of agents and police officers streaming in and shouting for Freya and me to drop our weapons. We both stepped back, guns and hands up—eyes locking through the sheer chaos. The most powerful feeling of trust I'd ever experienced in my life surged between us. And it wasn't adrenaline, but something richer and more compelling than that.

It was the supreme understanding that Freya and I were meant to be partners. We couldn't deny it, couldn't shake it. It was ingrained in us like our DNA. That trust and partnership had been there from the very day we'd met. But our naturally competitive natures had resisted it, shoved it back as hard as we could.

But send the two of us into a dark, claustrophobic basement filled with gun-toting book thieves and we'd end up on top. We always would.

How in the *hell* was I supposed to go back to the FBI without her?

"Special Agent Byrne?" It was a younger agent, rushing to me in the pandemonium. I nodded, rattled off my badge number. The man blew out a big breath, called back to his superior officer. "And that's Freya Evandale, from the Codex team," I said.

Ward groaned from the floor, and Freya toed around his body, grinning mischievously at the man who'd tried to kill me.

"Don't you worry your pretty little head about it, Dr. Ward," she said cheerfully. "You're going to love prison."

Officers dragged me off of Roy so he could receive medical attention from the paramedics crowding around us. It was madness confined to a former speakeasy. Out of the corner of my eye, I caught Cora and Thomas with twin haughty expressions. Every time the tiger roared, someone yelped. Ward was already shouting for his lawyer.

Freya and I kept staring at each other. It was impossible not to—she was pure, unbridled magnificence. She moved toward me through the crowd—we'd only have a second before being carted off for questioning. And my father would probably call at any moment.

None of that mattered.

"Did you just save my life, Evandale?" I asked.

"Only because you saved mine," she said. When she lifted her chin at me, I could see the thin trickle of blood from the letter opener.

"We need a medic over here," I called.

"Please, it's a scratch," she said, waving her hand through the air. The urge to comfort her was overwhelming.

"Those were some nice moves with Ward," I said.

"And you were a crack shot with Roy."

"My target practice skills are legendary." My lips twitched. "If you'll recall."

"Oh, I recall all right."

Abraham materialized next to us. He was immaculate, hair slicked back and suit perfectly pressed.

"Have you been here this whole time?" Freya asked, surprised.

He gave a curt nod. Reached out and touched her lightly on the shoulder. "I am pleased to see you are not harmed."

His expression was neutral. But his tone barely concealed his raw emotion.

She hugged him. "I love you too, boss," she said. "An antique letter opener can't take this girl out. Plus, Byrne was here."

"I had several guns on me at one point," I added. "Freya saved me."

"Well, you did promise to protect each other," Abe said, clearing his throat as Freya let him go. "I believe I've aged about ten years since the two of you got here. Delilah and Henry are outside in the car. They have both been suitably unhinged for the past ten minutes." He pinned me with a sincere look. "We're lucky the Bureau was here to help. I'm not sure the three of us could have handled this level of danger."

I eyed the chaos around us. "And I'm not sure we could have gotten those letters back without them."

"We couldn't hear what preceded Freya being grabbed," he said. "Were you recognized?"

I grimaced, scanning the audience for the masked man who'd revealed my true identity. I caught him with his wrists behind his back, being led down the hallway by a pair of agents.

"I'm pretty sure it was William Buchanan," I explained, "though I didn't see him when I came in. I was the lead on his case at Art Theft, and there was a three-month period where he saw my face every day. A mask can't hide the face of a person you hate. And that man hates me for putting him away." My chest ached with regret—with the missed opportunity to spot the danger lurking in the corners. "I thought he was still in prison."

"Good news is he's probably going back," Abe said mildly. "You couldn't have anticipated it, Sam."

I nodded, throat still tight. Freya grabbed Abe and pulled him onto the short stage. "Now here's the best part about not dying. We got the damn letters back."

Abe stared down at the glass case. Shook his head in slow disbelief.

"I'll bring you tacos for a year," he promised. His phone was to his ear not a second later.

"Scarlett?" he said, starting to walk away. "I'm staring at the George Sand letters. My agents recovered them from an underground auction. I think it's highly likely those other letters you're holding are forgeries."

"We'll probably lose the contract," Freya said next to me. "We got the letters back, but the press will be all over it. No top-secret return to Hollywood."

"I'm not sure we had a choice," I said, placing my palm on the glass case. They were tiny, insubstantial pieces of paper with words scrawled in uneven lines. So small for a rescue that was so big.

She leaned down, her breath fogging the glass. Her eyes shone with wonder, as they often did. "Do you know what happened to these two in the end?"

"I don't."

"Alfred grew ill with a mysterious sickness which he eventually recovered from," she explained. "And George left him for his doctor."

"Ice-cold," I said.

"Right?" she said, smiling. "But for this moment in time, as they wrote these words—hidden messages and all—the only thing that mattered was their passionate love. It's why they're beautiful. We hunt down a lot of epic historical tomes or great works of literature at Codex. These are mere records of our humanity, which makes them even more special."

"Do you think they loved each other, even if they argued constantly?" I asked.

"Yes, I do," she said. "I think, deep down, they only argued because they were afraid of how powerful their love was."

"Freya, listen," I started to say, voice ragged. Two police officers and a paramedic were moving quickly toward the stage.

"We did it," I said softly, redirecting. "You and me."

She cracked a cheeky smile. "I'm fucking happy, Sam."

I laughed. "Fuck, I mean...*me too*."

"How do you feel?"

I felt night and day from the way I'd felt during my "incident" at the Bureau. This feeling of joyful elation didn't even bear comparison.

"I feel accomplished," I admitted. "I feel like we did something good for the world."

"That's how I feel too," she agreed. "George the writer and Alfred the poet would be proud. Your mother loved poetry, didn't she?"

The unexpected mention of my mother brought instant happiness. I thought about her every day. But the week after she passed away, my father made it clear she was not to be spoken about in our house. My young, healthy, ever-vital mother had died from a brain aneurysm in her sleep when I was twelve—a swift, unexpected death that carved my father in half. He kept his external grief for her short. Secretive. For a long time, I'd try sharing memories of her on her birthday or during certain holidays. His responses were glacial and curt.

In many ways, I was starved to share her memory with anyone who would listen.

"She did love poetry," I finally said. "She read it every

single night. Sometimes she'd read poems to me before I fell asleep. But if I woke up, searching for her, she'd be sitting in the kitchen. Tea and a blanket. Just reading. She always said poetry influenced her dreams, made them more beautiful." I rubbed the back of my neck. "You remembered that?"

"You told me all about her once," Freya said. "During one of our late-night study sessions when we were loopy from lack of sleep. I always think about her when I'm in the poetry section of bookstores."

"You think of my mother?"

"Of course," she said.

A swell of emotion threatened to knock me down.

"I always think of you when I go to bookstores," I said. "I would go to that old bookstore you loved near the academy. If I was missing you."

She brushed the hair from her face. "Sam?"

"Yeah?"

"That love letter you told Cora about...was it for me?"

The police officers and the paramedic descended upon us—Abe alongside them. I knew it was going to be a long night—we'd be questioned and give our statements, and I wasn't going to be able to ignore the incoming call from my father. Besides, Freya and I might have dismantled an actual black-market antiquities ring. It was a big fucking deal.

My truth, however, demanded to be liberated.

"Ms. Evandale, I need to look at your throat," the paramedic was saying. And Abe was talking to the agents. And another agent was on the phone with the Bureau, confirming my badge number.

"I'll stay with Freya," Abe told me, with a look more knowing than I expected. "We'll probably see you at the closest police station. Scarlett is shocked and thrilled that we have the letters. But they'll need to be authenticated. And the story is going to be everywhere."

"I'm sorry, sir," I said. "Did we make all the wrong decisions? Make things messier?"

"Not at all," he said, clapping me on the shoulder. "You made all the right decisions."

I let out a massive sigh of gratitude. It had been years since I'd been told I'd done anything right at all.

"Special Agent Byrne?" That youngish-looking agent was extending a cell phone my way. "The Deputy Director of the FBI wants to speak with you?"

"I'll take it, thank you," I said, watching the paramedic as he examined Freya's throat. Abe was talking to her softly, and whatever she was saying was making him *and* the paramedic laugh.

"Sir," I said into the phone.

"Abraham informed me of tonight's outcome." My father's clipped tone lacked all emotion. "I heard the retrieval was a success."

"Yes, it was," I said. I didn't need to say more—he had staff members who'd relay all the pertinent details. I chewed on my next words carefully. "Thank you for the help and the resources. It was needed."

"As discussed, I'll expect you back in Virginia tomorrow," he replied. "The hearing will be in the morning."

I heard the clear, bell-like sound of Freya's joy, and it had my chest constricting with yearning. *I want more time.*

"I'm sure some events from this evening will shake out through the Bureau and end up on your desk in Art Theft," he said.

I watched Ward being hauled off in handcuffs. He looked *furious*. "Yes, sir, I believe they will."

"Eleven a.m. will be your hearing decision," my father said. "Please confirm you will be here."

Freya had a small bandage on her throat but looked otherwise unharmed. She kept glancing at me shyly as she answered the medic's questions. I couldn't actually process what it had been like to watch Roy put a sharp object to her beautiful throat. Our simulations at Quantico were fake. There was no real danger.

This had been the first time I'd ever felt her life was at risk. And the resulting emotions were immeasurable.

Fury. Fear.

Passion. Yearning.

Nothing could have stopped me from protecting her in that moment. Not ten guards or one hundred. I was unstoppable.

"Samuel," my father snapped. "I will see you tomorrow."

It wasn't a question. It was a barked command.

"I'll try my hardest but can't promise anything," I said and ended the call. The phone rang again, and I handed it back to the young officer. "You can ignore it."

I was escorted back through the basement, up the elevator, and out into a waiting squad car. I knew what was going to happen next—had conducted plenty of interviews myself—but I wanted Freya. Needed Freya. But as I glanced behind me one last time, the crowds of people converged in front of her and Abe.

And she vanished.

42

FREYA

The clap of thunder rattled my windowpanes. Minerva hissed and bolted as lightning lit the angry-looking sky.

"Candles, check," Delilah said. "Tea, check. Blankets, check." She touched my chin, looked at the bandage on my throat. "Pain meds?"

"Not needed," I said. "Honestly. It barely broke the skin."

After Sam and I had both been questioned by federal agents at the police station—separately—Delilah had taken me home. It was well past midnight, and a vicious summer storm had landed over the city of Philadelphia. Rain pelted the windows, and I was grateful for candles and a cozy mountain of blankets. The adrenaline was starting to ebb, and I felt drowsy and punch-drunk.

She rubbed my arms through the blankets with a look of concern. "Frey."

"Yeah?"

"I thought you were going to get hurt tonight," she said. "I don't know what I would have done if that had happened."

"Having you in my ear helped," I said. "I knew you had my back. You always do. I trusted you to save me. And I trusted..." I swallowed hard. "I trusted Sam to save me."

Her face softened with sympathy. "The connection the two of you have is practically tangible."

I bit my lip but didn't say a word.

"When did you have sex?"

I hid my face behind the blanket. "Can you read minds?"

"I can read my best friend."

I glanced at the pelting rain, wondering where Sam was right this very instant. I'd seen him on the phone, and based on his body language, I guessed it was his father.

"We had sex in the back seat of his car yesterday morning," I admitted.

Delilah smirked. "I've also enjoyed sex in a vehicle with Henry."

"Girl, I know it."

"It must have been very intense."

I started to make a joke—per the usual—but found I couldn't. It was late, and I was exhausted, and I'd had a knife pulled on me not three hours earlier.

"I'm terrified of my feelings for Sam," I said.

"Is he going back to Virginia?" she asked.

"There's no doubt in my mind that he will," I said. "He was born to be an FBI agent. It's in his blood."

"I'm not sure about that," Delilah said, standing and kissing the top of my head. "If you think you've been hiding your feelings for Sam, you have no idea how obvious *he's* been these past few days."

"What do you mean?"

"That man is in love with you, Freya," she said. "Like hearts-in-his-eyes love. So keep trusting. Because I'm guessing you'll figure it out."

I watched a drop of rain slide down the window. Lightning illuminated the framed picture of my mom and me, dressed up as FBI agents. "All those years," I said, "we did nothing but argue and fight and compete. But we were never apart from each other. I worked hard to convince myself I was annoyed by his presence. Except we waited for each other outside the library to study every night." I smiled at the memory, so sweet now. "Who willingly studies with their archnemesis every single night for *hours*?"

She grinned. "Nemeses in love, my dear."

I covered my face again. "We were fighting our feelings."

"I know," she said, mirth in her tone. "Henry knows. Even Abe knows. Strangers on the street know. The moment I saw the two of you together in our office, I would have bet my life savings you loved each other."

"*Oh, god,*" I wailed. "Henry and Abe *know*?"

Delilah crouched down until we were eye-level. I tugged the blanket down, blowing the messy hair from my forehead. "Frey." She was fighting amusement. "Frey. The man *shot someone* for you tonight. Sam's not your enemy."

My pulse fluttered like moth wings, body and mind fully accepting what I'd realized while kissing Sam Byrne in the elevator.

I'd let him into my heart. There was no going back for me.

"He's my love," I said.

Her smile widened. "He most certainly is."

"And he's amazing at sex."

"That is also extremely obvious."

"I have to tell him how I feel," I said, softly this time. Serious.

Delilah nodded. "You can do it," she said. "You were

extraordinary tonight. I'm truly proud to be your best friend, Frey. Always."

Her warm praise lit me up. I wrapped the blanket more tightly around my shoulders and beamed at her.

"Thank you," I said. "I never thought I'd have a real friend like you. When I was younger, I, you know, didn't always have the nicest time with friends. You taught me that friendship is real. And it means everything to me."

"Well, you can't get rid of me now," she teased. But her eyes were shining.

"I don't plan on it," I replied. I held her hand, squeezed it hard.

Delilah blew me a kiss before slipping out the door. I exhaled, forehead pressed to my knees, thoughts a riotous mess. The minute I'd looked up and spotted Sven and Ward with their guns on Sam, years of training and self-confidence had snapped back over my bones. I'd never felt stronger than slapping that gun from Ward's hand and punching him in the face.

But even more than that—Sam and I had *done it*. We'd gone undercover, together, as *book thieves*. Infiltrated a secret society. And we got the damn letters back. I'd done that with the man I loved. A man who believed in me.

I'd done it because I'd believed in myself.

The sharp knock was barely audible through the rumbling thunder. Blanket wrapped around myself, I shuffled like a burrito and opened the door.

It wasn't Delilah though.

It was Sam.

The lightning flashed, highlighting the muscled edges of his big body outlined in my doorway. He was soaked to the skin, the rain plastering his white tuxedo shirt to his broad, ridged chest.

"What are you doing here?" I breathed. He was the most magnificent thing I'd ever seen.

"I did write you a letter," he said. Another rumble of thunder. "The night that you left Quantico, I got drunk on contraband whiskey and wrote you a love letter."

Those words stopped me cold. "A love letter?"

"I didn't know that's what it was at the time," Sam said. "It had been years since I'd been allowed to fully feel my emotions. Which is why it was always easier to fight with you. Less complicated than kissing you. Less complicated than fucking you."

Both of us were staring, panting heavily. The rain fell in a sheet behind him, drenching the pavement.

"And much less complicated than falling in love with you."

"Sam," I said, voice wavering.

"In the letter I begged you to stay. Not because of your career. Not because of the FBI. I asked you to stay because the thought of not seeing you every day broke my fucking heart. And I was brokenhearted until the day I graduated. After that, I worked hard to forget that feeling. Too complicated, too messy. But the moment you walked into Abe's office and I saw you again…" He stopped, voice raw. "I've lived the last seven years in darkness. You turned on every light in my life. *You* are the light, Freya."

Tears spilled over, rolling down my cheeks. It was too much, this dismantling of the walls we'd built to protect us from our love.

Sam's fingers gripped my cheeks, brushing away the tears.

"I'd never known true fear until I thought Ward was going to shoot you," I whispered. "But until that point, I wasn't scared. Even with a knife to my neck. You're the person I trust the most in this world to save my life." I pressed a kiss to his palm. "Because I'm in love with you."

Then I grabbed his soaking wet shirt and yanked him into my house.

43

FREYA

Sam kicked the door closed and lifted me. My blanket fell to the floor, and my arms wrapped around his neck.

"Are you hurt?" he asked, studying the bandage.

"No," I said. "Not in the least. Nor am I fragile."

His muscles shook—and I knew it wasn't from effort. Sam Byrne could hold me over his head and run the bleachers of a stadium without breaking a sweat. He was restraining himself. And I didn't want restraint.

"What do you want?" he whispered.

In response, I tore off my glasses and crashed our lips together. Yanked on his hair and devoured his mouth with every ounce of my fear and trust and protection and gratitude that he was *alive*. And safe.

And mine—at least for the night. He responded just the way I wanted. Turning and slamming me against the nearest wall, shaking the bookshelves and various paperbacks. Another clap of thunder rolled past, muffling my cries as his hot mouth roamed my throat, cautious of the bandage. In a second, I was wet from the rainwater on his skin. Shivering at the onslaught of violent sensation. I needed to be naked and I needed Sam naked. As usual, my partner read my mind, sliding my body to the ground and raising my sweater over my head. He hissed as he took in my bare breasts, rubbing a hand across his mouth.

"Take off your fucking pants, Evandale," he rasped.

I did as I was told. I was completely bare, my hair down and loose around my shoulders.

The expression on his face was undeniable—it was love and hunger twisted so beautifully I could have cried. Sam—still clothed, still wet—dropped to his knees in front of me and pressed his face to my stomach, breathing in.

"If anything had happened to you," he murmured, "I don't know what I would have done. Freya. Freya, I don't—"

"Shh," I said, stroking his hair. "I'm here. And yours."

His mouth descended to my stomach with hungry, open kisses as his palms smoothed across my aching nipples. His mouth joined his fingers, and I held his head in place, body arching off the wall. It was a worship I'd never known—this wild, wanton devouring. He was noisy, groaning, whispering against my skin, lapping at my nipples with such skill my head spun with the pleasure of it. We were still in my fucking foyer, and I was already boneless and ready to be taken. With a growl of appreciation, he scooped me up and walked us into my living room. Laid me down easily on the soft rug, then stood over my body.

"Spread your legs," he ordered, loosening his tie. I did, marveling at the way his wet shirt clung to his pectoral muscles. His pants were tented by an erection I remembered well. He looked fucking *huge* towering like this, a dirty superhero about to do filthy things to the woman he loved.

"Slide that hand between your legs and touch your clit," he said.

Very, *very* dirty.

"Isn't that your job?" I sassed back.

"Fucking do it," he commanded.

Sam Byrne started slowly unbuttoning that soaked white shirt, and my hands were moving of their own volition. Every button revealed golden skin, ridged abs that flexed as he watched me. He shrugged, and the shirt fell from his magnificent shoulders. My finger landed on my clit, rubbing once, and I was already half-gone.

"I used to wonder about you at night. In the dorm room across from mine at the academy," he said, staring between my legs as I rubbed myself. He dropped his pants. Dropped his underwear. Fisted his own cock in time with my fingers. He was *gorgeous.* Thickly muscled thighs, abs for days, and that huge, perfect cock. "Did you ever touch yourself and think of me?"

"Yes," I whispered. "Yes, I did."

"I did too," he admitted. "All the time."

Sam fell to the floor, face directly in front of my cunt. He reached forward and stilled my fingers, licking from my entrance, over my finger, teasing.

"Sugar," he groaned. "You smell like sugar and you *taste* like goddamn sugar." He slapped my hand away and pinned my knees to the floor, opening me. The lightning crackled outside, making our naked bodies glow. The first swipe of his tongue through my folds was like nothing I'd ever experienced before. The sound he made—a guttural grunt, deep in his throat—had my back arching off the rug.

"Freya," he whispered against my clit, "tell me what you like."

"What I...what I like?"

His mouth kissed along my inner thighs until they were shaking. *Kiss.* Bite. *Kiss.* Bite. Pleasure, pain. A deep inhale of my sex again. Glancing down between my legs, I could see his broad shoulders prying my legs open. The round, muscular globes of his perfect ass.

And his perfect face, staring at me.

"Tell me."

"I need to be filled," I said.

He slid one finger inside, hooked upward.

"Goddammit, *yes*," I sighed, head falling back momentarily.

"Look at me."

I snapped back up.

"More?" he asked.

I nodded. He added another finger. I bit my lip, telegraphed my need.

He added a third finger.

Sweet *fuck,* it felt good being filled like that. His slick digits moved easily as his tongue kept gliding up and down my inner thighs.

"Then what?"

"I don't know," I admitted. His fingers were moving seamlessly, igniting a fire. "No one's ever...I've never come this way."

Sam's eyes closed briefly. He dipped his head back down and pressed a wet kiss to my clit. My hips surged off the floor. "I'm going to make you come with my mouth," he said.

"What if I can't?"

He licked my clit in slow, even strokes like he was enjoying the tip of an ice cream cone. The bolt of pleasure made me actually *scream*.

His grin was dark and devious. "I don't think that will be a problem," he said. And then his mouth descended, and I was lost. It was true—I'd had plenty of boyfriends, and plenty of sex, but none of them had been able to make me come through oral sex. Until this moment I hadn't known why.

It was that they hadn't been Sam Byrne, who went for my clit like he went after everything—with precision and motivation to succeed. Who knew a tongue could *move like that*? Fast and slow...even, then rapid...in circles and up and down. Sweet, filthy—all while maintaining the perfect rhythm of his fingers. I reached down and grabbed his hair, riding his tongue, and that seemed to turn him on even more. I could see his hips, rocking against the floor, like he needed to seek his own release as he was making me come. His gaze locked on mine as his lips latched onto my clit and *sucked*.

"Oh," I gasped, surprised. "Oh...*oh, oh, yes, I think...*"

He sucked rhythmically, increasing the pressure, and finger-fucked me fast. Faster. I was yanking his hair out, head back, spine curved. His lips let go of my clit. His tongue flattened against it, swirling in rapid circles, and my orgasm burst forth like radiant light. I wailed, shook, screamed as euphoric sensation lit me up with a surge of pleasure. I crashed down hard, plummeting back to reality, arms and legs splayed on the floor as I panted.

And when I opened my eyes, it was Sam's face peering down at me with more vulnerability than I could handle. He brushed my hair from my eyes with his careful fingers. And his mouth met mine in a kiss made of sighs. His thumbs swiped across my cheekbones, body lowering onto mine. And it felt delicious—his bare skin on my bare skin, the glorious weight of his hips pressing between my spread legs, his hands cupping my face. We weren't moving, just frozen like that, drinking each other in. His back muscles flexed beneath my wandering fingers—so hard, like they'd been carved from stone. When they reached his ass, I gripped him hard and felt him thrust his cock over my still-sensitive clit in response.

"I retract my statement," I said, laughing a little as he kissed my neck. He slid against my clit again, and I bit my lip. So good already—how was that possible? "You're the best at everything, and I'm not even mad about it."

His teeth coasted along my jawline. "Don't doubt your ability to accomplish anything you set your mind to."

I hummed a little, delighted.

"Especially with my head between your legs," he growled, teeth nipping. He gave me a harder rock of cock-against-clit. "And you should know my new mission in life is to have my tongue on you whenever you demand."

"This takes arguing with you to a whole new level," I said, a little delirious from the thrusting. I was gripping his perfect ass hard, meeting every stroke. We weren't even fucking, but this tease was too damn amazing.

His groan vibrated against my ear. "Imagine our sparring sessions," he whispered. "I'd tap out every time. You'd only need to pin me to the floor and lower that delicious pussy onto my face."

"*Jesus*, Sam," I panted. "*Sam*." His hot mouth landed on my breasts, sucking one, then the other, fully into his mouth. "Then you admit I can take you to the floor?"

His reaction was to hoist my legs high on his waist and pin my wrists to the floor. My partner knew everything I wanted—always. His lips teased mine.

"I'd like to see you try, Evandale."

44

SAM

I'd said it on purpose.

Freya knew I'd said it on purpose. And instead of resisting the competitive sides of our nature, I felt a shift between the two of us. An opening. And a hard shove from the beautiful naked woman beneath me.

My back hit the rug, wrists wrenched overhead. Her smirk swam into view, cheeks flushed. I allowed myself an honest grin—which I'd spent years restraining whenever she was in my presence. But now, moments after experiencing the perfection of her cries of orgasm as my tongue licked her clit, how could I deny myself *anything*? I'd never deny myself unfettered joy ever, ever again.

"Are you trying to best me?" I teased.

Her eyebrow lifted. "I demand it."

"What?" I asked. I pushed against her hands, loosening her hold. Immediately gripped her slim hips.

"Your tongue."

I yanked her up and over my mouth instantly. Inhaled the scent of her climax, her wet heat. She stared down at me beneath a veil of golden hair, and my light, fluttering tongue had her seizing above me.

"I can just *ask* for this?" She sighed, head falling back.

I licked inside of her sex, knowing she needed the pressure. Tongue-fucked her slowly as she rolled her hips above me. Languorous. Enjoying something she hadn't known she could.

"I would *never* deny you this, Freya," I promised.

"I want your cock."

The words were barely out of her mouth before I'd flipped her again, onto her side. I dragged her right leg over my waist, curled my arm around her back, bringing us face to face. I was still compelled to take it slow, to fully earn her trust before the wild beast of my sexuality was unleashed on her.

She kissed me, hands on my face, moaning and begging as I teased at her entrance. "Please," she whispered. "Sam. *Please*."

I gripped her ass and fucked into her once—hitting deep. She bit my lip.

"You feel good," I grunted, thrusting again. She practically tore my hair out. "You like it like this?"

"Like what?" she whispered, another tease.

I pinned her back to the rug, her legs out wide, and gave her a series of short, brutal strokes that did nothing to satisfy my baser instincts. My hands held down her wrists, and she met me thrust for thrust, crying my name every time.

"*Harder*," she whimpered, and I just about lost my damn mind.

I slipped her leg over my shoulder, sliding deeper. Her freed hand came to my back, and she raked her fingernails down my spine.

"You always push, don't you?" I said.

Another shove, and I was flipped back—being ridden by Freya with glorious speed. Propped onto my elbows, I thrust my hips up in time to her actions, allowing her to sink deeper every time she moved.

"I always push because I love what it does to you," she gasped.

I sat up, yanking her hair back as she hissed. We were rocking together, legs around my waist, but the sounds we were making were far from romantic.

"And what does it do to me?" I growled, biting the curve of her shoulder.

"Snaps your control. Lets me see the real you."

My mouth was on hers a second later—needing to claim this woman who was my greatest challenger and my greatest vulnerability.

"And who is that?" I whispered against her lips. I held her strong against my chest and stood up, dropping her on the closest table. Fucked her hard as the table legs rattled. She lay back, displaying her gorgeous body as I held her knees and fucked her fast and deep. In between baiting me she was crying, wailing, begging. I bent close, bit her jaw.

"Who is that?" I asked again.

"Tongue," she panted, slapping her hands down. "Tongue, tongue, *I need your tongue, Sam.*"

I didn't need to be asked twice. I dropped to my knees and ate her pussy on her table, her legs pressed to my ears as her hips went wild beneath my mouth. Her climax was one long release of moaning and sighs. It was a beautiful privilege—but I was too greedy to stop at two. Before she'd even come down, I turned her around.

"Palms on the table," I whispered at her ear. She complied, and as I watched my cock slide back inside her wet sex—still clenching with ecstasy—I understood the depths of my love for this woman. This coupling was too intense not to mean every damn thing in the world to me. As I fucked Freya, I turned her face toward mine and kissed her breathless.

"Who is that?" I asked softly, one last time.

"You're the man I love," she replied. We were too overcome with sensation to do anything but kiss and gasp and fall headfirst into climax. My orgasm ripped up my spine, stole my breath, had me whispering her name over and over against her lips. Her final orgasm seemed to light up her face, and she was still shuddering as I held her back to my chest, arm wrapped around her breasts, face pressed to her hair.

"I love you," I whispered. "I love you. I love you."

Freya turned in my arms and wrapped herself around me. The smile that broke across her face felt like a thousand glittering stars in the sky—it was that brilliant.

And then she laughed. "Being in love. *Finally* something the two of us can agree upon."

45

SAM

I woke up in paradise.

I blinked one eye open, then the other. Two blankets covered my naked body where we'd fallen asleep, limbs entwined, on Freya's couch. On the side table, Minerva perched on a stack of paperbacks, whiskers twitching. I stroked her neck, and she purred. Behind her, books were jammed into every available nook and cranny, tumbling out of the built-in shelves. Green leaves scratched against the window as the summer sun peeked through the clouds.

"Good morning." It was Freya's sultry voice, extra-raspy from the early hour. She stood in the doorway, completely naked, holding two mugs of steaming tea. Her blond hair was snarled and wild, lips swollen, face a beam of fucking sunshine.

"Come here," I said, holding out the blankets. She giggled, deposited our mugs on the table, and curled up next to me.

Would I ever get used to the sensation of our bare skin pressed together? With one hand, I pushed the mess of her hair out of her delighted face. Kissed her mouth. Kissed her cheek. Kissed her neck until she giggled. She arranged herself on my lap, dragging the blanket tightly around us.

"Are you sore from our night of marathon sex, Agent Byrne?" she asked.

"Never." I smirked. But I was. In the best way possible. My body ached from the adrenaline, the tension, the fear. And it ached from the hours we'd spent bringing each other to orgasm again and again.

"Liar."

"A little," I admitted. She bit my ear and growled. Chuckling, I pulled her closer, smelling her hair. Taking in the new, beautiful details of *Freya Evandale in the morning*.

Keeping our bodies close, she sat back, found her glasses, and placed them primly on her face. "Now I can see you."

"How do I look?"

"Like an insufferable jackass."

I tickled my fingers along her ribcage. "You like my insufferable face."

"I *do* like it." Biting her lip, she clasped her mug and sipped her tea quietly. Studying me with a look I very much recognized. "I love you, Sam."

It was so matter-of-fact, as if the words weren't the most vital ones I'd ever heard in my life. All night, we'd gasped and panted those same three words to each other. But those moments were fraught and scorching-hot, and the words felt unabashedly simple.

This—this quiet, domestic morning—felt even more intense. Even more *real*.

"I love you, too," I said, surprised at how easily they spilled from my mouth.

"Happy to hear it." Her smile was shy. "When are you leaving to go back to Virginia?"

I rubbed a hand down my face, deflated by the reminder. I picked up my watch from the floor—I had an hour, max, before I needed to hit the road.

I looked at the bespectacled goddess watching me.

More like an hour to decide *if I was hitting the road.*

"Should I go?" I asked.

"That depends," she said. "Do you want to tell me the truth of what happened before you came to Codex?" Her fingers found mine. She squeezed tight.

"There isn't much to say."

"I doubt that very much."

"You're gonna push, aren't you?" I flashed her a wry smile.

"Wouldn't you?" she countered.

I stared at our entwined fingers. Noticed the corresponding sense of peace her touch evoked.

"About a month ago, I was called to the Deputy Director's office for an urgent meeting," I said. "When I arrived, it wasn't only my father, but several high-ranking agents from the Office of Professional Responsibility. They wanted to ask me questions about Gregory Lowell, who'd been my partner in the Art Theft department for three years." The shock of seeing OPR agents was like stumbling into freezing-cold water. Blistering sensation, followed by numbness, and then...

"There was an incident," I said. She held my hand even tighter. "I was the incident, actually. The OPR agents informed me they'd opened an investigation into Gregory's alleged misconduct. He was a veteran agent, had worked Art Theft for a decade, at least." I cleared my throat. "He, uh... well, Gregory had this side-hustle he'd play. If we were planning on a suspect's arrest, Gregory would sometimes tip off the suspect that we were on our way. We'd arrive, only to find that the suspect had fled. And Gregory would receive a payout from the suspect."

"How often did he do this?" she asked.

"That's what the investigation is currently looking into. We had a decent close rate, so he obviously didn't run this game every time. He spread it out, made it hard to detect a pattern."

I was quiet, struggling to beat back the memory of my father's white-hot fury.

"I'm guessing your father thought differently," she said gently.

"You know how he is," I muttered. "He thought I'd been too *distracted* and not doing my damn job. The OPR agents were opening an investigation into whether or not I was complicit in these crimes. I wasn't, of course. And my father did believe me. But he also believed it was my fault Gregory had gotten away with it."

"Not Gregory's fault?" Freya's mouth twisted with anger.

"We were partners," I explained. "Other agents would have spotted his transgressions immediately."

"That sounds like some Andrew Byrne bullshit right there." She slid even closer, brushing the hair from my forehead. "What did he expect you to do? Bug your partner's phone? Tail him on the weekends?"

"My father believes you should treat everyone in your life like a potential suspect." I grimaced. "And it felt like a betrayal. It felt like—Jesus, it felt like every damn thing I'd ever worked for had been for nothing. My own partner didn't even believe in the values of the Bureau. Didn't believe in honor, in justice, didn't see our roles as crucial to upholding law and order. Who knows how many criminals slipped through my fingers because my own fucking partner was scheming behind my back?"

She didn't respond. Just kept stroking my hair. Finally, she asked, "What was the incident, Sam?"

"We were sitting at the table in my father's office," I said. "They told me about Gregory. Told me I was also being investigated. I stood up, kicked my chair away. Knocked over..." I swallowed. "I knocked over all these mugs of coffee, ruining the files I'd brought with me. Ruining *their* files. I couldn't breathe. I left, ran back to my own office. Everyone was *staring*. Meanwhile I thought I was going to pass out. Thought the walls were going to slam together and kill me. I kept throwing papers around, shoving things off my desk. I broke my computer, cracked a window. I still don't know why."

She pressed my hand between hers. Brought her lips down, kissed my fingers. "I think you had a panic attack."

"I think I did too," I replied after a beat. "My father followed me, demanded I take time to *fix myself*. Said he'd figure out a place to hide me during the investigation. Didn't want, well, he didn't want me to bring more shame to our family. Wanted me out of the FBI's spotlight."

"He called Abe?" she asked. I nodded. Understanding flooded her features. But she was still searching my gaze, searching for the deeper truths hidden behind Gregory's scandal.

"Before this panic attack," Freya started, "do you think you had others?"

I held her gaze. "Yes."

"At work?"

My jaw clenched. "Yes."

"How many hours a week do you think you were working?" she asked. Her fingers continued to soothe my body.

"About seventy," I said. "I never had a weekend off. I slept maybe…four hours a night? If I was lucky?"

"And how did you feel when you were there? When you worked cases?" she asked.

"Exhausted. Confused. I was anxious from the moment I got to work until I fell into bed at night."

Her eyes shone with unshed tears, but she kept her composure. "That's how I felt. Back at Quantico." She tipped forward, brushing our lips together in a sweet kiss. "I can't believe you've felt that way for years."

My throat was so tight I could barely swallow. "Not all the years. But…most of the years," I admitted. "Those kinds of feelings are pretty normalized at the Bureau."

"I know they are," she said. "Doesn't mean you have to work a job that makes you feel that way. Sounds a lot like burnout to me."

I flipped over her hand, traced my fingers inside her wrist. "I used to think I'd feel energized being an agent. Used to think the stress and anxiety were the same as flashing my FBI badge. Something to be proud of. Because it meant you worked hard, had a hard job worth doing. But I—"

I rubbed the back of my neck, suddenly embarrassed. "I felt happy working this case for Codex. And we still did the right thing. Caught the bad guy."

"Only broke a handful of laws." She smirked.

I grinned. "I wasn't aware it could feel this way. Fulfilled but not crouched beneath my desk panicking. Nothing was ever *done* at Art Theft. No tasks *ever* accomplished. Every case I closed only freed up my time to tackle the foot-high stack that sat on my desk, taunting me. I'm not sure the system is set up for you to feel healthy."

"Interestingly," Freya said, "I feel a little sad about your dad."

"Plot twist," I said.

"He *believes* in what you're saying. Believes in subverting happiness in pursuit of duty or honor, even if it affects your relationship with your son. I imagine it's tough being Andrew Byrne." She paused. "I still think he's a dick though."

I laughed softly. "I've laughed more with you in the past seventy-two hours than I have the past seven years."

"Laughter is the most important thing in this world," she said. "I'm sorry it's not been a part of your life."

"Fun hasn't been a priority," I explained.

"I can remedy that," she said. "And for what it's worth, you deserve a job that fulfills you without draining you dry."

"Like being a private detective?" I asked. The words opened my throat, loosened my chest.

Freya's lips parted, as if surprised. "You know my thoughts on this, Sam."

"We had fun, didn't we?" I asked. "Once we worked together?"

She sat back, sipped her tea. Chewed on her bottom lip. "We had the most fun. And I know how *I* feel about Codex. About the job we just did. But I don't want to muddy your thinking."

"Tell me why you chose it," I urged.

More lip-chewing. "Finding Codex felt like finding a second home. A second family. It's not like we don't work long hours or have high stress levels. But it's not as heavy, with much less pressure. And Abe is cautious of burnout and seeks to protect his staff at all costs. I don't think you find that with many supervisors at the FBI." Here, her pretty cheeks flushed. "*Once* you and I started working together, being partners again felt like..."

I waited her out. Waited until she said, "Being your partner made me feel like I could do anything. Like I'm good at my job. Like dropping out didn't mean I was a failure. Last night, beating Ward like that..." She murmured it under her breath like she couldn't believe it. "I knew. Knew you had my back. Knew I could best any thief in that room. Knew I was *exactly* where I was supposed to be."

I reached forward and dragged my ex-enemy—blankets and all—back into my lap.

"Being your partner is an honor, Evandale," I whispered against her mouth. "You've never been a failure a single day in your life."

She kissed my cheek. "There you go, being a superhero again."

"And you take my breath away."

That stilled her, had her staring at me for a long time.

"Sam?"

"Yeah?"

"I want you to know, regardless of what happens today, you shouldn't have to suffer to earn your father's love. Or his respect. From what you've told me of your mom, she really embraced life, didn't she?"

I nodded, unable to speak.

"I'm sorry your father took that from you," she said.

I rubbed a strand of her golden hair between my fingers, remembering all those arguments we used to have about my dad. How confused I'd feel, having to defend a man who infuriated me all the damn time. Who withheld his love, his affection, and his respect out of a distorted sense of honor and duty. The Bureau above all else.

Even your only child.

"My mother encouraged me to chase whatever happiness I discovered. To treasure the joy, no matter how small. She believed in changing your mind, starting over, trying new things. She was never rigid, always flexible. Losing her was the worst thing that's ever happened to me," I said.

"Your mother would be overjoyed to know we're having this conversation right now," Freya whispered, kissing my cheek. "I imagine she'd be cheering for you to blow up your life. Start fresh."

"Yeah," I agreed. "Yeah, she would." I tucked that knowledge away for safekeeping. A knowledge that couldn't be taken from me, that would be cherished. "When did you get so smart?"

"Oh, so you're admitting I'm *smarter* than you now, Byrne?"

"Yes. Or at least smart enough to listen to me when we're working an undercover case." I tickled her again as she shrieked with glorious laughter. But then she executed a complicated move, sending me flying off the couch and onto the floor. She landed on top of me with a happy *oof* and immediately pinned my wrists down.

"Who's the smart one now?" she teased. We were breathing heavily, for several reasons, and I mentally calculated how much time we had before we hit the road.

"How fast can you get ready?" I asked, skating my palms along her thighs.

"Five minutes, tops," she murmured. "I just need a sweater and my yoga pants."

"Good," I said. "You're coming with me."

"Where?"

"To Quantico, of course."

"And what will we be doing there?" she gasped. "Don't tell me we're finally gonna fuck in the library."

I sat up, bringing our mouths close together. The magnificent grin on her face was all the confidence I'd ever need.

"That can be arranged," I said. "But first, I'll need your help quitting the FBI."

Her mouth formed a surprised *O*. She tapped her chin. "Hmmm. If you quit the FBI, where on earth would you work?"

I closed the distance between our mouths, kissed her for a sweet, breathtaking moment. "I heard Codex is hiring."

My irritating, beautiful, genius rival tackled me to the floor in a bear hug.

46

SAM

At 10:59 a.m., I lowered myself into a chair in front of my father's desk at the FBI's Quantico offices in Virginia. The Deputy Director had cleared the room, shut the door—and now looked at me with a professionally neutral expression. With a casual air, he flipped the file on his desk open with one finger, scanned it. Nodded.

"The OPR's initial investigation into your role as Gregory's partner has come back favorably," he began. "They found not a shred of evidence of fraudulent activity. Gregory, however, was arrested on criminal charges late last night."

"Pleased to hear it," I said. With Freya's guidance, I'd driven down here wearing my ragged Princeton sweatshirt and sweatpants, feeling nothing but liberation from years of stuffy, ill-fitting suits. But his shrewd eye had scanned my wardrobe and clearly found me lacking.

"Are you sick?" he asked.

"No, sir," I replied. "Just wanted to be comfortable."

His eyes narrowed, but he left it unaddressed. "Given your successful role in the infiltration of this Empty House secret society, the Bureau is excited to welcome you back into the Art Theft division. I have assured them that your *outburst* was due to your shock at hearing the news of Gregory's actions. And that you've gotten your stress levels under control."

"All due respect, sir, but what I was feeling isn't something you can—"

"You'll begin with a brand-new partner," he spoke over me. "His name is Patrick, and he brings five years of experience working in white-collar crime. He's eager and looking forward to working with you. Your staff, additionally, informed me of their eagerness for you to return."

"I find that hard to believe," I said. "I barely know them."

"You're in charge. They don't need to know you."

I looked out his wide office window. The last time I'd sat in this office, I'd been overwrought, stress levels a mess, my body experiencing a combination of fear and shame. Funny that when he'd mentioned working for Codex, I had no idea that it would bring Freya and me back together. How insignificant, those words—*Abraham has offered to allow you to work for Codex until all of this blows over.* I'd nodded, accepted the terms of my punishment, and didn't think twice. I certainly didn't think it would reconnect me with the woman I loved.

"I won't be returning to the FBI," I said.

Interestingly, my body responded to these controversial words with nothing but calm, layered with happiness. I actually smiled at my father.

"You're not needed at Codex anymore," he continued. "Abe will finish the paperwork on his end. And you have much to do here concerning Bernard Allerton. You *are* returning. Today, in fact."

“I’m resigning from the FBI,” I said. More plainly this time. “So no, I won’t be returning.”

“That’s preposterous,” he barked.

I shrugged. “I’m not lying or exaggerating. I’ve already started the resignation process with human resources.”

For the first time in all the years I’d known him, my father was speechless.

“Thank you for everything,” I continued. “And thank you for ensuring the OPR investigation went smoothly. I’ll be moving to Philadelphia. You can visit whenever you’d like.”

“Doing what?” His tone was sharp.

“I’ll be joining Abe Royal’s team at Codex. As a private investigator.”

Freya and I had called Abe on the drive down. His voice on the phone was smooth—but pleased—when he said, *Why, Samuel, I was thinking it was time we added another member to our crime-fighting family.*

“You’ve been placed with a new partner,” my father countered.

I thought about the bespectacled goddess sitting outside these doors—probably chewing on a pen while reading a book.

“I have a partner, actually,” I said. “We worked together on The Empty House case. We’ve got good chemistry.”

“Who?” he asked.

I made my way to the door. I cracked it open six inches and spied Freya doing exactly what I imagined. My ex-enemy sat cross-legged on a chair, wearing a giant blue sweater with a halo of pens sticking out of her messy bun. When she felt me watching her, she caught my eye. Beamed a big, carefree grin my way. Flashed me the thumbs-up.

My father must have caught my expression because he looked for himself.

"Ah," he said shortly. "Ms. Evandale."

"You were right about her," I said. "She is the most talented field agent I've ever seen."

He cleared his throat, tightened his cufflink. "Serving this institution is in your blood, Samuel," he said quietly. "I envisioned you rising through the ranks here. One day being a director yourself. It would make me happy to see that."

He was still avoiding my gaze—but his body language indicated how uncomfortable he was.

"I understand what your intentions have always been," I said. "But you saw me the day you broke the news about Gregory. That's how I feel every day here. I don't want to feel like that. I want to feel good about my job. About my life."

For a moment, his expression softened. "You think working with Abraham will achieve that?"

"Yes, I do," I said. "Nothing is a guarantee. But I have to at least try."

He cast his gaze downward as if he was studying the most interesting thing on the floor. "Samuel," he said. "It would make me more than happy to see you stay here at the FBI. It would make me...proud. I *am* proud. I'm proud of you."

It was the most vulnerable display of emotion he'd ever shown me.

He hadn't cried when my mother passed away. He'd remained stoic and vigilant even at her funeral. But I'd never told him that I'd caught him that night, after her funeral, after the hundreds of weeping guests had finally left. I'd come down late at night, in need of a glass of water, and I could just make out his silhouette in our pantry. Crying quietly, as if worried he'd wake me.

I'd never mentioned it. And we'd never spoken of anything so fragile, or real, as the loss we'd gone through together. But even as he said the words I'd ached to hear my entire career—*I'm proud of you*—suddenly, they were no longer enough.

Working at Codex meant I'd be proud of myself. It was a crucial difference.

"Thanks, Dad," I said. The non-formal name startled him. "I'm proud of you too. And I'm proud of myself, whatever career path I choose. But this is no longer the right place for me. Besides, Abe will still work with the FBI whenever Codex needs the help. I'll be here in spirit."

My father ran a hand through his hair—a gesture I'd never seen before.

I hugged him. Just for two seconds. It was extremely awkward. We disengaged like two work acquaintances.

"Are you, um..." He coughed a little. "Are you and Ms. Evandale...more than work partners?"

Freya was walking toward us, book tucked beneath her arm. Seeing her like this, in FBI offices, was stirring waves of nostalgia. Of course, she used to wait outside the library to study with me every night. Of course, she'd bring me cookies when she saw I was sad. Of course, she'd wait patiently while I shattered my life—and started a new one.

She had always been there, waiting for me.

"We are," I said.

He slipped his hands into his pockets, gave a curt nod. "Your mother and I used to bicker constantly."

Now it was my turn to be startled.

"It's important to have a partner who challenges you," he said. "I'm sure that's what Ms. Evandale does."

"She is smarter than me," I said.

"What's this about me being smarter than you?" Freya said brightly, coming to join us. She shoved her glasses up her nose and gave my father a firm handshake.

"It's nice to see you in person again, Ms. Evandale," he said.

"Nice to see you, Mr. Byrne," she said. "Did Sam extend an invitation to visit the Codex team in Philadelphia?"

"He did," he replied. "I've always found the city of Philadelphia to be adequate to my liking."

"That's high praise," she said. "Adequate or not, you're always welcome."

My father checked his watch, frowning. "Yes, well, I'm late for my next meeting. I trust human resources will be in touch to finalize your plans."

"Yes, sir," I promised. With a slightly awkward pat on both my and Freya's shoulders, he closed the door to his office.

She spun on her heels. She mouthed *what happened?*

"I think my dad's going to miss me," I guessed. I looped an arm around her shoulders, turning her toward the exit. Catching the stares of every stressed-looking staff member of the office of the Deputy Director.

This time? I didn't care one bit.

47

FREYA

For the first time in seven years, I was back on the grounds of Quantico's Training Academy. The campus was directly next to the FBI field offices that housed the Deputy Director, Art Theft, and other divisions. While I'd left this place and joined a team of butt-kicking private detectives, Sam had stayed here. Stayed here and suffered, to hear him tell it.

We walked together across the large, green field, the sun setting his blond hair alight. The thought of Sam Byrne with anxiety and panic attacks, burnout and exhaustion, made me want to punch everyone here in the face. But he'd changed course—was changing his mind—and the two of us were about to become—

"Partners," he said, reading my thoughts as usual. I hooked our pinkies together, reveling in the new freedom of our intimacy. "I told my dad we were partners."

"What kind?" I asked. Even in gym clothes, he was broad-shouldered and brave-looking. There was *even* a hint of stubble on that strong jaw.

"I told him you and I would be partners at Codex. And that we were romantic partners."

I stopped, yanking him to a halt. "Samuel Byrne."

He was trying not to smile. "Freya Evandale."

"Are you my boyfriend?"

"Do you want me to be?"

"I don't know," I shrugged—even though my heart was racing. "What's in it for me?"

"Constant arguing."

I hummed a little. "Go on."

"Wild sex."

I arched a brow. "*Do* go on."

He leaned down until his lips were at my ear. "Love letters."

My toes curled.

"With or without encoded, raunchy messages?"

"With, of course. What am I, an amateur?"

I giggled—too breathtakingly happy to do otherwise. "Then...yes. We are partners. Of a romantic sort. Which is good to hear, since I'm still in love with you."

"Hasn't changed since this morning?"

"Nope," I said cheerfully.

He kissed my temple. "I love you too," he whispered.

We walked in contented silence for a moment.

"You know, Abe is going to lose his fucking mind when he finds out," I mused. "But if Henry and Delilah can be engaged, he'll have to deal with us too."

We were nearing the track—the site of unending physical battles between us. Just the sight of it sent a strange, nostalgic thrill along my spine.

"When we get back, I'm going to talk to Abe," I said. "Talk to him about keeping me out in the field as long as it doesn't interfere with my computer nerd duties."

"Back undercover?" Sam asked.

"I'm here to admit, with full confidence, that I'm fucking amazing as an undercover agent." God, it felt good to say that. To *feel* that. I waved a hand behind me, toward the building that had served as a source of so much displeasure for us both. "Not becoming an agent was painful. But allowing that to shape my own sense of my abilities was even worse. It's okay to let it go now."

I placed my palm directly over his heart, imagined I could feel it beating. He placed his hand over my own, entwining our fingers. Entwining our lives.

"What did you say to your dad?" I asked. When he'd emerged from that office, he'd looked light. Unshackled.

"He finally said that he was proud of me," he said. My fingers tightened over his heart. "But I still told him it was time for me to leave. Right for me to leave. I think one of the reasons he likes having me work in Art Theft is because he can't miss me. He can see me every day."

Sam's eyes were soft, but his resolve seemed strong. "But that doesn't mean I have to be an agent. I *want* to try something new. And he'll have to accept that."

"I'm proud of you too," I said, kissing his cheek. "Your mom would *definitely* be proud of you, Sam."

His answering smile was radiant with hope. "She would."

"We really are better together," I said. "Undercover. And in love."

He pressed his lips together. "When we go back to Codex, will we have to admit that Abe was right all along?"

"*Never*," I promised. He cracked a half grin, and my toes curled *again*.

"Is that Sam and Freya I see?"

We both turned to find one of our former physical

training instructors, whistle around his neck and ever-present clipboard at his side.

"Instructor McAvoy," Sam beamed, extending a hand. "What are you doing out here?"

"I think the better question is, what are you?" The man was still healthy and hale though I knew he was nearing his seventies. "We've got the next class coming through next week. Just getting the field set up."

Instructor McAvoy shook my hand as well. "It's lovely to see you both."

"Lovely to be seen," I said. "We're visiting the campus. Sam and I are heading back to Philadelphia soon. We're private investigators there."

"Ah," he said. "That's where you ended up."

Sam nodded while squeezing my hand. McAvoy caught the gesture. Chuckled as he began to walk back toward the field course. "There was a bet going on about you two. I'll have to tell everyone that I won."

I bit my lip, tucking a strand of hair behind my ear. "Did *everyone* think we would end up banging?" I hissed beneath my breath.

Sam called back out to our instructor. "Do you mind counting us down?"

"What?" I said. Just as McAvoy said, "Uh, what?"

"Come on," Sam said. "Let's race."

"No way," I said.

"Are you...scared?"

I tossed my bag and paperback on the ground. Rolled out my neck. "Okay, let's fucking do this, Byrne."

McAvoy was bemused. "Why do I need to count you down?"

"Because she'll cheat," Sam called back.

I crouched into a runner's stance, fingertips grazing the red track. "Such an arrogant ass."

"Last night, you liked my ass."

"Last night, you liked *my* ass."

"*On your marks,*" McAvoy called out.

Sam crouched next to me, face sly. Body loose. "You're not afraid to lose, are you? I mean, it wouldn't be the first time on this track."

I was starting to laugh—could feel it bubbling up in my chest. "Nope."

"Get set."

"You ready?" he taunted.

"Oh, I'm always ready to kick your—"

"*Go.*"

The whistle blew—and my body flew forward with muscle memory, ingrained from hours spent racing Sam in this exact same lane. McAvoy was already leaving us to our antics, which was fine. I only had eyes for the broad back *barely* in front of me.

"Not much of a runner anymore, Evandale?" Sam huffed over his shoulder.

I pushed harder, caught up to him.

"Too busy hunting down...book thieves...I guess..." I panted.

He was trying not to laugh. *I* was trying not to laugh. And as we rounded the first bend, Sam Byrne swooped in to grab me around the waist.

And we both tumbled to the grass.

"I need to file a complaint," I gasped. "*You're* the cheater."

He pinned me to the earth easily, muscular body landing gently on mine. I hooked my legs over his waist immediately, loving this new position of ours. His chest was heaving, blue eyes bright with mirth. Then he was crashing our lips together in a kiss that spun my world. My mouth opened for his, tasting him, feeling the scrape of his stubble across my skin.

"Too bad," he murmured. "You're the one who stole my heart."

I giggled, kissed his cheek noisily.

He blushed furiously. "Was that too cheesy? I'm new to flirting."

"It was perfect. Never stop flirting with me." When I licked my tongue back into his mouth, I tried my hardest to ease his worries. It would never be too much, this man that challenged me. Always. Pushed me, always. My former nemesis. My *new* partner.

My new everything.

"Some archnemesis you turned out to be," I said. "Being your partner is a privilege, Sam."

"How so?" he asked.

"Because you're the best agent I know. And the man I trust to always protect me."

Another kiss—firm lips, mouth moving, a sultry heat building between our bodies.

"Falling in love with my rival actually made my life better," he replied. "I wish I'd known that seven years ago."

"Another thing we agree on," I teased. "Now what do you say about finding that soundproof room in the library?"

EPILOGUE

Freya

One week later

Delilah and I walked into Abe's office for our weekly staff meeting—and both almost fell down.

"Are you sick?" Delilah asked him, red lips pursed.

"Have you been replaced by your evil twin, who's actually the *nice* boss?" I said, hand on my chest.

Abe, to his credit, gave a slow clap in appreciation. "You slay me. Now sit and eat all of this damn food I got you for being incredible." He indicated his desk, on which donuts *and* tacos were fanned out in a semi-circle. Donut, taco, donut, taco.

"I've never seen anything this beautiful in my life," I declared.

Behind me, Sam and Henry ambled in—both cheering

in surprise at the bounty in front of us. I heaped a plate filled with my favorite foods and sat next to Sam on the sofa. Ever since he officially joined the Codex team, we'd kept our hands to ourselves, and our bickering to a friendly minimum.

At night, Byrne and I were wild for each other, unfettered in our passion and craving. His knee brushed against mine, and the slight contact rocketed me back to the evening before. When I'd been naked and spread-eagle on my bed, served up for Sam to enjoy me like a decadent, three-course meal. Every orgasm earned me his husky voice at my ear. *"You're not tapping out on me, are you, Evandale?"*

I didn't. Not for hours.

"Why are we being celebrated for being incredible?" Delilah asked. "Or are we just generally amazing?"

"While you are, indeed, amazing," Abe said, "this is to celebrate the close of two extremely high-profile and lucrative cases." He sat behind his desk, hands clasped loosely in front of him. "We just received a call from Louisa, Henry's former boss, thanking us for recovering the missing *Tamerlane*. Which Interpol had failed to do."

Henry and Delilah exchanged a look of pure love.

"I'm extremely happy to hear it," Henry said. "And extremely happy it'll return to its rightful home at the McMaster's Library."

"As am I," Abe said. He pinned Sam and me with a proud look. "Thanks to a little pressure from Francisco, we'll be receiving full payment for recovering the Sand letters, even though we made a mess of things." A pause. "A mess of things in a good way."

"Sam and Freya—messing things up in a good way since freshman year," I teased, giving my coworkers an exaggerated wink.

Sam, however, surprised me by kissing my cheek. "Nice work, partner."

"You too," I grinned.

"I'll remind all of the couples currently in my office about my PDA policy," Abe said.

All four of us hid smiles.

"Any news on the forged letters the other private detective firm recovered?" Henry asked.

Abe flipped open a file on his desk. "Yes, actually. The FBI is working to find out who is responsible for that forgery, since it fooled everyone. Jim Dahl had been an intern for Francisco for six months before the theft. My theory is he had a forger he worked with on the side to pull it off. Stole the letters twice. Was paid twice."

"Smart," Delilah said, shaking her head. "The thieves are getting smarter. The forgeries are getting better."

The events at The Grand Dame that night had been big news—an elegant auction for wealthy criminals featuring a shoot-out and broken up by federal agents. Rare antiques being sold in the basement of a beloved hotel to undercover private detectives. The tiger had been rescued and was being returned to the big cat sanctuary it had been stolen from. The Gutenberg Bible, the *Tamerlane,* and all of the other antiques were similarly returned. In the back of that basement, authorities had discovered stacks of authentication papers for each item—also all forged. The FBI was beginning to unravel the intricate web of secrecy involved in this underground auction that involved art lovers and white-collar criminals alike.

It'd been a *hot* story, and Codex had received a slew of new cases in the past seven days because of it. We were lucky Sam was already studying to receive his private investigator's license—we were going to need his help as Codex grew.

"I spoke to my father yesterday," Sam said. "The FBI formally arrested Roy Edwards, Dr. Bradley Ward, and the Alexanders. As well as many others there that night. Roy's father hired one of the best criminal defense attorneys in the country. As did Ward and the Alexanders. We're not sure what type of trial or punishment they'll receive yet."

Abe nodded. "Par for the course for that crowd. If any of them serve real time, I'll be surprised."

"Ward did lose his position at the university. Made quite a splash," Sam said. "He claims, of course, that he is innocent of all charges."

"I'm sure *Thomas* thinks the arrest is all part of his curse," I said. "Some kind of punishment by the universe for stealing Ward's book."

Henry nodded. "Rare book librarians are generally an academic lot. But I will say, I've known many in my years who believed their departments were cursed by books or antiques."

I tapped my glasses. "Interesting. Maybe Thomas was right?"

"Curse or not," Sam jumped in, "The Empty House is a crumbling secret society. Bernard had Thomas and Cora steal *Don Quixote* from Ward and orchestrate the theft of the Sand letters. I'm sure Jim Dahl was their criminal contact for both thefts."

"Dahl remains missing," Abe added. "Or whoever he is, since we can assume that's an alias."

"That makes him a talented thief to be on the loose though," I mused.

"Indeed," he replied. "And Julian and Birdie never had the flu. I think they'd conned too many people. They've probably moved on with other identities and are opening a rare bookstore in another city as we speak. They backed out of attending the festival because they feared their misdeeds would come to light."

"Their accounts have all been deleted," I said. "Nothing on Under the Rose. No social media. Website and business pages closed. They fucked everyone over. Made money. Moved on." I paused. "I don't like having Dahl, Julian, and Birdie all unaccounted for."

Abe rubbed his jaw. "Neither do I. It's unsettling, to say the least."

"And then there's Roy's blackmail threat," Sam said. "He was a destabilizing factor from the beginning, turning against people and abusing their loyalty. Except Bernard Allerton doesn't seem to care at all about true loyalty either."

"Bernard demands loyalty *to* him," Abe said. "Loyalty to his criminal empire and the many ways in which he steals and sells rare books. But yes, if he's taking manuscripts from his own followers and carelessly burning bridges, he must be *extremely confident* that he's protected and safe. Especially since all four members of The Empty House could give up information on his whereabouts in exchange for a deal."

"He's extremely confident and extremely greedy," Henry said somberly. "Bernard plays the game, and he plays it well. But at the end of the day, he's a man consumed by his lust for power."

The frustration felt by both Henry and Abe was obvious. How much control did Bernard *truly* have? Based on the way The Empty House members spoke of him, they revered him as a morally bankrupt god—the man who led them to their darkest desires, who brought them power in exchange for their wealth. Bernard Allerton was comprised entirely of secrets.

Good thing Codex was quite adept at uncovering things that didn't want to be discovered.

"Well," Abe said, "this is all talk for another day. And Sam can keep us in the loop if the FBI uncovers anything else regarding Dahl, Julian, or Birdie. Until then, we've got cases coming, books to recover, and a new employee to get trained."

I raised my hand. "I volunteer to train Byrne."

"Wish granted," Abe said.

Next to me, Sam grumbled into a taco.

"You're welcome already," I said.

"We'll discuss this later tonight," he growled.

"Byrne never has taken nicely to my telling him what to do." I beamed.

"All joking aside," Abe said, "we are happy to have you onboard, Samuel. You and Freya make a marvelous pairing. Both professionally and...personally."

Sam and I shared a shy look that sent heat to my cheeks.

"I'm happy to have her as my partner," Sam said. "I do believe the two of us can accomplish anything we put our minds to."

I was in a full-on blush attack. Delilah and Henry were shooting me the cheekiest grins.

And even Abe looked *slightly* amused. "That's odd," he remarked casually. "It's almost as if I taught both of you at Quantico, knew your strengths and talents, and guessed that together you were an unstoppable force that would bring honor and prestige to my private detective firm." He shrugged, tossed a piece of donut into his mouth. "But what are you going to do?"

"Don't say it," Sam whispered next to me.

"How can I not?" I whispered back.

Abe merely waited with a passive expression.

"Okay, you were right about me and Sam," I blurted out.

Delilah snorted into her coffee.

"Thank you," he said. "I know how it pains you *both* to admit when you're wrong."

I looked over at Sam—couldn't believe that two weeks earlier, we were glaring at each other as Abe forced us to work the George Sand case.

"And while we're going around taking credit," Delilah said, "I'd also like to add a hearty *told you so*."

"Well..." I sighed. "I can't stay mad at *you*. You're too flawless, babe."

"Thank you," she winked. "Welcome to the chaos, Sam. We're happy to have you. Both personally and professionally."

"You got the damn book back," Henry added. "And on your first try. It's not easy, what we do here. But I think this team is the best one yet."

Sam shifted an inch until we were leaning against one another. My heart recognized the man next to me as the one I loved more than anything. More than tea and cookies and even books.

"Now go get to training," Abe said with mock sternness.

Sam and I pulled the door closed to Abe's office and stood in the large room.

"How about we—" I started.

But he swooped in and kissed me.

"Sorry," he murmured against my lips.

"I told you," I teased. "You don't have to apologize every time you kiss me."

He kissed me again—with more fervor than was *techni-*

cally professional. I gasped against his mouth, smiling as we parted.

"I love you, Byrne."

"I love you, Evandale."

His mischievous gaze found our sparring corner, with the long mat and punching bag.

"Are you trying to spar with me?" I asked.

"I have to start somewhere, don't I? I'm game if you are." That crooked, superhero smile was going to get me in a *lot* of trouble.

We both stepped forward. Shook each other's hands—no longer bickering trainees, vying for the top spot. But partners, vying for each other's trust. Astonished at the depths of our love.

I pulled him close. "May the best woman win."

THE END

BONUS EPILOGUE

Sam

One year later

It had been a week since I'd written my last love letter to Freya Evandale.

I found her working late at the Codex offices—of course. Abe had truly been right—together, the two of us were an unstoppable pair. Partnering with her undercover felt as simple as breathing, and just as vital.

That crushing feeling of dread I'd carried with me disappeared the moment Freya returned my kiss in that bathroom. And spending each workday catching thieves with my beautifully charming soulmate made those years of grueling struggle worth it. Because they had led me right back to her.

"Knock knock," I said, rapping my knuckles on her office door. Freya looked up from the couch and flashed me that grin—the one that never ceased to feel like the rays of the summer sun.

"If my boyfriend's here at work, who's watching our cat?"

Her bun had seven highlighters sticking out of it. A new record.

"Minerva is just fine," I promised. "Purring and spying on the neighbors out the window."

"A natural detective just like her parents," she replied. She crooked her finger at me, and I was helpless to resist, as usual. I sank onto the couch, pushing off the stacks of papers and pens. Then I dragged my former-rival onto my lap and buried my nose in her golden hair.

"Why aren't you home with me?" I asked. One month after joining Codex, I'd moved my meager possessions into Freya's colorful, paperback-filled rowhome. The only change I'd made was the punching bags and mats I installed for our sparring sessions.

Which always turned hot—and dirty—within minutes. *Wild sex* had been one of the things I'd promised her. And although a year had passed, our sex hadn't ceased in its wildness or passion. Neither had our good-natured bickering...which naturally led to our sparring mat...which naturally led right back to our bed. Or the shower. Or the kitchen counter.

"Because we need to crack this case, and my superhero boyfriend is much too tempting at home," she said. "Can't a girl concentrate on her case without her sweatpants-wearing nemesis walking around shirtless?"

"How descriptive," I said, kissing her neck. She squirmed, giggled. Sighed.

"Speaking of, did you enjoy my letter?" she asked. Freya and I hadn't let up on our final promise—that our relationship would be filled with love letters. Although she favored hot pink sticky notes with short messages that were as filthy as they were sweet. This morning I'd found one taped to the bottom of my coffee mug.

Thank you for always making me feel protected, she'd scribbled. *And thank you for waking me up with oral sex this morning.*

The feel of Freya on my lap—and the memory of my head between her legs beneath our bedsheets—had me quickly hardening. Which she quickly noticed.

"Ah," she whispered, rocking a little. "So you did enjoy it."

My palms skated up her thighs, slipping beneath her shirt to splay across her hips. "Making you feel protected is my religion, Evandale. As is making you come."

Her emerald eyes sparkled with mischief. "*Thus* why I had to come here to finish working, Byrne." But she was rocking against me more deliberately now.

"I didn't give you my letter yet." I pinched her chin, keeping her green eyes on mine. "Do you want it?"

"Please."

With a half smile, I slipped it from my pocket. While she used sticky notes, I preferred classic notebook paper. I tried often to use code words in my letters—but found blunt honesty was all I could manage. After years of subverting my feelings for this woman, the dam had broken. Only the truth spilled out.

"*Dear Freya,*" she read. "*This morning I watched you sip your tea at our little kitchen table by the sunny window. In the light, your hair shone brighter and your face was even more beautiful backlit by the sun. You were reading a book, gazing down at the pages like they held the secrets of the universe. Which is why I'm reminded to tell you, in this letter, that* you *are my entire universe. Love, Sam.*"

Her eyes were shining by the end of it, which happened every time she finished reading one of my letters. She placed the note carefully on the table behind her. Then she wrapped her arms around my neck. "The day I walked into this office and saw you sitting in my favorite chair was the best day of my life. You're my entire universe too, Sam." Then she kissed me.

Opening our lips wider, our tongues slid together, seeking a kiss that was deep, soulful. Real. After a long time, she pulled back. Swept the hair from my forehead with tender fingers. Gazed at me with open, ardent affection.

Watching Freya Evandale regain her confidence this past year had been exhilarating. My undercover partner—and gorgeous girlfriend—was a force to be reckoned with. Her genius hadn't dimmed eight years ago, it'd just been muted. She kicked ass every day, ate tacos with Delilah and Henry, joked around with Abe, caught criminals with me. She did it all with her good humor and silly laughter.

And she was mine. All mine.

"You know what I was doing right before you came in, Byrne?" she asked, stripping her shirt from her head. She was bare-breasted on my lap. Perfect. I pressed my lips to the hollow of her collarbone.

"What?" I asked, voice gravelly.

"Admiring your instincts on this case we're working on right now." She tilted her neck so I could put my teeth there. Moaned. "Turns out, I think you were right about which suspect we should be tailing."

I moved, pushing her down onto the couch. She arched her brow, arched her back—always the temptress. Always supportive. With her by my side, my career change had been fucking *effortless*. Fun and adventurous. Without the stress of being a special agent—and free from the burden of being Andrew Byrne's son—I could remember why I'd wanted to spend my life dedicated to justice. I could remember why the values of the FBI had resonated with me so strongly. At

Codex, our team was small but we trusted each other. Took care of one another. For the first time in my life, I'd found my real family.

The writhing goddess in front of me was the sole reason why.

"Is that so?" I asked, enjoying our natural competitiveness. "Because I swore you told me last week I was *absolutely, one hundred percent wrong* about everything."

She tapped her lip. "Was that me? Or the other hot blonde in our office?"

I chuckled. Then yanked her pants off, followed quickly by her underwear. "Do you think what we're about to do violates Abe's PDA policy?"

She eyed my very obvious erection. "Depends on what we're about to do, Agent Byrne."

With a smirk, I shed my clothes, needing to be skin to skin with the woman who would always push me to be my best. My lips traveled along her hips, up her rib cage, tasted her nipples, caressed her throat. As always, Evandale smelled like sugar, Earl Grey tea, and the pages of books.

"So I was right?" I wrapped her legs around my waist. Kissed her hard. Then seated my cock fully inside of her. A ragged groan escaped my lips, and she threw her head back with a satisfied gasp. Her hands landed on my ass as she pulled me closer. Deeper.

"Maybe," she panted. "Actually...yes. You're a fucking genius, as always."

I shifted on the couch and thrust deeper, hitting a spot that made her cry my name. "That's what I like to hear, Evandale."

"So...so smug." She sighed, laughing softly. "And so fucking *big*."

My lips landed at her ear. "I promised you wild sex,

didn't I?" I intertwined our hands, enjoyed the way we could always predict what each other truly desired.

"Really, it's like we're always *both* winning," Freya gasped.

We picked up a languid rhythm, knocking the couch against the wall as our bodies moved as one, both seeking the pleasure that came so gloriously to us now. We had loved each other since those early Princeton days—and now, finally together, we hadn't changed. In many ways, we were still just as passionate, just as headstrong, just as ambitious. The difference now was that we were a team. Partners in everything. The best together.

An hour later, we were still a panting, sweating mess of limbs on the couch.

"Okay, so having sex *twice* definitely means we broke the Codex rules." She giggled, biting my biceps.

"You always did promise to corrupt me, you little rule-breaker," I growled, kissing her cheek over and over as she continued to squeal.

"Operation Corrupt Samuel Byrne is officially a *success*," she said. "Now, the only thing that could make this night of love letters and hot sex even better would be a—"

"Delivery of your favorite tacos?"

Her green eyes widened. "Mind reader, as always."

I shrugged. "Or I ordered them when you took a water break a few minutes ago. They'll be here soon."

"Goddammit, I love you, Byrne."

"And I love you," I promised. "Turns out my stubborn, brilliant, beautiful rival was the woman of my dreams, all along."

A NOTE FROM THE AUTHOR

Dear Reader,

Didn't we once meet at Reichenbach Falls? It's been so wonderful to be back in the Codex world again! Intrigue, glamour, literary references, action, hot sex...these books bring me *a lot* of joy. I had an absolute blast writing Freya and Sam's zany adventure—and am beyond thrilled with their happily-ever-after!

Freya and Sam have lived in my head since I first created Codex and this merry band of private detectives. I always knew they'd be featured in the second book. I always knew they'd be lifelong rivals (with a dash of second chance). And I *always* knew they'd meet again—dramatically—in that first chapter. But what I loved the most about these two was their devoted friendship; that once their competition was stripped away, they were actually two people who had loved each other since their freshman year of college. Like Sam says *competitors can still be friends*. And deep down, that's what they were.

Also I really, really, *really* enjoyed creating the members of The Empty House. Thank you for coming along on this fun adventure of secret societies, and underground auctions and Sherlock Holmes-inspired code words.

A lot of research went into *Under the Rose.* Controversial author George Sand did write love letters to the French poet Alfred de Musset. Alfred even wrote an autobiographical novel about their affair. George did eventually leave Alfred for his doctor and *did* use basic cryptography to inscribe messages within the letters. However, many of the other details (the sexy hidden messages, their tempestuous relationship, the number thirteen) were imagined for this story.

I've been obsessed with the FBI's Training Academy at Quantico since my childhood spent watching *The X-Files*. That being said, many details surrounding the academy's training have been imagined for this story (although Hogan's Alley is real). Quantico is located in Virginia—however, it's important to note that I moved the offices of the Deputy Director. In real life, Sam's dad would have worked in Washington, D.C., not on the Quantico campus.

Philosopher's Hall is not a real place in Philadelphia—I based it on The Union League of Philadelphia. Sadly, The Grand Dame Hotel is also imagined (as were those tunnels!) and was based on The Bellevue Hotel. Both are incredibly beautiful places to see the next time you're in the City of Brotherly Love!

Finally, the conclusion to the Codex series will release summer of 2020! Abe will be back—and he's hunting their biggest thief yet. And he might fall head-over-heels in love during the process. So stay safe, get the damn book back. Don't do anything Victoria Whitney wouldn't do.

Love,

Kathryn

P.S. If you're dying to chat spoilers and theories for the Codex books, come join *Secret Passageways* on Facebook!

ACKNOWLEDGMENTS

Freya and Sam's love story would not be here without the team of incredible people that make my writing life so very wonderful.

Thank you to Faith—who pulls double duty as my best friend *and* developmental editor. And she's one hell of a brainstormer too. Her thoughtful feedback, edits and notes are the backbone of all of my novels. Two *X-Files* nerds cannot be stopped when they get together and plot!

Jodi, Julia and Bronwyn are my intrepid beta readers. And they're a gorgeous team. Combined, they catch every plot hole, every pacing issue, every character flaw. They'll answer my many questions and brainstorm with me over Facebook messenger. Plus, they make me laugh (and make me feel loved) while we're doing it.

A giant thank you goes to Joyce, Tammy, Lucy, Tim and Rick—who are the magical ingredients in this entire process. Also, they're all truly spectacular human beings.

Thank you to my community of brilliant authors, supportive writing pals and passionate readers. Every day your support lifts me up and makes this job possible—and fun. The same goes to my reader group, The Hippie Chicks, who astound me with their bravery and positivity. They were early adopters of Codex and kept me motivated when I needed it.

To my grandfather—losing you while writing this book changed everything. But your loving support before—and your loving memories after—kept me going. *Under the Rose* releases just four days before your 90th birthday. I'd give anything to be able to place this book into your hands.

To my barely-domesticated-coyote, Walter: thank you for demanding I pay attention to you while writing by placing your paw on my hand and physically dragging it off of my mouse. Our many long, daily walks, however, are where all of my best plot ideas come from.

And always, always for Rob. He really is the world's best husband and #1 Dog Dad. You deserve all the love letters in the world, and then some.

HANG OUT WITH KATHRYN!

Sign up for my newsletter and receive exclusive content, bonus scenes and more!
I've got a reader group on Facebook called **Kathryn Nolan's Hippie Chicks.** We're all about motivation, girl power, sexy short stories and empowerment! Come join us.

Let's be friends on
Website: authorkathrynnolan.com
Instagram at: kathrynnolanromance
Facebook at: KatNolanRomance
Follow me on BookBub
Follow me on Amazon

ABOUT KATHRYN

I'm an adventurous hippie chick that loves to write steamy romance. My specialty is slow-burn sexual tension with plenty of witty dialogue and tons of heart.

I started my writing career in elementary school, writing about *Star Wars* and *Harry Potter* and inventing love stories in my journals. And I blame my obsession with slow-burn on my similar obsession for The *X-Files*.

I'm a born-and-raised Philly girl, but left for Northern California right after college, where I met my adorably-bearded husband. After living there for eight years, we decided to embark on an epic, six-month road trip, traveling across the country with our little van, Van Morrison. Eighteen states and 17,000 miles later, we're back in my hometown of Philadelphia for a bit... but I know the next adventure is just around the corner.

When I'm not spending the (early) mornings writing steamy love scenes with a strong cup of coffee, you can find me outdoors -- hiking, camping, traveling, yoga-ing.

BOOKS BY KATHRYN

BOHEMIAN

LANDSLIDE

RIPTIDE

STRICTLY PROFESSIONAL

SEXY SHORTS

BEHIND THE VEIL

UNDER THE ROSE

IN THE CLEAR

WILD OPEN HEARTS

Made in the USA
Middletown, DE
12 January 2024